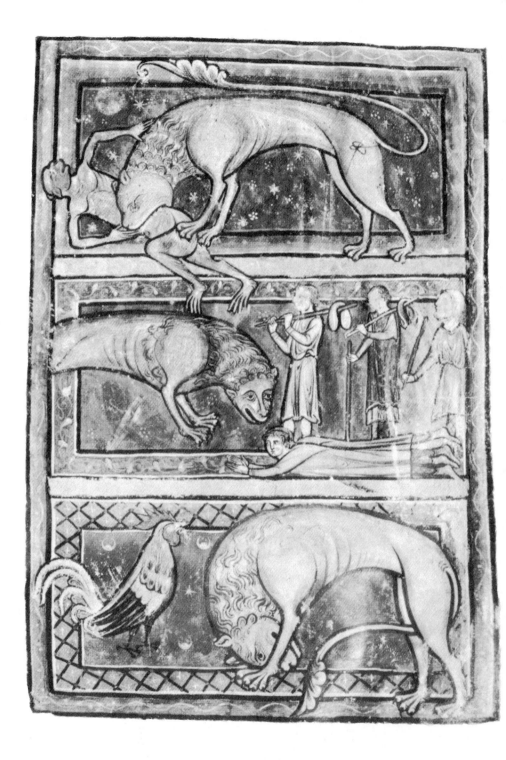

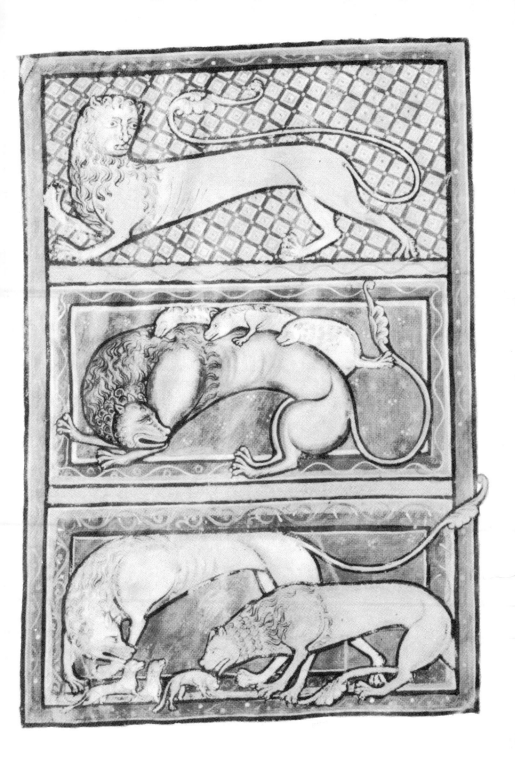

THE BOOK OF BEASTS

THE BOOK OF
BEASTS

BEING

A TRANSLATION FROM
A
LATIN BESTIARY
OF THE TWELFTH CENTURY
MADE AND EDITED BY

T. H. WHITE

'*Ancient traditions, when tested by the severe processes of modern investigation, commonly enough fade away into mere dreams: but it is singular how often the dream turns out to have been a half-waking one, presaging a reality.*' T. H. HUXLEY

'*And as dutifull Children let us cover the Naked-nesse of our Fathers with the Cloke of a favourable Interpretation.*' A. ROSS

DOVER PUBLICATIONS, INC.
NEW YORK

This Dover edition, first published in 1984, is an unabridged republication of the edition first published by G. P. Putnam's Sons, N.Y., in 1954. The original endpaper illustrations now appear on pages ii and iii.

International Standard Book Number: 0-486-24609-4

Manufactured in the United States of America
Dover Publications, Inc., 31 East 2nd Street, Mineola, N.Y. 11501

I

BEASTS

The Earth obey'd and straight
Op'ning her fertile womb teem'd at a birth
Innumerous living creatures, perfect forms,
Limb'd and full-grown . . .
The grassy clods now calv'd; now half appear'd
The tawny lion, pawing to get free
His hinder parts, then springs as broke from bonds,
And rampant shakes his brindled mane; the ounce,
The libbard and the tiger, as the mole
Rising, the crumbl'd earth above them threw
In hillocks; the swift stag from under ground
Bore up his branching head; scarce from his mould
Behemoth biggest born of earth upheav'd
His vastness; fleec't the flocks and bleating rose
As plants; ambiguous between sea and land
The river-horse and scaly crocodile.

PARADISE LOST, vii, 453 *sqq.*

E O the Lion, mightiest of beasts, will stand up to anybody.

The word 'beasts' should properly be used about lions, leopards, tigers, wolves, foxes, dogs, monkeys and others which rage about with tooth and claw—with the exception of snakes. They are called Beasts because of the violence with which they rage, and are known as 'wild' (*ferus*) because they are accustomed to freedom by nature and are governed (*ferantur*) by their own wishes. They wander hither and thither, fancy free, and they go wherever they want to go.

The name 'Lion' (*leo*) has been turned into Latin from a Greek root, for it is called '*leon*' in Greek—but this is a muddled name, partly corrupted, since '*leon*' has also been translated as 'king' from Greek into Latin, owing to the fact that he is the Prince of All Animals.

They say that the litters of these creatures come in threes. The short ones with curly manes are peaceful: the tall ones with plain hair are fierce.

The nature of their brows and tail-tufts is an index to their disposition. Their courage is seated in their hearts, while their constancy is in their heads. They fear the creaking of wheels, but are frightened by fires even more so.

A lion, proud in the strength of his own nature, knows not how to mingle his ferocity with all and sundry, but, like the king he is, disdains to have a lot of different wives.

Scientists say that Leo has three principal characteristics. His first feature is that he loves to saunter on the tops of mountains. Then, if he should happen to be pursued by hunting men, the smell of the hunters reaches up to him, and he disguises his spoor behind him with his tail. Thus the sportsmen cannot track him.

It was in this way that our Saviour (i.e. the Spiritual Lion of the Tribe of Judah, the Rod of Jesse, the Lord of Lords, the Son of God) once hid the spoor of his love in the high places, until, being sent by the Father, he came down into the womb of the Virgin Mary and saved the human race which had perished. Ignorant of the fact that his spoor could be concealed, the Devil (i.e. the hunter of humankind) dared to pursue him with temptations like a mere man. Even the angels themselves who were on high, not recognizing his spoor, said to those who were going up with him when he ascended to his reward: 'Who is this King of Glory?'

The Lion's second feature is, that when he sleeps, he seems to keep his eyes open.

In this very way, Our Lord also, while sleeping in the body, was buried after being crucified—yet his Godhead was awake. As it is said in the *Song of Songs*, 'I am asleep and my heart is awake', or, in the Psalm, 'Behold, he that keepeth Israel shall neither slumber nor sleep.'

The third feature is this, that when a lioness gives birth to her cubs, she brings them forth dead and lays them up lifeless for three days—until their father, coming on the third day, breathes in their faces and makes them alive.[1]

Just so did the Father Omnipotent raise Our Lord Jesus Christ from the dead on the third day. Quoth

[1] E. P. Evans understands that they revive them with a roar.

Jacob: 'He shall sleep like a lion, and the lion's whelp shall be raised.'

So far as their relations with men are concerned, the nature of lions is that they do not get angry unless they are wounded.

Any decent human ought to pay attention to this. For men do get angry when they are not wounded, and they oppress the innocent although the law of Christ bids them to let even the guilty go free.

The compassion of lions, on the contrary, is clear from innumerable examples—for they spare the prostrate;[1] they allow such captives as they come across to go back to their own country; they prey on men rather than on women, and they do not kill children except when they are very hungry.

Furthermore, lions abstain from over-eating: in the first place, because they only take food and drink on alternate days—and frequently, if digestion has not followed, they are even in the habit of putting off the day for dinner. In the second place, they pop their paws carefully into their mouths and pull out the meat of their own accord, when they have eaten too much. Indeed, when they have to run away from somebody, they perform the same action if they are full up.

Lack of teeth is a sign of old age in lions.

[1] Dr Johnson's Mrs Thrale narrated an interesting anecdote about one of her ancestors (*Hayward*, ii, 8) without being aware that it derived from the bestiarists. The ancestor was a Sir Henry de Salusbury, who bore 'the Bavarian Lion' in his shield. An opponent whom he had conquered in battle prostrated himself before Sir Henry, observing: *Sat est prostrasse leoni*. Charmed by this tactful and apposite quotation, which shows that the bestiaries must have been familiar to both combatants, Sir Henry spared his suppliant: and must have repeated the story rather frequently afterwards, to have impressed it on the family mind to a generation so distant as that of Mrs Thrale.

They copulate the backward way. Nor are they the only ones, but also Lynxes, Camels, Elephants, Rhinoceroses, Tigers and Hyaenas.[1]

When they first have babies, they produce five whelps.[2] Then, one by one, they reduce the number in succeeding years. Finally, when they have come down to one, the maternal fertility disappears and they become sterile for ever afterward.

A lion turns up its nose at yesterday's dinner, and will

---

[1] Sir Thomas Browne observes (*Vulgar Errors*, Bk 5, xix): 'We are unwilling to question the Royall supporters of England, that is, the approved descriptions of the Lion and the Unicorne; although, if in the Lion the position of the pizell be proper, and that the naturall situation, it will be hard to make out their retrocopulation, or their coupling and pissing backward, according to the determination of Aristotle. All that urine backward do copulate πυγηδόν, *cluniatim*, or aversely, as Lions, Hares, Linxes.' In Bk 3, xvii, he deals with the subject more fully. 'The last foundation was Retromingency or pissing backward, for men observing both sexes (of some animals) to urine backward, or aversely between their legs, they might conceive there was a foeminine part in both. Wherein they are deceived by the ignorance of the just and proper site of the Pizell or part designed unto the Excretion of urine, which in the Hare holds not the common position, but is aversely seated, and in its distension enclines unto the coccix or scut. Now from the nature of this position, there ensueth a necessitie of Retrocopulation, which also promoteth the conceit. For some observing them to couple without ascension, have not been able to judge of male or female, or to determine the proper sex in either. And to speak generally, this way of copulation is not appropriate (i.e. confined) unto hares, nor is there one, but many ways of Coition, according to divers shapes and different conformations. For some couple laterally or sidewise as wormes; some circularly or by complication as Serpents; some pronely, that is by contaction of prone parts in both, as Apes, Porcupines, Hedgehogges, and such as are termed Mollia, as the Cuttlefish and the Purple; some mixtly, that is, the male ascending the female, or by application of the prone parts of one unto the postick parts of the other, as most Quadrupes; some aversely, as all Crustaceous Animals, Lobsters, Shrimps and Crevises, and also Retromingents, as Panthers, Tigers and Hares. This is the constant Law of their Coition, this they observe and transgresse not. Only the vitiositie of man hath acted the varieties thereof—not content with a digression from sex or species, hath in his own kind run through the Anomalies of venery, and been so bold, not only to act, but represent to view, the Irregular ways of lust.'

[2] See Appendix.

10

go away hungry from food which has been left over.[1]

What creature dares declare himself an enemy to this beast, in whose roar there is such natural terribleness that many animals, which could escape its charge by their speed, fail to get away from the very sound of its voice—as if dumbfounded and overcome by brute force!

A sick lion searches for a monkey to eat, by which means he can be cured.

A lion fears a cock, especially a white one.[2]

A lion, although he is the king of beasts, gets harassed by the tiny sting of a scorpion, and snake poison kills him.

We read about certain creatures of moderate size, called Leontophontes,[3] which people burn when they get them. They burn them so that they may kill lions with meat which has been tainted by a sprinkling of their ash, and thrown down at crossroads between converging tracks, should the lions eat the least little bit of it. Consequently lions instinctively pursue these creatures with hatred, and, when they get a chance, they do not actually bite them, but they lacerate and kill them with the weight of their paws.

[1] ' 'Tis the royal disposition of that beast
To prey on nothing that doth seem as dead.' AS YOU LIKE IT, IV, iii.

[2] The end-papers show the lion indulging his various habits. 1. Eating a monkey for medicine. 2. Sparing prostrate captives. 3. Being frightened by a white cock. 4. Waving his tail on a mountain. 5. His wife sleeping open-eyed, with three babies not yet animated. 6. Breathing on the babies.

[3] Aldrovandus says that nobody has given a sufficient description of these animals to identify them, but he suggests that they may be insects or plants. There is a plant called Leopard's bane, also known as Arnica, while the dandelion (*dent de lion*) belongs to the genus Leontodon.

TIGRIS the Tiger gets his name from his speedy pace; for the Persians, Greeks and Medes used to call an arrow 'tygris'.

The beast can be distinguished by his manifold specklings, by his courage and by his wonderful velocity. And from him the River Tigris is named, because it is the most rapid of all rivers.

Hyrcania is his principal home.

Now the Tigress, when she finds the empty lair of one of her cubs that has been stolen, instantly presses along the tracks of the thief. But this person who has stolen the cub, seeing that even though carried by a swiftly galloping horse he is on the point of being destroyed by the speed of the tigress, and seeing that no safety can be expected from flight, cunningly invents the following ruse. When he perceives that the mother is close, he throws down a glass ball, and she, taken in by her own reflection, assumes that the image of herself in the glass is her little one. She pulls up, hoping to collect the infant. But after she has been delayed by the hollow mockery, she again throws herself with all her might into the pursuit of the horseman, and, goaded by rage, quickly threatens to catch up with the fugitive. Again he delays the pursuer by throwing down a second ball, nor does the memory of his former trick prevent the mother's tender care. She curls herself round the vain reflection and lies down as if to suckle the cub. And so, deceived by the zeal of her own dutifulness, she loses both her revenge and her baby.

The PARD[1] is a parti-coloured species, very swift and strongly inclined to bloodshed. It leaps to the kill with a bound.

Leo-pards are born from the adultery of a lioness with

[1] Bartholomeus Anglicus tells us that the Pard and the Pardal are the same as the Panther. 'The perde varieth not fro the pantera, but the pantera hath moo white speckes'. Trevisa's translation. All three of them are the same as the Leopard. The explanation is that there were two latin names for leopard: *panthera* and *pardus*. The names reached England before the animals did. Gesner agrees with Bartholomeus, and adds a fifth variant, the Pordalis.

a pard, which produces this third kind of animal. Thus Pliny says in his *Natural History* that the lion lies with the female pard, or the pard with the lioness, and in either case there are created inferior offspring, like the Mule and the Hinny.

There is an animal called a PANTHER which has a truly variegated colour, and it is most beautiful and excessively kind. Physiologus says that the only animal which it considers as an enemy is the Dragon.

When a Panther has dined and is full up, it hides away in its own den and goes to sleep. After three days it wakes up again and emits a loud belch,[1] and there comes a very sweet smell from its mouth, like the smell of allspice. When the other animals have heard the noise, they follow wherever it goes, because of the sweetness of

[1] 'On the third day when he wakes, a lofty, sweet, ringing sound comes from his mouth, and with the song a most delightful stream of sweet-smelling breath, more grateful than all the blooms of herbs and blossoms of the trees'. The Panther, in the *Exeter Book*, trans. Stopford Brooke.

In 1656 a (sweet-smelling?) drug called Panther was selling at £2 the pound.

this smell. But the Dragon only, hearing the sound, flees into the caves of the earth, being smitten with fear. There, unable to bear the smell, it becomes torpid and half asleep, and remains motionless, as if dead.

The true Panther,[1] Our Lord Jesus Christ, snatched us from the power of the dragon-devil on descending from the heavens. He associated us with himself as sons by his incarnation, accepting all, and gave gifts to men, leading captivity captive.

What Solomon pointed out about Christ is symbolized by the panther being an animal of so many colours that by the wisdom of God the Father he is the Apprehensible Spirit, the Only Wise, the Manifold, the True, the Sweet, the Suitable, the Clement, the Constant, the Established, the Untroubled, the Omnipotent, the All-Seeing.

And because it is a beautiful animal, the Lord God says of Christ: 'He is beautiful in form among the sons of men'.

Isaiah also, because it is a kindly animal, cries: 'Rejoice and be glad, O daughter of Sion, proclaim, O daughter of Jerusalem, because thy kindly king comes to thee'.

When the Panther-Christ was satiated with his incarnation, he hid himself away in Jewish mockeries: in whippings, boxes on the ear, insults, contumelies, thorns, being hung up by the hands on the cross, fixed by nails, given gall and vinegar to drink, and transfixed by the lance. Dying, he reposed in the den-tomb and descended into Hell, there binding the Great Dragon. But on the third day he rose from sleep and emitted a mighty noise breathing sweetness.

[1] 'In this connection it may be mentioned as a singular coincidence that, according to an ancient tradition, the real father of Jesus was a Roman soldier named Panthera'. E. P. EVANS, *Animal Symbolism in Ecclesiastical Architecture*.

Thus David sings of Our Lord Jesus Christ rising from the dead: 'The Lord is aroused as if he had been sleeping, mighty as if he had been refreshed with wine'.[1] Also: 'And he cried out with a loud voice so that his voice was heard in every land and his words at the end of the earth.'

And just as there comes an odour of sweetness from the mouth of the panther so that all beasts meet together to follow it, both those which are near and those which are far, so also the Jews—who have sometimes had the senses of beasts but who were near to him on account of the Law—and also those who were far away, i.e. the Gentiles —who were outside the Law—both these, on hearing the

---

[1] The phrase is '*crapulatus a vino*'. Sir Thomas Browne, like the psalmist, seems to have approved of a medicinal use in liquor. 'That 'tis good to be drunk once a month,' he says, 'is a common flattery of sensuality, supporting itself upon physick and the healthfull effects of inebriation. This indeed seems plainly affirmed by Avicenna, a Physitian of great Authority, and whose religion prohibiting Wine should lesse extenuate ebriety. But Averroes, a man of his owne faith, was of another beliefe, restraining his ebriety unto hilarity, and in effect making no more thereof then Seneca commendeth and was allowable in Cato; that is, a sober incalescence and regulated aestuation from wine, or what may be conceived betweene Joseph and his bretheren, when the Text expresseth they were merry, or dranke largely; and whereby indeed the commodities set down by Avicenna, that is, Alleviation of spirits, resolution of superfluities, provocation of sweat and urine may also ensue. But as for dementation, sopition of reason and the diviner particle from drinke, though American religion approve, and Pagan piety of old hath practised even at their sacrifices, Christian morality and the Doctrine of Christ will not allow.' In this Sir Thomas Browne is supported by a fourteenth-century observation on the fly-leaf of a thirteenth-century Bible in the possession of Sir Sydney Cockerell:

proprietates ebrii
{
Primo letus et gaudens
Secundo sanctus et sapiens
Tercio tristis et amans
Quarto Debilis—Fine stultus
et moriens, et omni sensu et
omni bono carens.

It is to be hoped that none of these stages could be covered by the holy description '*crapulatus*' in the text, whatever the American Religion may approve, and that Our Lord in the psalm here quoted, unlike his ancestor Lot, had gone no further than a sober incalescence.

voice of Christ, follow him saying: 'How sweet are thy words unto my taste! Yea, sweeter than honey to my mouth'. Likewise, concerning the same thing: 'In thy lips pleasantness is diffused, therefore God hath blessed thee forever'. Solomon says: 'The smell of thy ointments is above all spices'. Item, from the same author: 'We shall run to the smell of thy ointments'. And a little further on: 'The King has led me into his chamber'.

Hence we may conclude that it behoves us like little creatures, i.e. like souls renewed in baptism, to run to the sweet-smelling ointment of Christ's commands, and to flee from earthly things to heavenly, so that the King may lead us into his palace, into Jerusalem the divine city of virtues, and into the mount of all the saints.

The Panther is an animal with small spots daubed all over it, so that it can be distinguished by the circled dots upon the tawny and also by its black and white variegation.

It only has babies once. The reason for this is obvious, because, when three cubs have struck root in the mother's womb and begin to wax with the strength of birth, they become impatient of the delays of time. So they tear the infant-burdened womb in which they are, as being an obstacle to delivery. This pours out or rather discharges the litter, since it is spurred by pain. Thus, when the seed of generation is infused into it at a later date, this does not adhere to the damaged and scarred parts and is not accepted, but vainly jumps out again. Pliny says that animals with sharp claws cannot bear babies frequently, since they get damaged inside when the pups move about.

The ANTALOPS is an animal of incomparable celerity, so much so that no hunter can ever get near it.

It has long horns shaped like a saw, with the result that
it can even cut down very big trees and fell them to the
ground.

When it is thirsty, it goes to the great River Euphrates,
and drinks. Now there is in those parts a shrub called
Herecine, which has subtile, long twigs. Coming therefore to the shrub, it begins to play with the Herecine
with its horns, and, while it plays, it entangles the horns
in the twigs. When it cannot get free after a long struggle,
it cries with a loud bellow.[1]

---

[1] Dr Ansell Robin states that unicorns may be captured by making them run
their horns into trees, behind which the huntsman has dodged. This is a very early
offshoot of the Antalop legend, a mistaken reading which was not only to be
followed by Shakespeare, but also by Chapman and by Spenser (*Faerie Queene*,
II. V. 10).

But the hunter, hearing its voice, comes and kills it.[1]

Do thus also, O Man of God, thou who dost endeavour to be sober and chaste and to live spiritually! Your two horns are the two Testaments, with which you can prune and saw off all fleshly vices from yourself, that is to say, adultery, fornication, avarice, envy, pride, homicide, slander, drunkenness, lust and all the pomps of this world. Thus will the angels reward you with the virtues of heaven.

But beware, O Man of God, of the shrub Booze, and do not be entangled in the Herecine pleasure of Lust, so as not to be slain by the Devil. Wine and Women are great turners-away from God.

[1] The leaf describing ANTALOPS is missing from C.U.L. 11.4.26. It is here translated from Laud. Misc. 247, and the picture is taken from Brit. Mus. 12, C.XIX.

The N.E.D. derives the Antelope as follows: 'O Fr. *antelop* (also *antelu*), ad. L. *ant(h)alop-us* (Damianus, a 1072), Gr. ανθόροψ ανθόροπ–(Eusthasius of Antioch, *c.* 336), original language and meaning unknown. Med. Latin forms were also *talopus, calopus.* The coptic is '*Panthalops*'.

It is an astonishing fact that Aldrovandus does not describe any animal under any of these names, in all the 78 lb. 4 oz. avoirdupois, which is the exact weight of erudition presented by his eleven tomes.

The creature was probably an elk, eland or reindeer–but the great naturalist had confused himself about these species, under the names of Tragelaphus, Tarandus, Rangiferus, Alce and Alcida *inter alia.* Fabricius wrote to tell him that a reindeer did indeed have saw-shaped horns and that its expanding hoofs were the reason for its celerity. These helped it to escape from the pursuer in soft snow. Moreover, there were many deer which did entangle their horns, either in trees when rubbing off the velvet or fighting with each other.

The Herecine shrub might be translated as 'the Antalop-tree', for the 'antalop' was said to resemble a goat and a deer–'*quod animal sit hirco atque cervo simile*'. It was probably the Hircuscervus tree (*hircus-cervus*). But the Ericaceae are a family of shrubs including Heath (Erica), which may have been available to reindeer.

19

UNICORNIS the Unicorn,[1] which is also called
Rhinoceros[2] by the Greeks, is of the following nature.

He is a very small animal like a kid, excessively swift,
with one horn in the middle of his forehead, and no

[1] Text from Harl, 4751, picture from Bodl. Laud. Misc. 247.

'He loves to hear,' says Shakespeare in *Julius Caesar* II, i, 'That unicorns
may be betrayed with trees, And bears with glasses.' In fact, he was confusing
Unicorn with Antalop, and Bear with Tiger.

Although Shakespeare generally gives the impression of having been a universal
genius who knew everything, it is evident that he had never read a *Bestiary*.
His natural history is of his personal observation, or else what he might have heard
discussed in any country tavern. He has heard somebody mention that tigers
come from Hyrcania (*Macbeth*, III, iv), or that elephants have no joints (*Troilus
and Cressida*, II, iii), but he seldom refers to the odder tenents of the bestiarists,
nor does he mention the more outlandish beasts familiar to Milton, which would
certainly have interested him if he had known about them. No full English
translation of a Latin Prose Bestiary existed for him to consult—though he might
have been acquainted with Trevisa, Du Bartas or Topsell—and Ben Jonson seems
to have been right about his latinity, which would have kept him from the
sources. 'I think we can take it,' says J. A. K. Thompson in *Shakespeare and the
Classics* (1952), 'that Shakespeare did not consult *De Generatione Animalium*'.

[2] See Monoceros.

hunter can catch him. But he can be trapped by the following stratagem.

A virgin girl is led to where he lurks, and there she is sent off by herself into the wood. He soon leaps into her lap when he sees her, and embraces her, and hence he gets caught.

Our Lord Jesus Christ is also a Unicorn spiritually, about whom it is said: 'And he was beloved like the Son of the Unicorns'. And in another psalm: 'He hath raised up a horn of salvation for us in the house of his son David'.

The fact that it has just one horn on its head means what he himself said: 'I and the Father are One'. Also, according to the Apostle: 'The head of Christ is the Lord'.

It says that he is very swift because neither Principalities, nor Powers, nor Thrones, nor Dominations could keep up with him, nor could Hell contain him, nor could the most subtle Devil prevail to catch or comprehend him; but, by the sole will of the Father, he came down into the virgin womb for our salvation.

It is described as a tiny animal on account of the lowliness of his incarnation, as he said himself: 'Learn from me, because I am mild and lowly of heart'.

It is like a kid or scapegoat because the Saviour himself was made in the likeness of sinful flesh, and from sin he condemned sin.

The Unicorn often fights with elephants, and conquers them by wounding them in the belly.

LINCIS the Lynx is called this because he is a kind of wolf (λύγξ, λύκος). The brute is distinguished by spots on the back like a Pard, but he looks like a wolf. They say that his urine hardens into a precious stone called Ligurius,[1] and it is established that the Lynxes themselves realize this, by the following fact. When they have pissed the liquid, they cover it up in the sand as much as they can. They do this from a certain constitutional meanness, for fear that the piss should be useful as an ornament to the human race.

Pliny says that Lynxes only have one baby.

This is called a GRIFFIN[2] because it is a winged quadruped. This kind of wild animal is born in Hyperborean parts, or in mountains. All its bodily members

---

[1] Ligurius is simply Lync-urius, lynx-piss. Isidorus says that it is the carbuncle, and it takes seven days to set.

[2] One is tempted to say, with Lewis Carroll in *Alice in Wonderland*, 'If you don't know what a Griffin is, look at the picture'. It is evidently something of a Hieroglyphin. A sphinx-god who has strayed out of Egyptian art into natural history, a mythological monster from Assyria where the winged bulls were, a Persian Senmurv who united heaven and earth, the Simargl from Russia or the Garuda in the Mahabharata: he is simply one of the composite animals of religion about which some explanation will be found in the Appendix. Even St Mark and St Luke are depicted in many of our churches as winged lions and winged bulls. Sir Thomas Browne tried to identify him with the Griffon Vulture, and we have a dog nowadays which has inherited his name; but it is easier to accept

him as a fabulous animal pure and simple, like the mysterious Dodo of Thomas
Lovell Beddoes:

> 'I'll not be a fool, like the nightingale
> Who sits up all midnight without any ale,
>   Making a noise with his nose;
> Nor a camel, although 'tis a beautiful back;
> Nor a duck, notwithstanding the music of quack,
>   And the webby, mud-patting toes.
> I'll be a new bird with the head of an ass,
>   Two pigs' feet, two men's feet, and two of a hen;
> Devil-winged; dragon-bellied; grave-jawed, because grass
>   Is a beard that's soon shaved, and grows seldom again
> Before it is summer; so cow all the rest:
>   The new Dodo is finished. O! Come to my nest.'

Death's Jest Book, 1850

The Griffin, however, was a serious animal and a more terrible one than the
imaginations of Beddoes. It does not pay to be supercilious about the creatures
in a Bestiary.

23

are like a lion's, but its wings and mask are like an eagle's. [1]

It is vehemently hostile to horses. But it will also tear to pieces any human beings which it happens to come across.

[1] 'In the swift Rank of these fell Rovers, flies
The *Indian Griffin* with the glistring eyes.'
Sylvester's *Du Bartas*.

There is an animal called an ELEPHANT, which has no desire to copulate.

People say that it is called an Elephant by the Greeks on account of its size, for it approaches the form of a mountain: you see, a mountain is called '*eliphio*' in Greek. In the Indies, however, it is known by the name of '*barrus*' because of its voice—whence both the voice is called '*bari*tone' and the tusks are called 'ivory' (*ebur*). Its nose is called a proboscis (for the bushes), because it carries its leaf-food to its mouth with it, and it looks like a snake.[1]

Elephants protect themselves with ivory tusks. No larger animals can be found. The Persians and the Indians, collected into wooden towers on them, sometimes fight each other with javelins as if from a castle. They possess vast intelligence and memory. They march about in herds. And they copulate back-to-back.[2]

Elephants remain pregnant for two years, nor do they have babies more than once, nor do they have several at a time, but only one. They live three hundred years. If one of them wants to have a baby, he goes eastward toward Paradise, and there is a tree there called

---

[1] Pro-boscis—for the bushes!
'Th' unwieldy Elephant
To make them mirth us'd all his might, and wreathd
His Lithe Proboscis.'
                        Paradise Lost, IV, 347

[2] The copulation of elephants was a matter for speculation in the dark ages, and still is, as it is rarely witnessed. Solinus quotes Pliny to the effect that their genitals, like those mentioned by Sir Thomas Browne in his note on hares, were put on backward. It was supposed that, being modest, they preferred to look the other way while they were about it. Albertus Magnus held that they copulated like other quadrupeds, but that, owing to the great weight of the husband, he either had to dig a pit for his wife to stand in or else he had to float himself over her in a lake, where his gravity would naturally be less. In fact, they copulate in the ordinary way and, according to Lieut.-Colonel C. H. Williams, more gracefully than most.

Mandragora,[1] and he goes with his wife. She first takes of the tree and then gives some to her spouse. When they munch it up, it seduces them, and she immediately conceives in her womb. When the proper time for being delivered arrives, she walks out into a lake, and the water comes up to the mother's udders. Meanwhile the father-elephant guards her while she is in labour, because there is a certain dragon which is inimical to elephants. Moreover, if a serpent happens by, the father kills and tramples on it till dead. He is also formidable to bulls—but he is frightened of mice, for all that.

The Elephant's nature is that if he tumbles down he cannot get up again. Hence it comes that he leans against a tree when he wants to go to sleep, for he has no joints in his knees. This is the reason why a hunter partly saws through a tree, so that the elephant, when he leans against it, may fall down at the same time as the tree.[2] As he falls, he calls out loudly; and immediately a large elephant appears, but it is not able to lift him up. At this they both cry out, and twelve more elephants arrive upon the scene: but even they cannot lift up the one who has fallen down. Then they all shout for help, and at once there comes a very Insignificant Elephant, and he

---

[1] Mandrake. There is still a genus of plants called the Mandragora, said to be emetic, narcotic and 'fertilizing'. 'The mandrakes which Reuben found in the field were used by his mother Leah for venereal purposes (Gen. xxx. 14-16), and this precious peculiarity is enlarged upon in rabbinical literature. The Greeks spoke of them as anthropomorphic; and according to popular superstition they spring from human sperm spilled on the ground, and are so full of animal life and consciousness that they shriek when torn out of the earth, so "that living mortals, hearing them, run mad".' E. P. Evans.

[2] Julius Caesar, in his *Gallic War*, relates the same fable about the elks (*alces*). The present translator is informed by Captain A. A. F. Minchin of the Indian Forest Service that elephants do have, as it were, scratching posts at their watering places, and that the hunter is able to forecast the size of his quarry by the height of the mud rubbed off against these trees.

puts his mouth with the proboscis under the big one, and lifts him up. This little elephant has, moreover, the property that nothing evil can come near his hairs and bones when they have been reduced to ashes, not even a Dragon.

Now the Elephant and his wife represent Adam and Eve. For when they were pleasing to God, before their provocation in the flesh, they knew nothing about copulation nor had they knowledge of sin. When, however, the wife ate of the Tree of Knowledge, which is what the Mandragora means, and gave one of the fruits to her man, she was immediately made a wanderer and they had to clear out of Paradise on account of it. For, all the time that they were in Paradise, Adam did not know her. But then, the Scriptures say: 'Adam went in to his wife and she conceived and bore Cain, upon the waters of tribulation'. Of which waters the Psalmist cries: 'Save me, O God, for the waters have entered in even unto my soul'. And immediately the dragon subverted them and made them strangers to God's refuge. That is what comes of not pleasing God.

When the Big Elephant arrives, i.e. the Hebrew Law, and fails to lift up the fallen, it is the same as when the Pharisee failed with the fellow who had fallen among thieves. Nor could the Twelve Elephants, i.e. the Band of the Prophets, lift him up, just as the Levite did not lift the man we mentioned. But it means that Our Lord Jesus Christ, although he was the greatest, was made the most Insignificant of All the Elephants. He humiliated himself, and was made obedient even unto death, in order that he might raise men up.

The little elephant also symbolizes the Samaritan who put the man on his mare. For he himself, wounded, took over our infirmities and carried them from us. Moreover, this heavenly Samaritan is interpreted as the Defender about whom David writes: 'The Lord defending the lowly ones'. Also, with reference to the little elephant's ashes: 'Where the Lord is present, no devil can come nigh'.

It is a fact that Elephants smash whatever they wind their noses round, like the fall of some prodigious ruin, and whatever they squash with their feet they blot out.

They never quarrel about their wives, for adultery is unknown to them. There is a mild gentleness about them, for, if they happen to come across a forwandered man in the deserts, they offer to lead him back into familiar paths. If they are gathered together into crowded herds, they make way for themselves with tender and placid trunks, lest any of their tusks should happen to kill some animal on the road. If by chance they do become involved in battles, they take no little care of the casualties, for they collect the wounded and exhausted into the middle of the herd.

This is an animal called C A S T O R the Beaver, none more gentle, and his testicles make a capital medicine. For this reason, so Physiologus says, when he notices that he is being pursued by the hunter, he removes his own testicles with a bite, and casts them before the sportsman, and thus escapes by flight. What is more, if he should again happen to be chased by a second hunter, he lifts himself up and shows his members to him. And the latter, when he perceives the testicles to be missing, leaves the beaver alone.[1]

Hence every man who inclines toward the commandment of God and who wants to live chastely, must cut off from himself all vices, all motions of lewdness, and must cast them from him in the Devil's face. Thereupon the Devil, seeing him to have nothing of his own about him, goes away from him confused. That man truly lives in God and is not captured by the Devil who says: 'I shall persevere and attain these things'.

The creature is called a Beaver (Castor) because of the castration.

[1] The medicine was called 'castoreum'. It was situated not in the testicles, but in a different gland. The testicles of a beaver are internal and cannot be bitten off. 'The originall of the conceit,' says Sir Thomas Browne, 'was probably Hieroglyphicall, which after became Mythologicall unto the Greeks and so set down by Aesop, and by process of tradition stole into a totall verity'.

There is an animal called I B E X the Chamois, which has two horns. And such is the strength of these that, if it is hurled down from a high mountain peak to the very depths, its whole body will be preserved unhurt by these two.[1]

The Ibex symbolizes learned men, who are accustomed to shock-absorb whatever adversities befall them with a harmonization of the two Testaments, as if with some protecting braking-action. They prop up the good which they do on two things: the testimony of the Old Testament and the reading of the Gospel.

[1] 'It seemeth that this Haebrew name Iaall [see Yale], is derived of climbing, and (*Isidorus* saith) that Ibices are *quasi Avices*, that is like Birdes, because like Fowles of the ayre, they inhabit the toppes of cliftes'. TOPSELL. Ibex has of course been confused with Ibis.

This is an animal called the Y E N A, which is accustomed

to live in the sepulchres of the dead and to devour their bodies. Its nature is that at one moment it is masculine and at another moment feminine, and hence it is a dirty brute.[1]

It is unable to turn round, except by a complete reversal of its body, because its spine is rigid and is all in one piece. Solinus relates many wonders about it. First, it frequents the sheepfolds of shepherds and walks round the houses of a night and studies the tone of voice of those inside with careful ear, for it is able to do imitations of the human voice. In order that it may prey upon men called out at night by this ruse, it copies the sound of human vomiting.[2]

Such dogs as it has called out like this, it gobbles up with hypocritical sobs. And if by chance the sporting dogs should cross its shadow while they are hunting it, they lose their voices and cannot give tongue. This same Hyaena digs up graves in quest of buried corpses.

The Children of Israel, who served the living God at first, are compared to this brute. Afterwards, given up to riches and luxuries, they paid respect to dead idols; whence the Prophet compared the Synagogue to a dirty

[1] This animal has never been popular. Sir Walter Raleigh, in his *History of the World* (1614), excludes hybrids from Noah's Ark, and mentions hyaenas as belonging to this class. He asserts that only pure species were saved, and not mongrels. After the Deluge, hyaenas, he says, were reproduced by a cross between the dog and the cat.

[2] The Hyaena is not listed by Aldrovandus under that name, but as Gulo the glutton. Gesner says that it gorges on corpses until its stomach is blown up like a drum, upon which it seeks out two stones or trees and squashes itself between them, extruding its repast by this means at both ends. Then it begins again. The question of vomiting is therefore of importance to hyaenas, and medical opinion, according to Crollius, valued their products for vomits and purges. Whether this is the sound mentioned in the text, or whether the word is intended to describe the ululation of the laughing hyaena, is not clear.

animal, saying: 'My inheritance is made for me like the cave of the Yena'. Yes, those of you who serve wantonness and avarice are compared to this monster.

Since they are neither male nor female, they are neither faithful nor pagan, but are obviously the people concerning whom Solomon said: 'A man of double mind is inconstant in all his ways'. About whom also the Lord said: 'Thou canst not serve God and Mammon'.

This beast has a stone in its eye, also called an Yena, which is believed to make a person able to foresee the future if he keeps it under his tongue. It is true that if an Yena walks round any animal three times, the animal cannot move. For this reason they affirm that it has some sort of magic skill about it.

In part of Ethiopia it copulates with a lioness, from whence is born a monster known as a Crotote.[1] This can produce the voices of humans in the same way. It is said not to be able to turn its eyes backward, owing to its rigid backbone, and to be blind in that direction unless it turns round. It has no gums in its mouth. It has one rigid tooth-bone all the way along, which shuts like a little box, so that it cannot be blunted by anything.

[1] Leucrota (q.v.). Other names for derivatives of the hyaena species were Rosomacha, Crocuta, Corocotta, Leucrocuta, Akabo, Alzabo, Zabo, Ana, Belbus, Lupus vesperitinus, Zilis and Lacta. Shakespeare calls it a Hyen. 'I will laugh like a hyen, and that when thou art inclined to sleep.' *As You Like It*, IV, i.

An animal is born in Asia which they call a B O N N A-
C O N, and he has a bullish head and from then on the
rest of his body like a horse's mane. The horns are curled
round upon themselves with such a multiple convolution
that if anybody bumps against them he does not get hurt.

But however much his front end does not defend this
monster, his belly end is amply sufficient. For when he
turns to run away he emits a fart with the contents of his
large intestine which covers three acres. And any tree
that it reaches catches fire. Thus he drives away his pur-
suers with noxious excrement.[1]

[1] Bonnacon is the Bonasus, i.e. the bison or aurochs. Many animals do void
their excrements when escaping.

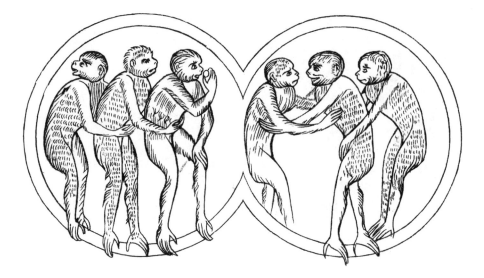

They are called MONKEYS (Simia) in the latin language because people notice a great *similitude* to human reason in them. Wise in the lore of the elements, these creatures grow merry at the time of the new moon. At half and full moon they are depressed. Such is the nature of a monkey that, when she gives birth to twins, she esteems one of them highly but scorns the other. Hence, if it ever happens that she gets chased by a sportsman she clasps the one she likes in her arms in front of her, and carries the one she detests with its arms round her neck, pickaback. But for this very reason, when she is exhausted by running on her hind legs, she has to throw away the one she loves, and carries the one she hates, willy-nilly.

A monkey has no tail (*cauda*). The Devil resembles these beasts; for he has a head, but no scripture (*caudex*).

Admitting that the whole of a monkey is disgraceful,

yet their bottoms really are excessively disgraceful and horrible. In the same way, the Devil had a sound *foundation* when he was among the angels of heaven, but he was hypocritical and cunning inside himself, and so he lost his cauda-caudex as a sign that all of him would perish in the end. As the Apostle says: 'Whom the Lord Jesus Christ will kill with the breath of his mouth'.

'Simia' is a Greek word, meaning 'with squashed nostrils'. Hence we call monkeys this, because they have turned-up noses and a hideous countenance, with wrinkles lewdly puffing like bellows. It is also said to be a characteristic of goats to have a turned-up nose.

Cercopitheci[1] do have tails. These are the only ones to be discreet, among those previously mentioned.

Cynocephali[2] are also numbered among monkeys. They are very common in Ethiopia. They are violent in leaping and fierce in biting. They never get tame enough not to be rather ferocious.

Sphinxes[3] also are reckoned as monkeys. They are shaggy, defenceless, and docilely ready to forget their wild freedom.

[1] Aldrovandus says that the English is 'marmuset'.

[2] The Baboon, the dog-headed ape, possibly the Egyptian god Anubis.

[3] According to Gesner, the sphinx is a real monkey, and the Sphinx of art, woman in front and lion behind, is merely an imaginary representation of it made by painters and sculptors. Perhaps he is not so wrong in this as he seems. At any rate, the Guinea Baboon is called a sphinx to this day.

A note on fabulous animals will be found in the Appendix.

There are others which they call S A T Y R S,[1] with a quite agreeable figure but with movements of ceaseless pantomime. The Callitrices[2] differ from the rest in nearly their whole appearance. They have a beard on the face and a copious tail. It is not difficult to catch them, but rare to find them. Nor do they live in any other parts than Ethiopia, and there in the open air.

[1] These mythological companions of Pan and Bacchus were also, we are informed by the N.E.D., 'a kind of ape (so Gr. σατυρος); in modern use, the orang-utan, *Simia Satyrus*'. 'Some ape', says Trevisa's Bartholomew, 'is called Satirus, plesynge in face wyth mery meuynges and playenges'. But ape and ancestor, myth and monkey, biology, anthropology and ancient religions are inextricably mixed together. They have good-humouredly lent each other their names. 'Horace did not realize', says Mr Robert Graves, 'that Centaurs, Silenians, Satyrs, and the like were merely Pelasgions, pictographically identified as belonging to the Horse, Goat or other totemistic fraternities'.

Pliny stated that the Satyrs got their name from σαθή, the membrum virile, because they were always prone to lust. Presumably this would be Shakespeare's reading (*Hamlet* I, ii) when he referred to Hamlet's father-in-law. Aldrovandus was inclined to place them among the sylvan deities of mythology, but was willing to compound with Petrus Martyr, who identified them with *Homines Sylvestris*— the Wild Men of the Woods. The latter, he says, used to inhabit inelegant subterranean hovels, lived on vegetables, and refused to have anything to do with other humans. However kindly they were treated it was impossible to civilize them, because they refused to recognize law and order. There were an almost infinite number of them in Ireland.

[2] Bearded monkeys. Perhaps Barbary apes.

A STAG is called 'Cervus' from its habit of snuffing up the Cerastes—which are horned snakes—or else from being 'horn-bearing', for horns are called *'cerata'* in Greek.[1]

These creatures are enemies to serpents. When they feel themselves to be weighed down by illness, they suck snakes from their holes with a snort of the nostrils and, the danger of their venom having been survived, the stags are restored to health by a meal of them.

The plant called Dittany offers them the same sort of medical food, for, when they have fed on it, they can shake off any arrows which they may have received.

[1] It is needless to mention that nearly all the derivations made by the Bestiarist were imaginative. In this case the scribe seems scarcely to have understood the explanation himself. Whenever he has made rubbish of his dictation, which he does very often, writing *'comici'* for *'ocimi'*, or *'a radicos'* for *'Arcadicos'*, the present translator has tried to restore the sense without comment, provided that he has traced it elsewhere. A Bestiary is not a great work of literary art, and it would be pedantic to reproduce it verbatim, with its innumerable 'verilys' and 'moreovers'. Nor is it reasonable to be incomprehensibly accurate in translating a scribe who is himself inaccurate. In the section on Serpents, the Bestiarist quotes six times from Lucan. He quotes him correctly only twice.

Stags listen admiringly to the music of rustic pipes.[1]
With their ears pricked, they hear acutely; with the ears
lowered, not at all.

Also these animals have the following peculiarity: that
when they change their feeding grounds for love of a
foreign pasture, and browse along on the way there, if
by any chance they have to cross huge rivers or seas,
each rests his head on the haunches of the one in front,
and, since the one behind does the same thing for him in
turn, they suffer no trouble from the weight. And, when
they have mounted their heads upon those parts, they
hurry across with the greatest possible speed for fear of
getting befouled.

Stags have another feature too, for, after a dinner of
snake, they shed their coats and all their old age with
them.

These peculiarities seem to fit in with people who are
devoted to the Holy Church, by a congruous and com-
petent symbolism. For when Christians leave their
pasture, i.e. this world, for the love of heavenly pastures,
they support each other, i.e. the more perfect carry along
and sustain the weight of the less perfect by their example
and good works. And if they come across some occasion
for sin they hurry over it at once. Also, after snuffing
up the devil-snake, i.e. after the perpetration of sin, they

---

[1] Even Aristotle, a genuine observer, states that they like music. Pigs were
also notorious for this foible. 'Arion', says Burton in his *Anatomy of Melancholy*,
'made fish follow him, which, as common experience evinceth, are much affected
with musick. All singing birds are much pleased with it, especially nightingales,
if we may beleeve Calcagninus; and bees among the rest, though they be flying
away, when they hear any tingling sound, will tarry behinde. Harts, hinds,
horses, dogs, bears, are exceedingly delighted with it, Scal. exerc. 302. Elephants,
Aggrippa addes, lib. 2. cap. 24. and in Lydia in the midst of a lake there be
certain floating ilands (if ye will beleeve it) that, after musick, will dance'.

run with Confession to Our Lord Jesus Christ, who is the true fountain, and, drinking the precepts laid down by him, our Christians are renovated—the Old Age of Sin having been shed.

When the appointed season inclines the Stag to rut, the males of this species bell with a fury of concupiscence. Although the females may be impregnated beforehand, they do not conceive until the time of the star Arcturus. Nor do they bring forth their babies just anywhere, but they hide them with tender care, and, having tucked them up in some deep shrubbery or undergrowth, they admonish them with a stamp of the foot to keep hidden. When the powers of the little ones have become strong enough for running, they teach them to trot by practise and accustom them to leap over high places.

Upon hearing the cry of hounds, Stags place themselves with a following wind, so that their scent may blow away with them. All stand stock still, for which reason they make themselves an easier mark for archers.

The one of the horns which is on the right of the head is the more useful one for healing things. To keep snakes away, you can burn either of them.

Teeth give away their age, when there are found to be few or none. To estimate their longevity, Alexander the Great once ringed a large number of stags which, when recaptured after a hundred years, did not show signs of senility.

The young of stags are called Hinnuli (fawns) from '*innuere*—to nod, or make a sign', because they hide at a nod from their mother. The rennet of a fawn killed in its mother's womb is capital against poisons.

It is known that stags never get feverish, so, for this

reason, ointments made from their marrow will settle heats in sick men. We read that many people who have been accustomed to eat venison from their early days have been immortal, and immune to fevers, but it fails them in the end if they happen to get killed by a single wound.[1]

[1] 'Mithradates, he died old.' A. E. HOUSMAN.

CAPER the Goat is an animal who gets called this because she strives to attain the mountain crags (aspera *cap*tet).

Others call her Caprea, because of the rattling (*a crepita*).[1] But the latter are Wild Goats, which the Greeks used to call Dorcas[2] because they can see so very acutely. These linger on the highest mountains and can recognize approaching people from far away, distinguishing the wayfarer from the sportsman.

Thus Our Lord Jesus Christ is partial to high mountains, i.e. to Prophets and Apostles, for it is said in the *Song of Songs:* 'Behold my cousin cometh like a he-goat leaping on the mountains, crossing the little hills, and like a goat he is pastured in the valleys'. Our Lord is pastured in the Church—you see, the good works of Christians are food for him—and it was he who said: 'I hungered and you gave me to eat, I thirsted and you gave me to drink'.

By the valleys of the mountains, the Churches in various parts are intended. It is said in the *Song of Songs:* 'Behold, my cousin inclineth to me and let him be like a kid or the fawn of a deer'.

Because the sharpness of a goat's eyes is very acute, and they see everything and know men from afar, this symbolizes Our Lord, who is the Lord God of all knowing. And from another scriptural passage, when the High God looks down to the humble and gazes upon the haughty from afar—he who created all things and founded and rules and sees and examines and as it were perceives and knows absolutely anything which arises in our hearts—then indeed that Holy Goat does recognize the approaching sportsman from afar.

[1] i.e. the rattling of the dry droppings entangled in the pelt—or of her hoofs?

[2] Dorcas is δορκάς, the deer or gazelle. The word 'gazelle' comes from the Arabic '*ghazāl*'. The word 'gaze' is of unknown origin. If the ancient philologist was here pursuing a pun, perhaps this has something to do with it.

41

In the same way Christ, perceiving the wiles of his betrayer, said: 'Behold, the man who shall betray me is approaching'.

The WILD GOAT (*Caprea*) has the following peculiarities: that he moves higher and higher as he pastures; that he chooses good herbs from bad ones by the sharpness of his eyes; that he ruminates these herbs, and that, if wounded, he runs to the plant Dittany,[1] after reaching which he is cured.

---

[1] 'The Englishmen (call it) Dittander, Ditany, and Pepperwoort.' GERARDE's *Herbal*.

Thus good Preachers, feeding on the Law of God and on good works, as if delighting in this sort of pasture, rise up and up from one virtue to another. They choose out good thoughts from bad ones with the eyes of the heart. They ruminate the selected ones, i.e. they thoroughly examine the good and commit their ruminations to memory. If they are wounded by sin, they run to Jesus Christ in confession and are healed by the herb dogma. And thus may Jesus well be called most-gracious, when he so closely resembles this herb-o'grace.[1] For just as the Dittany expels the sword from the wound, and the wound heals, so does Jesus Christ forgive sins and expel the devil by means of confession.

[1] Just as the previous moralization is among the least strained, so is the present play-upon-words among the more successful of the holy puns in the Bestiary. Christ heals: dittany heals. Christ is to be called '*bene-ditantius*' [*sic*]: the latin for dittany is here '*ditannus*'.

The MONOCEROS[1] is a monster with a horrible howl, with a horse-like body, with feet like an elephant, and with a tail like a stag's.[2]

[1] Lo! in the mute, mid wilderness,
   What wondrous Creature?—of no kind;—
   His burning hair doth largely press—
   Gaze fixt—and feeding on the wind?
   His fell is of the desert dye,
   And tissue adust, dun-yellow and dry,
   Compact of living sands; his eye
   Black luminary, soft and mild,
   With its dark lustre cools the wild.
   From his stately forehead springs,
   Piercing to heaven, a radiant horn!
   Lo, the compeer of lion-kings,
   The steed self-armed, the Unicorn.'
                    GEORGE DARLEY, 1835

[2] Bright Scolopendraes arm'd with silver scales;
   Mighty Monoceros with immeasured tayles.
                    SPENSER, *Faerie Queene*, II, xii, 23

A horn sticks out from the middle of its forehead with astonishing splendour to the distance of four feet, so sharp that whatever it charges is easily perforated by it. Not a single one has ever come alive into the hands of man, and, although it is possible to kill them, it is not possible to capture them.[1]

[1] Since the Monoceros or Unicorn was simply an animal with one horn on its nose, there was naturally a good deal of discussion about the particular animal intended. There is no reason to regard it as a mythological one. Indeed, there are a very large number of single-horned animals in nature: beetles named after the rhinoceros, fishes like the sword-fish or the narwhal, quadrupeds like the African rhino, crested reptiles, even birds with a hard growth on the nares. The one point about which Aldrovandus, Browne and even Alexander Ross were agreed, was that they themselves did not intend the true rhinoceros, with which animal they were well acquainted.

The reason why there are two unicorns described in this Bestiary is that Aelian believed there were two species—a solid-footed, donkey-sized one identified with 'the Indian Asse'; and a cloven-footed creature identified with the oryx.

The whole subject, however, is so complicated—apart from the heading Rhinoceros under '*Bisulcis*', Aldrovandus devotes no less than sixty-seven of his enormous pages to the Unicorn—that those who wish to pursue it must do so elsewhere than here. To put it briefly, the idea of the unicorn probably orginated in travellers' tales about the rhinoceros whose horn was so much valued in Asia as an aphrodisiac. These tales about the scarce horn were given an impetus by the teeth of narwhal found on beaches. The famous medieval ones at Paris, Venice, Antwerp and in England, and those belonging to the King of Poland and the Duke of Mantua, with what Sir Thomas Browne calls their 'anfractuous spires and chocleary turnings', were narwhal horns. They were supposed also to have great virtue against poisons, particularly arsenic, but of their medical value Sir Thomas observes with dubiety: 'With what security a man may rely on this

URSUS the Bear, connected with the word '*Orsus*' (a beginning), is said to get her name because she sculptures her brood with her mouth (*ore*). For they say that these creatures produce a formless foetus, giving birth to something like a bit of pulp, and this the mother-bear arranges into the proper legs and arms by licking it. This is because of the prematurity of the birth. In short, she pups on the thirtieth day, from whence it comes that a hasty, unformed creation is brought forth.

A bear's head is feeble: the greatest strength is in the arms and loins, for which reason they sometimes stand upright.

Nor do they neglect the healer's art. Indeed, if they

---

remedy, the mistresse of fooles hath already instructed some; and to wisdome (which is never too wise to learne) it is not too late to consider'.

Single-horned animals have existed and do exist. 'It was not until Cuvier in the early nineteenth century laid it down as a rule of nature that, because the bone of its forehead was divided, it was impossible for an animal with a cleft hoof to have a horn growing in the middle of its forehead, that science turned against the unicorn,' PETER LUM, *Fabulous Beasts*, 1952.

The same authoress mentions 'a fascinating experiment recently performed in America by Dr Dove and described by Willy Ley in *The Lungfish, the Dodo, and the Unicorn*. In this experiment the two normal horn buds of a young calf were grafted together and transplanted to the centre of the forehead, where they grew into a single and straight horn. Even more interesting than this was the result of the operation on the character of the bull. He grew to be stronger than the normal two-horned bulls, so that he naturally took over the leadership of the herd; at the same time, sure of his power, he became unusually gentle and mild, thus displaying exactly the great strength and gentle nature of the legendary unicorn.'

are afflicted with a serious injury and damaged by wounds, they know how to doctor themselves by stroking their sores with a herb whose name is Flomus,[1] as the Greeks call it, so that they are cured by the mere touch.

A sick bear eats ants.

Numidian bears excel others so far as the thickness of their shaggy hair is concerned, but the creature itself is the same wherever they breed.

They do not make love like other quadrupeds, but, being joined in mutual embraces, they copulate in the human way. The winter season provokes their inclination to lust. The males respect the pregnant females with the decency of a private room, and, though in the same lairs for their lying-in, these are divided by earth-works into separate beds. The period of gestation is short, since the thirtieth day relieves the womb. This is why the precipitate childbirth creates shapeless fruits. They bring forth very tiny pulps of a white colour, with no eyes. They gradually sculpture these by licking;[2] and meanwhile they cherish them to their bosoms so as to draw up the animal spirit, being warmed by this careful incubation. During this time, with absolutely no food for the first fourteen days, the sleepless she-bears get so deeply drowsy that they cannot be woken up, even by wounds, and they lie hid after bearing for three months. Then, after coming out into the free daylight, they suffer so much from being unaccustomed to the light that you would take them to be struck blind.

[1] φλόμος, mullein.

[2] A learned doctor, in her book on *Alexander Pope*, has recently found a 'hell-born inspiration', indeed a 'smoky and appalling beauty', in the amiable lines from the *Dunciad*:

> So watchful Bruin forms, with plastic care,
> Each growing lump, and brings it to a bear.

Bears look out for the hives of bees and long for the honeycombs very much. Nor do they grab anything else more greedily than honey.

When they have eaten the fruits of the mandrake they die—unless they hurry off, for fear that the poison should grow strong enough to destroy them, and eat ants to recuperate their health.

If ever they attack bulls, they know by what parts to bring them down most readily, nor will they go for anything but the horns or the nostrils—the nostrils, because the sharper pain comes in the tenderer place.

Presumably the doctor discovers these infernal terrors in some construction of her own, by which the slavering omnivore makes unmentionable meat-patties for dinner and hands them round the company ('brings them to a bear.'). In fact, poor Bruin's tender care was only to fashion her formless babies into the right shape for growing up, and she was watchful because she had to keep awake to do it. She was 'licking them into shape'.

The first use quoted by the N.E.D. for the word 'licking' in the sense of 'flogging' is dated 1756. Until that period, the parents or schoolmasters who proposed to lick the young idea into shape were offering no threat: they were, on the contrary, referring to the gentle and maternal solicitude which Pope mentions playfully in his couplet, and to which Shakespeare refers in 3 *Henry VI*, iii, ii: 'like to a chaos, or an unlicked bear-whelp'.

There was a reasonable substratum of truth for the medieval belief. Bear cubs really are born blind and hairless, and remain so for no less than five weeks. Naked, born in a jealous seclusion which made observation almost impossible, and constantly licked by their dam as bitches clean their puppies, the idea that the cubs were produced as a kind of mola was not absolutely preposterous. 'The cub comes forth involved in the Chorion,' says Sir Thomas Browne, 'a thick and tough membrane obscuring the formation, and which the Dam doth after bite and teare asunder, (so that) the beholder at first sight conceives it a rude and informous lumpe of flesh, and imputes the ensuing shape unto the mouthing of the Dam'.

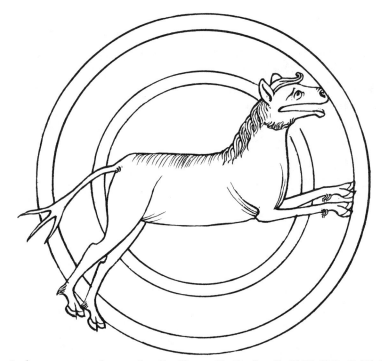

A beast gets born in India called the LEUCROTA,[1] and it exceeds in velocity all the wild animals there are. It has the size of a donkey, the haunches of a stag, the breast and shins of a lion, the head of a horse, a cloven hoof, and a mouth opening as far as its ears. Instead of

[1] See Yena. Aldrovandus gives it up. It must be a mythical animal, he says, like the Griffin, Sphinx and Mantichora.

Topsell, indeed, in his version of Gesner (1607), states that it *is* the Mantichora. After describing the latter beast more or less as we have it on p. 51, he proceeds to mix it up with the porcupine—'with her taile she woundeth her Hunters whether they come before her or behind her, and presently when the quils are cast forth, new ones grow up in their roome'—and also with the 'marico-morion' (mermecoleon?). He concludes: 'This also (the Mantichora) is the same beast which is called *Leucrocuta*, about the bigness of a wilde Asse, being in legs and hoofes like a Hart, having his mouth reaching on both sides to his eares, and the head and face of a female like unto a Badger's. It is called also *Martiora*, which in the Persian tongue signifieth a devourer of men.' Topsell's picture of a Mantichora will be found on p. 247.

48

teeth, there is one continuous bone: but this is only as to shape, for in voice it comes near to the sounds of people talking.

This is called a COCODRYLLUS from its crocus or saffron colour. It breeds in the River Nile: an animal with four feet, amphibious, generally about thirty feet long, armed with horrible teeth and claws. So great is the hardness of its skin that no blow can hurt a crocodile, not even if hefty stones are bounced on its back. It lies in the water by night, on land by day.

It incubates its eggs in the earth. The male and female take turns. Certain fishes which have a saw-like dorsal fin destroy it, ripping up the tender parts of its belly. Moreover, alone among animals, it moves its upper jaw, keeping the lower one quite motionless.[1] Its dung provides an ointment with which old and wrinkled whores anoint their figures and are made beautiful, until the flowing sweat of their efforts washes it away.[2]

Hypocritical, dissolute and avaricious people have the same nature as this brute—also any people who are puffed up with the vice of pride, dirtied with the corruption of luxury, or haunted with the disease of avarice—even if they do make a show of falling in with the justifications of the Law, pretending in the sight of men to be upright and indeed very saintly.

[1] 'This was the common belief of the ancients. Cuvier thus accounts for the error: "The lower jaw being prolonged behind the skull, the upper seems to be movable, and the ancients have so recorded it; but it moves only with the whole head".' Dr W. OGLE.

Aristotle himself fell into this error.

The articulation of jaws in crocodiles was responsible for a certain amount of acrobatics in the eighteenth century. 'The under jaw in man', says Goldsmith's *History of the Earth and Animated Nature*, 'possesses a great variety of motions; while the upper has been thought, by many, to be quite immovable. However, that it moves in man, a very easy experiment will suffice to convince us. If we keep the head fixed, with anything between our teeth, the edge of a table for instance, and then open our mouths, we shall find that both jaws recede from it at the same time; the upper jaw rises, and the lower falls, and the table remains untouched between them.'

[2] Francis Bacon, who held that 'some Putrefactions and Excrements do yield excellent Odors,' pointed out that: 'We finde also, that places where men Urine commonly have some smell of Violets. And Urine, if one hath eaten Nutmeg, hath so too'.

The scented dung was thought to come from a special kind of crocodile living in 'the Province of Xanagarra'. It was better than musk. As the sweet-smelling Panther also inhabited those parts, it was conjectured that perhaps the habitat was responsible for the smell. Galen considered that crocodile dung was good for freckles. Aetius recommended that it should be lighted and the smoke puffed into snake-holes. Kiranides held that the teeth were aphrodisiac, but they had to be taken out alive.

Crocodiles lie by night in the water, by day on land, because hypocrites, however luxuriously they live by night, delight to be said to live holily and justly by day. Conscious of their wickedness in doing so, they beat their breasts: yes, but with use, habit always brings to light the things which they have done.

The monster moves his upper jaws because these people hold up the higher examples of the Fathers and an abundance of precepts in speech to others, while they show in their lower selves all too little of what they say.

An ointment is made of its evil dung because bad people are often admired and praised by the inexperienced for the evil they have done, and extolled by the plaudits of this world, as if beautified by an ointment. But when the Judgement, sweated out by the evils perpetrated, moves its anger to the striking, then all that elegance of flattery vanishes like a smoke.

A beast is born in the Indies called a MANTICORA. It has a threefold row of teeth meeting alternately: the face of a man, with gleaming, blood-red eyes: a lion's body: a tail like the sting of a scorpion, and a shrill voice which is so sibilant that it resembles the notes of flutes. It hankers after human flesh most ravenously. It is so strong in the foot, so powerful with its leaps, that not the most extensive space

nor the most lofty obstacle can contain it.[1]

[1] When Skelton cursed the cat which had killed poor Phyllyp Sparowe, he expressed the wish that

'The mantycors of the montaynes
Might fede them on thy braynes.'

The name is derived from an old Persian word meaning 'man-eater', and some have suggested that the Manticore is simply a man-eating tiger. There is a fabulous Indian beast called the Makara. Another suggestion is man-tiger, i.e. an uncanny creature like the Werewolf. In Haiti at the present day there is a voodoo animal called the *Cigouave*, which resembles the Manticora, and, since the Bestiaries are connected with an African origin, it is just within the distant bounds of possibility that the Manticora may have had some similar supernatural ancestry. The beast is probably an eastern hieroglyphic, or god, or piece of sculpture like the man-headed bulls of Assyria, or a combination of all these and others also, which has found its way into natural history with the Griffin.

Whatever the Manticora was, it is not extinct. Mr David Garnett informs the present translator that his friend Mr Richard Strachey was mistaken for one by the villagers of Ugijar, Andalusia, in 1930, who mobbed him on that hypothesis.

The confusion among the parts of these composite beasts in the Bestiaries is sometimes due to the etymologist. One reason why we are now puzzled about things like Serra (q.v.) and Basiliok and Manticora is that the medieval philologue has often, by his own conjecture, managed to mix them together in pursuit of a verbal derivation in his own head. There is even, for instance, a Mantiserra in a Will of 1494 at Somerset House. Mermaids, mermecoleons, manticoras, mantiserras and half a dozen others have at one time or another been scrambled together by interpreters like Isidore of Seville, not in pursuit of natural history, but in that of language, or even in that of morals. See Appendix.

Ethiopia produces an animal called a P A R-A N D R U S, which has the slot of an Ibex, branching horns, the head of a stag, the colour of a bear, and, like a bear, it has a deep shaggy coat.

People say that this Parandrus runs away

when it is frightened, and, when it hides somewhere, it gets changed into the likeness of whatever it is close to—either white against a stone or green against a bush or in any other way it likes.[1]

[1] This animal belongs to the same puzzle as the 'antalops'. It does not figure in the N.E.D. Gesner says that certain barbarian authors have corruptly written 'parandrus' for 'tarandus', which was either the elk or the reindeer. Its chameleon-like ability to copy its background was simply the reindeer's talent for assuming a spring or autumn coat in relation to the snow.

VULPIS the fox gets his name from the person who winds wool (*volupis*)—for he is a creature with circuitous pug marks who never runs straight but goes on his way with tortuous windings.

He is a fraudulent and ingenious animal. When he is hungry and nothing turns up for him to devour, he rolls

53

himself in red mud so that he looks as if he were stained with blood. Then he throws himself on the ground and holds his breath, so that he positively does not seem to breathe. The birds, seeing that he is not breathing, and that he looks as if he were covered with blood with his tongue hanging out, think he is dead and come down to sit on him. Well, thus he grabs them and gobbles them up.[1]

The Devil has the nature of this same.

With all those who are living according to the flesh he feigns himself to be dead until he gets them in his gullet and punishes them. But for spiritual men of faith he is truly dead and reduced to nothing.

Furthermore, those who wish to follow the devil's works perish, as the Apostle says: 'Know this, since if you live after the flesh you shall die, but if you mortify the doings of the foxy body according to the spirit you shall live'. And the Lord God says: 'They will go into the lower parts of the earth, they will be given over to the power of the sword, they will become a portion for foxes'.

[1] The same fable was reported of cats with rats in the Middle Ages, and by Francis Meres in *Palladis Tamia* (1598) of leopards with monkeys.

There is a beast called a Y A L E, which is as big as a horse, has the tail of an elephant, its colour black and with the jowls of a boar. It carries outlandishly long horns which are adjusted to move at will. They are not fixed, but are moved as the needs of battle dictate, and, when it fights, it points one of them forward and folds the other one back, so that, if it hurts the tip of this one with any

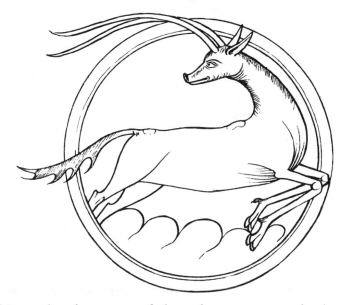

blow, the sharpness of the other one can take its place.[1]

[1] The Eale or Yale was popular in Heraldry (argent bezanty), and furnished the supporters of the arms of Christ's College, Cambridge, among others. It had spots and tushes. Pliny was the first to describe the creature, and it has been suggested that he was thinking of the Antelope Gnu: but he also describes the latter animal under the name of Catoblepas. 'This Ethiopian wild beast [the Catoblepas], according to Pliny (VIII, 77) was of moderate dimensions, except for a head so heavy that it hung down towards the ground—fortunately for the human race, because all who met its gaze expired immediately. Aelian (VII, 5) adds that it was like a bull, which suggests "an animal of the antelope kind" (Liddell and Scott), or more probably the Gnu'. Dr Ansell Robin.

Pliny's description of the Catoblepas is immediately followed by the statement: 'The basilisk has the same power [of killing with its glance]'. The result is that later copyists or translators have sometimes confused the one with the other.

The Yale appears in French bestiaries as '*la Centicore*'. Sir Arthur Shipley 'tracked it back to Egypt' and Mr G. C. Druce dealt with it very fully in a paper published by the *Archaeological Journal* in 1911. It seems to be the opinion of Druce that the Yale cannot be identified with any living animal. It may be a hieroglyphic one depicted in silhouette, which would turn one horn forward and the other backward. Or it may be some antelope which flicks its ears.

According to the magazine *Life* (7 May 1951), '*ya-'el*' means 'mountain goat' in Hebrew. Mr G. W. B. Huntingford, however, publishing a report for the Colonial Office later in the same year, states that there is a cow among the Nandi tribe of Kenya, known as a Kamari cow, and he who does not own one is 'ashamed, and sits silent at his beer-drinking'. One horn points forward and the other back. Sometimes the cows are born with this deformity. Sometimes it is induced by training the horns with thongs.

The word LUPUS, a Wolf,[1] is brought into our Latin
language from a Greek derivation, for they call a Lupus
a *Licus* (λύκος). And they are called λύκος in Greek on
account of their bites, because they massacre anybody
who passes by with a fury of greediness. Others maintain
that they are called 'Lupus' from 'Lion-paws', because,
as with lions, their powers are in their paws. Whatever
they pounce on, dies.

Wolves are known for their rapacity, and for this reason
we call prostitutes wolves, because they devastate the
possessions of their lovers. Moreover, a wolf is a rapaci-
ous beast, and hankering for gore. He keeps his strength
in his chest and jaws: in his loins there is really very

[1] Once upon a time there was a Wolf who had heard great things about the
clergy in monasteries, and how they did very little work, lived easy and had
lamb for dinner. So he decided to be a religious. His friends told him that he
would have to go through the proper training for this, which would mean going
to the abbey school for his education. He did so, and there was a schoolmaster
there who had to teach him his alphabet. The master had a birch and Wolf had
a pointer with which he had to pick out the letters. They got over A, and they

little. His neck is never able to turn backward. He is said sometimes to live on prey, sometimes on earth, and sometimes even on air.

The female wolf does not whelp in any other month than May, and then in thundery weather. So great is her cunning that she does not catch food for her whelps near home, but from far away. And if it is needful to take prey at night, she goes like a tame dog to the fold, at a foot's pace, and, lest the sheepdog should notice the smell of her breath or the shepherds wake up, she goes upwind. And if a twig or anything else should make a noise when

---

got over B. It was hard going. Then they arrived at the third letter. 'What does that stand for?' asked the master. Poor Wolf, who thought that this might surely be it at last, cried out enthusiastically: 'Lamb!'

But they only turned him out, on the score that he was a humbug.
> 'And thus it haps ofttimes to each,
> That his secret thought is by his speech
> Revealed, and, ere he is aware,
> It is out of his lips and in the air.'

The story is narrated by Marie de France:
> '*Une prestres volt jadis aprendre*
> *I lou a letres fere entendre.*
> *A dist li prestres. – A dist li leus*
> *Qui mult est fel et engingneux.*
> *B dist li prestres, di o moi.*
> *B dist li leux, la letre voi.*
> *C dist li prestres, di avant.*
> *C dist le leus. Ail dont tant,*
> *Respont li prestres, or di par toi.*
> *Li leu respont: Je ne sai coi.*
> *Di que te semble, si espel.*
> *Respont li leus: Aignel, aignel!*
> *Li prestres dist: que verte touche;*
> *Tel on penser, tel en la bouche.*
> *De pensons, le voit l'en souvent;*
> *Ce dont il pensent durement,*
> *Est par la bouche conneu.*
> *Ainçois que d'autre soit seu,*
> *La bouche monstre le penser;*
> *Tout doit ele de li parler.'*

her foot presses it, she punishes her own foot with a regular nip.

A Wolf's eyes shine at night like lamps, and its nature is that, if it sees a man first, it strikes him dumb and triumphs over him like a victor over the voiceless.[1] But, also, if it feels itself to have been seen first, it loses its own ferocity and cannot run.

Solinus, who has much to say about the nature of things, reports that on the backside of this animal there is a small patch of aphrodisiac hair, which it plucks off with its teeth if it happens to be afraid of being caught, nor is this aphrodisiac hair for which people are trying to catch it of any use unless taken off alive.[2]

[1] That the sudden sight of a man-eater causes obmutency need be no fable. Artemidorus the grammarian, Burton informs us, lost his wits by the unexpected sight of a crocodile. The leopard of Rudrapryag, which was finally shot by Colonel Corbett, was able to make off with its victims, without sound or cry, from among assemblies of people. Big-game hunters who have been mauled by lions and have survived it, state that they felt neither fear nor pain. Birds which fall into the clutches of cats or other raptors remain mute, and seem anaesthetized. Rabbits are paralysed by stoats. 'The ground or occasional original hereof', says Sir Thomas Browne, was probably 'a vehement fear which naturally produceth obmutence, and sometimes irrecoverable silence: thus birds are silent in the presence of an hawk.'

[2] 'Rhasis was being frivolous when he reported concerning wolves' hair: "If the eyebrows are anointed with the same, mixed with rose-water, the anointed one will be adored by the beholder." And really I think it even more ridiculous and merry when it is said that backward men and women can be brought to lust by the tie of a wolf's pizzle (dried in an oven). This is like the statement about a wolf-skin pouch, which, if worn with a dove's heart tied up inside it, saves one from falling into the snares of Venus. Rather of the same sort is the story of Rhasis, who cites ten disciples of Democritus, people who certainly escaped safely from the enemy by carrying the scrotum of a wolf on their lances. In the same way, Sextus tells us about the Traveller who made his journey safely by carrying with him the end bit of a wolf's tail. Also, according to Vuecherius, if one hangs up the brush or the pelt or the head of a wolf over the stall, the beasts will not eat unless it is taken away. With the same tail, so Albertus Magnus says, if it is tied above the mangers of sheep and cattle, the wolf itself can be frightened off: and that is why people bury them in farms, to keep these brutes away.' *Ulyssis Aldrovandi, de Quadrup. Digit. Vivip.* Lib. I, 172.

The devil bears the similitude of a wolf: he who is always looking over the human race with his evil eye, and darkly prowling round the sheepfolds of the faithful so that he may afflict and ruin their souls.

That a wolf should be born during the first thunder of the month of May symbolizes that the Devil fell from heaven in the first motion of his pride.

Moreover, since this creature keeps its strength in its fore parts and not in its backward parts, it signifies that this same Satan was at first forward among the angels of light and was only made an apostate by the hindward way.

Its eyes shine in the night like lamps because the works of the devil are everywhere thought to seem beautiful and salubrious, by darkened and fatuous human beings.

When it whelps, it only takes its prey from far off, because the Devil fosters those of whom he is sure, as being near to him, with temporal blessings, knowing that they are going to suffer torments with him in the dens of hell anyway. But he anxiously pursues such people as take themselves far away from him by good works. In this sense it can be read of the Blessed Job, from whom the Devil took away all his substance and even his sons and daughters, in order that his heart might renege from God.

Because a wolf is never able to turn its neck backward, except with a movement of the whole body, it means that the Devil never turns back to lay hold on repentance.

Now what on earth can a man do, from whom the Wolf has stolen away the strength to shout and who even lacks the power of speech and consequently cannot get the help of distant people? If he is able to do anything,

59

let him drop down his clothes to be trampled underfoot and take two stones in his hands, which he must beat together.[1] Seeing this, the Wolf, losing the courage of his convictions, will run away; and the man, saved by his own ingenuity, will be as free as he was in the beginning.

Now all this is to be understood in a spiritual manner, and you have to say it allegorically, to the higher sense. For what can we mean by the Wolf except the Devil, what by the man except sin, what by the stones except the apostles or other saints or Our Lord himself? All the prophets have been called stones of adamant. And he himself, Our Lord Jesus Christ, has been called in the Law 'a stumbling block and a rock of scandal'. The Prophet says about him: 'I saw One standing upon an adamant mountain'.

Before we were redeemed, we were under the power of the Enemy and we had lost the shouting voice. We, though our sins needed it, were inaudible and did not cry out to the saints to help us. But after the all-merciful God had qualified us in the person of his Son, we threw off the old man in baptism, i.e. the clothes, and with his acts we put on the new man, who is created according to God. At this point we picked up stones in our hands, which we strike against each other. This is how we reverberate the saints of God, who are already reigning in heaven with Jesus Christ our Lord, with the exhortation of our mouths. We do this in order to strike the ears of the Judge and to obtain pardon for our sins—lest Cerberus,

---

[1] Aldrovandus explains that the wolf is allergic to noises like singing or the clashing of cymbals. But it is not the noise which frightens the animal in this case. It is the stone itself. Wolves detest stones, he says, because, when people throw them at them, the bruises of the impact breed worms.

whom we cannot outspeak, rejoicing at our demise, should swallow us up.

Wolves only copulate on twelve days in the whole year. They can suffer hunger for a long time, and after much fasting they eat a lot.

Ethiopia[1] produces a kind of wolf which is maned on the neck and so variegated that no colour is missing, they say. It is a characteristic of Ethiopian wolves that they are as able as a bird in leaping, so that they do not cover more ground by running than by flying. But they never attack man. They are hairy at the winter solstice, naked in the summer. The Ethiopians call them *'Theas'*.[2]

[1] If an animal was of doubtful authenticity, it was generally placed in Ethiopia. The simplest translation of the word would be simply 'Africa'.

[2] Quare 'dyas'—a beast which does both things, to run and to fly. Perhaps they were flying foxes.

The Latin name of CANIS the Dog is seen to have a Greek etymology. For in Greek it is called *Canos*. But we must grant that some hold it to be named from the melody (*canor*) of its barking, since it howls deeply and is said to sing (*canere*).

Now none is more sagacious than Dog, for he has more perception than other animals and he

alone recognizes his own name. He esteems his Master highly.

There are numerous breeds of dogs. Some track down the wild creatures of the woods to catch them. Others guard the flocks of sheep vigilantly against infestations of wolves. Others, the house-dogs, look after the palisade of their masters, lest it should be robbed in the night by thieves, and these will stand up for their owners to the death. They gladly dash out hunting with Master, and will even guard his body when dead, and not leave it. In sum, it is a part of their nature that they cannot live without men.

So much do dogs adore their owners, that one can read how, when King Garamantes[1] was captured by his enemies and sold into slavery, two hundred of his hounds, having made up a party, rescued him from exile out of the middle of the whole battle-line of his foes, and fought those who resisted.

When Jason was killed in a quarrel, his dog refused food and died of hunger.

The hound of King Lisimachus threw itself into the flames when its master's funeral pyre had been lighted and was burnt up by the fire in company with him.

In the days when Appius and Junius Pictimus were consuls, a dog which could not be driven away accompanied its master—who had been condemned into prison—and followed him howling after he had been executed. And when, from the compassion of the Roman people, food was offered to it, it carried the victuals to the mouth of the dead man. At last, when the corpse was thrown into the Tyber, it tried to hold the body up, swimming beside it.

---

[1] According to the *Hereford Mappa Mundi*, the Garamantes live in a country whose waters boil by day and freeze by night. See the note on 'Birds', p. 103.

When a dog comes across the track of a hare or a stag, and reaches the branching of the trail, or the criss-cross of the trail because it has split into more parts, then the

dog puzzles silently with himself, seeking along the beginnings of each different track. He shows his sagacity
in following the scent, as if enunciating a syllogism.
'Either it has gone this way,' says he to himself, 'or that
way, or, indeed, it may have turned twisting in that other
direction. But as it has neither entered into this road, nor
that road, obviously it must have taken the third one!'
And so, by rejecting error, Dog finds the truth.[1]

Dogs, moreover, have often produced evidence to con-
vict culprits with proofs of murder done—to such an
extent that their mute testimony has frequently been
believed.[2]

They say that a man was murdered in Antioch, in a
remote part of the city, at dusk, who had his dog on a

---

[1] Jews did not like dogs, and the attitude of the Bible to these charming
creatures is uniformly revolting. Only Tobias, in the Apocrypha, gives them
their due. But in the Middle Ages, and even in the Dark Ages, there was a
tenderer attitude to animals and children than has sometimes developed since.
Few Masters of Foxhounds in the twentieth century would trouble to insist, as
the noble Master who was killed at Agincourt did, that a 'dog-boy' ought to sleep
permanently in the kennels, in order to keep the hounds happy. 'Also I will
teach the child', wrote the Duke of York in his *Master of Game*, 'to lead out the
hounds to scombre twice in the day in the morning and in the evening, so that
the sun be up, especially in the winter. Then should he let them run and play
long in a meadow in the sun, and then comb every hound after the other, and
wipe them with a great wisp of straw, and this he shall do every morning. And
then he shall lead them into some fair place where tender grass grows as corn and
other things, that therewith they may feed themselves as it is medicine for them.'
Thus, since the boy's 'heart and his business be with the hounds,' the hounds
themselves will become 'goodly and kindly and clean, glad and joyful and playful,
and goodly to all manner of folks save to the wild beasts, to whom they should be
fierce, eager and spiteful'.

It is a fact which may give pleasure to the kindly, that our Bestiarist has devoted
more space to horses and hounds and bees than to any other animals; and this
because he loved them in return, for being the friends of man. Even the N.E.D.
gives them nearly three pages.

[2] A leaf is here missing from C.U.L. ii.4.26, which probably showed two
full-page illustrations of the story which follows.

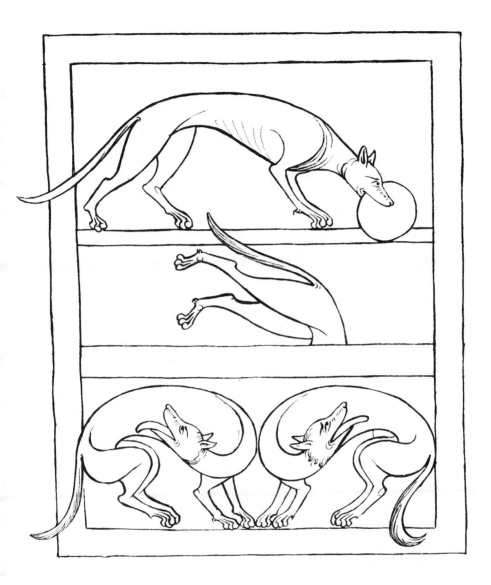

lead. A certain soldier, servant to the dead man, had done the killing in the hope of plunder. Hidden by the now gathering dusk, this fellow had cleared off elsewhere.

The body lay unburied. The crowd of onlookers was dense. The dog stood by. He was weeping for his master's woe with a piteous howl. Now it chanced that he who had committed the murder—such is the deviousness of human cunning—had innocently joined the mob of spectators and approached the corpse as if in mourning, so that he might lay claim to confidence by assuming authority in the middle of the fuss. At this the dog, putting aside its lamentation for a little while, took up the weapons of revenge, and gripped the fellow tight, and, wailing a keen that sounded like some heart-breaking tragic epilogue, reduced everybody to tears. And what gave weight to the proof was that the dog only held up this one person from among so many, and would not let him go. At length the wretch became terrified, for he did not know how to refute such an obvious testimony— not even by objecting that there was hatred, unfriendliness, envy or malice among the bystanders—and he no longer knew how to deny the fact. Thereupon, because it was all very difficult, he was put to the torture: in which he was not able to maintain his innocence.

In licking a wound, the tongue of a dog heals the same.

Its way of life is reported to be perfectly temperate, you see. What is more, the tongue of a puppy makes a salve for men's intestines, if they are wounded.

The dog's nature is that it returns to its own vomit and gobbles it up again.

And if it happens to cross a river carrying some meat or anything of that sort, when it sees its reflection it opens its mouth and, while it hastens to pick up the other bit of meat, it loses the one which it had.

In certain ways, Priests are like watchdogs. They

66

always drive away the wiles of the trespassing Devil with admonishments—and by doing the right thing—lest he should steal away the treasury of God, i.e. the souls of Christians.

The tongue of a dog cures a wound by licking it. This is because the wounds of sinners are cleansed, when they are laid bare in confession, by the penance imposed by the Priest. Also the tongue of a puppy cures the insides of men, because the inside secrets of the heart are often purified by the work and preaching of these learned men.

The dog is said to be very temperate in its diet, because that man only is truly on his guard who excels others in wisdom and studies: and that is the fellow who must shun all satiety—for Sodom perished of surfeit. Indeed, by no entry can the Enemy take possession of man so quickly as through a voracious gullet.

The fact that a dog returns to its vomit signifies that human beings, after a complete confession, often return incautiously to the crimes which they have perpetrated.

Because it leaves the true food in the river out of greed for the shadow, it symbolizes those silly people who often leave that which is peculiarly of the Law out of desire for some unknown thing. Whence it comes that, while they are not able to obtain what they hanker after, what they had before floats uselessly away to loss.

Some dogs are called LICISCI the Wolf Hounds,[1] because they are born of a wolf and a dog (*licus-canis*), when

[1] Baxter and Johnson translate '*licisca*' as 'greyhound bitch', but Pliny calls them wolf-hounds. One of the dogs of Acteon was named Lycitus. Mrs Piozzi wrote to Sir James Fellowes in 1821, to say that the most interesting circumstance of Parry's polar voyage had been 'an account given by one of the officers, how his Irish setter, a tall smooth spaniel, attracted the attentions of a she-wolf on

these have married one another by chance. And the bitches which are born of that union are accustomed to give admission to tiger-beasts, when involved by night in the woods—by whom they get overleaped, and then they give birth from that cross to an even fiercer kind of dog, and strong withal, so much so that it can outface lions.

 WHENSOEVER[1] the sinner wishes to please his Maker, it is useful and necessary that he should look for three Spiritual Guides. And these three bring together three Spiritual Governors, with three Spiritual Gifts for man's reconciliation with his Creator. These Guides and Governors, with their Spiritual Gifts, are thus arranged:

The first Guide is Weeping of the Heart, the second True Confession, the third Real Penitence. Their Governors are Love of God, Right Intentions and Good Deeds. The Spiritual Gifts are Cleanness of Body and Soul, Chaste Speech and Perseverance in Good Work.

And these Governors and Guides with Spiritual Gifts appear before the Trinity as follows:

[1] The moralization, beginning '*Quocienscumque peccator*', is accustomed to appear at various places in Bestiaries, or to be omitted. It seems to bear little relation to the text at this or any point, unless the 'sinner' is to represent the dog and his 'maker' the dog's master. Toward the end of this short sermon, there is another leaf missing from C.U.L. 11.4.26, which has been supplied from Sloane 3544, while the picture of Adam naming the animals is from Brit. Mus. Harl. 3244. We return to our own manuscript four lines from the end of Adam.

Melville Island, who made love to the handsome dandy, and seduced him at length to end his days with her and her rough-haired family, refusing every invitation to return to the ship'. This was 'a certain proof', added the learned lady, 'that dog, fox, jackal, etc. are only accidental varieties; while lupo is head of the house, penkennedil, as Welsh and Cornish people call it'.

Before God the Father appears Weeping of the Heart with Love of God, presenting Cleanness of Body and Soul. Before the Son, comes True Confession with Right Intentions, presenting Chaste Speech. Before the Holy Ghost comes Real Penitence with Good Deeds, presenting Perseverance in Good Work.

Just as medicines are necessary to a sick body to heal its infirmities, so is medicine needful to a sinful soul, by means of which its spiritual corruption may be healed. Now the Medicine of the Soul is made out of four ingredients, i.e. Weeping of the Heart, True Confession, Real Penitence, Good Deeds. And it is useful for curing our ills for the following reason: because, when the soul is anointed with it, it is immediately healed from its infirmities.

But if the Soul-patient, after cure, is without a decent covering, however it might be presented in the heavenly gathering where it has to be offered before its maker, it would be passed over. It is necessary therefore that he who undertakes to carry the cured soul back to God should so clothe it, both decently and sufficiently, that he may be able to present it laudably before the angels of heaven. Verily, the first covering with which the soul ought to be dressed is Purity. For nothing, either now or in the future, can be presented in the heavenly gathering if it is not clean. Other necessary coverings are: piety, charity and various other virtues with which it ought to be clothed.

It is then indeed that, with such clothes, together with the three Guides, i.e., Pure Thought, Chaste Word and Perfect Deed, the soul can decently be introduced into the heavenly kingdom, where it will be rewarded with that beatitude which the angels enjoy. It was to obtain this that God created Man and assigned him his three Councillors, viz, the Spiritual Mind, the Power of Behaving Properly, and Wisdom. If Man had stuck to these things, the heavenly kingdom would not have turned him away, but, because he did not stick to them, he has let slip his inheritance.

It was A D A M[1] who first gave names to animals, calling each and all of them something or other, by trial and error, according to the sort of nature which each of them had. Moreover, people addressed these animals in the First of Languages. For Adam did not award the names according to the Latin tongue, nor the Greek one, nor

---

[1] 'It may be remarked that man is the only animal which can live and multiply in every country from the equator to the poles. The hog seems to approach the nearest to our species in that privilege.' GIBBON.

according to any other barbarous speech, but in that language which was current to everybody before the Flood: that is to say, Hebrew.[1]

In Latin, the words for animals—'*animalia*' or '*animantia*'—come from the life of animation and the spirit of movement.

Quadrupeds are called this because they go on four feet; but of these creatures—although they are rather like the herds under human care—the ones which we call stags, fallow deer, wild asses and so forth are neither Beasts (like lions) nor Domestic Animals (like those which can lend themselves to the uses of man) but are, on the contrary, the kind who disdain the voice or countenance of any master.

Properly speaking, the word 'herd' is applied to those animals which are bred for food (like sheep) or which are otherwise suitable for the use of man (like horses and cows). The word '*pecus*' can be used either for solitary or gregarious animals: since the ancients commonly used '*pecora*' or '*pecudes*' to indicate all animals—whether they were creatures to eat, like sheep, or creatures which were named thus because they grazed (*a pascendo*).

Beasts of burden are so called because they aid the burdens of men by their assistance under the yoke; for the ox draws his cart or ploughs the hardest furrows, the horse and the ass carry packs and ease the human task as they pace along. Thus they are called '*jumenta*' because they '*juvent homines*'.[2] They are animals of great strength.

---

[1] The Jews claim to have had a natural history by Adam, who as the first man created . . . might therefore be regarded as an original and infallible authority on the subject.' E. P. EVANS.

[2] 'Say poor,' says Burton sadly, 'and say all: they are born to labour, to misery, to carry burdens like juments, *pistum stercus comedere*, with Ulysses companions, and (as Chremylus objected in Aristophanes) *salem lingere*, lick salt, to empty

The final word for 'herds'—*armenta*—comes either because they are capable of fighting with their horns (*armis*), or else because like horses they are actually used in war (*in armis*). Others explain the '*armenta*' of cattle from their ploughing (*ab arando*), as if they were spiders weaving a web-pattern on the soil (*quasi aranienta*). Or else you could say that they are 'armed' (*armata*) with horns.

Anyway, there is a difference between the herds called '*armenta*' and the flocks called '*greges*'. The herds or '*armenta*' are of horses or cattle, while the flocks or '*greges*' are of goats and sheep.

The gentle flock of OVIS the sheep, woolly, defenceless in body and placid in mind, gets its name '*ab oblatione*'—from the burnt sacrifice—because in the old days among the ancients it was not bulls but sheep which were offered up.

They call some of them 'bidents', and these are the ones which have two longer teeth among the eight. It was

---

jakes, fay channels, carry out dirt and dunghills, sweep chimnies, rub horse-heels, etc. I say nothing of Turks galley-slaves, which are bought and sold like juments. . . . *Others eat to live, but they live to drudge.*'

these which the Gentiles used principally to offer in sacrifice.

On the approach of winter a sheep gets hungry at pasture and it roots up the grass insatiably—because it foresees the severity of the winter before it, and hopes to stuff itself with green fodder before all herbage shall fail it under the nipping frost.

VERVEX the Wether is so called either from his powers (*a viribus*) because he is stronger than the other sheep: or else it is because he is a man (*vir*), i.e. masculine: or else it is because he has maggots (*vermes*) in his noddle. It is from the itch occasioned by the worms that these creatures mutually rush together and collide with a great impetus, butting.

ARIES the Ram perhaps gets his name by aphaeresis[1] from Ares, the God of War—and from hence, among us, the males among the flocks are sometimes called in Latin '*mares*' (Mars). Or else the beast may get its name

---

[1] The manuscript seems to say: '*Aries vel* (or '*ut*') *aitotoapeoc i. amarte vocatus.*' It does sometimes become tiresome to have to unravel these readings.

because it was originally immolated on altars—from whence 'aries' because he was sacrificed '*aris*' (with altars) —and thus we get that ram in scripture who was offered up at the altar (*ad aram*).

AGNUS the Lamb is called so in Latin with the sense of 'pius'. But some people think it has got the name because it recognizes (*agnoscat*) its own mother among the other animals —to such an extent that even if it gets lost in a big flock it immediately identifies the parental voice by her bleat, and hastens to Mammy.

What is more, a lamb demands those particular dugs of the maternal milk with which it is familiar. It is also true that the mother recognizes her own baby only, among many thousand lambkins. There comes the one same baa-ing from ever so many, yet she picks out her own offspring none the less, and only takes notice of her unique son, with what a lovely show of natural piety!

HRYCUS the He-Goat is a lascivious and butting animal who is always burning for coition. His eyes are transverse slits because he is so randy. It is thence that

he gets his name, for the Hyrci are slit-eyed too, according to Suetonius.[1]

The nature of goats is so extremely hot that a stone of adamant,[2] which neither fire nor iron implement can alter, is dissolved merely by the blood of one of these creatures.

Kids (*Hedi*) are so called from the word '*edendum*'

---

[1] The philologist seems to be thinking that the Hyrci were the Hyrcani, or mongolian inhabitants of Hyrcania, and that the reference of Suetonius was to these people. If, however, the reference is that of Suet. Lib. 45, it refers to goats themselves.

[2] Adamant, ἀδάμας, started as the name of a hard metal like steel. Hence it began to mean the hardest of objects, thus emery-stone, thus sapphire, and finally diamond. It also became confused with the lodestone and magnet; but 'diamond' finally prevailed.

'Chalybean tempered steel, and frock of mail
Adamantean proof.' MILTON.

(meet to be eaten) because these little ones are very fat and of an agreeable taste.

And that is why our own abbey here, in which I am writing this—our '*edes*'—is also called 'spiritually nourishing' (*edulium*).

We get the name of A P E R the Wild Boar from its savagery (*a feritate*), by leaving out the letter F and putting P instead. In the same way, among the Greeks, it is called S U A G R O S, the boorish or country pig. For everything which is wild and rude we loosely call 'boorish'.

J U V E N T U S the Bullock or Ox is called so because, being useful for tilling the soil, he begins to help man (*juvare*). Or it may be because among the Gentiles it was

always the bul-
lock and never
the bull who was
everywhere sac-
rificed to 'Jove'.
Even their age
used to be con-
sidered in choos-
ing the victims.
   With Indian
Bulls the colour
is tawny and the

speed is like that of flight. Their hair grows against the
nap all over the head. They can swing round their horns
with whatever flexibility they want.[1] They can repel
every weapon by the thickness of their hides. They are
endowed with such a ferocious wildness that, when somebody catches them, they lose their minds with rage.

[1] The intention here is not that they can move their horns like the Yale, but
that, unlike the Hyena, they can swing their necks round easily, as the animal is
doing in the illustration. The animal couch discovered in Tutankhamen's tomb
was spotted like a yale.

The Greeks call B O S the Ox by the name of '*boaen*'
and the Latins call these creatures '*triones*' because they
tread the Earth underfoot like the stars of that name.[2]
The kindness of oxen for their comrades is extraordinary,
for each of them demands the company of that other one
with whom he has been accustomed to draw the plough
by the neck—and, if by any chance the second one is

[2] The Great and Little Bear were called the Triones, since these constellations
were supposed to resemble a waggon (King Charles' Wain) with the oxen
harnessed to it.

absent, then the firstone's kindly disposition is testified by frequent mooing.

When rain is impending, oxen know that they ought to keep themselves at home in their stables. Moreover, when they foresee by natural instinct a change for the better in the sky, they look out carefully and stick their necks from the stalls, all gazing out at once, in order to show themselves willing to go forth.

There are fierce bulls of the Wild Ox in Germany, which have such immense horns that, at the royal tables, which have a notable capacity for booze, the people make the receptacles for drink out of them.

There are single-horned or unicorn bulls in India, with solid hooves not cloven, but these are very fearful.

'Bubali', the Buffaloes or Wild Oxen, derive their name because they resemble 'Bos' the Ox, though they are so unbiddable that they will not accept the yoke. 'Vacca' the Cow is really '*Boacca*', for this is a transferable generic name, like 'Lion-Lioness'. 'Vitulus' and 'Vitula', the calf and the heifer, are named from their greenness (*a viriditate*) i.e. from their greenhorn age, like a virgin's, for a Vitula is a very little maid and not vigorous, though her mother the 'Juventa', i.e. the 'Vacca', is vigorous.

Adam gave their name to CAMELS (*camelis*) with good reason, for when they are being loaded up they kneel down and make themselves lower or humbler—and the Greek for low or humble is '*cam*'. Or else it is because the creature is humped on the back and the word '*camur*' means 'curved' in Greek.

Although other regions produce them, yet Arabia does so most. The Bactrians breed the strongest camels, but Arabia breeds the largest number. The two kinds differ in this, that the Arabians have humps on the back.

These Bactrians never wear away their hoofs. They have fleshy soles with certain concertina-like pads, and from these there is a cushioning counteraction for the walkers, with no hard impediment to putting down the foot.

They are kept for two purposes. Some are accommodated to carry a burden. Others are more speedy, but cannot be given loads beyond what is fitting, nor are the latter willing to do more than the accustomed distances.

When they come into season, they are so unbridled by the matter that they run mad for the want of love.

They detest horses.

They are good at putting up with the weariness of thirst, and indeed, when the chance of drinking is given them, they fill up with enough both for the past want and for whatever lack may come in the future for a long time. They go for dirty waters and avoid clean ones. In fact, unless there should be fouler drink available, they themselves stir up the slime with busy trampling, in order that it should be muddied.

They live for a hundred years.

If they happen to be sold to a stranger they grow ill, disgusted at the price.

Females are provided in warfare, but it is so arranged that their desire for copulation is frustrated: for they are thought to do more valiantly if they are prevented from coition.

The DROMEDARY is a species of camel, but smaller in stature and more swift. And that is the way it

gets its name, for 'racing' and 'speed' are called '*dromos*' in Greek.[1] It is accustomed to cover a hundred miles and more in a day.

This creature, like the sheep and the bull and the camel, ruminates. The word 'rumination' is got from the gullet (*a ruma*)—the top part of the neck—through which food etc. is brought up again by animals, after being swallowed down.

---

[1] On the other hand, Levins called them 'drumbledaries' in 1570, while to call a thief a 'Purple Dromedary' in the cant of 1700 was to insult him as a bungler.

The DONKEY
and the LITTLE
ASS (*asinus et asel-
lus*) are so named
from being sat upon
—as if from the word
'seat' or 'saddle' (*a
sede*). These crea-
tures got the name,
which would have
been more suitable
for horses, because
men domesticated
them before horses.[1]
People captured
the Donkey by the following stratagem. Being forsooth
a tardy beast and having no sense at all, it surrendered as
soon as men surrounded it!

Arcadian donkeys get their name because the big, tall
ones were first ridden in Arcadia.

The Little Ass, although smaller than the Wild Ass, is
more useful, because it puts up with work and does not
take exception to almost unlimited neglect.

[1] The word 'donkey' is of recent origin, appearing in the eighteenth century.
Originally it rhymed with 'monkey'.

The ONAGER is said to be the Wild Ass. The Greeks,
to be sure, called the Ass '*on*' and they called wild '*agra*'.
Africa breeds these creatures—large and untameable and
wandering about in the desert.

One male at a time presides over the herds of females.
When little males are born, the fathers get jealous of them

and remove their testicles with a bite—for fear of which, the mothers hide them in secret places.

Physiologus says of the Wild Ass that, when twenty-five days of March have passed, it brays twelve times in the night and the same number in the day. From this the season is recognized as the 'Equinox'[1] and people can tell, hour by hour, the time of day or night by counting the brays of the ass.

Now the Devil is symbolized by this animal, for he brays about the place night and day, hour by hour, seeking his prey. He does this when he knows night and day to be equal, i.e. when he knows that the number of those who walk in darkness is equal to the number of the sons of light. For the Wild Ass does not bray unless it wants its dinner. As Job says, 'Doth the Wild Ass bray when he hath grass?' Wherefore the Apostle also: 'Our

[1] The earliest text of *Physiologus* (see Appendix), upon which the bestiaries are based, here names an Egyptian month, according to the *Encyclopaedia Britannica*. If the date is there stated with precision, it seems just possible that an astronomer who was acquainted with the history of the calendar and with the alterations of the equinox might be able to give an approximate date at which the *Physiologus* was written—a date which at present can only be debated between the second and fifth centuries A.D.

The performance of a certain action every hour is also related of the Cynocephalus (q.v.) by John Maplet in his *Diall of Destiny*. It 'pisseth twelve tymes in the day, and twelve tymes in the night. And that in the wane of the Moone (durynge all the tyme that shee is darkened) hee continually lamenteth never eatynge anything at all'.

83

adversary the Devil, as a roaring lion, walketh about, seeking whom he may devour'.

HORSES (*Equi*) get that name because, when they are teamed in fours, they are 'levelled' (*equabantur*) and those which are pairs in shape and equals in pace are matched together. The word 'caballus' comes from its hollow hoof mark (*a cavo pede*) because, in walking, the passing hoof-frog leaves a sort of dent in the ground which other animals do not leave.

The spiritedness of horses is great. They exult in battlefields; they sniff the combat; they are excited to the

fight by the sound of a trumpet. Inflamed by the war-yell, they are spurred to charge. They are miserable when conquered and delighted when they have won. They recognize their enemies in battle to such an extent that they go for their adversaries with a bite. Some of them, moreover, will only recognize their proper masters, and will stop being tame if these are changed. Some will let nobody on their back except their master. We will give an example.

The horse of Alexander the Great, called Bucephalus—either because of his wild-bull-like appearance, or else because of Alexander's badge, for the latter used to have a bull's head stamped on his harness, or else because a sort of armour of horns used to be stuck out from the horse's forehead—although at other times he was accustomed to be ridden by his groom, and quietly so, once the royal saddle had been put on, that horse would never deign to carry anybody except his Master. There are many stories of him in battles, in which by his own effort he brought Alexander safe out of the most terrible scrimmages.

The horse of Caius Caesar would have nobody but Caesar on his back. When a victorious adversary was trying to plunder the King of the Scythians after being engaged in single combat, he was cut to pieces with kicks and bites by the king's mount. When King Nicomedes had been killed, his steed rid itself of life by fasting. When Antiochus conquered the Galatae in battle, in order to go on fighting he jumped upon the horse of their general who had fallen in the field, by name Cintaretus.[1] But it spurned the bridle to such an extent that,

[1] In Pliny, Centeretrius. In Aelian, Centoaratus.

85

falling down on purpose, it dashed to bits both itself and its rider, by the fall.

In this particular kind of animal, the length of life is greater in the male. Indeed, we read of a horse having lived to be seventy years of age. We also find it noted that a horse called Opus[1] went on copulating to the age of forty.

The virility of horses is extinguished when their manes are cut.

At birth, a love charm is delivered with the foal, which they carry on their foreheads when they are dropped. It is of a tawny colour, similar to a dried fig, and is called Hippomanes.[2] And if this were taken away, it would immediately happen that the mother would not on any account give her udders to the foal to be suckled.

The deeper a horse dips his nostrils when drinking, the better his prospects as a sire.

When their master is dead or dying, horses shed tears—for they say that only the horse can weep for man and feel the emotion of sorrow. And hence in Centaurs the nature of men and horses can be mixed.[3]

People who are going to fight a battle are wont to prophesy what the event will be, from the low or high spirits of their steeds.

It is a common belief that four things are necessary, or so the Ancients say, in well-bred horses. These are:

[1] It was because he came from a Greek town of that name, not because he worked so hard.

[2] The present translator has seen the same charm pocketed by an English farm labourer at the delivery of a foal in 1934.

[3] But Lucretius declares that Centaurs are impossible. Since men and horses live to different ages, he says, a man-horse would find that one end of him had died of old age while the other end was in its prime.

figure, beauty, merit and colour. Figure: the body powerful and solid in strength, the height convenient to it, the flank long and narrow, the haunches very large and round, the chest spreading widely, the whole knotted with a mass of muscles and the hoof dry and firmed with an arched horn. Beauty: that the head be small and sound with the skin holding close to the bone, the ears short and lively, the eyes big, the nostrils wide, the neck erect, the mane and tail dense, and a firm curve on the hoofs. Merit: that it should be audacious in spirit, swift of foot and trembling in its limbs. The latter is an indication of courage, because then it is easily excited from a state of deepest repose and, once speed has been got up, it can be maintained without difficulty. Incidentally, the pace of a horse is judged from the twitching of the ears, its spirit from the twitching of the limbs. Colour to be looked for principally in these animals: bay, golden, ruddy, chestnut, deer-coloured, pale yellow, grey, roan, hoary, silver, white, flea-bitten, black. Next in order there comes a mixed colour on a ground of black or bay. Lastly, a piebald or a stripe is the worst.

Now the Ancients[1] used to consider the chestnut the best colour, because it matches better with other animals. This colour is also known as 'nut-brown' (*spadix*), which others call 'Phoenicatus' (a purple-red, from the Phoenician dye) and that is named from the date-palm-tree colour which the Syrians call the *Spadix*. Blue-grey (*glaucus*) is the colour of human eyes, yet shot through with a kind of brilliance. Pale yellow (*gilvus*) is a better colour

[1] The manuscript in the following paragraph is complicated by the fact that colours can seldom be described in terms of other colours, particularly not in dead languages, and the scribe himself has grown confused and bored. He soon begins to write '*contubitum*' for '*concubitum*', and is shortly contented to offer '*aquarum*' when he means '*equorum*'. But the general sense can be discerned.

, .r a horse when it is sub-whitish. Flea-bitten (*guttatus*) is white with black spots all over. Silver (*candidus*) and white (*albus*) are different from each other: for white is of a certain paleness, but silver is snowy and shines with pure light. Hoary (*canus*) is called this because it is composed of silver and black. *Scutulatus* (checkered or roan?) is named after 'shields' (but he implies the pun '*scutulatus*'—'*scutum*') because these have argents between purples. Piebalds have patches of different colours. Of these, those which have white feet are deemed feeble, but those which have white blazes are fiery. Deer-coloured (*cervinus*) are the horses which they call '*gaurans*' (garrons?) in the vulgar tongue. '*Dosinus*' is an ass-coloured horse (*de asino*) and also means 'ashen'. The latter are sprung from a rustic breed which we call Wild Horses, and consequently they cannot aspire to town rank. The Moor (an Arab steed) is black, for the Greeks call a black man a '*moor*'. The *Mannus* (a Gaulish cob) is a smaller horse and is commonly 'brown'. The Ancients named the cart-horse '*veredus*' because these used to draw (*veherent*) the waggons, i.e. drag them along, or else because such horses ply upon the public roads, along which one is accustomed to drive waggons.

There are three main kinds of horse: one of them noble in battle and a grand weight-carrier; the second vulgar and common, meet for pulling though not for riding; while the third is sprung from a mixture of diverse stocks, and is indeed called a 'hybrid' (*bigener*) because it is produced from differing varieties, like the Mule.

MULUS the Mule has a name taken from the Greek. He is called this in Greek possibly because, being put under the yoke of the millers, he draws the slow mill-stones (*molas*) in a circle for their grinding.

The Jews affirm that Anas himself, the son of a great-grandchild of Esau, was the first man to cause herds of horses to be covered by asses in the desert—so that thence this new kind of animal might be born from many of them, against nature. Further to this, they say that Wild Asses were let in to the ordinary Asses and in this way the same kind of cross-breeding was brought about, so that out of this particular cross the most speedy kind of asses were born.

Human industry, to be sure, has forced unlikely animals to coition, and has thus produced a new sort by the adulterous mixture.

And in this way Jacob procured the similarities of colours, also unnaturally. For his ewes used to conceive offspring corresponding to the reflected images of the rams which they saw mounting them from behind, in the mirror of the rivers in which they stood. In the end, the same thing was caused to be done among the herds of horses, so that the mares should throw noble foals by catching a reflected glimpse of the sire at the moment of conception, by which they might be able to take in and create his likeness. Pigeon fanciers also put the most beautifully coloured pigeons in the places where they are turned out together, by catching sight of which the females give birth to similar ones. This is why people tell pregnant women not to look any of the very disgusting animals in the face—like dog-headed apes or monkeys—lest they should give birth to children similar in appearance to those they met. For such is said to be the nature of females that whatever they view, or even if they imagine it in the mind during the extreme heat of lust while they are conceiving, just so do they procreate the progeny. Animals in the act of venery translate images from outside inward, and, fertilized by the imaginary figure, they transform the apparition into a real quality.

Among living creatures, the Mongrels are those which are born from two different varieties—as the Mule from the mare and the ass, the Hinny from the stallion and the she-ass, the Hybrid[1] from the Wild Boar and the sow, the Tyrius[2] from the sheep and the he-goat, and the Musimo[3] from the she-goat and the ram which is the leader of the flock.

[1] 'There is no creature ingenders so soon with wild of the kind as doth swine: and verily such hogs in old time they called Hybrides, as a man would say, halfe wild.' HOLLAND's *Pliny* II, 231.

[2] Perhaps a species bred in Tyre; but Tyrrheus was the shepherd of King Latinus in *Vergil* and the Tyrrhidae were his sons. The word does not figure in Aldrovandus, N.E.D., Baxter and Johnson or Lewis and Short—except in the latter case as an inhabitant of Tyre.

[3] *Ovis musimon* is the Moufflon, the wild sheep of Corsica.

She is called MOUSER because she is fatal to mice. The vulgar call her CATUS the Cat because she catches things (*a captura*) while others say that it is because she lies in wait (*captat*) i.e. because she 'watches'. So acutely does she glare that her eye penetrates the shades of darkness with a gleam of light. Hence from the Greek comes '*catus*', i.e. 'acute'.

MUS the Mouse, a puny animal, comes from a Greek word: although it may have become Latin, it really comes from that. Others say it is 'mice' (*mures*) because they are generated from the dampness of the soil (*ex humore*). For '*humus*' is '*hu-Mus*', you see?

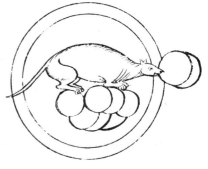

The liver of these creatures gets bigger at full moon, just as certain seashores rise and fall with the waning moon.[1]

[1] 'Aelian declares that the liver of mice waxes and wanes with the waxing and waning of the moon. As for their temperament, Pliny maintains that among creatures of the earth, mice, and swallows among the creatures of the sky, are the two most unbiddable. Here we have Porta saying that their flesh if put in one's food begets oblivion. And there we have Aelian asserting that they make many holes, so that if one of them is shut up they can betake themselves to another, and also that if a number of them tumble into the water they all catch hold of each other's tails, so that when one gets out the rest can heave after. But allow me to doubt the statement of Albertus, for he really does seem to be drawing the long bow a little, when he says that he himself was acquainted with a mouse in Upper Germany, which, on a sign from its master, acted as a candlestick for him by holding the candle in its mouth. No, no, in my opinion it must have been an Alpine mouse! Finally there is the sad fact—such is the nature of these creatures that they do not live long to enjoy the light of day. That was why the little mouse in Horace said of his friend: *Vive memor, quam sis aevi brevis.' Ulyssis Aldrovandi, De Quadrup. Digit. Vivip.* Lib. II, 418.

'It is for his bignes a verie ravenour or greedigut.' JOHN MAPLET, 1567.

She is called a WEASEL (*mustela*) as if she were an elongated mouse, for the Greeks say '*theon*' for 'long'.[2]

[2] But Isidore explains that she is a *mus* (mouse) who is as long as a *telum* (spear).

 When she lives in a house, she moves from place to place with subtle cunning after she has had her babies, and always lies at night in a different lair.

She pursues snakes and mice.[1] There are two kinds. One kind keeps far off in the forest— the Greeks call these *Ictides*[2]— and the other wanders about in houses.

Some say that they conceive through the ear and give birth through the mouth, while, on the other hand, others declare that they conceive by mouth and give birth by ear.[3]

---

[1] The Bestiarist comprises under Mustela the whole family of ferrets, from stoats to weasels, and probably the mongoose as well.

[2] Aldrovandus excels himself in identifying the *Ictides*, mainly under the heading of *Mustela sylvestris*. He suggests '*martes*' (the *marten*), '*putorius*' (something that smells, like a skunk or polecat), '*viverra*' (translated by Lewis and Short as 'ferret'), '*furonis*' (some vicious member of the tribe, a fury, probably the weasel) and '*pholitam*', which seems to defeat all commentators. Straying into other languages than the classical, he states that the *Ictides* are known in Spanish as '*pholentas*', in Hebrew '*oach*', in French '*furette*', in German '*frett*' and in English either '*fret*' or '*sitche*'. Evidently '*fret*' is 'ferret' and '*sitche*' may be Shakespeare's 'fitchew'—the polecat.

[3] 'This horrible bloomer of the ancient naturalists is perhaps explained by the fable of Galanthis, that maid-servant of the mother of Hercules who was changed into a weasel—so Ovid relates. The poet tells us how the Goddess Lucina was invoked—the goddess who was said to preside over childbirth—at a time when Alcmena was in labour with her son Hercules and when the child's delivery seemed difficult. And Lucina, he says, taking the shape of an old hag, was sent to the labour by the command of Juno, not to help but to hinder. So Lucina sat down at Alcmena's front door, holding her own knees shut with her fingers interlaced like a trellis. But Galanthis, Alcmena's maid, suspecting by that gesture that Lucina was being an impediment to the birth, approached as if to thank her for her assistance and falsely announced that the lady had been successfully delivered. When the goddess heard this, she relaxed and stood up— and instantly Alcmena managed to produce Hercules. At this the goddess,

Weasels are said to be so skilled in medicine that, if by any chance their babies are killed, they can make them come alive again if they can get at them.

Now these creatures signify not a few of you fellows, who willingly accept by ear the seed of God's word, but who, shackled by the love of earthly things, put it away in the wrong place and dissimulate what you hear.

E R I C I U S the Hedgehog is an animal which is covered with spikes, and that is how it gets its name; for it curls itself up and is inclosed in the spikes[1] with which it is protected against stratagems in all directions. As soon as it gets a presentiment of anything nasty, first it bristles

---

[1] '*Ericius*' also means by transference a *cheval-de-frise*. The philologist seems to think that the urchin is named from the engine, not the engine from the urchin.

---

exasperated by the take-in, turned Galanthis into a weasel—with the added curse that the girl would always have to bear her own children through that ear by which she had deceived the goddess.' *Ulyssis Aldrovandi, De Quadrup. Digit. Vivip.* Lib. II, 314.

All the same, Greek fables were generally invented to account for what they took to be natural phenomena, not the other way about. The theory concerning the weasel's ear may yet be explained by the field-naturalist.

The patristic writers and some later theologians really did believe that 'the conception of Christ was effected supernaturally through the Virgin's ear. . . . As God spoke the world into existence, so the voice of the Most High uttering salutation through the mouth of the angel caused the Virgin to conceive, 'and the Word was made flesh'. But as spoken words are addressed to the ear, and through this organ find lodgement in the mind and thus bear fruit, it was assumed that the incarnation of the Logos was accomplished in the same manner.' E. P. EVANS.

'*Deus per angelum loquebatur et Virgo per aurem impregnabatur.*' ST AUGUSTINE.
'*Gaude Virgo, mater Christi,*
Quae par aurem concepisti.'
—attributed to St Thomas à Becket.

93

up and then tucks itself together, rolled up in a ball.[1]

This creature has a kind of prudence, for, when a bunch of grapes comes off the vine, it rolls itself upside

[1] 'When the Foxe Pursueth him, the *Hedg-hogge* rowleth him selfe (as men say) within his prickles, as the Chesnut is enclosed within his hull. And by that meanes he keepeth him there enclosed, so that he cannot be any whit hurted.' *The Schoole of Beastes,* 1585.

down on top of the bunch, and thus delivers it to its babies.[1]

It is also called an Urchin (*echinus*). This same Urchin, provident for the future, provides itself with double breathing holes, so that, when it suspects the north wind is going to blow, it can shut up the northern one, and, when it seems to detect a mixture of airs, it can betake itself to the north one, to avoid the exposed blasts and those which are likely to be harmful because of their direction.

[1] '*Pliny* in his natural history reporteth of *Hedg-hogs*, that having been abroad to *provide* their store, and returning home *laden* with nuts and fruit, if the least *Filbert* fall but off, they will in a pettish humour, *fling* down all the rest, and *beat* the ground for very anger with their bristles.' WILLIAM BARLOW, 1658.

The pettish humour of these creatures has its lighter moments, however. 'And whan he feleth hym selfe lade as moche as he may bere,' says the *Myrrour and Descrypcyon of the Worlde,* 'he gothe his way with them syngynge and maketh his deluyte.'

The Hedgehog constructs a humble nest in ditches, and there it hibernates. In 1939, the present translator dug out such a nest, near an orchard, with an Irish labouring companion who proceeded to tell him that hedgehogs carried apples to their nests on their spines—an anecdote which the translator had just been reading in this manuscript, eight hundred years older than the Irishman. The latter asserted the truth of his statement with passion, pointing to the apples, which were indeed there, and had punctured bruises on them. But the creature had probably trundled them there with its nose, subsequently making the punctures when it curled up to sleep on top of them. That urchins should be met, however, in vine-growing countries, with desiccating grapes upon their spines, is not improbable. They are untidy, or possibly camouflage-loving animals, who often have a collection of leaves and detritus upon their spikes among the fleas.

The M O L E is called Talpa because it is condemned to perpetual blindness in dark places. It is without eyes.[1] It always digs through the

[1] The Mole was formerly called a Moldiwarp. 'Be silent then,' says Burton the anatomist; 'rest satisfied; *desine, intuensque in aliorum infortunia, solare mentem;* comfort they self with other men's

ground and carries out the soil, and it gobbles up the roots beneath the fruits, wherefore the Greeks call it '*aphala*'.[1]

[1] ἄφᾱλος means 'without the boss in which the plume of a helmet is fixed'. Perhaps this might apply to a plant with no roots. Or perhaps the reference is to φαλλός, in which case the mole is regarded as emasculating the plants. The previous hint that the animal is called '*talpa*' because it digs, is, in fact, correct; since '*talpa*' and '*scalpere*' (to dig) derive from the same Greek root.

The A N T has three peculiarities.[2]

[2] The unfinished picture of the ant-hills appears as above in the manuscript, showing that the scribe worked before the limner. But it is interesting to note that the picture of bee-hives was also left unfinished. The Bestiarist seems to be describing *Messor barbarus*.

---

misfortunes; and, as the moldiwarpe in Aesop told the fox, complaining for want of a tail, and the rest of his companions, *tacete, quando me oculis captum videtis;* you complain of toies; but I am blind; be quiet; I say to thee be thou satisfied'.

Not only does Shakespeare seem to have been unacquainted with the Bestiaries, but there is some slight reason to believe that his keen, pragmatic, countryman's eye for fact may have been impatient of the old-fashioned tenets which they contain. At any rate, one of his characters in 1 *Henry IV*, iii, i, the testy Hotspur, is outraged by Glendower's ancient biology:

> *Mort.* Fie, cousin Percy! how you cross my father!
> *Hot.* I cannot choose: sometime he angers me
> With telling of the moldwarp and the ant,
> Of the dreamer Merlin and his prophecies,
> And of a dragon, and a finless fish,
> A clip-wing'd griffin and a moulten raven,
> A crouching lion and a ramping cat,
> And a deal of scimble-scamble stuff
> As puts me from my faith.

What was annoying Hotspur, however, was not the question of natural history, but the symbolical, Welsh, heraldic visions which the old gentleman had evidently been relating to him out of the Arthurian cycle.

The first is that these creatures walk in a line, and each of them carries one grain in his mouth. Their comrades do not say 'give us of your grains' to the loaded ones, but they go along the tracks of the latter to the place where they found the corn, and they carry back their own grain to the nest.

Mere words, you see, are not an indication of being provident. Provident people, like ants, betake themselves to that place where they will get their future reward.

The second peculiarity is that when an ant stores seeds in the nest it divides them into two, lest by chance they should be soaked with rain in winter, and the seeds should germinate, and the ant die of hunger.[1]

O Man, divide you also the words of the Bible in this way, i.e. discern between the spiritual and carnal meanings, lest the Letter of the Law should be the death of you. It is as the Apostle observes: 'For the Letter kills, but the Spirit gives life'. The Jews, attending only to the letter, and scorning the spiritual meaning, have been killed with hunger.

The third peculiarity is that in time of harvest an ant walks about among the crops and feels with its mouth whether the stem is one of barley or one of wheat. If it should be barley, it goes off to another stem and investigates; and if this feels as if it were wheat, it climbs up to

---

[1] The fact that ants can arrest the germination of seeds, though well known to Aelian in A.D. 200, gradually dropped out of sight and had to be rediscovered by a Mr J. Traherne Moggridge in 1873. Sir Thomas Browne, however, had experimented on the subject with his usual accuracy.

the top of the stem and, taking thence the grain, carries it to its habitation. For barley is the food for bigger beasts.

This was why Job said: 'Instead of wheat, it produced barley to men'—that is to say, the doctrine of heretics did. For those things which shatter and kill the souls of men are like barley, and meet to be thrown far away. Fly, O Christian, from all heretics, whose dogmas are false and inimical to the truth.

The Scriptures say, moreover: 'Go to the ant, thou sluggard; consider her ways and be wise. Which having no guide, overseer or ruler, provideth her meat in the summer, and gathereth her food in the harvest.' And she lays up a harvest to herself out of thy labours. And while thou art in need for the most part, she lacks not. She has no locked barns, no impenetrable guards, no inviolable stores. The human custodian sees her thefts, which he does not dare to prohibit; the owner perceives his losses and does not take vengeance.

Once the booty has been collected in a black heap, the ants swarm through the fields along the pathway in a convoy of travellers, and when they cannot hold a grain in their narrow mouths those grains are transferred on their shoulders. The owner of the harvest looks on, and blushes to deny the gleanings of industry to such a thrifty sense of duty.

The ant also knows how to exploit the periods of good weather. For when it notices that its stores are growing damp and wetted with rain, after having examined the atmosphere very diligently and having decided that it looks as if the settled weather may serve, it carries its grain-heaps back again and takes them out of doors from the tunnels on its shoulders, so that the corn can be dried in a steady sun.

Finally, you will never on any day see the showers burst from the clouds, unless the ant has first carried back her fruits to the granaries.[1]

[1] This ends the section on Beasts. The manuscript goes straight on, without pause and without an illustration, to the section on Birds.

THE BOOK OF BEASTS

II

BIRDS

'*Moult est a dire et a retraire*
Es essamples del Bestiare,
Qui sunt de bestes et de oiseaus,
Moult profitables, boens et beaus.
Et le livre si nous enseigne
En quel guise le mal remaigne,
Et la veie que deit tenir
Cil qui a Deu veut revertir.'

PHILIPPE DE THAUN

num Now all B I R D S are called Birds, but there are a lot of them—for, just as they differ from one another in species, so do they in diversity of nature. Some are simple-minded like the pigeon, others astute like the partridge; some subject themselves to the hand of man like the hawks, others shun it like the Garamantes;[1] some are delighted with human society like the swallow, others, like the rock-dove, prefer a secret way of life in desert places; some only feed on the corn which they find, like the goose, while others eat flesh and turn their minds to thieving, like the kite; some congregate, i.e. fly in flocks like starlings and quail, others are solitary, i.e. go singly, pillaging by cunning, like the eagle, the hawk and others of that sort; some squeak like the swallow, others breathe out the most beautiful songs like the swan and the black-bird—while others again imitate the words and voices of men, like the parrot and the magpie. There are number-less more, differing as to kind and custom; for there are so many sorts of birds that it is not possible to learn every one, nor indeed is there anybody who can pene-trate all the deserts of Scythia and India and Ethiopia, to know their species according to the differences of them.

They are called Birds (*A-ves*) because they do not

---

[1] Neither this word nor anything closely resembling it is to be found as a bird in Liddell and Scott, Lewis and Short, Baxter and Johnson, N.E.D., *Enc. Brit.*, nor even in Aldrovandus.

The Garamantes were a tribe mentioned in Herodotus, whose capital was supposed to be Garama in Phazania, now Fezzan.

The Pheasant is supposed to have orginated from Phasis, a river in Asia Minor. Hence φᾱσιαν-ός; O.F., *Fesan*; M.E. *Fesant*.

If the pheasant originated from Phazania, and not from Phasis, there would be some ground for translating 'garamantes' as 'pheasants'.

follow straight roads (*vias*), but stray through any by-way. They are called the Winged Ones (*alites*) because they mount with wings (*alis*) to the high places and reach the heavens with a rowing of plumes. They are called Fowls (*volucres*) from their ability to fly. You see, we use the verb 'to wing' from 'wings', just as we say 'to leg it' from 'legs'—and the '*Vola*' or palm is the middle part of our hand or foot, while in birds it is the middle part of the wing, by the motion of whose feathers they are propelled: hence '*volucres*'.

The children of all birds are called '*Pulli*' or poults. However, the offspring of four-footed beasts are also called '*pulli*' and a baby boy is called '*pullus*' too. In fact, all recently born creatures are called '*pulli*', because they are born dirty or polluted. Whence our dirty clothes are also called '*pulla*'.

The 'wings' are the things in which the feathers, after being placed in order, allow the exercise of flight. Moreover, they are called wings (*alae*) because the birds nourish (*alant*) and foster their chicks with them, by folding them up in these.

The 'feather' (*pinna*) is given its name from 'hovering' (*a pendendo*), i.e. from flying, whence also comes 'to suspend' (*pendere*)—for birds are kept up by the aid of feathers when they launch themselves on the air.

'Plumes' get their name from hairs (*pluma quasi piluma*), because just as there are hairs on the body of a quadruped so there are plumes on birds.

It is known that the names of many birds are invented from the sound of their voices, e.g. Grus, Corvus, Cignus, Bubo, Milvus, Ulula, Cuculus, Garrulus, Graculus, etc. (Crane, Crow, Swan, Owl, Kite, Screech-owl, Cuckoo, Starling, Daw, etc.). The particular kind of song they have suggests what men should call them.[1]

AQUILA the Eagle is called so from the acuteness (*acumine*) of his eyes, for he is said to have such wonderful eyesight that, when he is poised above the seas on motionless plume—not even visible to the human gaze—yet from such a height he can see the little fishes swimming, and, coming down like a thunderbolt, he can carry off his captured prey to the shore, on the wing.[2]
And it is a true fact that when the eagle grows old and his wings become heavy and his eyes become darkened with a mist, then he goes in search of a fountain, and, over against it, he flies up to the height of heaven, even unto the circle of the sun;[3] and there he singes his wings and at the same time evaporates the fog of his eyes, in a ray of the sun. Then at length, taking a header down into the fountain, he dips himself three times in it, and instantly he is renewed with a great vigour of plumage and splendour of vision.

Do the same thing, O Man, you who are clothed in the old garment and have the eyes of your heart growing foggy. Seek for the spiritual fountain of the Lord and

[1] 'Why did the owl 'owl' is an accurate piece of etymology. Its name in most languages is of echoic origin.

[2] Sir Thomas Browne reflects adversely upon the eyesight of the eagle. 'It much disadvantageth the Panegyrick of Synesius, and is no small disparagement unto baldnesse, if it bee true what is related by Aelian concerning Aeschilus, whose balde pate was mistaken for a rock, and so was brained by a Tortoise which an Eagle let fall upon it. Certainely, it was a very great mistake in the perspicacity of that Animall. . . .'

[2] 'Your vulgar writer is always most vulgar the higher his subject, as the man who shewed the menagerie at Pidcock's was wont to say,—"This, gentlemen, is the *eagle* of the *sun*, from Archangel in Russia; the *otterer* it is the *igherer* he flies".' BYRON, 1821.

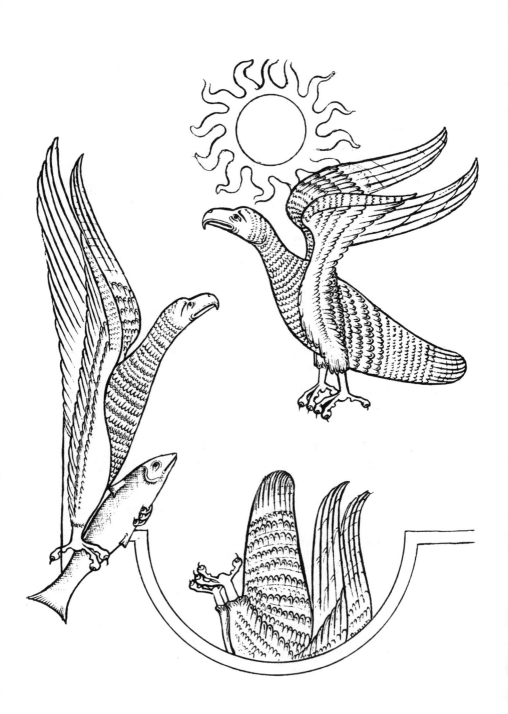

lift up your mind's eyes to God—who is the fount of justice—and then your youth will be renewed like the eagle's.

It is claimed that an eagle presents his young to the sunbeams, and holds the children up to them in middle air with his talon. And if one of them, when stricken with the sun's light, uses a fearless gaze of his eyes, with an uninjured power of staring at it, that one is made much of, because it has proved the truth of its nature.[1] But the one which turns away its eyes from the sunbeam is thrown out as being degenerate and not deserving of such reward. Nor is it considered worth educating such a molly-coddle, as if it were not worth bothering about it.

The parent does not condemn his child from hardness of heart, but from the integrity of his judgement, nor does he abandon it like one of his own but as if he were rejecting some stranger.

All the same—and this has been seen by many—the mercy of a certain mere plebeian bird softens this spartan behaviour in the royal fowl. A bird whose name is COOT, and who is called 'Fene' in Greek,[2] picks the baby up, whether it has been thrown out or just not

---

[1] Several of these statements about the eagle are not without some foundation. The 'mist' on the eyes probably refers to the nictitating membrane: the upward glance toward the sun has been noticed by all falconers or austringers, as their captive, cocking his head on one side, gazes upward without a blink, generally at some other raptor: and the renewal of youth is an attempt to account for moulting. The Greek Physiologus relates that the beaks of elderly eagles grow long, thus preventing them from eating, and that they break the tips of them off against a stone. Falconers still have to pare the beaks of their hawks.

[2] ΦΕΝΑΞ, ᾱκος, ὁ a cheat, quack, impostor. Ar.—Liddell & Scott. E. P. Evans understands *Fulica* to mean heron, not coot.

recognized, and adopts the child of the eagle with her own little ones and feeds it and nourishes it with the very same maternal zeal as she shows for her own offspring, and with the same kind of food.

Very well, there you have the Coot supporting strangers, while we humans turn our own kin away with unfriendly cruelty!

The eagle, if she does turn it away, does not do so as her own—but as if she did not recognize the degenerate one—yet we, which is worse, disown those whom we do recognize.

The VULTURE is thought to have been named from its slow flight (*a volatu tardo*).

To be sure, it does not make rapid flights, on account of the size of its body.

Now Vultures, like Eagles, notice cadavers even when they are beyond the seas. They see from a height, while flying, many things which are hidden from us by the mountains in between.

Vultures are said not to go in for copulation, and not to mingle in a conjugal manner by way of nuptial intercourse. The females conceive without any assistance from the males and generate without conjunction. The children thus born continue to a great age, so that the course of their life is prolonged even to a hundred years, nor does the end of life's brief span steal upon them easily.

What would those people say, who are accustomed to laugh at Mysteries, when they hear that a virgin vulture brought forth—those people who think that childbirth is impossible for an unmarried woman whose decency has had no knowledge of man? They actually suppose that the Mother of God cannot do what vultures do![1]

The bird can breed without a male, and nobody disproves it. Yet when the betrothed Virgin Mary herself so produces, people question her modesty!

Vultures are accustomed to foretell the death of men by certain signs. The augurs are warned by these signs, whenever two lines of battle are drawn up against each other in lamentable war—for the birds follow in a long column, and they show by the length of this column how

---

[1] Whatever the fact about vultures, it must indeed be a formidable thought for the heretic that so many creatures like the aphids are capable of parthenogenesis.

many soldiers are to die in the struggle. They show, in fact, how many men are destined to be the booty of the vultures themselves.[1]

[1] On 18 and 20 July 1812, before the Battle of Salamanca, the armies of Wellington and Marmont marched in parallel columns, within gunshot, 'while swarms of vultures cruised overhead'. 'I was frequently impressed with the horror of being wounded without the power to keep them off.' (TOMKINSON).

G R U S the Crane takes its name from its peculiar note. For it is with such a cry (grus) that they make a low, continual muttering sound to each other.

And I would like to tell you how they manage their campaigns. They go about in proper military formations. And, lest there should be a high wind which might prevent their light bodies from going straight ahead to their destination, they eat sand and pick up small stones of moderate weight, to give themselves ballast.[1] Then they rise quickly to the heights, so that, from a greater altitude, they can see the territory which they want to reach. What is more, while they hurry along, they explicitly follow one particular pathfinder, and she, confident of her navigation, flies at the front of the formation. She reproves the laggards as she flies, and controls the column with her voice. Whenever she becomes hoarse, another leader takes her place.[2]

All cranes are agreed in the matter of the tired ones who begin to fall out from exhaustion. They close in upon them and give them a lift, until the weary ones are rested.[3]

Cranes keep a watchful guard at night. You can see sentries placed in an orderly way, and, while the remainder of the comrade-army is sleeping, these march round and round to investigate whether there are any ambushes being attempted from anywhere. They provide complete protection. When the sentry's time on guard is over and he has finished his watch, he at last composes

---

[1] The same stratagem was related of bees and sea-urchins. In fact, the crops of birds do require roughage for scouring and digestion.

[2] 'I hear the *Crane* (if I mistake not) cry:
Who in the Clouds forming the forked Y,
By the brave orders practiz'd under her,
Instructeth Souldiers in the Art of War. . . .
A front each Band a forward Captain flies,
Whose pointed Bill cuts passage through the skies;
Two skilfull Sergeants keep the Ranks aright,
And with their voyce hasten their tardy Flight.'
SYLVESTER's *Du Bartas.*

[3] It was claimed in 1952 that two American fighter-pilots in Korea were able to sustain a third fighter in the air, whose pilot had lost consciousness, by using the air-flow over their own wings to cushion the air-flow under his: a claim which Mr T. Rose, the test pilot, has since described as unexpected.

himself to sleep, but only after giving a loud squawk to wake up the next man, whose turn it is to come on duty.

And, may I tell you, the next fellow willingly accepts his lot—not reluctantly, like us human sleepy-heads. He is out of bed as soon as called. For it is thus that cranes return with care and courtesy whatever good turn they have themselves received. There is no dereliction of duty, because there is natural affection. There is a safe watch, because there is free choice.

They keep themselves awake for their sentry-go by holding stones in their claws, and share the night-watches equally, taking over in turn.[1]

If there is an emergency, the sentries shout.

You can tell a crane's age by its colour, for in old age it becomes black.

[1] When the stone is dropped through drowsiness, this wakes up the sentinel. He can be seen holding one in the illustration. But the English cricketer will be unable to help hoping that the stones were also used to count the hours, by which the overs of duty were divided, as the cricket umpire still counts the pennies in his pocket. The text gives little support to this idea, unfortunately.

It is only from India that one can get a PSITIACUS or Parrot, which is a green bird with a red collar and a large tongue. The tongue is broader than in other birds and it makes distinct sounds with it.[1] If

[1] Aristotle pointed out that the tongue of a parrot resembles that of a man.

you did not see it, you would think it was a real man talking. It greets people of its own accord, saying 'What-cheer?' or 'Toodle-oo!'[1] It learns other words by teaching. Hence the story of the man who paid a compliment to Caesar by giving him a parrot which had been taught to say: 'I, a parrot, am willing to learn the names of others from you. This I learnt by myself to say—Hail Caesar!'[2] A parrot's beak is so hard that if you throw down the bird from a height on a rock, it saves itself by landing on its beak with its mouth tight shut, using the beak as a kind of foundation for the shock. Actually its whole skull is so thick that, if it has to be taught anything, it needs to be admonished with blows. Although it really does try to copy what its teacher is saying, it wants an occasional crack with an iron bar. While young, and up

---

[1] *Ex natura autem salutat dicens ave vel kere.*

[2] The story is from Martial. George Crabbe relates a sadder one in *The Parish Register:*

> Her neat small room, adorn'd with maiden-taste,
> A clipp'd French puppy, first of favourites, graced:
> A parrot next, but dead and stuff'd with art;
> (For Poll, when living, lost the Lady's heart,
> And then his life; for he was heard to speak
> Such frightful words as tinged his Lady's cheek:)
> Unhappy bird! who had no power to prove,
> Save by such speech, his gratitude and love.

'I was the other day', writes Abraham de la Pryme in his diary of 23 April 1698 'with Mr. Wesley, minister of Epworth, the famous author of the poem of the Life of Christ. He says, that while he was at London, he knew a parrot that by its long hanging in a cage in Billingsgate Street (where all the worst language in the city is most commonly spoke), had learned to curse and swear, and to use all the most bawdy expressions imaginable. But, to reform it, they sent it to a coffy-house in another street, where, before half-a-year was at an end, it had forgot all its wicked expressions, and was so full of coffy-house language that it could say nothing but "Bring a dish of coffy"; "Where's the news", and such like. When it was thus thoroughly converted, they sent it home again, but within a week's time it got all its cursings and swearings and its old expressions as pat as ever.' DANIEL GEORGE, *Alphabetical Order*, 1949.

to two years old, it learns what you point out to it quickly enough, and retains it tenaciously; but after that it begins to be distrait and unteachable.[1]

[1] Miss Nancy Price informs us (*Bright Pinions*, 1952) that the Maharajah of Nawanagar had a parrot aged 115 who went about in a Rolls Royce and had an international passport. 'It was often necessary for diplomatic reasons that the Maharajah should visit certain countries, and no parrot meant no Maharajah.' 'His Majesty King George V enjoyed the friendship of one of these companionable birds, Charlotte by name. When a midshipman, King George V had acquired Charlotte, who was an African grey, during a call his ship made at Port Said, and she remained a close companion throughout his life. She viewed State and confidential documents with a critical eye from her favourite perch on the King's shoulder, and sometimes, when feeling that matters demanded active intervention, she would call out in a strident seafaring voice, "What about it?" Charlotte loved the sea. In the *Britannia* at Cowes she was a centre of attraction, and her voice was continually heard shouting "Where's the Captain?" And during the King's illness Charlotte spent hours disconsolately muttering the same question. She was the first visitor admitted during the King's convalescence: she danced with delight at again enjoying the companionship of her beloved friend, and immediately perched on his shoulder, calling out at intervals, "Bless my buttons! Bless my buttons! All's well!"' 'It has always', writes Miss Price, 'been of interest to me that a parrot is included among the company of the illustrious dead in Westminster Abbey. This bird was the companion of the Duchess of Richmond, Francis Theresa, "*la Belle* Stuart". It is probably the oldest stuffed bird in existence, as well as the most honoured. The Duchess left instructions that when she died her effigy should be modelled in wax and dressed in the robes she had worn at the coronation of Queen Anne. The parrot, who had been her companion for forty years, died of grief a few days after her passing, and it was felt to be worthy of a place beside her.'

One of the most curious instances of a talking bird is that recorded by the German explorer Humboldt, who states that in South America he met with a venerable bird who had the sole knowledge of a dead language, the whole tribe of Indians (Atures) who alone spoke it having become extinct.

The CALADRIUS, as Physiologus calls the crea-
ture,[1] is a completely white bird without a speck of black.
Its dung is good for eye-trouble.

Now this bird is generally to be found in the halls of
kings, owing to its peculiar properties. For if anybody is
very ill indeed, you can tell from a Caladrius whether
the patient is going to live or die. When the sickness is
mortal, as soon as the Caladrius sees the patient he turns
his back on him, and then everybody knows that the
fellow is doomed. If on the other hand it is not a mortal
illness, the Caladrius faces the patient. It takes the whole
infirmity of the man upon itself, flies up toward the sun,

[1] G. C. Druce dealt very fully with the Caladrius or Charadrius in a paper
published by the *Archaeological Journal* in 1913. It would be impossible to
summarize any of Mr Druce's papers (see Bibliography) in a footnote. The bird
has been assumed by antiquity to be everything from a white parrot to a woodpecker or a seagull, but there was a general agreement that it was a bird of the
rivers. The present translator inclines to the belief that it was a white wagtail
(*Motacilla alba Linn.*) for wagtails are still regarded in Ireland with a super-
stitious dread. The markings of their heads are skull-like. In the jargon of the
scientists, the Charadiidae and the Charadriinae are the Plovers and Phalaropes,
while the Charadriformes cover many other species up to Bustards.

picks up the man's infirmity and disperses it into the air.
Then the patient is cured.[1]

Caladrius is like Our Saviour. Our Lord is entirely
white, having nothing black about him, and he committed no sin nor was there any deceit in his mouth.
Moreover, Our Lord from heaven turns his face from
the Jews,[2] because of their unbelief, but turns toward the
people of our own sort, bearing our infirmities and
taking away our sins. Then he ascends on high, on the
wood of the cross, leading captivity captive and giving
his gifts to men.

But you may want to remark that, because a Caladrius
is an unclean beast according to the Law, it ought not to
be likened to Christ. As to that, St John aptly said: 'As
Moses lifted up the serpent in the Wilderness, so must
the Son of Man be lifted up.' Yet it says in the Law that
the serpent is the most prudent 'of all beasts'. Besides,
the Lion and the Eagle are also beasts, yet they get
likened to Christ in the matter of their royal grandeur—
for the Lion is the King of Beasts, and the Eagle is the
King of Birds.

---

[1] The diagnostic value of the Caladrius caused it to be a troublesome com-
modity for the bird-seller. The ailing purchaser had only to enter a bird-shop,
ask to see a Caladrius, note whether it looked at him or away from him, and then,
making some excuse about the purchase price, he could go away with all he
wanted to know, without buying the Caladrius. The result was that few dealers
were willing to display their goods without cash down, a fact which may account
for the difficulty in identifying this particular bird.

[2] The British Museum M.S. Harl. 273 is a *Bestiare d'Amour* (see Appendix).
Its symbolism, that is to say, is explained in terms of secular love, not in terms of
clerical Christianity. The gentleman in that Bestiary reproaches the lady for
turning away her face, like a charadrius. She opines that it is safer to do so.
She wants no part in taking man's infirmities upon herself. 'Ha! True God!
Guard me from conceiving anything which would be dangerous to bring forth.'

CICONIAE the Storks are called so from the clacking note which they make, like the clacking of a ciconia or tolleno—one of those beams for drawing water out of wells. We know that this note comes from the beak, not from the larynx, and they make it by shaking their heads. It is said that they have no tongues.

These messengers of Spring, these brotherly comrades, these enemies of serpents, can migrate across the oceans and, having collected themselves into column of route, can go straight through to Asia.[1] Crows fly in front of them as pathfinders, and the storks follow like a squadron.

They are exceedingly dutiful toward their babies and incubate the nests so tirelessly that they lose their own feathers.[2] What is more, when they have moulted in this

[1] Although the facts about bird migration are generally supposed to have been 'discovered' in the eighteenth century, it is clear that the discovery was a belated one. The facts were never wholly unknown: it was only that people did not know which birds migrated. At that time, the swallow was the talking point. Defoe's teacher proved in a book that they flew to the moon, but Defoe himself, with his sturdy common sense, thought that they followed their food, the insects, to warmer climes. Dr Johnson was more conservative. 'Swallows', he explained tremendously, 'certainly sleep all the winter. A number of them conglobulate together, by flying round and round, and then all in a heap throw themselves under water, and lie in the bed of a river.'

[2] Pliny says: 'Storks return to the same nests'. They do. Neckham adds that they are monogamous. They are. Sylvester considers the Stork and the Pelican a 'Praise-worthy Paire'.

way, they in turn are looked after by the babies, for a time corresponding in length to the time which they themselves have spent in bringing up and cherishing their offspring.

O LO R the Swan is a bird which the Greeks call a *Cygnus*. It is called Olor because its feathers are *all* white. Who on earth ever heard of a black swan? You see, the Greek for 'all' is '*holos*'.

It is called *Cygnus* (κυκνος) in Greek on account of its song,[1] for it pours out a sweetness of music with melodious notes. They say, moreover, that the

---

[1] i.e., by onomatopoeia.
  'And on the bankes each cypress bow'd his head
  To heare the swan sing her own epiced.' BROWNE.

  'Praise-worthy Payre; which pure examples yield
  Of faithfull Father, and officious Childe:
  Th' one quites (in time) her Parents love exceeding,
  From whom she had her birth and tender breeding,
  Not onely brooding under her warm brest
  Their age-chill'd bodies bed-rid in the nest;
  Nor onely bearing them upon her back
  Through the empty Aire when their owne wings they lack;
  But also sparing (This let Children note)
  Her daintiest food from her own hungry throat,
  To feed at home her feeble Parents, held
  From forraging, with heavie Gyves of Eld.'

reason why this bird sings so beautifully is because it has a long, curved neck, and it is obvious that the vibrating voice must give out a rich music as it goes round and round through the lengthy bend. They also say that in the Northern parts of the world, once the lute players have tuned up, a great many swans are invited in, and they play a concert together in strict measure.

Olor is the Latin name, and *Cygnus* the Greek one.

Sailors quite rightly say that this bird brings good luck. '*Cygnus* is a fowl most cheerful in auguries', as Emilianus remarks. The reason why sailors are fond of it is because it does not plunge itself beneath the waves.[1]

[1] Sailors have always been averse to being plunged beneath the wave fast by their native shore.

There is a bird called the YBIS (Ibis) which cleans out its bowels with its own beak. It enjoys eating corpses or snakes' eggs, and from such things it takes food home for its young, which comes most acceptable. It walks about near the seashore by day and night, looking for little dead fish or other bodies which have been thrown up by the waves. It is afraid to enter the water because it cannot swim.

This bird is typical of Carnal Man, who goes in for deadly dealings as if they were good spiritual food—by which his miserable soul gets nourished for punishment.

You, on the other hand, good Christian fellow—who are born again by water and the Holy Spirit to enter into the spiritual oceans of God's mysteries—on you he bestows the very finest food which he mentioned to the apostles, saying: 'The fruit of the Spirit moreover is affection, praise, peace, forbearance, long suffering, etc.'

Now if the sun and moon do not throw out their cruciform rays, they do not shine: if the birds do not spread their wings like a cross, they cannot fly. Just so, Man, if you do not protect yourself by the sign of the cross and spread your yard-arm wings of love, you will not be able to go through the tempests of this world to the quiet haven of the heavenly land.[1]

Finally, when Moses raised his arms like a bird, Israel prevailed: when he lowered his arms, Amalech conquered.

[1] 'Who can blot out the cross, which th' instrument
Of God dewed (dowed?) on me in the sacrament?
Who can deny me power and liberty
To stretch mine arms, and mine own cross to be?
Swim, and at every stroke thou art a cross!
The mast and yard make one when seas do toss.
Look down, thou spy'st ever crosses in small things;
Look up, thou seest birds raised on crossed wings.
All the globe's frame and sphere is nothing else
But the meridian's crossing parallels.'
DONNE.

There is an animal called an A S S I D A (ostrich),[1] which the Greeks call *Struthio-camelus*. Actually, the Latins call it a *Struthio* too. This bird has really got wings, but it does not fly. Furthermore, it has feet like a camel. Now when the time comes for it to lay some eggs, the  ostrich raises its eyes to heaven and looks to see whether those stars which are called the Pleiades are visible. Nor will it lay until the Pleiades appear. When, however, it perceives that constellation, round about the month of June, it digs a hole in the earth, and there it deposits the eggs and covers them with sand. Then it gets up, instantly forgets all about them, and never comes back any more.

[1] In the first part of *King Henry IV*, IV, i, there is a description of knights-in-armour at line 99. Dr Ansell Robin reads this as:

'All plumed like estridges that with the wind
Baited, like eagles having lately bathed.'

Another reading is:

'All plumed like estridges that wing the wind,
Baited like eagles having lately bathed.'

In the first place, the Ostrich or Estridge has at times been confused with the Ostour or Goshawk (*Astur palumbarius*). 'Thay be calde Ostregis that kepe Goshawkys or Tercellis'. *Boke of St Albans*, 1486. In the second place, the word 'baited' can have two meanings. Hawks which fly from the fist in a rage are said to have bated: animals which have been refreshed are said to have been baited, as in 'Livery and Bait Stables'. In the third place, both the ostrich and the goshawk were well known to Shakespeare's contemporaries. Dekker, for instance, wrote with reference to the true ostrich in *Fortunatus*:

A certain clemency and mildness of the atmosphere is noticeable in June, and so the sand, being warmed by the hot weather, incubates the eggs and hatches out the young.[1]

Now if the Ostrich knows its times and seasons, and, disregarding earthly things, cleaves to the heavenly ones—even unto the forgetting of its own offspring—how much the more should you, O Man, strive after the reward of the starry calling, on account of which God was made man that he might enlighten you from the powers of darkness and place you with the chiefs of his people in the glorious kingdom of the heavens.

[1] Ostriches swallow roughage to assist the gizzard, and their eggs are partly hatched by the sun. The male broods at night, the female by day.

'From beggary
I plumed thee like an estrich: like that estrich
Thou has eaten metals and abused my gifts,'
while Shakespeare himself was a knowledgeable austringer, as can be seen in *The Taming of the Shrew*. He would have known that a high wind sometimes annoys the carried hawk enough to make him bate, and also that hawks, after bathing, will flap, rustle or wing the wind in order to dry their plumage. So the lines about the crested knights can be taken in various ways. Either they were like ostriches annoyed and fluffed up by the wind—in which case they bated from anger: or they were like goshawks and eagles, refreshed after a bath (baited), and in that case the word is 'wing' not 'with'. Intermediate readings are equally possible.

The FULICA (coot) is a fowl which is very intelligent and foresighted,[2] and it does *not* eat corpses. Nor does it

[2] Skelton does not think so well of Fulica:
'The doterell, that folyshe pek,
And also the mad coote,
With a bald face to toote.'

gad about and stray from place to place. On the contrary, it stays in one place and persists in remaining there all its life. There it gets its food and there it sticks.

In just the same way do the faithful live, all knit together in one flock. *They* do not go wandering hither and thither, flapping about in different directions as the heretics do. *They* are not delighted with secular longings and desires. *They* always keep together in one place and rest in the catholic church.

There Our Lord causes them to live 'with one mind in the house'. There they get their daily sustenance, the food and drink of immortality, verily the precious blood of Christ, restoring them by the words of God which are sweeter than honey and the honeycomb.

The ALTION (halcyon) is a sea-bird, which hatches its young on the beaches. It lays its eggs in the sand, in the very middle of winter—for that is the season which destiny has chosen for the business—and it produces them just when the

sea normally rises to its roughest on the shores, and when the waves are most boisterously dashed against them.

Now the object of all this is, that the mother-love of the halcyon may be illustrified by an unexpected celebration of kindness.

For when the full-waved sea reaches the position of the eggs it suddenly moderates, and the violent winds fall, and the booming of the breeze softens, and the sea stands calm in the light airs, while the halcyon warms her eggs. What is more, there follow seven quiet hatching days, until, when these are over, the mother lets her chicks out and stops sitting. Then there are seven more days during which she feeds the young, while they are beginning to grow up. You may perhaps wonder at such a short infancy, when the brooding time was also so short.

People say that during those fourteen days sailors take it for granted that there will be fine weather. They call these days 'the Halcyon Days', in which there is no tide and the sea is not rough.[1]

[1] It will be noticed that this is not the classical story of Halcyone, whose nest should properly be on the sea itself, thus accounting for the seven halcyon days when 'birds of calm sit brooding on the charmèd wave'. Here the nest is on the beach, like that of the ringed plover. Perhaps the medieval version is more interesting than the classical one, for it seems to link the Greek legend with a real phenomenon, the neap tides. The mid-winter neaps are the tides at which the rise and fall between high-tide and low-tide would be at a minimum, thus causing less disturbance to a bird nesting near the tide line, and the numbers seven and fourteen are, moreover, evidently connected with lunar calculations, hence with tides.

The tides of the Mediterranean, from which sea the legend originated, are not pronounced like ours, however, and Oppian could place the incubation of these birds between sea and shore. 'They are so fond of the sea that they put their nests alongside the waves, and though they wet their breasts, they lay their tails on dry land.' (Auc. Bk. 2).

Birds of the tide-line do have a very short infancy, like many others which are hatched at ground level.

FENIX[1] the Bird of Arabia is called this because of its reddish purple colour (*phoeniceus*). It is unique: it is unparalleled in the whole world. It lives beyond five hundred years. When it notices that it is growing old, it builds itself a funeral pyre, after  collecting some spice branches, and on this, turning its body toward the rays of the sun and flapping its wings, it sets fire to itself of its own accord until it burns itself up. Then verily, on the ninth day afterward, it rises from its own ashes!

[1] Many identities have been suggested for the Phoenix, from the Bird of Paradise to the Flamingo. It has also been stated that the creature was a self-fertile and everlasting palm tree, of the same name. Aldrovandus devotes a chapter to it and so does Sir Thomas Browne.

Herodotus claimed that the Phoenix was to be seen at Heliopolis in Egypt. The fact seems to be that a sacred symbol used in the Sun worship at Heliopolis was a *benu*, said by the *Encyclopaedia Britannica* to have been a 'stork, heron or egret'. This symbol represented the sun, which died in its own fires every night and rose from them again in the morning—rose from the east of Egypt, i.e. from Arabia. The theory is supported by the fact that in Greek the word Phoenix can mean 'palm tree', and so does *benu* have the alternative meaning of 'palm tree' in Egyptian. Perhaps the *benu* and the Phoenix, both symbols of the sun-god, are really the Purple Heron (*Ardea purpurea*). *Phoeniceus* means 'purple', as our Bestiarist has pointed out. In that case, our fable seems likely to mean that a Purple Heron was ceremoniously sacrificed by the priests of Heliopolis at a grand celebration once every five hundred years.

Now Our Lord Jesus Christ exhibits the character of this bird,[1] who says: 'I have the power to lay down my life and to take it up again'. If the Phoenix has the power to die and rise again, why, silly man, are you scandalized at the word of God—who is the true Son of God—when he says that he came down from heaven for men and for our salvation, and who filled his wings with the odours of sweetness from the New and the Old Testaments, and who offered himself on the altar of the cross to suffer for us and on the third day rise again?

We repeat that the Phoenix is a bird which is stated to pass its time in the regions of Arabia, and that in length of age it reaches even unto five hundred years: also that when it observes its life to be coming to an end, it makes a coffin for itself of frankincense and myrrh and other spices, into which, its life being over, it enters and dies.

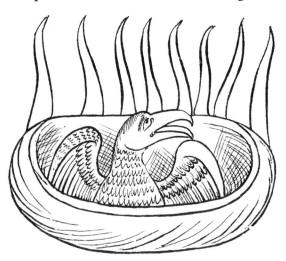

From the liquid of its body a worm now emerges, and this gradually grows to maturity, until, in the appointed cycle of time, the Phoenix itself assumes the oarage of its wings, and there it is again in its previous species and form!

[1] As the Egyptian God, if our previous note is to be believed, had done before him.

The symbolism of this bird therefore teaches us to believe in the resurrection.

This bird, without anybody to explain things to it, without even the power of reason, goes through the very facts of the resurrection—and that, in spite of the fact that birds exist for the good of men, not men for birds. Let it be an example to us, therefore, that the author and creator of mere birds did not arrange for his holy ones to be destroyed for ever, but wishes the seed to be renewed by rising again.

Who tells the simple Phoenix the day of its death—so that it makes its coffin and fills it with fine spices and gets inside and dies in a place where the stink of corruption can be effaced by agreeable smells?

How much the more should you, Man, both make your coffin of faith and—putting off the old man—put on the new coffin! Christ is your coffin: the sheath which protects you and hides you in the day of trouble. Should you wish to be assured that the coffin means protection, it is written 'in which I have protected him'. Verily, your faith is your coffin. Fill it then with the good spices of your virtues—which are chastity, compassion and justice—and thus enter safe into the sweet innermost chambers, with the odours of noble deeds.

May your departure from this life find you clothed in that same faith, so that your bones may wax fat and be like a well-watered garden, whose seeds are quickly raised.

Know therefore the day of your death, just as St Paul knew it when he said: 'I have fought the good fight, I have finished the course, I have kept the faith, the crown of justice is restored to me'.

He, like the good Phoenix, entered thereafter into his coffin, which he fills with the pleasant smell of a martyr.[1]

[1] Neither Shakespeare nor Chaucer seems to have been interested in Bestiaries as such. Although Chaucer quotes once from Neckham, perhaps from memory, and although he claimed to own sixty books, a large number for the fourteenth century, his only overt mention of anything approaching a natural history is in the *Parlement of Foules*, v, 316–and this although the Bestiaries were among the most popular books of the Middle Ages. Chaucer was a man of the Renaissance. His books would have been the classics. Also, since he was himself an observer of living nature with his own eye, he had no need to read the old wives' tales about it. In the *Parlement of Foules*, from line 316 to line 368, we are given his index of the birds of the air, yet there is no Phoenix, no Cinomolgus, no Hoopoe, none of the sensational oddities of the Physiologus. The only birds which have even the most oblique reference to the common tenets of the Bestiary are the Eagle, for his eyesight, and the wedded Turtle, for her 'herte trewe'.

An hour with a Shakespeare Concordance will show that the same thing is true of the dramatist (see note, p. 20). There are no Manticores in Shakespeare, no Aspidodelones, no Amphisbaenae with a head at each end. Had the bard heard of these fascinating creatures, it seems likely that he would have mentioned them, as Milton did.

This is one of the arguments by internal evidence that the poem called *The Phoenix and the Turtle*, which was attributed to Shakespeare, may not have been by him.

For whoever did write *The Phoenix and the Turtle* looks more like a student of the Bestiaries; or at any rate he must have had a passing knowledge of Trevisa or Du Bartas or Topsell. The birds of Physiologus do seem to appear in that. The Phoenix is in the first verse, the Chaladrius may be in the second, and certain medieval peculiarities of swans, sable-gendered crows or widowed doves are understood throughout the threnody. There is no Caladrius elsewhere in Shakespeare, although the Phoenix, a much commoner object for conversation from his day to ours, does appear about seven times.

The extended influence of the Bestiaries in general has been so prodigious that it is not possible to say who has read them at first hand and who at second. Everybody has heard of the Phoenix, and half the poets who have written have mentioned it. The only way to come closer to a solution of the question seems to be to choose the rarer creatures like the Leucrota, and to look for them. Spenser, as can be seen from the quotation on page 163, was well acquainted with uncommon beasts. But who would have expected that both Tennyson and Pope should mention the Amphisbaena?

Another Arabian bird, the C I N O M O L G U S,[1] is called this because he builds his nests in the very highest trees, making them out of Cinnamon. Since people are not able to climb to such a height, owing to the altitude and fragility of the branches, they try to hit the nests with weighted missiles, and so to bring down the cinnamon. The nests sell for very high prices, because merchants prize these cinnamon fruits more than most.

[1] The Cinomolgus has been thought to be the same bird as the Phoenix. It does not appear in the N.E.D.

The Emperor Heliogabulus (218-222 A.D.) shared his name of 'Helio' with the sun, the sun city and the sun bird. A glutton and a debauchee, 'his rice was steamed with pearls, his peas mixed with shavings of gold and his other vegetables with amber and different precious stones. He was particularly fond of the brains of certain birds, together with the crests cut from living cocks, the tongues of peacocks and the heads of flamingoes.' PETER LUM. But what the Emperor coveted most was a dish of the Phoenix or Cinnamon-bird, whose longevity and uniquity might be assimilated by digestion. As a Phoenician himself, he would have had a special partiality. A very rare bird was finally obtained for him, probably a bird of paradise, and this he instantly immolated, like any other collector of rare birds. One is thankful to know that he was murdered very shortly afterwards.

ERCINEE birds (Bohemian Jays?) are called after the vast Hercynian Forest of Germany, where they are born. Their feathers shine so brightly in the darkness that, however densely the night may be overcast, their wings shed a phosphorescence. They shine on the ground so as to make safe the route which has to be flown, and the bird's journey can be followed by the tell-tale glow of its shining feathers.[1]

[1] Aldrovandus and others remark with some doubt that a bird which had been sitting on a decaying nest might become phosphorescent.

By the sixteenth century some such bird had become transferred to the New World.

> 'NEW-SPAIN's *Cucuio*, in his forehead brings
> Two burning Lamps, two underneath his wings;
> Whose shining Rayes serve oft, in darkest night,
> Th' imbroiderer's hand in royall Works to light. . . .
> The Usurer to count his glistring treasures;
> The learned Scribe to limn his golden measures.'
> SYLVESTER's *Du Bartas*.

There is a bird called the EPOPUS (Hoopoe) which, when it sees that its parents are growing elderly,[1] preens their feathers for them, keeps them warm and licks their eyes. Thus the parents feel restored. It looks as if it were saying to its father and mother: 'Just as you worked hard to nourish me, I am going to do the same for you'.

Now observe: if these birds, being without the faculty

[1] See Note on Stork, p. 118.

of reason, do these mutual kindnesses to each other, how much the more ought rational men to return the care of their parents?

Because the Law says: 'He who speaks evil of his father and his mother shall die the death'. It is the equivalent of parricide and matricide.

PELICANUS the Pelican is a bird which lives in the solitude of the River Nile, whence it takes its name. The point is that, in Greek, Egypt is called *Can*opos. The Pelican is excessively devoted to its children. But when these have been born and begin to grow up, they flap their parents in the face with their wings, and the parents, striking back, kill them. Three days afterward the mother pierces her breast, opens her side, and lays herself across her young, pouring out her blood over the dead bodies. This brings them to life again.

In the same way, Our Lord Jesus Christ, who is the originator and maker of all created things, begets us and calls us into being out of nothing. We, on the contrary, strike him in the face. As the prophet Isaiah says: 'I have borne children and exalted them and truly they have scorned me'. We have struck him in the face by devoting ourselves to the creation rather than the creator.

That was why he ascended into the height of the cross, and, his side having been pierced, there came from it blood and water for our salvation and eternal life.[1]

[1] Just as certain unreal birds of mythology have passed into the Bestiaries, so have certain real birds from the Bestiaries passed out again into the abstract science of heraldry. The pelican was a favourite among the ecclesiastical symbols in this art, and, as we learn from Boutell, the bird 'represented as standing above its nest, having its wings addorsed, and nourishing its young with its blood, is blazoned as *a Pelican in its Piety*'. It was suggested by a Mr A. D. Bartlett (*Proc. Zool. Soc.* 1869, p. 146) that the pelican of piety was really the flamingo, which does eject 'a curious bloody secretion from the mouth'. But probably the ordinary ejection of food from the pelican's pouch may account for the legend. It will be noticed that in our illustration the bird on the right is reviving its young by a gush from the mouth, not from the breast.

NOCTUA the Owl is called a Noctua because it flies about by night (*nox*). It cannot see by day, because its sight is weakened by the rising splendour of the sun.

Notice that Noctua the Little Owl is not Bubo the Eagle Owl, for the latter is larger. Nycticorax the Night Heron is itself an owl, because it loves the darkness.[1] It is a light-shunning bird, and cannot stand daylight.

Owls are symbolical of the Jews, who repulse Our Saviour when he comes to redeem them, saying: 'We have no King but Caesar'. They value darkness more than light.

Therefore Our Lord turns to us Gentiles, and sheds his rays upon us who are sitting in darkness and the shadow of death—concerning which it is written: 'The people whom I knew not shall serve me'. And in another prophet: 'I will call them my people who were not my people and her beloved which was not beloved'.

[1] Nycticorax has also been translated as the 'night raven'. 'The eared owl is like an ordinary owl, only that it has feathers about its ears; by some it is called the night raven'. ARISTOTLE, H.A., II, 509a.

The SIRENAE (Sirens), so Physiologus says, are deadly creatures who are made like human beings from the head to the navel, while their lower parts down to the feet are winged. They give forth musical songs in a melodious manner, which songs are very lovely, and thus they charm the ears of sailormen and allure them to themselves. They entice the hearing of these poor chaps by a wonderful sweetness of rhythm, and put them to sleep. At last, when they see that the sailors are deeply slumbering, they pounce upon them and tear them to bits.

That's the way in which ignorant and incautious human beings get tricked by pretty voices, when they are charmed by indelicacies, ostentations and pleasures, or when they become licentious with comedies, tragedies and various ditties. They lose their whole mental vigour,

134

as if in a deep sleep, and suddenly the reaving pounce of the Enemy is upon them.[1]

[1] Although the lady in the illustration is drawn with a fish tail, it is to be noted that this does not accord with the text. The true Sirens were not Mermaids. Aldrovandus thinks that they were Nightingales, and that the name of the mythological songstresses who charmed Ulysses had become attached to these birds, because they were the most lovely of the feathered musicians. Perhaps it was the other way about. If we analyse their anatomy in the text rather than the picture, they are simply human-headed birds, i.e. birds who would be able to sing as beautifully as women, with human cadenze, because they had the human thorax and the same ideas about music. The allegory would then be: seamen who hear the magic music of the nightingale along the shores of the Mediterranean are liable to approach the rocks too closely and to get wrecked. Should this be the correct explanation of their identity, we can answer at least one of the conundrums posed by Sir Thomas Browne. Dr Ludwig Koch would be able to tell him what song the Sirens sang, by means of a gramophone record, even if he could not also conjecture what name Achilles assumed when he hid himself among women.

PERDIX the Part-ridge gets its name because it makes that sort of noise.

It is a cunning, disgusting bird.

The male sometimes mounts the male, and thus the chief sensual appetite forgets the laws of sex. Moreover, it is such a perverted creature that the female will go and steal the eggs of another female. Yes, and in spite of the cheat she does not get any good of it. For, when the young are hatched and hear the call of their real mother, they instinctively run away from the one who is brooding them and return to the one who laid them.

The Devil is an example of this sort of thing. He tries to steal the children of the Eternal Creator, and, if they are foolish or lacking in a sense of their own strength, Satan is able to collect some of them somehow, and he cherishes them with the allurements of the body. But when the call of Christ is heard, the wise ones, growing their spiritual plumage, fly away and put their trust in Jesus.

Partridges secure protective coloration by clever camouflage. They cover their setts with thorny shrubs, so that animals which might attack them are kept off by the sharpness of the twigs. Dust is used as a covering for

the eggs, and the birds
return to the nest circuit-
ously. The females mostly
carry away their young
to trick their husbands
because the latter often
attack the young ones
when they are fawning
on them impatiently.

Frequent intercourse
tires them out. The males
fight each other for their
mate, and it is believed that the conquered male submits
to venery like a female.

Desire torments the females so much that even if a wind
blows toward them from the males they become pregnant
by the smell.

Another thing is that if a man comes near the place
where a partridge is brooding, the mother, having gone
out to meet him, shows herself of her own accord, and
feigning feebleness of foot and wing as if she might be
caught at any moment, invents all sorts of ways to hasten
slowly away. By this stratagem she entices and deludes
the passer-by until he is coaxed away from the nest, by
being moved further off. So you see they are not slow in
employing zeal to guard their babies.

When partridges notice that they have been spied out,
they turn over on their backs, lift clods of earth with their
feet, and spread these so skilfully to cover themselves that
they lie hidden from detection.

The word P I C A E (magpies) stands for 'poeticae' (imitators) because they can imitate words in a distinct voice like a man. Even if they are not able to speak real talk, as they hang down through the middle of the tree branches uttering their unseemly chatter,[1] yet they do imitate the sound of the human voice. Concerning this, a certain writer[2] aptly says: 'I, Magpie, a talker, greet thee, Lord, with definite speech, and if you don't see me you refuse to believe that I am a bird'.

[1] 'Not pious in its proper sense,
    But chattering like a bird,
    Of sin and grace–in such a case
    Magpiety's the word.'   Thomas Hood
[2] Martial.

The P I C U S (woodpecker) gets its name from Picus the son of Saturn, because he used the creature in auguries. For they say that this bird is something of a soothsayer by the following evidence, viz: in the trees on which it builds its nest, one cannot stick a nail where it sat, or anything else that remains fixed for a long time, without its falling out at once.

A C C I P I T E R the Hawk is a bird which is even better equipped in its spirit than in its talons, for it shows very great courage in a very small body. It gets its name from 'accipiendo'

138

(accepting), i.e. '*a capiendo*' (from seizing). For it is an avid bird at seizing upon others, whence it is called Accipiter, i.e. Raptor—the ravisher, the thief. It is in this sense that St Paul says you must bear with the matter '*siquis accipit vos*'—meaning '*siquis rapit*', though he said '*siquis accipit*'.

People say that the Hawk is unnaturally spartan toward his offspring, for, when he sees that the youngsters are fit to try flying, he offers them no food in the nest but beats them with his wings and throws them out and drives them from the nursery to destruction, so that they shall not turn into sluggish adults. He takes care that they shall not be slow-coaches in their tender age, so that later on they shall not be debauched by pleasures; so that they shall not get flabby from inactivity; so that they shall not learn to expect more food than they can win for themselves; and so that they shall not grow up to be a discredit to his own vim.

He gives up feeding them, to make them audacious in the art of robbery.

The Nightingale bird, LU-CINA, takes this name because she is accustomed to herald the dawn of a new day with her song, as a lamp does (*lucerna*).

She is an ever-watchful guardian, too, for she warms her eggs with a certain hollow of the body and with her breast. She tempers the sleepless labour of her long night's work by the sweetness of her song, and hence it is seen that the summit of her ambition is to cherish her young and to warm the eggs, to the best of her ability, not less by her sweet tones than by the heat of her body.

In imitation of this bird, the poor but honest working woman, as she toils with her arm at the thumped grindstone so that a subsistence of bread may not be lacking for her babies, yet lightens the burden of poverty by her nightly song, and, however unable she may be to imitate the lovely measures of the nightingale, yet she does imitate it nevertheless by the diligence of her devotion.[1]

[1] 'The broke-heart of a Nightingale
Ore-come in musicke.'
HERRICK.

Of bird-song it is impossible not to quote what Audubon heard from a French peasant of the nightingale:

'*Le bon Dieu m'a donné une femme*
Que j'ai tant, tant, tant, tant battue
Que s'il m'en donne une autre
Je ne la batterais plus, plus, plus, plus,
Qu'un petit, qu'un petit, qu'un petit!'

Another memorable piece of onomatopeia is Sylvester's imitation of the skylark:

'The pretty *Lark*, climbing the Welkin clear,
Chaunts with a cheer, *Heer peer I near my Dear*;
Then stooping thence (seeming her fall to rew)
Adieu (she saith) *adieu, deer Deer, adieu.*'

VESPERTILIO the Bat is a paltry animal. It takes its name from the evening (*vesper*).

It has wings, but at the same time it is a quadruped and uses teeth—a thing which one does not usually find in other birds.

The Bat parturates like a quadruped, bringing forth, not eggs, but living young. Moreover, it does not fly with wings, but is[1] supported by a membrane, poised on which just as if on a flight of feathers it moves and weaves about.

There is one other thing about these undistinguished animals, and this is that they hang on to each other alternately, and depend from any place like a cluster of grapes. If the top one let go, they would be all scattered. And this they do from a certain duty of affection, of a kind which it is difficult to find in man.

[1] At this point a leaf is missing from C.U.L. 11.4.26. The text and illustrations for Raven, Crow and Dove are supplied from Add. 11283 in the British Museum. Our own manuscript resumes half way through Dove.

The RAVEN, Corvus or Corax, takes its name from the sound of its gutteral throat, because its voice croaks.

It is said to be a bird which refuses to feed its children properly until it recognizes in them the appearance of the real black colour in the wings.[1] But after it sees them

[1] Konrad Lorenz the naturalist relates that Jackdaws will attack anybody seen to be carrying anything black. They assume that he has been preying upon their species. They make an attack even if a known friend like Dr Lorenz handles

to be sable feathered, it feeds those which it recognizes, generously.[1]

This bird goes for the eye first when eating corpses.

[1] 'He giveth to the beast his food, and to the young ravens which cry.' Ps. cxlvii, 9. If the young ravens are not properly fed by their parents until they are black-penned, who but God can support them? In spite of this forgotten peculiarity, the word 'ravenous' has a different derivation.

That old bird the CROW (*cornix*) is called by its Greek name among the Latins.

Soothsayers declare that it has to do with the troubles of men by omens, that it discloses the paths of treachery, and that it predicts the future.

It is very wrong to believe that God entrusts his secrets to crows.

Among the many omens attributed to this bird, they specially mention the foretelling of rain by its voice. Hence we get the quotation: 'Then the crow announces a cloud burst with a vulgar caw'.[2]

Let men learn to love their children from the example and from the sense of duty of crows. They diligently

[2] Virgil.

their young *after these are black-penned*. 'When I took the babies from the nest and presented them (unfledged) to their parents on the palm of my hand, it left them quite unmoved. But the very day that the small feathers on the nestling burst through their quills, changing their colour into black, there followed a furious attack by the parents on my outstretched hand. . . . In most respects, all this applies to crows.' *King Solomon's Ring*, Methuen, 1952.

follow their sons as an escort when they fly, and, fearing that the babies might possibly pine away, food is laid in, and they do not neglect this chore of feeding for a long time.

Now, on the other hand, the women of our own race quickly wean even those whom they love, and, if they are of the richer classes, they actually scorn to suckle them. If they are of the poorer classes, they reject their offspring and these are exposed and they refuse to acknowledge the ones which are found. What is more, the rich ones kill their own children in the belly, so that the inheritance may not be divided among many, and with murdering medicines they destroy the tokens of the unborn baby in the fruitful womb. Life is destroyed before it is delivered.

Who but Man has preached the abandoning of children? Who but he has devised such harsh customs for fathers? Who made brothers unequal among the fraternal relationships of Nature?

Our sons have to yield their place to the isolated fortune of a single rich one. The first of them is overwhelmed with the whole paternal inheritance: the second deplores the exhaustion of a rich patrimony and laments his penniless dower. But did not Nature divide equally among sons? Nature assigns equally to all, that they may have the wherewithal for being born and for living.

This should teach you people not to make unequal in their patrimony those whom you have made equal by the title of brotherhood, and whom, indeed, you have made to be both alike by the accident of birth. You ought not to grudge their having in common a thing to which they are common heirs.

COLUMBA the Dove is a simple fowl and free from gall, and it asks for love with its eye. (In the same way, Preachers are free from gall or acrimoniousness, because although they may be in a rage, it is not to be called  anger when they are exasperated with good reason.) The dove has a groan instead of a song. (Thus Preachers, being far from provocative songs and from the fashion of the times, groan over the sins of themselves and of others.) Nor does this bird mangle things with its beak, and this fact well applies to Preachers, who do not falsify the sacred scriptures as the heretics do. The dove picks out the better grains: the Preachers choose the better maxims from holy writ. The bird brings up the young of others: the Preachers by their preachings nourish the young of this generation—who are quite perverted by sin—and draw them to Christ. The bird sits near streams so that on seeing a hawk it can dive in and escape: similarly the Preachers live near the blessed scriptures so that, on seeing an attack and temptation from the Devil, they can dive into the scriptures—i.e. by acting according to the precepts of these same scriptures—and thus escape. The bird defends itself with its wings: so do the Preachers fortify and defend themselves with the opinions of the Fathers. It nests in a hole in the rock: so do the Preachers take refuge—i.e. by faith—in. those wounds of Christ, of whom it is said: 'The Rock moreover was Jesus'. They make a nest there for themselves and others. The bird has the peculiarity of recovering its lost sight: the Preachers of the Church, if some special gift of the Holy Ghost has been lost through sin, recover it, like the bird, by the spirit of prophecy. It flies about in flocks: in the same way, flocks of Preachers belonging to the Catholic faith follow in the steps of good works and virtues.

For, by so many good works as we do, by so many steps do we hasten to God.[1]

[1] 'He (Wordsworth) said, once in a wood, Mrs. Wordsworth and a lady were walking, when the stock dove was cooing. A farmer's wife coming by said to herself, "Oh, I do like stock doves". Mrs. Wordsworth, in all her enthusiasm for Wordsworth's poetry, took the old woman to her heart. "But", continued the old woman, "some like them in a pie; for my part, there's nothing like 'em stewed in onions".' R. B. HAYDON.

TURTUR the Turtle-dove gets her name from her cooing. She is a shy creature and always lives in the crests of the mountains, where she dwells in lonely solitude; for she shuns the houses of men or any intercourse with them, and takes to the woods.

In the winter time, when she has moulted, she is said to live in the hollow trunks of trees.

For fear that some wolf should attack her young in the nest, the Turtledove spreads the leaves of squills over it, knowing that wolves do not like this kind of leaf.

It is truly believed that when a turtle-dove is widowed by the loss of her spouse, she takes a dread against the marriage bed and against the very name of matrimony. For the first love has deceived and disappointed her by

145

the death of her darling one, and, since he has now become unfaithful for ever, she grows bitter about love
itself—which produces more sorrow out of death than
sweetness out of loving. So she refuses to repeat the
experience, nor does she break the bonds of chastity or
forget the rights of her wedded husband. She keeps her
love for him alone, for him she guards the name of wife.

Know then, O Woman, how much widowhood is es-
teemed, when it is shown forth even in birds.

Who gave such laws to turtle-doves? If I look for a
man who did, I cannot find one. For no man has dared,
not even Paul dared, to prescribe laws about widowhood.
He only says that he wishes the young to marry in order
to bear sons, in order to be the mothers of a family and in
order to give no opportunity to the Enemy. And elsewhere he says: 'It is good if they remain even as He.
Because they are not continent, they should marry. It
is better to marry than to burn.' Paul would like women
to have that chastity which is kept by turtle-doves, but
in other respects he urges the custom of matrimony, because mere women are seldom able to come up to the
standard of doves.

God poured out his grace and disposition on Turtur,
and gave her this virtue of continence. He also is able
to lay down what all should follow. The flower of youth
does not burn up the turtle-dove, nor is she allured by the
temptations of occasion. She has no skill to betray her
troth, for she knows how to preserve the married chastity
which she plighted when she was a newly-wed.

HIRUNDO the Swallow is called this because it does not take its dinner sitting down, but seizes and eats it in the air. (Hir-undo: Aër-undo.)

It is a chittering bird which sweeps about in twisting and winding circles, and it is very clever at nest-building as well as at bringing up its children. Also it has a sort of second-sight, because it leaves the nest when this will not stick to the roof-ridge and is going to tumble down.

It is not endangered by birds of prey, nor does it ever fall a victim to them as it flies across the sea. And there overseas it lives during the winter.[1]

Bodily it is rather a small bird, but it is exalted by an uncommonly devout state of mind, heedful to all sorts of things. It constructs nests more precious than gold—for it builds wisely, and the nest of wisdom is indeed better than gold. What is wiser than that it should achieve freedom of flight in migration? That it should trust its young to the dwellings and roofs of men, where no one attacks them? For it is a beautiful fact that it accustoms its children from their earliest days to the company of man, and this preserves them safe from the wiles of the raptors.

Now here is another plain fact: that it builds itself a four-walled home, without elegance, but with real craftsmanship. It gathers straw with its mouth and spreads it

[1] See note on page 117. Here is a plain statement of the migration of swallows which remained partly a mystery even to the immortal Gilbert White. In 1703 it was the naturalist Morton who stated that they migrated to the moon.

with mud to make it gum together. And because it is not able to carry mud in its feet, it gets water on its wings so that the dust sticks to them easily and mud is made. Into this it gradually binds the straw and the twigs which it has collected, and makes them adhere. By this means it makes the fabric for the whole nest, so that its children can live on a hard floor as if they were in their own houses, with nothing to be afraid of and nobody able to put a foot through the cracks and the cold not able to creep upon the tender young.

This obligation of parental care is properly common to many birds, but this particular bird is unique in its noble attention to duty, and because there really seems to be a conscious understanding in craftsmanship.

It also has a certain knowledge of medical skill, for when its children go blind or their eyes are pricked, it has a remedy by which it is able to restore their vision.

COTURNIX the Quail is named after his call-note, and the Greeks call him *Ortygia* because quails were first seen on the island of *Ortygia* (Delos).[1]

When the summer is over, they cross the sea. The one who leads the host is called *Ortycumetra*, the quail-mother.[2] If a hawk sees her approaching the land, he seizes her, for which reason it is everybody's business to protect the leader from enemy formations, and for that the front rank is responsible.

[1] 'First' probably means first on migration.

[2] But *Ortycumetra* also means a Landrail. Perhaps we are to understand that the flight of quails is led by a landrail, just as the pathfinder of the storks was a crow.

The food they are fondest of is poisonous seed,[1] for which reason the ancients forbade them to be eaten. Finally, they are the only animals which suffer from the falling sickness like man.[2]

[1] Quails fattened themselves with poison, it was believed, as we take tonics of strychnine and arsenic. Aristotle said that they ate henbane and hellebore.

[2] It is a fact that if a heron can be stalked and surprised at close quarters, it will fall down in a kind of fit. The present translator has seen this.

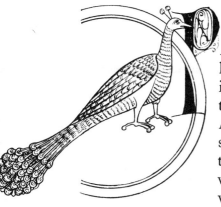

A V O the Peacock is named after his voice. His flesh is so hard that it is scarcely subject to putrefaction,[3] and it is not easily cooked. About this bird a certain poet[4] sings: 'How can you be surprised that he often ruffles his jewelled wings at you, O you hard-hearted woman, when you can find it in your heart to hand him over to the cruel cook?'

[3] St Augustine remarked, 'Who except God, the Creator of all things, endowed the flesh of the dead peacock with the power of never decaying?' *De Civ. Dei.* 'There is a tradition that the acute and inquisitive suffragan of Hippo (St Augustine) experimented with the flesh of this fowl, and found the popular superstition to be correct'. E. P. Evans.

[4] Martial. The Bestiarist has unfortunately omitted to tell us that peacocks are shy about their feet. 'When he sees his feet, he screams wildly, thinking that they are not in keeping with the rest of his body'. Epiphanius.
'The proud sun-bearing Peacock with his feathers
    Walkes all along, thinking himself a king,
And with his voice prognosticates all weathers,
    Although God knowes but badly he doth sing;
But when he lookes downe to his base blacke Feete,
He droopes and is asham'd of things unmeete.'
                                        Chester, *Love's Martyr.*

149

The Greeks named this bird UPUPA (The Hoopoe)[1] because it lines its nest with human dung. The filthy creature feeds on stinking excrement. He lives on this in graves.

His helmet is topped with a crest of feathers which stick out.

If anybody smears himself with the blood of this bird on his way to bed, he will have nightmares about suffocating devils.

[1] The Epopus, which we have seen on page 131 is thought to be the same as the Upupa, and both to be the Hoopoe. It will be noticed that animals are liable to repeat themselves in Bestiaries—for instance, the crocodile does. This might happen in the course of the expansion and re-arrangement explained in the Appendix, though in some cases, such as that of the unicorn, there were two species.

It is a fact that the real Hoopoe is an insanitary bird. 'Pleasing', says the *Encyclopaedia Britannica*, 'as is the appearance of the hoopoe as it fearlessly parades its showy plumage, some of its habits are much the reverse. All observers agree in stating that it delights to find its food among filth of the most abominable description.' The Bestiarist does not explain how the word Upupa is supposed to be derived from the Greek. The name is in fact onomatopoeic, deriving from the bird's cry of 'Up-up' or 'Hoop-hoop'.

The COCK (*gallus*) is called the cock because it gets castrated. It is the only member of the bird family whose testicles are removed. Indeed, the ancients used to call the Galli (the priests of Cybele) the 'cut-offs'.

Just as a lioness takes her name from a lion or a

dragoness from a dragon, so does a hen take hers (*gallina*) from the cock (*gallinus*).

Their limbs, they say, are eaten mixed with liquid gold.[1]

Cockcrow is a pleasant thing of a night, and not only pleasant but useful. It is nice to have it about the place. It wakes the sleeping, it forewarns the anxious, it consoles the traveller by bearing witness to the passage of time with tuneful notes. At the cock's crowing the robber leaves his wiles, the morning star himself wakes up and shines upon the sky. At his singing the frightened sailor lays aside his cares and the tempest often moderates, waking up from last night's storm. At his crowing the devoted mind rises to prayer and the priest begins again to read his office. By testifying devotedly after the cock-crow Peter washed away the sin of the Church, which he had incurred by denying Christ before it crowed. It is by this song that hope returns to the sick, trouble is turned to advantage, the pain of wounds is relieved, the burning of fever is lessened, faith is restored to the fallen, Christ turns his face to the wavering or reforms the erring, wandering of mind departs and negation is driven out. Confession follows. Scripture teaches that this did not happen by chance, but by the will of our Lord.

[1] i.e. as a medicine. Of this prescription Aldrovandus remarks: '*Sciteque dixit Trincavella, olim praeceptor meus, aurem exhilarare spiritus omnes, cum quis in crumena eo abundaverit.*' Well, look you, Dr Trincavella used to say, who was once my tutor, gold cheers everybody up, doesn't it—when they have enough in their pockets?

ANAS the Duck achieves his appropriate name by his constant application to swimming (*a natandi*). One of his

species is called Graminia, because it feeds more than others do on couch-grass (*gramen*).

The Duck gives its name to the Goose (*anser*) by derivation, or else by similarity, for the goose itself is constantly swimming about.

The latter birds mark the watches of the night by a steady repetition of their.cackling. Another thing is that no animals notice the scent of men so well as the geese do, and for this reason the climbing of the Gauls into the Capitol was detected from their outcry.

AN ODD THING is that the offspring of all birds are born twice: first when the eggs are laid, then when they are formed and hatched by the heat of the mother's body.

EGGS (*ova*) are called this because they are full of liquid inside. You see, a thing which has liquid outside is wet (*humidus*) while a thing which has liquid on the inside is 'juicy' (*uvidus*). However, some people think that the name of Egg has a Greek origin—and indeed those people do call them OA, with the V left out.

Some eggs are created in a wind at the fundament, but then they are not fertile unless they are conceived with male intercourse and penetrated by the semen.

They say that the power of eggs is so great that wood which has been sprinkled with them does not burn hotly, and if a garment is put close to a fire of that sort it will not scorch.

Mixed with chalk, they are used to glue pieces of glass together.

BEES[1] are called Apes either because they cling to things with their feet (*a pedibus*) or else because they are born without feet, for they only grow their feet and wings later on.

They are skilled in the art of making honey. They live in definite houses. They build their homes with indescribable dexterity, making them out of various flowers and filling innumerable cells with woven wax. They have kings. They have armies. They go to war.

Bees flee from smoke and are irritated by noise.

Many people have proved that these creatures are born from the corpses of cows. The flesh of dead calves is beaten in order to bring them forth, so that out of the rotting blood maggots may be created which finally turn into bees.[2] As a matter of fact, one ought more accurately to say that bees are born from oxen, hornets from horses, drones from mules and wasps from donkeys.[3]

The Greeks call the ones which are produced in the outer part of the honeycomb '*castros*', the drones (workers?) or castrated ones, though some people think they are called 'kings' because they lead the hive.

[1] The illustration, like that attached to Ants, was not completed contemporaneously with the manuscript. A good contemporary picture can be found in Roy: 12.c.xix.

[2] 'Out of the eater came forth meat, and out of the strong came forth sweetness.' Judges xiv. 14.

[3] Ovid.

Alone among every species of living thing, the bees have children which are common to all. All inhabit the same dwelling, all are enclosed within the threshold of one fatherland. Work is common to all, food is in common, labour and the habit and enjoyment of flight are all in common. Procreation and virginity are common to all, and so is birth, which is not shared among them with any sexual intercourse nor troubled with any unlawful desire, nor are they harassed with the griefs of childbirth. For they suddenly produce the greatest swarm of progeny, picking up the grubs with the mouth from leaves and grasses.

They arrange their own king for themselves. They create a popular state, and, although they are placed under a king, they are free. For the king does not merely hold the privilege of giving judgement, but he also excites a feeling of allegiance, both because the Bees love him on the ground that he was appointed by themselves and also because they honour him for being at the head of so great a swarm. Moreover, the king does not become their leader by lot, for in casting lots there is the element of chance rather than good judgement, and often by the irrational misfortune of luck somebody who is worse gets preferred to better men. A King Bee, on the contrary, is formed with clear natural signs, so that he can be distinguished by the size of his body and by his appearance.[1] What is more, the peculiarity of a king is the

---

[1] Queen bees were believed to be kings until the late seventeenth or eighteenth century. Shakespeare thought of them as Emperors.

'Therefore doth heaven divide
The state of man in divers functions,
Setting endeavour in continual motion;
To which is fixed as an aim or butt
Obedience: for so work the honey-bees,

154

clemency of his character, for even if he has a sting he does not use it in punishment—since there are unwritten laws in Nature, not laid down but customary, to the effect that those who have the greatest power should be the most lenient.

Such bees as are disobedient to the laws of the king punish themselves, on being condemned to penance, so that they die by the wounds of their own stings. They say that the people of Persia do likewise to this day, carrying out the sentence of death upon themselves, in proportion to their deserts. Thus none possess such a king as the bees, unless it be the Persians who have the severest laws against insubordinate people, or the Indians, or perhaps the people of Sarmatia.[1]

Bees observe such a tremendous reverence of respect that none dare leave the nest to swarm to other pastures unless the king shall have gone forth in front of them and claimed the first rank of flight for himself. Then the

[1] Scythians—Russians, more or less.

> Creatures that by a rule in nature teach
> The act of order to a peopled kingdom.
> They have a king and officers of sorts;
> Where some, like magistrates, correct at home,
> Others, like merchants, venture trade abroad,
> Others, like soldiers, armed in their stings,
> Make boot upon the summer's velvet buds,
> Which pillage they with merry march bring home
> To the tent-royal of their Emperor;
> Who, busied in his majesty, surveys
> The singing masons building roofs of gold,
> The civil citizens kneading up the honey,
> The poor mechanic porters crowding in
> Their heavy burdens at his narrow gate,
> The sad-eyed justice, with his surly hum,
> Delivering o'er to executors pale
> The lazy yawning drone.'
>
> *Henry V*, i. ii. 183 *sqq*

advance is through sweet-smelling territories where there are gardens fragrant with flowers, where the river is flowing through grassy places among the pleasaunces of its banks. There takes place the game of active youth, there the exercise on the plain, there trouble is made little. Work is pleasant there, and from flowers and sweet herbs the foundations of the new hive are laid.

What indeed is a honey hive except a sort of camp? For these enclosures the bee-wax of the bees is laid up. What four-walled houses can show so much skill and beauty as the frame-work of their combs shows, in which small round apartments are supported by sticking one to the other? What architect taught them to fit together six-sided chambers with their sides undistinguishably equal? To suspend thin wax cells inside the walls of their tenements? To compress honey-dew and make the flower-granaries to swell with a kind of nectar?

You can see bees all vying with each other in their tasks. You can see some watchful in the search for food, others showing an anxious guardianship over the hive, others on the lookout for coming showers and studying the way the clouds run together, others making wax from flowers, and others collecting in their mouths the honey-water which has been infused on the blossoms. Yet none of them is encroaching on the work of his neighbours, and none is getting his living by robberies. Would indeed that they had not themselves to fear the tricks of robbers!

Bees have stings and can produce poison as well as honey, if they are provoked.[1] In their thirst for revenge,

---

[1] Readers who do not share the Bestiarist's affection for the honey bee may find the following charm effective, from *Caltha Poetarum, or The Bumble Bee*, composed by T. Cutwode Esq. (1599):

156

they lay down their own lives in the wounds which they
make.

Avaunt from us false bumble Bee
    in thy busie buzzing:
And come not here thou craftie Flee,
    harme not in thy huzing.
Fly farre inough prodigious Fowle,
    in they bitter stinging:
Worse then the scrytching ougly Owle,
    never good luck bringing.
In thy comming or thy bumming
If thou commest hither humming,
    thou false bumble Bee,
In thy swarming and thy harming,
If thou chance within my charming,
        Exorciso te.
Beware I say thou little bird,
    of my leather flee flap:
And come not here nor hitherward,
    least it reach a sound rap:
For it shall beate thy litle bum
    Here me pretie fellow,
And clap it thriftly if thou come,
    harken what I tell you.
In thy comming or thy bumming
If thou commest hither humming,
    thou false bumble Bee,
In thy swarming and thy harming,
If thou chance within my charming,
        Exorciso te.
In nomine O domine,
    defend us from this Drone:
And charme this hurtfull hony Bee,
    to let us here alone.
Away thou fowle and fearefull spright,
    and thou litel divell:
I charge thee come not in our sight,
    for to do us evil.
In thy comming or thy bumming,
If thou commest hither humming,
    thou false bumble Bee,
In thy swarming and thy harming,
If thou chance within my charming,
        Exorciso te.

The moisture of honey-dew is poured into the midmost recesses of the hives and little by little, as time goes by, it is refined into honey. Although it was liquid in the first place, it begins to take on the sweet mellifluous smell by the thickening of the wax and the scent of the flowers.

How right the Scripture is, in proclaiming the bee to be a good worker, when it says: 'Go to the bee and mark its handiwork and copy the operation thereof'. In what a remarkable industry does the bee deal, when our kings and commons take its produce for the sake of their health! Worthy it is to be desired of all men and dear to them! Do you hear what the Prophet says? 'He sends you verily that you may follow the example of that little bee, and that you may imitate its labour.' See how industrious, how agreeable it is. What it manufactures is desired and sought after by all, nor is this valued by men for the sake of variety, but in its unvaried deliciousness it grows sugary with equal sweetness for kings and commons alike.

Not only is honey delightful, but it is healthy. It mollifies the throat, it heals wounds, it is administered as a medicine for internal ulcers.[1]

And so, although bees may be weak in physical strength, they are strong in the vigour of wisdom and the love of virtue. Finally, they guard their king to the top of protection and think it beautiful to die for him.

---

[1] Also, according to Aldrovandus, one can stimulate the growth of one's beard by applying to the chin a mixture of the ashes of burnt bees compounded with the excrement of shrew mice. He devotes four pages to the medicinal virtues of honey.

While their king is safe, they never alter decisions or change their minds. But if the king is lost, they abandon the trust of preserving his kingdom and tear themselves away from his honey-store, because he who held the office of Chief is destroyed.

Where others scarcely bring forth one brood in a year, bees reproduce themselves twofold and preponderate over other animals with a double fruitfulness.

The PERINDEUS is a tree in India. Its fruit is very sweet and exceedingly agreeable. Doves delight in the produce of this tree, and live in it, feeding on its fruits.

Now the dragon is an enemy to doves, but it fears the tree they live in, and its shade too, nor can it approach either the tree or its shadow. Indeed, if the shadow of the tree falls to the west, the dragon betakes himself to the east, and if the shadow comes to the east, he flees to the west. If, however, a dove happens to be found outside the tree-shade then the dragon kills it.[1]

[1] The Perindeus does not appear in the N.E.D. Aelian informs us, in the second century, that 'the people of the City of Apollo, who are a division of the Tenterites, catch crocodiles in a drag net, and having hung them up on persea-trees, they beat them with many blows and flog them as men are flogged, while the animals whimper and shed tears; then they cut them down and feast on them.' If the Persea is the same as the Perindeus, this treatment might account for the antipathy felt for it by reptiles: or perhaps that tree is selected because of the existing antipathy.

Aldrovandus, however, says that the Perindeus or Peridexion was really the 'deadly white hellebore' or Christmas Rose, which was famous in the Dark Ages as a purge, a poison, a heart stimulant and a medicine for insanity. One of its active principles, Helleborëin, does act similarly to digitalis.

The Upas Tree of Java (*Antiaris toxicaria*) contains Antiarin, which is also a cardiac stimulant. If this link, and the fact that they both come from the East, is worth consideration, perhaps the Peridexion was connected with the Upas—that fabulous member of the fig family which was said to destroy all life within a radius of fifteen miles.

Understand that the tree is God the Father and the shade is God the Son, for Gabriel said to Mary: 'The Holy Ghost shall come upon thee, and the shade of the all-highest shall overshadow thee'. The fruit of the tree is heavenly wisdom, i.e. of the Lord. The dove is the Holy Ghost.

Look to it, therefore, O Man, lest before you can receive the Holy Ghost, which is the spiritual and heavenly dove descending and abiding in you, you do not remain for eternity outside the Father, Son and Holy Ghost. Look to it lest the Dragon destroy you, i.e. the Devil.

Now if you have the Holy Ghost, the Dragon cannot come nigh you. O Man, then turn toward the Catholic faith and remain in it and there live. Persevere there in the one Catholic Church. Take as much care as you can not to be caught outside the doors of your refuge. Take care lest that Dragon, the serpent of old, should seize you and gobble you up like Judas—who, as soon as he went out from the Lord and his brother apostles, was instantly devoured by a demon and perished.

III

REPTILES AND FISHES

'*Scorpion and Asp, and Amphisbaena dire,*
Cerastes horn'd, Hydrus and Ellops drear,
And Dipsas.'

PARADISE LOST, X, 523.

'*Spring-headed hydraes, and sea-shouldering Whales;*
Great whirlpooles, which all fishes make to flee;
Bright scolopendraes arm'd with silver scales;
Mighty Monoceros with immeasured tayles;
The dreadful Fish that hath deserved the name
Of Death, and like him lookes in dreadfull hew;
The griesly Wasserman, that makes his game
The flying ships with swiftnesse to pursew;
The horrible Sea-satyre that doth shew
His fearefull face in time of greatest storme;
Huge Ziffius, whom mariners eschew
No less than rockes (as travellers informe),
And greedy Rosmarines with visages deforme.'

FAERIE QUEENE, ii, 12.

NGUIS (the Snake, but also the star Draco) is the origin of all serpents, because they can be folded and bent, and hence snakes are called 'anguis' since they are angular and never straight.

COLUBER (another name for snake) is called this because *'colat umbras'*—it inhabits shady places—or else because it glides with serpentine coils (*colubrosus*) into slippery courses. It is known as 'the slippery one' because it slips away crawling, and, like a fish, the more so the tighter it is held.

SERPENS gets its name because it creeps (*serpit*) by secret approaches and not by open steps. It moves along by very small pressures of its scales.

The ones which have four legs like lizards and newts are not called serpents but reptiles. Serpents are reptiles which crawl on the belly and breast.

Of these creatures how many poisons there are, how many species, how many calamities, how many griefs, and what a lot of different colours they have got!

DRACO the Dragon[1] is the biggest of all serpents, in fact of all living things on earth. The Greeks call it

---

[1] Aldrovandus gives fifty-nine folio pages to dragons, and turns up much interesting material in the process. He deals with humans of the name of Draco, with sea-serpents, tarantulas, plants, trees, stars, devils, quicksilver, mountains, traps, fistulae, sirens, Hydras, anacondas, whales, leviathan, fossils, heiroglyphs and even with an early form of aircraft called a Dragon, though not manufactured by De Havilland, which flew. He adds that it is possible for unscrupulous people to forge a dragon, by plastic surgery on the cadaver of a Giant Ray. But his main point is that the words 'dragon' and 'serpent' are interchangeable. He points out that the reptile which attacked Laocoon is called by Virgil a serpent in one place and a dragon in another. 'Why', wrote Kingsley in 1849, 'should not these dragons have been simply what the Greek word dragon means—what . . . the superstitions of the peasantry in many parts of England to this day assert them to have been—"mighty worms", huge snakes?' This is the proper way to regard them. 'Dragon' was simply the medieval word for a large reptile, and the

'*draconta*' (δρακων) and hence it has been turned into Latin under the name 'draco'.

When this dragon has come out of its cave, it is often carried into the sky, and the air near it becomes ardent. It has a crest, a small mouth and a narrow gullet through which it draws breath or puts out its tongue. Moreover, its strength is not in its teeth but in its tail, and it inflicts injury by blows rather than by stinging. So it is harmless as regards poison. But they point out that poisons are not necessary to it for killing, since if it winds round anyone it kills him like that. Even the Elephant is not protected from it by the size of its body; for the dragon, lying in wait near the paths along which the elephants

---

more one regards it as not being a joke from the fairy stories, the more interesting the following pages may prove to be. The very first definition of 'dragon' in the N.E.D. is 'A huge serpent or snake; a python. *Obs.*' In modern zoology the dragon is a flying lizard forming the genus *Draco*, belonging to the family *Agamidae*, and there are twenty species.

usually saunter, lassoes their legs in a knot with its tail and destroys them by suffocation.[1]

They are bred in Ethiopia and India, in places where there is perpetual heat.

The Devil, who is the most enormous of all reptiles, is like this dragon. He is often borne into the air from his den, and the air round him blazes, for the Devil in raising himself from the lower regions translates himself into an angel of light and misleads the foolish with false hopes of glory and worldly bliss. He is said to have a crest or crown because he is the King of Pride, and his strength is not in his teeth but in his tail because he beguiles those whom he draws to him by deceit, their strength being destroyed. He lies hidden round the paths on which they saunter, because their way to heaven is encumbered by the knots of their sins, and he strangles them to death. For if anybody is ensnared by the toils of crime he dies, and no doubt he goes to Hell.

[1] 'Then suddenly, the Dragon slips his hold
From th' *Elephant,* and sliding down doth fold
About his fore-legs, fetter'd in such order,
That stocked there he now can stir no further;
While th' *Elephant* (but to no purpose) strives
With's winding Trunk t'undoe his wounding gyves,
His furious foe thrusts in his nose, his nose;
Then head and all; and there-withall doth close
His breathing passage: but, his victory
He joyes not long; for his huge Enemy
Falling down dead, doth with his weighty Fall
Crush him to death, that caus'd his death withall.'
SYLVESTER'S *Du Bartas.*

The BASILISK is translated in Greek and Latin as 'Regulus' (a prince) because it is the king of serpents—so much so, that people who see it run for their lives, because it can kill them merely by its smell. Even if it looks at a man, it destroys him. At the mere sight of a Basilisk, any bird which is flying past cannot get across unhurt, but, although it may be far from the creature's mouth, it gets frizzled up and is devoured.[1]

Nevertheless, Basilisks are conquered by weasels.[2] Men put these into the lairs in which they lie hid, and

---

[1] Sir Thomas Browne, the least credulous of naturalists, was a firm believer in the Basilisk. The Cocatrice, he said, was 'rather an Hieroglyphicall fancy' but the Basilisk, though not born from a cock's egg and not incubated by a toad, did exist as a real serpent. He considered it possible, moreover, that the creature could kill with a look—with an airborne poison, as it were. Were not 'plagues and pestilentiall Atomes' carried in the air?

In 1646, Pepys was reporting in his diary that, 'discoursing of the nature of serpents, he told us some that in the waste places of Lancashire do grow to a great bigness, and that do feed on larks, which they take thus: They observe when the lark is soared to the highest, and do crawl to be just underneath them; and there they place themselves with their mouths uppermost, and there, as is conceived, they do eject poyson up to the bird; for the bird do suddenly come down again in its course of a circle, and falls directly into the mouth of a serpent; which is very strange.'

The pictures of Basilisks in Aldrovandus look like scorpions, or like crowned snakes or like hooded ones. Before dismissing the creature as fabulous, it is worth reflecting that several venomous reptiles do spit their poison. Carolus Clusius suggests that it was the hooded cobra, and Avicenna that it was some kind of horned viper.

[2] Perhaps the weasel was the mongoose. A mongoose belongs to the genus Ichneumon. 'The Indian ichneumon or mungoos . . . is considerably smaller than the Egyptian form.' *Enc. Brit.* 1881.

thus, on seeing the weasel, the Basilisk runs away. The weasel follows and kills it. God never makes anything without a remedy. Finally, a Basilisk is striped lengthwise with white marks six inches in size.

The Basilisk, moreover, like the scorpion, also frequents desert places, and before people can get to the rivers it gives them hydrophobia and sends them mad. Its hiss is the same as that of the Regulus, for it can kill with its noise and burn people up, as it were, before it bites them.[1]

---

[1] The Basilisk has since the fourteenth century been confused with the Cockatrice, and the subject is now a complicated one. The position is briefly as follows.

At the time of our own manuscript, the basilisk was merely the king of serpents, and might readily have been identified with some kind of cobra. The naturalist Neckham (c. 1180) seems to have introduced the story that it was hatched from the egg of an aged cock. (Aristotle had correctly pointed out that elderly roosters do develop a sort of egg: 'substances resembling the egg . . . have been found in the cock when cut open, underneath the midriff where the hen hath her eggs, and these are entirely yellow in appearance and of the same size as ordinary eggs', H.A. VI, 559b.) The picture in our manuscript shows that even before Neckham the idea was present. In 1382, Wycliffe's bible translated basilisk into cockatrice. Words like 'basili-coc' had already appeared. It was approximately at this stage that the endless confusions of etymology began to interfere with natural history. The medieval philologist had no inhibitions about mixing languages, and for him the basili-coc might just as well have been a King Cock as a King Cobra. (βασιλεύς means King.) Unfortunately, the word Cocodrillus (the crocodile) also sounded a little like cock and cockatrice, while there was a bird called a Trochilus which entered the jaws of crocodiles to pick their teeth, and perhaps this was a cock bird too. The etymological tangle was further exasperated by physical coincidences, e.g. between the mongoose which killed the basilisk and the hydrus which killed the crocodile; also between the combs of cocks, the crests of some serpents and the dorsal fins of some fish. For the Serra (q.v.) had been swept into the maelstrom by now. The fact is that translation and identification were responsible for the muddle, and grammar had bred the cockatrice.

A long, complicated and misleading note in the N.E.D. under Cockatrice sets out to explain the confusion which now exists among Ichneumon, Enhydris, Hydrus, Cocatris, Crocodile and Basilisk. The tangle has been brilliantly unpicked by Dr Ansell Robin in *Animal Lore in English Literature* (1932). For our present purposes we can assume that the basilisk is a snake whose enemy is the mongoose, ichneumon or enhydris; while the crocodile's friend is the

The VIPER (*vipera*) is called this because it brings forth in violence (*vi*). The reason is that when its belly is yearning for delivery, the young snakes, not waiting for the timely discharge of birth, gnaw through the mother's sides and burst out to her destruction.

It is said, moreover, that the male puts his head into the female's mouth and spits the semen into it. Then she, angered by his lust, bites off his head when he tries to take it out again.

Thus both parents perish, the male when he copulates, and the female when she gives birth.

According to St Ambrose, the viper is the most villainous kind of beast, and particularly because it is the cunningest of all species when it feels the lust for coition. It decides to have a bastard union with the sea eel (Murena) and makes ready for this unnatural copulation. Having gone down to the seashore and made its presence known with a wolf-whistle, it calls the Murena out of the waters for a conjugal embrace. The invited eel does not fail him, but offers the desired uses of her coupling to the venomous reptile.

Now what can anybody make of a sermon like this, unless it is to show up the habits of married couples, and,

---

Trochilus, its enemy some kind of aquatic creature known as hydrus or serra; and the cockatrice itself is simply a medieval muddle. See, in our manuscript, the Hydrus, the Dolphin, the two descriptions of Serra and the two of Crocodile.

if you do not get the point, it shall now be explained to you.

Your husband, I admit, may be uncouth, undependable, disorderly, slippery and tipsy—but what is worse than the ill which the murena-mistress does not shun in him, once he has called her? *She* does not fail him. *She* embraces the slipperiness of the serpent with careful zeal. *She* puts up with your troubles and offers the comfort of womanly good cheer. But you, O Woman, like the lady-snake who bites off his head, are not able to support your own man.

Adam was deceived by Eve, not Eve by Adam. Consequently it is only good sense that the man, who was first got into trouble by the woman, should now take the leadership, for fear that he should once again be ruined by feminine whims.

But he is rough and savage, you will say: in short, he has ceased to please.

Well, is a man always to be choosing new wives? Even a horse loves truly and an ox seeks one single mate. And if one ox is changed in a yoke of oxen, the other one cannot drag the yoke but feels uncomfortable. Yet you women put away your husbands and think that you ought to be changing frequently. And if he happens to be away for one day, you give him a rival on mere suspicion, as if his inconstancy were proved. You do an injury to modesty.

A mere viper searches for his absent one, he calls his absent one, he cries out to her with a flattering note. And when he senses his partner approaching, he bashfully sicks up his poison, in reverence to the lady and in nuptial gratitude. You women, on the contrary, reject the coming union from afar, with insults. The viper even looks toward the sea, looks forward to the coming of his lady-friend. You women impede with contumely the approaches of your men.

But there is a catch in this for you too, my dear Man. You do *not* sick up your poisons when you excite the marriage girdle. In its season you ferment the fearful poison of the conjugal embrace, nor do you blush at the nuptials, nor feel respect for marriage.

Lay aside, O Man, the pride of your heart and the harshness of your conduct when that diligent wife does hasten to you.[1] Drive away the sulks when that solicitous wife does excite your affection. You are not her lord, but her husband, nor have you chosen a female slave, but a wife. God wants you to be the director of the weaker sex, but not by brute force. Return sympathy for her misfortunes, kindness for her love. Sometimes, where the viper is able to get rid of his poison, you are not able to get rid of the hard-heartedness of your mind. Well, if you have a natural coldness, you ought to temper it out of respect for the institution of marriage; you ought to lay aside the savagery of your brain out of respect to the union. Thus you may be able to get her to accept you after all!

Man! do not seek a corrupt union. Do not lie in wait for a different connection. Adultery is unpleasant, it is an injury to Nature.[2] God first made two people, Adam

---

[1] Pepys would have added 'poor wretch'.

[2] Eels are not the only creatures of the sea who misbehave themselves in another element.
> 'Th' adulterous *Sargus* [a sea-bream] doth not only change
> Wives every day, in the deep streams; but (strange)
> As if the honey of Sea-loves delights
> Could not suffice his ranging appetites,
> Courting the Shee-Goats on the grassie shore,
> Would horn their Husbands that had horns before.'
> SYLVESTER's *Du Bartas.*

and Eve, and they were to be man and wife. She was made from the rib of Adam and both were ordained to be in one body and to live in one spirit. So why separate the body, why divide the mind? It is adultery to Nature.

You see, this story of the Murena and the Viper shows that they do not copulate for the sake of procreation, but from a delight in the lusty fondlings of desire.

Notice, O Man, how the human male tries to make up to a strange concubine. He wants to adopt the same concupiscence as an eel has, and to that reptile he may well be compared! He hurries to that she-eel of his and pours himself into her bosom, not by the straight road of truth but by the slippery paths of love. He hurries to her, only to get back his own poison like a viper—for, by the very act of union with her, he takes back his own wickedness, just as the viper, so they say, afterwards sups the poison up again, which it had first vomited out.

The ASP gets its name because it injects and spreads poison with its bite. For the Greeks call venom '*Ios*', and hence comes 'Aspis', since it destroys with a venomous sting. Indeed, it always runs about with its mouth wide open and steaming, the effect of which is to injure other sorts and kinds and species of animals.

Now, it is said, when an Asp realizes that it is being enchanted by a musical snake-charmer, who summons it with his own particular incantations to get it out of its hole, that the Asp, being unwilling to come out, presses one ear to the ground and closes the other ear by sticking its tail in it, to shut it up. Thus, not hearing the magical noises, it does not go forth to the chanting.

Such indeed are the men of this world, who press down one ear to worldly desires, and truly by stuffing up the other one they do not hear the voice of the Lord saying 'He who will not renounce everything which he possesses cannot be my disciple or servant'. Apart from men, asps are the only other creatures which do such a thing, namely, refuse to listen. Men make their own eyes blind, so that they do not see heaven, nor do they call to mind the works of the Lord.

The DIPSAS is a species of asp which is called a 'water bucket' in Latin, because anybody whom it bites dies of thirst.[1]

[1] Hence also the dipsomaniac.

The HYPNALE is a species of asp, so called because it kills by making you sleepy. Cleopatra put this asp to her side and was released by that kind of death, as if in sleep.

The asp EMORRORIS is named because it sweats out your blood (haemorrhage). Anybody who is bitten by it becomes so weak that whatever life there is in him gets drawn out with the blood, once the veins have burst. In Greek, blood is called 'emath' ($a\iota\mu a$).

PRESTER is the asp which always rushes about with its mouth open, emitting steam. It is of this creature that the poet[1] sings: 'Gaping its reeking mouth, the greedy Prester . . .' Anybody who gets struck by this animal swells to a prodigious size and is destroyed by corpulence, and putrefaction follows the swelling.

[1] Lucan. Prester John, a Christian king of the east in the Middle Ages, is said to have derived his soubriquet from 'presbyter' or 'priest'. He was thought to dwell in Ethiopia, a land then particularly associated with intense heat and terrible animals, and the word 'prester' ($\pi\rho\eta\sigma\tau\eta\rho$) means in Greek 'a fiery (or scorching) whirlwind, also a kind of venomous serpent'. N.E.D. Perhaps the eastern potentate was as much of a scorcher as he was a presbyter, although by 1400 he was already accepted as the latter.

The SPECTAFICUS is an asp which consumes a man away at once, when it has stung him, so that he is completely rotted by the serpent's bite.

The CERASTES, a horned snake, is so called because it has horns on its head like a ram (*ceras*=horn). Moreover, they are called *Kerastes* in Greek. This reptile has four horns, by displaying which, as if they were a kind of bait, it attracts other animals and destroys them. It buries its whole body in the sand, showing nothing except the horns, by which means it captures the birds and beasts thus attracted. It is also more twisty than other serpents, so that it looks as if it had no spine.[1]

[1]   '. . . dreadful was the din
Of hissing through the hall, thick swarming now
With complicated monsters head and tail,
Scorpion and asp, and amphisbaena dire,
Cerastes horned, hydrus and ellop drear,
And dipsas.'

MILTON, *Paradise Lost*, Bk. x.

The snake SCITALIS gets that name because it is so splendid in the variegation of its skin (*scitulus*= elegant) that a man stops dead on seeing the beautiful markings. Owing to the fact that it is a sluggish crawler and has not the power to overtake people by chasing them, it captures them as they stand stupefied by its splendour. Moreover, it glows so much that even in winter time it displays the blazing skin of its body. About this creature Lucan sings:

'And the Scytale herself, even now in the lands of
the hoarfrost,
Is about to slough off her spot-speckled skin.'

This is called an AMPHIVENA (Amphisbena) because it has two heads. One head is in the right place and the other is in its tail. With one head holding the other,

176

it can bowl along in either direction like a hoop.[1] This is the only snake which stands the cold well, and it is the first to come out of hibernation. Lucan writes of it:

'Rising on twin-born heads comes dangerous
      Amphisbaena
And her eyes shine like lamps.'[2]

[1] Literally: 'running with either head first, and its trailing body bent round'. But see the illustration.

[2] The paper on Amphisbaena by G. C. Druce (*Arch. Journal* 1910) is perhaps the most interesting of his eighteen papers devoted to Bestiaries. A very brief précis of his findings may serve as an introduction to this interesting commentator. Druce begins with a translation of the relevant passage in Physiologus and continues with a summary of the seven pages in Aldrovandus, from which we learn among other things that Cassandra compared Clytemnestra to one in Aeschylus, that Nicander described it fully in the second century B.C., that Lucan's mention appears in *Pharsalia* IX, 719, that Pliny recommends its skin as a remedy for the cold shivers, that a pregnant woman will miscarry if she steps over it, that Aelian mentions it in the third century and that Albertus Magnus did so in the thirteenth. In 1552 was published a translation of Nicander by a Dr Peter Jacob Steve, who stated that the amphisbaena was the size of an earth worm, that it stung like a flea, but worse, and that it had bad eyesight. In 1557 John Gorraeus said that the story of two heads was due to the equal thickness of the body at each end. It was good for chilblains. A military bootlace, tipped with brass at both ends, was called after it. There is then a discussion about the possibility of accounting for it as a freak birth, and a four-headed snake from Taprobane (Ceylon) is mentioned, which used to point north, east, south and west. The twenty-five authorities cited by Aldrovandus are listed by name. It is noted that when hatching its eggs, one head of the amphisbaena wakes the other one up, if it is time to take over. Druce then quotes from *Reptiles of the World* by R. L. Ditmars, as follows: 'The Indian sand-boa or "two-headed" snake (*Eryx Johnii*) may be told by the almost uniform brown hue and the curious tail, that member looking as if it had been mostly amputated and healed in a rounded stump. A big specimen is two and a half feet long. Owing to the blunt character of the tail, the name, "two-headed" snake, has arisen. A novice might for a moment mistake

the two extremities unless closely inspected and the tiny eyes discovered. The Hindoos practise a deception with this species by painting a mouth and eyes on the blunt tail and exploiting it as a serpent with two independent heads, explaining that while one sleeps the other watches in an endeavour to protect the animal from harm.' It has now begun to be possible that the amphisbaena may have been a real creature, so Mr Druce betakes himself to the South Kensington Museum, where he is delighted to find that it is still listed by the scientists, that it is in reality a legless lizard twenty inches long, of which two kinds are there preserved: *A. alba* and *A. fulginosa*. Their eyes are functionless: they have no ears: if annoyed, they lift the tail in menace like a head: they are found in America, the West Indies, Africa and European Mediterranean countries. Druce clinches his perfect research with a quotation from the British Museum Official Guide: 'The Amphisbaenas (family amphisbaenidas) are worm-like and for the most part limbless tropical lizards which take their name from their power of progressing either forwards or backwards. They are degraded or perhaps specialized types; and are characterized by having the body covered with soft skin which forms numerous rings and shows only vestiges of scales. . . . Amphisbaenas live an underground burrowing existence, like worms; and are often found in ants' nests and refuse heaps. Their movements are worm-like, the soft-ringed skin enabling them to move with equal facility in either direction. Unlike other limbless lizards and snakes, which move in lateral undulations, amphisbaenas crawl in a straight line with slight vertical folds of the body.'

There is an animal in the River Nile which is called HY-DRUS, and it lives in the water. The Greeks call water '*hydros*'. That is why it is known as an aquatic snake. People swell up with the dropsy from its venom, and some call their illness 'the boa' (cow-pox) be-cause it can be remedied by the excrement of cows.

The Hydra Dragon, on the other hand, is one with lots of heads—such as there used to be in the Island of Lerna or in the marshy province of Arcadia. This one was called the Excedra in Latin, because, when you had cut off one of its heads, then three heads used to grow in its place. (*Excedere*=to outbid.) But that is just a fable. It is well known that there was a place where the River Hydra, spewing forth its waters, was laying waste the neighbouring countryside because the main channel to the sea was closed and many others were therefore bursting out. Seeing this, Hercules cleaned out the places where the main channel hindered the flow. For the River Hydra also gets its name from 'water'.[1]

Now the real Hydrus is sufficiently hostile to crocodiles, and it has the following habit and disposition, viz., that when it sees a crocodile sleeping on the shore with its mouth open, it dashes off and rolls itself in the mud. By means of the slippery mud it is easily able to slide down the crocodile's throat. The crocodile then, suddenly waking up, gulps it down, and the Hydrus, splitting all the crocodile's guts into two parts, not only remains alive but comes out safely at the other end.[2]

[1] Zoologically speaking, the Hydrozoa are fresh-water polyps nowadays, whole tentacles represent the numerous heads of the fable. And, like the Hydra, they do spring up again when cut off, for 'if cut transversally into several segments, each will in time become a perfect animal, so that thirty or forty Hydrae may thus be produced by the section of one'. CARPENTER.

[2] Many versions assume that the mud coating of the Hydrus is not for lubrication, but to make itself a carapace or armoured coat, when the mud has dried. Du Bartas takes it so.

Dr Ansell Robin has made it clear that where the weasel or ichneumon or mongoose or Egyptian rat (all the same animal) is the enemy of the basilisk, the enemy of the crocodile is variously described as the Hydrus or the Enhydrus: and these he takes to be two animals, a water-snake and an otter. In the present text the enemy is clearly a water-snake.

Thus is the crocodile symbolical of Death and Hell, whose hydrus-enemy is our Lord Jesus Christ. For it was he who, assuming human flesh, descended into Hell and, breaking asunder all its internal arrangements, led out those people who were unjustly imprisoned in it. He destroyed Death itself by rising from the dead, so that the Prophet mocked it, saying: 'O Death, I shall be thy death, I shall be your grief here below'.

The BOA is an Italian snake which pursues herds of oxen or large crowds of buffaloes, and clings to their udders full of much milk. It destroys them by suckling.

And hence from the ravaging of cattle (*boves*), Boa receives its name.

aculvſ JACULUS is a flying serpent of which Lucan writes 'and the fleet Jaculi'. They jump up into trees and if any animal passes that way they fling themselves down and destroy it, whence they are called Jaculi—javelins.[1]

[1] Goldsmith, of whom Dr Johnson remarked 'if he can distinguish a cow from a horse, that, I believe, may be the extent of his knowledge of natural history', states that: 'the manner of progression in ... the Jaculus, is by instantly coiling itself upon its tail and darting from thence to its full extent.'

Moreover, there are in Arabia certain white snakes with wings which are known as S Y R E N S.[1] These can go faster than horses and are even said to fly as well. Their venom is so fierce that you die before you feel the pain of the bite.

[1] These serpents appeared in Isaiah xiii, 22 (Vulgate).

S E P S is a tiny snake which not only destroys your body with its poison, but even your bones.[1] It is the one the poet (Lucan) mentions, in 'And the corroding Seps, destroying the bones with the body'.

[1] Hence 'septic'.

The Serpent D I P S A is stated to be so small that when you step on him you do not see him. His poison also destroys before it is felt, so that the face of the doomed man, even when death has already taken place, does not look sad. Of this one, the poet (Lucan) reports:
  'The Dipsa, trodden upon, twisted back, seized
      and stung the young Ensign
   Aulus, Tyrrhenian by blood. And the pain or the
      feel of the fang-bite
   Scarcely was felt.'

LACERTUS is a species of reptile, called thus because it has arms (*lacertus*=arm muscle).[1] There are many kinds of Lacertus, such as the Botrax,[2] the Salamander, the Lizard and the Newt.

The Botrax gets its name because it has a face like a frog, since the Greeks call the frog '*botraca*' (βάτραχος).

[1] The Lacert is an obsolete name for a muscle, probably the Biceps. Just as the word 'muscle' itself (see p. 219) was supposed to derive from 'mouse', so the biceps, as it scampered to and fro beneath the skin, got its title from a lizard. 'Lyke as those two beestes (the lizard and the mouse) are byg in the middle and schlender towarde the tayle so is the muscle or lacerte'. COPLAND, 1541.

[2] An unspecified batrachian.

The SALAMANDRA has its name because it prevails against fire.

Of all poisonous creatures its strength is the greatest, for, although others may kill things one at a time, the Salamander kills most at one blow. If it slowly twines itself about a tree, all the fruits get infected with venom, and thus it kills the people who eat them. Even if it falls into a well the power of its toxin slays those who drink the water.

This animal is the only one which puts the flames out,

fire-fighting. Indeed, it lives in the middle of the blaze without being hurt and without being burnt—and not only because the fire does not consume it, but because it actually puts out the fire itself.[1]

[1] 'Further, we are by Pliny told
This serpent is extremely cold.' SWIFT.
Aristotle recorded that the salamander 'not only walks through fire, but puts it out in doing so'. The modern representative is a small, tailed batrachian which makes its home in damp places and hibernates in dead wood. When frightened, it exudes a milky liquid. If a log containing a wintering salamander were thrown upon a weak fire, Aristotle's phenomenon might take place. Pliny was responsible for exaggerating the story, which became very popular. When asbestos was discovered, it was assumed to be the wool of this creature. Prester John had a robe made from it: the 'Emperor of India' possessed a suit made from a thousand skins: and Pope Alexander III had a tunic which he valued highly. 'This Salemandre berith wulle, of which is made cloth and gyrdles that may not brenne in the fyre'. CAXTON, 1481. 'I have some of the hair, or down of the Salamander, which I have several times put in the Fire, and made it red hot, and after taken it out, which being cold, yet remained perfect wool'. HOLME, 1688. It was known at an early date that the way to clean asbestos was by putting it in the fire. Needless to say, the salamander is not poisonous to man and if kept in a fire would burn: as Pliny must very well have known, for he burned one, to made medicine from its ashes.

S A U R A the Lizard is a Lacertus which goes blind when it gets old. Then it goes into a hole in the wall facing east, stretches itself toward the rising sun, and its sight is restored.

S T E L L I O the Newt has been given its name because of

its colour, as it is in fact ornamented on its back with shiny spots like stars. Ovid sings of it:
'Studded with colour it has its name
Being starry in body with various spots.'
This animal is so destructive to scorpions that the mere sight of it, people say, scares them into a stupor.

There are also other species of the serpent tribe which put one in mind of Elephants and Camedragons.

To cut a long story short, the names of the various reptiles are as numerous as the names of the dead.[1]

[1] The difficulty in identifying genera and species among the reptiles mentioned in this section is increased by the fact that most of the classical names are still used in serious herpetology, though they do not always relate nowadays to their original proprietors. *Cerastes cornutus* is till the Horned Viper: *Lacerta* has become a genus of twenty species: *Hydrus* and *Boa* are also the names of genera: and the *Dipsades* form a whole group of genera.

The royal Basilisk was probably the King Cobra, that regal serpent the *Uraeus* which used to appear upon the head-dress of the Pharoah. 'It seems,' says Ditmars, 'that in striking the snake simultaneously compresses the poison glands by a contraction of the jaw and muscles and ejects the poison, though quite accidentally, in the direction of its annoyance. If the fluid should enter the eyes, blindness or death are probable consequences.' Their *Viper* may have been the common English adder, which is viviparous. Their *Asps* seem to have been regarded as a genus whose species were (a) *Dipsas*, possibly the Krait, (b) *Hypnale*, some snake like the mamba, whose poison is neurotoxic, (c) *Emorroris*, a snake of haemolytic venom such as that used by the rattlesnakes of America, (d) *Prester*, some other haemolytic snake with a wide gape like the Puff Adder (*B. arietans*), (e) *Spectaficus*, a Spectacled Cobra (?) and (f) *Cerastes*, the Horned Viper (*C. Cornutas*).

Then we get *Scitalis*, which may have been some sort of 'coral' snake found outside the Americas, or any beautiful serpent like the superbly marked Rhinoceros Viper. (In connection with the Rhinoceros Viper, it is not amiss to remember the Bestiarist's remark that: 'There are also other species of the serpent tribe which put one in mind of Elephants etc.') The *Amphisbaena* has already been identified. The *Hydrus* in its serpent form was a poisonous water-snake, but became confused with the Ichneumon, the animal like an otter, because the Greek for 'otter' also meant 'water-snake'. This Ichneumon (see p. 169) was 'a small brownish coloured slender-bodied carnivorous quadruped, *Herpestes* (formerly *Viverra*) *ichneumon*, closely allied to the mongoose, and resembling the weasel tribe in form and habits. It is found in Egypt, where it feeds on small

Now all SERPENTS are cold by nature. They do not strike people unless they are warm, for, when cold, they touch nothing. This is the reason why their venom is more injurious by day than by night. Exposure to the night's cold numbs them, and no wonder, what with the nocturnal dew. Obviously the plague of cold and the frigid, icy elements draw out the warmth of a body to themselves. So, although in summer snakes are on the loose, in winter they remain torpid in their nests.

It is for this sort of reason that a man who gets stung with the poison of a serpent first becomes numbed, and is only destroyed later on, when the poison has become warm in him and has begun to glow.

Poison is called 'venom' because it runs through the veins (*per venas*). The deadly ill which has been injected rushes in all directions through the arteries with increasing speed, and drives out the breath of life. Hence

---

mammals and reptiles, but is especially noted for destroying the eggs of the crocodile, on which account it was held in veneration by the ancient Egyptians.' N.E.D. The *Boa* may have been *Eryx Conicus*. The *Jaculus* was not the fer-de-lance but may have been *Eryx jaculus;* though several other serpents are better jumpers. For instance, the flying *Syren* may have resembled *Chrysopelea ornata*, the Gold and Black Tree Snake. 'A number of people' say Curran and Kauffeld, 'have seen a gold and black tree snake spring from one tree to another or from the window of a house to a tree. . . . The flights are evidently accomplished by flattening the abdomen in such a way that the underside becomes concave and offers considerable resistance to the air.' *Seps*, like *Dipsas*, may also have been the Krait (*B. caeruleus*). *Lacertus* is still a genus of lizards, among whose twenty-one species *Botrax*, *Salamandra* and *Saura* may have belonged. According to the scientific slang of the twentieth century, the Salamandridae still comprise a semi-poisonous form of terrestial newts; so these may be related to *Stellio* the Newt, who follows them, and who shows, in the illustration, the series of tubercles through which this kind of creature was supposed to be able to discharge the fluid which extinguished fires. The *Stellio*'s enemy, the *Scorpion*, will no doubt feign death or be 'scared into a stupor' by the presence of an adversary—like the spiders to whom he is closely allied.

snake-poison cannot hurt unless it reaches a man's blood. Lucan says: 'The bane of serpents noxious is, when mixed with gore'.

All venom is icy-cold, and that is why the fiery soul of man flies away before it.

In certain natural powers which we see to be common to ourselves and even to other living things which lack the faculty of reason, the serpent excels by having a queer tenacity of life. That is why we read in Genesis: 'Moreover the serpent was wiser than all cattle upon earth'.

Believe it, S N A K E S have three odd things about them. The first odd thing is that when they are getting old their eyes grow blind, and if they want to renovate themselves, they go away somewhere and fast for a long time until their skins are loose. Then they look for a tight crack in the rocks, and go in, and lay aside the old skin by scraping it off. Thus we, through much tribulation and abstinence for the sake of Christ, put off the old man and his garment. In this way we may seek the spiritual Rock, Jesus, and the tight crack, i.e. the Strait Gate.

The second odd thing about a snake is that when it goes to the river to drink water, it does not take its poison with it, but spews it into a hole. Thus we, when we come to get the living water and, drawing upon the eternal, come to hear the heavenly word in Church, we also ought to cast the poison out of ourselves, i.e. bad and earthly longings.

The third odd thing is that if a snake sees a naked man, it is afraid of him, but if it sees him with his clothes on, it springs upon him. We can understand the spiritual sense of this if we reflect that when the first man Adam was naked in Paradise, the Serpent was not able to spring upon him. But after he was dressed in the mortality of the body, the Serpent did spring. Just so, if you are wearing the mortal garment, i.e. the old man, and if you are long-standingly of evil days, the Serpent will pounce on you. But if you rid yourself from the garb worn by the Principalities and Powers of Darkness in this generation, then the Serpent will not be able to pounce, i.e. the Devil.

Further facts about reptiles are: By a diet of fennel, snakes can cure themselves of prolonged blindness, and thus, when they feel that their eyes are getting overcast, they seek for the well-known remedies, nor are they disappointed in the result.

The Tortoise, which is nourished through entrails similar to those of a serpent,[1] protects itself by eating marjoram when it sees a venomous creature snaking up to it.[2]

---

[1] Aldrovandus queries whether some kinds of Dragon may not be born by the conjunction of a snake and a tortoise, because both animals have the same kind of viscera. Pope Gregory XIII, he explains, in whose escutcheon there was a shining dragon, must have been thinking of a tortoise when he chose for his motto *'Festina Lente'*.

[2] This action has been actually observed.' ARISTOTLE (H.A. IX, 612a).

If a serpent swallows the spittle of a fasting man, it dies.

It is believed, so Pliny says, that if a snake can get away with only two finger's length of body attached to the head, it will survive. This is why it presents its whole body foremost, in front of its head, when a person goes to hit it.

All snakes suffer from bad eyesight, and they seldom see forward. Nor is this fortuitous, since their eyes are not in their faces but in their temples—so that they can hear better than see.

No animal flickers its tongue so fast as a snake does, and for this reason they seem to have triple tongues where there is really only one.

The bodies of snakes are damp, so that they mark the road by which they go with slime. Their tracks are such that they seem to have no feet. But they do crawl with the pressure of the scales on the end of their ribs, which are arranged equally from the top of the throat to the lower belly. The scales are like claws, which rest on the ribs as if on legs. When any part of the body from the belly to the head is struck with a blow, the snake is disabled and unable to get back into its course, because wherever the blow fell it broke the spine—by which the rib-feet and the whole movement of the body are propelled.[1]

[1] It seems possible that a qualified herpetologist might be surprised, not by the puerilities of the Physiologus, but by his accuracies. Snakes do have necks, bodies and tails, do crawl as stated, and do puzzle amateurs about the places where the tails begin.

After Sir Thomas Browne had exploded many of the 'tenents' held by the scholars of the Middle Ages, there rose up a Scotsman called Alexander Ross to the defence of ancient science. His book, the *Arcana Microcosmi*, is not very common. Ross himself is a pig-headed and comic figure. He will assert indefensible statements with vigour, in his zeal for the old writers, and he is not ashamed to join issue with Dr Harvey himself, the discoverer of the blood-stream.

189

Snakes are said to live for a long time, the reason being that, when they have sloughed off their old skins, it is granted to them to cast off their old age and to return to youth. The skins are called 'Exuviae' because when they get old they take them off (*exuunt*). You see, dresses and clothes are called dresses and clothes because you dress yourself in them and clothe yourself in them.

Pythagoras says: 'Serpents are created out of the spinal marrow of corpses'—a thing which Ovid also calls to mind in the books of the Metamorphoses, when he says:

He will affirm that a blown bladder is lighter than an empty one, or that goat's blood softens diamonds, or anything else which had been previously reported. On the other hand, his willing credulity offers a healthy antidote to the doubts of the twentieth century. One is startled to discover that he was already, in 1652, interested by such things as hypnotism and allergy. Among his chapter-headings, there are to be found the following evocative captions:

Why Eunuchs fatter, weaker, colder.
Hearing fails last in drowned men.
Monethly bloud in men.
The Roses smell (allergy).
Fascination by words (hypnotism).
Amphisbaena proved, and the contrary objections answered.
Hels fire truly black; brimstone causeth blackness.
In laughter there is sorrow: in weeping joy (psychiatry).
What the Ancients have written of Griffins may be true.
Fishes are cunning and docible creatures.
Publick and private calamities presaged by dogs.
The same Soul in a subventaneous and prolificall egge.
Of souls and spirits.
The Lord Bacons opinion refuted. Of holding the breath when wee hearken. . . . Of motion after the head is off.
The Lord Bacons opinions confuted concerning snow . . . the sperm of drunkards . . . the hedgehog.

The assertive and pedantic old Scotsman was in fact an amusing scholar whose book is well worth reading. For him, it was not good game to run down the Bestiarists. It was his business rather to defend them with filial piety. At the end of his third volume, this amiable Struldbrug offers the following charming and impressive admonition, which the present translator has constantly tried to bear in mind: 'Let prodigals forsake their husks, and leave them to swine, they will find bread enough at home. And as dutifull children let us cover the naked-nesse of our Fathers with the Cloke of a favourable Interpretation.'

'Some there are who believe that sealed in the grave, the spine rotting,
Marrows of humankind do turn themselves into serpents.'
And this, if it is to be credited, is all very appropriate: that just as Man's death was first brought about by a Snake, so by the death of man a snake should be brought about.

VERMIS the Worm is an animal which is mostly germinated, without sexual intercourse, out of meat or wood or any earthly thing. People agree that, like the scorpion, they are never born from eggs. There are earth worms and water worms and air worms and flesh worms and leaf worms, also wood worms and clothes worms.

A Spider is an air worm, as it is provided with nourishment from the air, which a long thread catches down to its small body. Its web is always tight. It never stops working, cutting out all loss of time without interruption in its skill.

The earth Millipede gets its name from the number of its legs, and this is the one which hides in large numbers under flower-pots, rolled up in a ball.

Sanguinea the Leech is a water worm, so called because it sucks blood. It also lies in wait for people who are taking a drink of water and, when it slips down their throats or manages to catch on anywhere, it sups their gore. When it is gorged with blood it spews it up again, so that it can start once more with fresh.

The Scorpion is a land worm which we classify with worms rather than with snakes. It is a stinging creature, and is called the Archer in the Greek language because it plunges in its tail and injects its poisons with a curving wound (*aculeus: arcuatus*). The oddest thing about a scorpion is that it will not bite you in the palm of your hand.[1]

Bombocis the Silkworm is a worm of leaves, from whose productions silken garments are made (*bombycina*). It is also called this (*bombus*= a hollow sound) because it empties itself out while it is spinning the threads, and only air remains inside it.

Eruca the Caterpillar[2] is another worm of leaves. After rolling up young vine shoots, it is believed to fatten itself by eating them away (*ab erodendo*). Plautus makes mention of it as follows: 'It curls itself round the young shoots like a nasty, malignant beast, nor does it buzz off like the locust, which wanders from place to place when it has half dined, but it sticks to the same growing fruits and gobbles the whole thing up with a tardy slither and slothful nibbles.'

---

[1] This fancy derives from Pliny. But since the blow is inflicted downwards, the palm of the hand and the sole of the foot do seem less likely to be wounded than their opposite sides.

[2] The word 'caterpillar' seems to be derived either from '*chatepelose*' (hairy cat) or '*chat-pilour*' (plundering cat). But why should a worm-like creature always be compared to a mammal? Even among the caterpillars of our own childhood, the most popular was the Woolly Bear.

The Greeks call wood worms *'Teredonas'*, because they eat by grinding (*terendo*). We call them Termites. The Latins call them Vermes. Trees which are felled in the wrong season breed them.

The clothes worm is called Tinea because it gnaws (*terat*), and whenever this one gets in, it eats the thing away. Hence it is a pertinacious creature, for it sticks to the same thing all the time.

Flesh worms include Emigramus, Lumbricus, Ascaridae, Costae, Pediculi, Pulices, Lendex, Tarmus, Ricinus, Usia and Cimex.

Emigramus is known as a head worm.

Lumbricus is a stomach worm, *quasi 'lumbicus'*, because it is slipped in; or else because it lives in the loins (*in lumbis*).

Pediculi the Lice are flesh worms which are named from 'feet' (*a pedibus*)—and lousy people (*pediculosi*) also get their name from this root. They swarm with them.

Fleas are rightly called fleas (*pulices*) because they are mainly nourished by dust (*ex pulvere*).

Tarmus is a lard worm.

Ricinus the Tick is a worm called after the dog, because it clings to dogs' ears. (The pun seems to be, *Ri-cinus: Auriscanis*.) Also, *Kunos* is the Greek for dog.

Usia (probably *'urica'*, the canker) is known as a pig worm, because its bite burns (*urit*). The place where it has bitten gets so fiery that you make water on the spot, when it has bitten you. (There is an obscure pun here about 'urine'.)

Cimex the Bug gets its name from its similarity to a certain herb, whose offensive smell it has.[1] Appropriately enough, this worm is born on rotting meat.

You get the Tinea in clothes, the Eruca in vegetables, the Teredo in wood and the Tarmus in earth.

Worms do not crawl by plain wriggles like snakes, nor by pressing on their scales, because they do not have the same rigidity of the spine that snakes have.[2] Instead, by contracting the parts of their small bodies into a straight line and then expanding them, their movement develops by dragging the stretched parts along and by crawling with this concertina action.

---

[1] Either *'cummin'* or *'cyma'*, a young cabbage.

[2] The ancient category of 'worms' was more extensive than the modern one. They included the serpent which stung Cleopatra, the maggots which bred in corpses, the malignities which destroyed Herod, and many other creepers or crawlers. In Golding's translation of Solinus we find the sunshun: 'It is a verie little Worme and like a Spyder in shape, and it is called a *Shunsunne* because it shunneth the daie light. It lyeth most in Sylver Mynes. . . . It creepeth privily, and casteth the plague uppon such as sitte upon it unawares.'

**ilccl** FISH (*pisces*), like cattle (*pecus*), get
their name because they browse in flocks (*a
pascendo*). Moreover, they are known as reptiles (*reptilia*) because they have the same
shape and natural disposition for swimming
about (*quod reptandi*). However deeply they
can plunge into the abyss, yet in swimming
itself they are slow movers (*repunt*). This
is why David says 'In the sea great and
spacious in power there are reptiles of which
there is no number'.

AMPHIVIA are a kind of fish which get this name because they have the habit of walking about on dry land or swimming about in the sea. The point is that in Greek the word '*Amphi*' means 'both'; i.e. they live in the water or on the shore, like seals, crocodiles and hippos.

There is an ocean monster which is called an ASPIDO DELONE in Greek. On the other hand, it is called an 'Aspido-Tortoise' in Latin. It is also called a WHALE (*cetus*) because of the frightfulness of its body and because it was this animal which swallowed (*excepit*) Jonah, and its belly was so great that people took it to be Hell. Jonah himself remarked: 'He heard me out of the belly of Hell'.

This animal lifts its back out of the open sea above the watery waves, and then it anchors itself in the one place; and on its back, what with the shingle of the ocean drawn there by the gales, a level lawn gets made and bushes begin to grow there. Sailing ships that happen to be going that way take it to be an island, and land on it. Then they make themselves a fireplace. But the Whale, feeling the hotness of the fire, suddenly plunges down into the depths of the deep, and pulls down the anchored ship with it into the profound.[1]

---

[1] When a mirage or fairy island is perceived off the West Coast of Ireland, it is still customary to row thither with a coal of fire, or a lighted tobacco pipe, and to shake out the embers upon the soil. The moment a fire has been lit there, the fairy ground solidifies into a real one and can be occupied. 'Among the other islands,' wrote Giraldus Cambrensis in his *Topography of Ireland* in 1187, 'is one newly formed, which they call the phantom isle, which had its origin in this manner. One calm day, a large mass of earth rose to the surface of the sea, where no land had ever been seen before, to the great amazement of the islanders who observed it. Some of them said that it was a whale, or other immense sea-monster; others, remarking that it remained motionless, said, 'No; it is land'. In order, therefore, to reduce their doubts to certainty, some picked young men of the island determined to approach nearer the spot in a boat. When, however, they came so near to it that they thought they could go on shore, the island sank in the water and entirely vanished from sight. The next day it re-appeared, and again mocked the same youths with the like delusion. At length upon their rowing towards it on the third day, they followed the advice of an older man, and let fly an arrow, barbed with red-hot steel, against the island; and then landing, found it stationary and habitable. This adds one to the many proofs that fire is the greatest of enemies to every sort of phantom.' Perhaps the

Now this is just the way in which unbelievers get paid out, I mean the people who are ignorant of the wiles of the Devil and place their hopes in him and in his works. They anchor themselves to him, and down they go into the fires of Hell.

The nature of this monster is that whenever it feels hungry it opens its mouth and blows out a sort of pleasantly-smelling breath, and, when the smaller fishes notice the odour of this, they crowd together in the mouth. Naturally, when the monster feels his mouth to be full, he shuts it at once. Thus he swallows them down.

That is the way in which human people who are lacking in faith get addicted to pleasures. They pander to their grub as if it were perfume. Then suddenly the Devil gobbles them up.

 alene The B A L E N A E (whales) are animals of prodigious size, and they get their name from blowing or spouting waters. They puff the water higher than other beasts of the sea. In Greek, '*ballein*' means 'to throw out'. The mate of a female whale is the M U S C U L U S, for

---

mariners of our Bestiary were lighting their fire in the hope of solidifying an uncharted Leviathan.

The word Kraken was introduced from Norway in 1752, and may have been a giant squid.

> 'Ye are mad, ye have taken
> A slumbering Kraken
> For firm land of the Past.'
> LOWELL, *Ode to France*, 1848.

the lady whale is not permitted to conceive by coition.[1]

[1] This confusion about the copulation of whales arises from a misreading of Pliny. The 'musculus' was a pilot fish which was believed to swim in front of these creatures. It was 'the companion of the whale'–hence its mate–hence *'masculus balenae est musculus'*. 'Of the whale and his friend Musculus', Sylvester writes:

> 'But for the little *Musculus* (his friend)
> A little Fish, that swimming still before,
> Directs him safe from Rock, from Shelf and Shore:
> Much like a childe that loving leads about
> His aged Father when his eyes be out.'

 There is a beast in the sea which we call a S E R R A and it has enormous fins. When this monster sees a ship sailing on the sea, it erects its wings and tries to outfly the ship, up to about two hundred yards. Then it cannot keep up the effort; so it folds up its fins and draws them in, after which, bored by being out of the water, it dives back into the ocean.[1]

This peculiar animal is exactly like human beings today. Naturally the ship symbolizes the Righteous, who sail through the squalls and tempests of this world without danger of shipwreck in their faith. The Serra, on the contrary, is the monster which could not keep up with the righteous ship. It symbolizes the people who start off trying to devote themselves to good works, but afterwards, not keeping it up, they get vanquished by various kinds of nasty habits and, undependable as the to-fro waves of the sea, they drive down to Hell.

[1] Most of the authorities quoted by Aldrovandus identify the Serra with the Sawfish. But surely this is a plain description of the Flying Fish (*exocaetus spilopus*)? See G. C. Druce (Bibliography).

You do not get anywhere by starting. You get there by pressing on.

OLPHINS, the Delfines, have that particular name either as a description because they follow the human voice or else because they will assemble together in schools for a symphony concert.[1]

Nothing in the sea is faster than they are, for they often outrun ships, leaping out of the water. When they are sporting in the waves and smashing themselves into the masses of combers with a headlong leap, they are thought to portend storms.

They are properly called 'Simones'.[2]

[1] The explanation seems to be that they either follow the human voice like an oracle (of Delphi) or gather to hear musical instruments (for there was an organ called a Delphinus). Apollo took the form of a dolphin when he founded the Oracle of Delphi.

[2] Snub-nosed $=\sigma\iota\mu\delta\varsigma$. Pliny informs us that certain fishermen, with the cry of 'Simo', used to summon dolphins to help them in fishing. 'In the daies of *Augustus Caesar* the Emperour, there was a Dolphin entered the gulfe or poole of Lucrinus, which loved wonderous well a certain boy, a poore mans sonne: who using to go every day to schoole from Baianum to Puteoli, was woont also about noone-tide to stay at the water side, and to call unto the Dolphin, *Simo*, *Simo*, and many times would give him fragments of bread, which of purpose hee ever brought with him, and by this meane allured the Dolphin to come ordinarily unto him at his call. . . . Well, in processe of time, at what houre soever of the day, this boy lured for him and called *Simo*, were the Dolphin never so close hidden in any secret and blind corner, out he would and come abroad, yea and skud amaine to this lad: and taking bread and other victuals at his hand, would gently offer him his backe to mount upon, and then downe went the sharpe pointed prickes of his finnes, which he would put up as it were within a sheathe for feare of hurting the boy. Thus when he had him once on his back, he would carry him over the broad arme of the sea as farre as Puteoli to schoole; and in like manner convey him backe again home: and thus he continued for many yeeres together, so long as the child lived. But when the boy was falne sicke and dead, yet the Dolphin gave not over his haunt, but usually came to the woonted place, and missing the lad, seemed to be heavie and mourne again,

There is a species of Dolphin in the River Nile, with a saw-shaped dorsal fin, which destroys Crocodiles by slicing up the soft parts of the belly.

PORCI MARINI, the Dugongs, are known as *Suilli* or Swine by the vulgar, because they snout up earth under the water when they eat, like pigs. Their mouth is beneath the chin, so that unless they plunge the snout into the mud they cannot collect food.

GLADIUS the sword-fish is so named because he has a sharp-pointed beak which he sticks into ships and sinks them.

SERRA is called this because he has a serrated cock's-comb and, swimming under the vessels, he saws them up.

SCORPIO the sea-scorpion gets his title because he stings when held in the hand. They say that if ten crabs are pounded together with a handful of Basil[1] all the

[1] The scribe writes '*comici*' when he means '*ocimi*,' a form of transcription which does not help the translator. Basil and Basilisk both derive from the same Greek root, meaning Royal, so the one was presumed to be the antidote or complement to the other. Hence its efficacy with scorpions also. It is good, says Turner's *Herbal*, 'for the stryking of a se dragon'. Cogan states that 'a certaine Italian, by often smelling to Basil, had a scorpion bred in his braine'.

untill for verie griefe and sorrow (as it is doubtless to be presumed) he also was found dead upon the shore.' HOLLAND's *Pliny*.

This story is by no means so improbable as it sounds. At the Marine Studios in Florida, in 1952, a porpoise called Flippy has already been taught to retrieve, to ring a bell, to jump through hoops and to tow a surf board with a lady standing on it.

scorpions of the neighbourhood will gather round the bait.[1]

[1] For the Scorpion-fish the best Tarentino bait was as follows: 'Of mulberry-wood shavings, Colocynth and Sandarach take eight drachms of each; add cabbage stalks to the number of five; these being mixed with thoroughly pulverized wheat-flour and sand-filtered water, the fish may be enticed by a paste kneaded therefrom'. ALDROVANDUS. Perhaps this bait may be of interest to carp fishermen.

ROCODILE is so called from its saffron or crocus colour. It is born in the River Nile, an amphibious animal with four legs: generally twenty cubits[2] in length: armed with an awfulness of teeth and claws. Such is the toughness of its hide that however much a blow of massive stones strikes upon its back, it does not hurt it. It reposes in the water by night, on land by day. It hatches its eggs in the sand. The male and female protect the eggs by turns. Certain fish which have a serrated crest destroy it, ripping up the tender parts of the belly.[3]

[2] A cubit was the length of the arm from the elbow to the tip of the middle finger—between eighteen and twenty-two inches.

[3] Among various suggestions from Pliny, Rondeletius and others, Aldrovandus mentions that the Serra may have been the *Pristis* or *Pistris*, which is translated by Lewis and Short as 'any sea monster'. This might account for the contradictory descriptions given by the Bestiarist. Its saw could have been on its nose or on its back, its size variable, and its habitat fresh or salt water, since it was evidently several fishes. G. C. Druce is the authority on the Serra.

His wolfish greed has given the name of LUPIS[4] to the Pike, and it is difficult to catch him. When he is encircled by the net, they say that he ploughs up the sand

[4] Lupus is probably Lucius (*Esox lucius*), the 'luce' of heraldry.

with his tail and thus, lying hidden, manages to escape the meshes.[1]

[1] The difficulty of catching fish has always been a source of lamentation to anglers. Christian fishermen, however, may console themselves by considering a discriminating fish mentioned by Edward Webbe in his *Rare and most Wonderful Things.* 'In the land of Syria', he says, 'there is a river that no Jew can catch any fish in at all, and yet in the same river there is a great store of fish like unto salmon trouts. But let a Christian or a Turk come thither and fish for them and either of them shall catch them in abundance.'

MULLUS, the Red Mullet, is called that because it is soft (*mollis*) and very tender. They say that lust can be cooled by eating it,[2] and they also dull the eyesight. People who frequently consume mullet smell of fish. If a Mullus is drowned in wine, those who drink the stuff afterwards get a loathing for wine-drinking.

[2] The Mullet, according to Juvenal, was used to punish adulterers—but, if our text can be trusted, perhaps it was intended to cure them?

MUGIL, the Grey Mullet, is so named because it is very nimble (*multum agilis*). For, when it perceives that the snares of the fishermen have been set, it instantly turns round and leaps over the net, so that you can watch it flip through the air.[3]

So you see there are innumerable habits and numberless species of fish. Some beget from an egg, as is the case with the mottled large ones which we call trout, and these entrust the egg to the waters for hatching. The water animates and creates and still carries on the work confided to it, as if by the Universal Law, for it is a kind of fondling mother to all living things. Others, such as the mighty whales, dolphins, seals and the rest of that sort,

[3] Mullet fishermen will know that the creatures are very shy and do have very tender mouths.

bring forth live offspring from their bodies. These, when they have given birth, if by chance in their dread of traps they sense some kind of danger in any way contriving against their babies, then, when they want to protect or tenderly soothe the fears of childhood with maternal affection, they are said to open their mouths and thus hold the little ones with a harmless tooth—or even to receive them back again into the body and hide them in the fruitful womb.

WHAT human love can compare with the compassion of fishes? For us the kisses of the mouth are enough. For them it is not too much to open their whole insides for the reception of their children, to bring them out again unharmed, to reanimate them as it were with the warmth of their own heat, to revive them with their own spirit, and for two to live in one body. So they go on, until they have either cheered the babies up or defended them from dangers by interposing their own bulk.

What person, on seeing these things and being able to prove them, must not give pride of place to the wonderful piety of fishes? Who is not amazed and astonished that Nature should exhibit in them what she does not exhibit in us men?

For lots of human mothers, driven to distrust by malevolent hatreds, kill their own offspring; others of bad repute, as we read, have actually eaten up their young, so that the mother has become the grave of her human children. The inside of the mamma-fish, on the contrary, is a wall with ramparts to the babes, in which she preserves the child undisturbed in her innermost organs.

Well, different species of fish have different customs. Some produce eggs, others bring forth formed and living young. Those who lay eggs do not build nests as birds do, nor do they engage in the lengthy labour of hatching eggs, nor do they trouble to feed them. The egg is simply dropped, because Water like a pleasant wet-nurse brings it up by her own nature, in her bosom as it were, and vivifies it into an animal by rapid incubation. Animated by a touch of its parent the Ocean, the egg finally falls apart and a fish comes out.

How pure and unsullied is the succession among fishes, consequently, where none is cross-bred except with a member of its own race! They are indeed ignorant of adulterous contacts with strange fish, unlike those of us who go in for adultery.

Before the intervention of men, the great clans of donkeys and horses continued uninterruptedly among themselves. But now, on the contrary, donkeys are crossed with horses, bastardizing nature. This is certainly a greater sin than mere fornication, because it is committed contrary to nature: it injures natural affinity, apart from the injury in respect of the person.

You, O Man, manage these things like a pander to adulterous horses and you think the new animal valuable more because it is counterfeit than because it is genuine. You mix up strange species; you mingle opposite semen and frequently collect together the unwilling victims to a forbidden coitus, and you call this husbandry!

Because you are not able to do this with men themselves, inasmuch as human offspring cannot mix with contrary species, you think of another thing to do. You take away what a man is born with and remove his man-hood, and, cutting off part of his body, you destroy sex to create an eunuch. So, what Nature did not produce among men, your shamelessness produces! What would good Mother Water say to all this?

Man, you have taught children the renunciation of their fathers, you have taught them separations, hatreds and enmity. Now learn what the relationship of parents and children could be. Fishes do not seek to live without Water, to be separated from the fellowship of their parents, to be parted from the nourishment of the mother. It is their nature that, if separated from the sea, they die immediately.

Now what can we say about the bigness of fish-teeth? They do not have large teeth in one part of the mouth like sheep and oxen, but each jaw is equipped with teeth of various size all along. If they chewed their food for a long time and did not quickly despatch it, the food could take itself off and be washed away from the mouth by the current of water. For this reason they have strong and sharp incisors so that they can cut quickly and easily finish the food, despatching it without delay. In short, they do not ruminate.

SCARUS the scar,[1] however, is said to be the one fish which does ruminate, and with him it was either an accident or by practise or because of a fondness for holding things in his mouth.

Fish of course do not escape the violence of power from their own kind. The smaller are subject to the larger or

[1] See Escarius.

to the more powerful, for whoever is weaker is liable to be captured by the stronger. There are, indeed, many who feed on vegetation, but the littler among these is food for the bigger, and again the bigger is seized in its turn by a still stronger one and becomes his food: one plunderer falling to another plunderer. And so it is the usual thing that when one fish has devoured another, itself is devoured by yet another, and both of them meet in the same belly, the devoured and its devourer, and there they are together—a fellowship of rapine and vengeance in the same interior.

Now this wickedness comes to pass in Fish spontaneously or by chance—just as in our own case it came to pass with us—and not out of Nature but out of greed; or perhaps because fish are given to us as a parable for the instruction of men.[1] Perhaps they behave like this so that in them we may see the imperfections of our own customs and be warned by their example—warned that the stronger should never attack the weaker, lest he

[1] 'O watry Citizens, what Umpeer bounded
    Your liquid Livings? O! what Monarch mounded
    With walls your City? What severest Law
    Keeps your huge armies in so certain aw,
    That you encroch not on the neighbouring Borders
    Of your swim-bretheren? . . .
    What learned *Chalde* (skild in fortune-telling)
    What cunning Prophet your fit time doth show?
    What Heralds Trumpet summons you to go?
    What Guide conducteth, Day and Night, your Legions
    Through path-less paths in unacquainted Regions?
    Surely the same that made you first of Nought,
    Who in your Nature some *Ideas* wrought
    Of Good and Evill; to the end that we,
    Following the Good, might from the Evill flee.'
                                    SYLVESTER'S *Du Bartas.*

should, by doing so, offer a precedent in wrong-doing to a Greater than himself. He who injures another prepares a rod for his own back. You yourself are a fish who gobbles other gobblers, who overpowers the weak and who chases the Believer down to the depths. Take care then that while you follow your prey you do not yourself meet with a Stronger than yourself, who may chase you down into a toil of his own. Remember the littler fellow who is scared about you chasing him—regardless of the fact that Somebody Else may be chasing you.

ESCARIUS the scar[1] gets his name because he alone is said to ruminate food (*esca*) and other fish do not. They say that he is a clever one. For when he is trapped in a pot he does not dash out to the front, nor does he put his head into the unsafe withies, but, turning round, he undoes the gates with frequent blows of his tail, thus going out backward. If by any chance another Escarius sees him struggling, it seizes his tail with its teeth and assists in the work of breaking out.

[1] A species of Wrasse. They are labrus fish, with thick lips. Sylvester calls them 'Golden-eye'.

ECHENEIS the Remora is a little creature six inches long, which gets its name because it holds a ship fast by clinging to it.[2] Oh, the ocean wave may roll and the stormy winds may blow—but nevertheless the ship is seen to stand stock still in the sea, as if rooted to the spot, and is unable to move. The fish does this, not by a grip, but by sucking very hard. The Latins call this fish by

[2] Ship-detaining $= \epsilon\chi\epsilon\nu\eta\acute{\iota}s$. Pliny affirms that Anthony's galley was detained by a remora at the Battle of Actium.

the name of Mora, because it compels vessels to stay motionless (*mora*=a delay).[1]

[1] Spenser refers to 'the dreadful fish that hath deserved the name of death', and Dr Ansell Robin says that this is 'evidently the morse or walrus, which Spenser fancifully associated with the Latin *mors* (death)'. But surely the fanciful association is more likely to be an earlier one than that? *Mors–mora*.

ANGUILLAE the Eels are similar to snakes, and thus they derive their name (*anguis*=serpent). They are engendered from mud and for this reason, if you catch hold of an eel, the creature is so slippery that the harder you press it the more quickly it slips away. They say that in the eastern River Ganges eels are born measuring thirty feet. If eels are drowned in wine, those who drink of it get a loathing for liquor.

The Greeks called the MURENA '*muriena*', because this eel rolls itself into a circle.[2] They state that the females are so highly sexed that they will become pregnant to a serpent. On that account the Murena is summoned by fishermen with a hiss like that of a serpent and is thus captured. Moreover, it can only be killed with difficulty by a cudgel-blow, but with a whip you can kill it at once. It is an established fact that a Murena has life in its tail, for hitting it on the head does not kill it unless the tail is despatched at the same time.[3]

[2] There was a necklace called a Murenula, but that was because the necklace resembled the eel, not the eel the necklace. Or perhaps the reference is to *Murus*, the wall which encircles a city.

[3] Many of the prehistoric reptilia did have a nervous system at both ends.

Once an unidentified eel, the Murena is now a Lamprey. Those which were eaten by King Henry I when he died of a surfeit, might have consoled themselves by reflecting that these fish were not used only to fatten people. People were once used to fatten them. 'Hee caused certain slaves condemned to die, to be put into the stewes where these Lampries or Muraenas were kept.' HOLLAND'S *Pliny* (1601). 'Could we have dug out of Herculaneum or Pompeii a muraena fattened on Syrian slaves.' SIR J. ROSS, 1835.

209

POILIPPUS the Polypus[1] is called Many-legged because he has such a lot of coils. This clever creature, eagerly making for a fish-hook, circles it in a grip with his arms and does not let go until he has gnawed the food all round.

[1] The octopus.

TORPEDO the Electric Ray or Eel gets its name because it makes one's body grow numb (*torpescere*) if one touches it when alive. Pliny the younger relates: 'If the electric ray out of the indigo sea is touched, even from a distance, even with a spear or a stick, the arm-muscles, howsoever mighty, will be paralysed and the feet, however swift in running, will be struck still'.[2] So great is its power, moreover, that even the radiation of its body affects the limbs.

[2] 'Like the fish Torpedo, which being towchd sends her venime alongst line and angle rod, till it cease on the finger, and so mar a fisher for ever.' HARVEY, 1589.
   In this respect, the Torpedo seems to be the marine counterpart of the Basilisk.
    'What though the Moor the basilisk has slain
    And pinned him lifeless to the sandy plain,
    Up through the spear the subtle venom flies,
    The hand imbibes it, and the victor dies.'
                TRANSLATION FROM LUCAN

CANCER the Crab goes in for a cunning stratagem, due to his greed. He is very fond of oysters and likes to get himself a banquet of their flesh.[3] But, although eager for dinner, he understands the danger, since the pursuit is as difficult as it is hazardous. It is difficult because the inner flesh of the oyster is contained within very strong shells, as if Nature its maker had by her imperial command fortified the soft part of the body with walls. She

[3] 'Who first an oyster eat, was a bold dog.' P. PINDAR, 1812.

feeds and cherishes this flesh in a kind of arched dome in the middle of the shell: disposes it, as it were, in a sort of hollow. For this reason, the handling of oysters has to be done carefully, because nothing can open the closed oyster by force, and thus it is dangerous for the crab to insert his claw. Betaking himself to artfulness, therefore, the crab lays an ambush with a new plot of his own. Because all species delight in relaxing themselves, the crab investigates to find out whether at any time the oyster opens that double shell of his in places remote from all wind and safe from the rays of the sun, or whether it unlocks the fastenings of its gates, so that it may pleasure its internal organs in the free air. Then the crab, secretly casting in a pebble, prevents the closing of the oyster, and thus, finding the lock forced, inserts his claws safely and feeds on the internal flesh.

Now is not that just like Men—those corrupt creatures who follow the habit of the crab, creep into the practise of unnatural trickery and eke out the weakness of their real powers by a sort of cunning! They join deceit to cruelty and are fed upon the distress of others. Do you, therefore, be content with your own things and do not seek the injury of your neighbours to support you.

The simple fare of a man who does no harm is the right food. Having his own property he knows not how to plot against his fellow man's, not does he burn with the flames of avarice. Covetousness is to him only a loss of virtue and an incentive to greed. And so, blessed is that poverty which truthfully sticks to its own goods, and meet it is to be preferred above all riches. 'Better is little with the fear of the Lord than great treasure and trouble therewith: better is a dinner of herbs where love is, than a stalled ox and hatred therewith.'

Let us then devote ourselves to acquiring merit and to maintaining what is wholesome, not to the cheating of another's innocence. Let it be left to us to make use of the marine example in perfecting our own well-being, not in the undoing of our neighbour.

E C H I N U S the Sea-Urchin is said to be a poor, paltry and contemptible animal. He is very frequently the herald of a coming tempest to sailors, or the announcer of a calm. When he senses a storm of wind he seizes a stout stone and carries it as ballast, or drags it as an anchor, so as not to be tossed about by the waves. Thus he is saved, not by his own strength, but held firm by an outside help and by the weight which he carries. Sailors snatch eagerly at this information as a sign of the coming disturbance and take care that no hurricane shall suddenly find them unprepared.

What mathematician, what astrologer, or what Chaldean can understand the course of the stars or the movement and signs of the heavens so well? By what natural quality does the sea-urchin comprehend what is taught among us by learned men? Who was the interpreter to it of so great an augury?

Men often see the disorder of the atmosphere and are deceived—for the clouds frequently disperse without a storm. Echinus is not deceived, the signs never escape Echinus. There is so much science in this one poor animal that it foretells the future. Since there is nothing more in it than this one bit of wisdom, we must believe that it is through the tenderness of God to all things that the urchin also gets his function of prescience. Moreover, if God makes lovely the grass of the field so that we marvel; if he feeds the birds and provides food for the ravens, whose young are truly turned toward the Lord; if he gave women the knowledge of weaving and does not leave even the spider destitute of that wisdom, who now minutely and skilfully hangs his roomy webs in the doorways; if God himself gives courage to the horse and unharnesses fear from his neck—so that he leaps about on the plains and is pleasing to kings as he gallops—that horse who detects war from a distance by the smell, and is excited by the sound of the trumpet; and if there are so many unreasoning things and others of no account, such as herbs, such as the lilies which are filled with the ordering of their own knowledge: can we doubt then that he also assigns to Echinus the service of this foresight? God leaves nothing unexplored, nothing unnoticed. He who feeds all things sees all things. He completes all things in wisdom. As it is written: 'He makes everything with knowledge'.

And thus, if he does not neglect poor, blind Echinus, if he takes care of him and trains him in the signs of the future, will he not carefully consider your things too, O Man? Indeed, he truly takes care of you when his divine wisdom is called upon, saying: 'If he has regard to the birds of the air, if he feeds them, are you not more than they? If God adorns the grass of the field, which today is and tomorrow is cast into the fire, how much more will he consider you, O ye of little faith?'

CONCHA[1] and Conchula, the larger and smaller bivalves, get these names because they grow hollow in a

[1] Concha=Cunnus, Plaut. Rud. 3,3,42.

waning moon, i.e. they are emptied out. Like all closed sea-animals and shell-fish, they increase bit by bit during a waxing moon: in a waning one they are emptied. When the moon is on the increase, it causes certain humours to rise; when it is declining the humours diminish, so the Doctors say. And 'concha' or 'cunnus' is the name of our first situation.

Conchula is a diminutive of Concha, just as Circulus is a diminutive of Circlus.

There are many species of shellfish, and among them are the Pearl-oysters which are often called O C C E O - L A E, in the flesh of which a precious stone solidifies. The people who write about the nature of living things relate, concerning these oysters, that they approach the shores at night-time and conceive a pearl from the celestial dew; hence they are named 'occeloe'.[1]

[1] The pun is presumably 'ob coelum'. This passage about the oyster is a confusing one. Apart from the mistakes in the manuscript, there is an underlying confusion in the mind of the scribe, of which the mistakes are probably a symptom. Dr M. R. James, in his Introduction to the Roxburghe copy of this Bestiary, wrote: 'The other section I wish to comment on is the last in *Laud* (another bestiary), which begins thus: "*Item lapis est in mare qui dicitur latine MERMECOLION, grece conca sabea, quia concava est et rotunda.*" After which we have a disquisition on the pearl oyster and the manner of the generation of pearls out of the dew and the sun's rays. This corresponds in part to Physiologus 44, of the Agate and the Pearl. . . . In *Laud* the agate has disappeared, and the discourse is far longer than in the Greek. But why the name Mermecolion? Physiologus 20 is a chapter περὶ μυρμηκολέοντος, of the ant-lion. I cannot resist quoting the greater part of it: "*Eliphaz the king of the Temanites says, 'The ant-lion perished because it had no food.' The Physiologus said: It had the face (or fore-part) of a lion and the hinder parts of an ant. Its father eats flesh, but its mother grains. If then they engender the ant-lion, they engender a thing of two natures, such that it cannot eat flesh because of the nature of its mother, nor grains because of the nature of its father. It perishes, therefore, because it has no nutriment. So is every double-minded man, unstable in all his ways, etc.*" This conception of the ant-lion as the offspring of the lion and the ant, and of its career, so closely paralleled by that of the Bread and Butter Fly, soon proved too much for editors. It vanished from the Latin versions, except in that of a Leyden MS cent. XII

MURICA the purple-fish is a sea-snail which is named from its sharp point and from its acuity.[1] It is also called by another name, 'Conchylium', because when cut out with a knife it gives out drops of a purple colour, from which the imperial purple is dyed. Hence also the other name, 'Ostrum',[2] for the dye is drawn from the liquid of the shell.

[1] 'Murex' also means a spike, a fierce bit for a horse, or a caltrop. The shell is pointed.

[2] 'Ostreum' is a rare name for oyster or sea-snail: 'ostrum' and 'conchylium' mean both that, and purple.

CRABS are so called because they are shellfish with legs.[3] These animals are hostile to oysters, for they live on the flesh of those by a wonderful stratagem. Because they cannot open the strong shell, they puzzle out how to pick the lock. They privily insert a stone and, the closing of the oyster being prevented, eat away the flesh. Some people relate that if ten crabs are compounded with a handful of basil all scorpions in the neighbourhood will

[3] The idea seems to be that Can-cer=Concha crura (habens)?

---

edited by Land: perhaps, too, a relic of it is in the MS. C.10 (Cahier is obscure here). A notice of the real ant-lion was appended to an article on the ant; and by some process of reasoning which I am quite unable to follow, the name Merme-colion became attached to the pearl oyster.'

The process was surely not one of reasoning, but of etymology and translation? In the five lines of our own passage, we find the punster spelling his shellfish as 'occeola' and 'occeloa', while he struggles with a derivation from 'ob coelum' and also, it seems, with an impossible past participle of 'occelare'–to conceal, as the pearl is concealed. Is it not possible that at some stage in the development of the bestiary some other etymologist has entangled Mermecolion with 'mare' and 'occeola', ant-lions with sea-oysters?

be gathered to that place.[1] There are two kinds of crab, river ones and sea ones.

[1] Some of the repetitions which we have noticed, about crocodile, crab, unicorn, scar, etc., are due to the fact that the Bestiary is a kind of animal scrap-book or compilation. (See Appendix.) When extracts from Physiologus, Solinus, Isidore, Ambrose and other bestiaries are stuck together, the same statement is liable to crop up in different extracts.

OSTREA the Oyster is named from the shell by which its soft inner flesh is concealed. The Greeks call a shell *'ostreon'*.[2]

[2] So here we have an additional confusion to add to the imbroglio over Mermecolion. *Ostrea* or *Ostreum* is now either *'ob testam'* (because of its shell), or from the Greek word ὄστρεον, or because *'ostrum'* means purple, or from some past participle of the late Latin verb *'occelare'*, to conceal. There is also *'ob coelum'*. As if this were not enough, the scholars of the Middle Ages managed to mix up the pearl (*margarite*) with the flower (*marguerite*)–'casting pearls before swine' may mean feeding them on daisies. (The pearl-oyster is still called *Meleagrina margaritifera*, while the edible oyster is one of the *Ostraedae*.) Where such a state of confusion exists, it seems no great aberration for the early philologist to have added to the Mer-maids a Mer-oyster. (But see the *Encyclopaedia Britannica*, Eleventh Edition, under Physiologus.)

MUSCULI the sea-mussels are water-snails. Oysters conceive from their milt. They are called Musculi because they are masculine.

TESTUDO the Tortoise is so named because his shell acts as a pot (*testa*) to cover him, like an arch. There are various kinds: Land Tortoises, Sea Tortoises, Mud Tortoises living filthily in a marsh, and a fourth species, found in rivers, which delights to inhabit the water. Some people relate an incredible fact, namely that ships go more slowly when carrying the right foot of a tortoise on board!

R A N E the Frogs are called so because of their croaking voices,[1] for they rattle round the mating ponds and make a row with their exasperating cries. Some frogs are aquatic, some pertain to the marshes, some are called Toads because they live in bramble bushes—and these are larger than the others.[2] Some are called Calamites or Green Frogs, and live among the reeds (*calami*) and little trees. The smallest of all and the greenest are dumb and voiceless. Very small frogs living in dry places or in fields are called Egredulae. Some say that dogs to whom a live frog is given in a lump of food do not bark thereafter.

[1] By onomatopoeia.

[2] '*Rubeta*' means both the bramble-thicket and the venomous toad which lives in it. These toads may be reddish or bramble coloured.

Among all the kinds of animal living in the sea, we have knowledge of one hundred and forty-four.

Pliny says that they are separated into the following divisions: monsters; serpents common to land and water; crabs, shellfish, lobsters, giant mussels; the polypi; flat fish, and muscular ones like the rockfish or those similar to it.[3]

RBozum   [3] The next three leaves of the bestiary are devoted to a section on Trees, followed by ten leaves on Nature and Man. These pages consist of an almost interminable quotation from the *Etymologiae* of Isidore, the early seventh-century Archbishop of Seville. Their interest is slight. There are no illustrations, except one picture of the scribe himself. The present translator proposes to spare the reader the trouble of wading through them in full, by preserving whatever of interest there may be in one longish footnote. The general plan of the holy man had been to enumerate every possible adjunct of Man or Tree, to define its function, and to explain, or rather in most cases to misconstrue, the reason why it had been given its name.

The chapter on Trees begins with the definitions of vegetables, trees, shrubs, orchards, groves, nurseries, cuttings, seeds, roots, trunks, bark, wood, branches, twigs, bushes, foliage, flowers, fruit, and so forth. It then proceeds to brief and somewhat platitudinous descriptions of individual species. We are told, for instance, that the oak is long-lived, or that the alder grows near water. There are, however, several passages which may seem worth translation.

'In the south wind,' we learn, 'the flowers fall: in a west wind they bloom.'

'The Palm-tree is so called because the Goddess of Victory holds it in her hand (palm-hand: the pun goes equally well in English) or else because its branches are spread like fingers from the palm of the hand. Rightly is this tree a token of victory, with its long and decorous leaves and evergreen foliage, for it preserves its fronds undefeated by new greenery. The Greeks call it '*Phoenix*' because it lasts a long time, after the name of that Arabian bird which is said to live many years. Its fruits are called Dates (*dactyles*) from their likeness to fingers (in Greek δάκτυλος means finger).'

Laurus the Laurel is so named from "*laus*" meaning "glory". With this the heads of victors used to be crowned.

The Bay tree is, of all, "the one believed by people to conduct lightning least".

The wood of the Fig-tree, "if put into water, sinks immediately, but when it has lain for some time in the mud it rises to the surface. This is contrary to nature, for when it is wet it ought to sink. . . . It is said that if figs are taken as food very often by old people their wrinkles will fill out again."

Mulberry leaves kill snakes, if thrown over them.

Cypress-wood "has a pleasant scent and lasts for a long time, nor is it ever destroyed by the worm. The resin is called *Cedria*, and this is useful in preserving books, for, if smeared with this, they do not suffer from worms nor do they decay through the ages."

Juniper-wood retains fire. If a juniper fire is smoored with its own ashes, it will remain smouldering for a year.

Abraham used to sit under an oak-tree which lasted to the reign of the Emperor Constantine. (Abraham, *c.* 2000 b.c.(?): Constantine, *c.* a.d. 330).

The Ash is useful for spears.

Such is the nature of the seed of the willow that "if anyone drinks it concocted in a goblet, he does not have children and it makes women unfruitful".

The poplar, the willow and the lime, being of soft material, are fit for sculpture.

The sections on Nature and Man begin with definitions of nature, life, man, soul, body, mind, intellect, memory, reason, sensation, flesh and the five senses. They are illuminated by a few flashes of interest.

'Man (*homo*) is properly derived from Mud (*humo*). The Greeks called him *Anthropos* because, being raised from the dust, he alone among animals looks upward to the contemplation of his Maker.'

We learn that flesh is composed of earth, air, fire and water, and that sight is a glassy liquid which comes out of the eyes, not into them. The Bestiarist considers that sight is the most important of the senses and is interested by the fact that 'we use the imperative of the verb "to see" of objects which pertain to the other senses, as, e.g. we commonly say, "see what it tastes like".'

218

There now follows a remorseless catalogue of about 170 parts of the human body, with their function and the derivation of their names. Nineteen pages after bidding good-bye to the trees, we have added little more to our stock of curious knowledge than that:

'The most important finger is the thumb, which among other things is strong in virtue and power. The second is the forefinger, which is not only serviceable but is used for giving directions, because we generally salute or show or point out with it. The third is the middle finger, by means of which the pursuit of dishonour is indicated. The fourth finger is the ring finger, because the ring is worn on it. This finger is also medicinal, because the common eye-salves are applied with it by doctors. The fifth finger is called the '*aurist*' because we scratch the ear with it.'

'We laugh with the spleen, we are enraged with the gall-bladder, we have discernment with the heart and we love with the liver.' (Incidentally, the Bestiarist knew that blood moved, though he was not acquainted with the circulation, for: 'The veins are so called because they are the paths of swimming blood and distinct streams through the whole body by which all the limbs are supplied.' It was thought that there were two distinct bloodstreams which pulsed back and forth with a piston action.)

He tells us that the muscles derive their name from mice, because they move about under the skin as mice move under the earth; and finally, it may be of interest to notice that 'the seat of wantonness in women is the navel'.

At leaf 73a, we resume the full translation of the manuscript at what Shakespeare called the Seven Ages of Man; though the physiologist adds them up to six.

RADUG The stages of man's life are six: Infancy, Boyhood, Adolescence, Manhood, Maturity and Old Age.

The first is the age of childhood, of the little one growing toward the light of day, and this goes on for seven years. The second is boyhood, which is innocent, that is to say pure and not yet able to beget children, which continues until fourteen. The third, adolescence, is grown up enough to be a sire, and this stretches to twenty-eight.[1] Manhood, the fourth, is the healthiest

[1] The Romeo-and-Juliet love convention, which has prevailed from the Renaissance to the age of Hollywood, is not of ancient origin. Before the Renaissance, a love affair was regarded as being more or less puerile or at least adolescent until what the critic of the cinematograph might now call the verge of middle

of all ages, finishing at fifty. The fifth state of the older man is Maturity, which is a decline from youth into age, not yet old but no longer young—for the rank of an older man was what the Greeks called '*Presbiter*', while they called the truly old one, not *Presbiter*, but '*Geron*'. This age, beginning in the fiftieth year, is ended in the seventieth. The sixth period, or Old Age, is not bounded by any particular time in years. It extends, after the first five stages, so long as life remains, until it is ended by senectitude. Decline is the final stage of old age (*senectutis*) and is called so because it is the end of the sixth one (*sextae aetatis*). Into these six divisions have the philosophers parcelled out our human life, by which it changes and slips away and tends toward the conclusion of the grave.

We pursue the aforementioned categories briefly, showing their etymologies in relation to man. In his first stage he is called an in-fant because up till now he cannot talk or explain (*fari*). With his teeth not yet properly arranged, the expression of his discourse is a minus quantity. Puer the boy is known as such because of his purity (*a puritate*), for he is smooth and has not yet the down and first soft flowering upon his cheeks. These are the Ephebi, named after Phoebus, gentle little fellows who are still not over the threshold of manhood. The word '*puer*' is used in three ways—a child at birth, as Isaiah uses it, in 'Unto us a child is born'; a child aged up to

---

age. 'But nowadayes', says Sir Thomas Malory, 'men can nat love sevennyght but they muste have all their desyres. That love may nat endure by reson, for where they bethe sone accorded and hasty, heete sone keelyth. And right so faryth the love nowadayes, sone hot sone colde. Thys ys no stabylyté. But the olde love was nat so. For men and women coude love togydirs seven yerys, and no lycoures lustis was betwyxte them, and than was love, trouthe and faythefulnes.'

eighteen, whence we get the quotation '*Jam puerile jugum tenera cervice gerebat*';[1] and by reason of the subject's biddableness or purity of faith, as we get it when God said to the prophet, 'Thou art my child (*puer*), fear not etc.'.

The little tiny girl (*puella*) is called so because she is a chicken (*pulla*); and for a like reason we call foundlings '*pupilli*', not from their situation but from their tender age. Pupilli are also known as such as if they were 'without eyes' (*sine oculis*)—that is, bereaved of their parents. Those whose fathers and mothers have gone before they got a name from them are properly called '*pupilli*', while the rest are said to be 'orphans'. Orphans are the same as foundlings really; for the one is a Greek word, the other a Latin one. It is in the Psalms, where we find: 'Thou art a helper to the fatherless (*pupillo*)', while the Greek reads '*orphano*'.

Growing children (*pubes*) are named from the bush of puberty, i.e. from the privates, for they say that these parts are the first to grow downy. Some people deem that 'puberty' comes from that swelling (*bubum*) which appears at the fourteenth year, although it grows very slowly. Anyway, it is certain that the sign of fertility is what grows out of the bodily habit at puberty, which is now fit for begetting children. These signs are what appear with the advance of childhood's years. Hence also we find in Horace: '*Laudatur primo jam prole puerpera nato*'.[2] And his fertile young matrons are called '*puerperae*' either because they are fertilized at the first

---

[1] 'Now with a tender neck he carried the yoke of his boyhood.'

[2] Three cheers for the fertile girl who has just had her first little man-child.

beginnings of their maturity or else because the first off-spring they give birth to are boys.

The adolescent is given that description because he or she is old enough (*adultus*) for childbearing, for to increase and to fertilize.

The young man (*juvenis*) gets his label because he is beginning to be able to look after himself (*juvare*), in the same way as, among cattle, the bullocks (*juvenci*) leave the calves. The young man is situated at the same coming-of-age and is ready to co-operate. For, among men, '*juvare*' means doing any work where two or more are gathered together. And just as the thirtieth year is the peak one among humans, so, among cattle and beasts of burden, the third is the most robust.

A man is called Vir because there is more worth (*virtus*) in him than there is in women. Hence also he gets the name of courage, or else because he governs his women by force (*vi*).

Mulier the Woman is derived from 'weakness', since '*mollior*' (weaker), with a letter taken away or changed, becomes 'mulier'. They are differentiated from man both in courage and in imbecility of body. Man has the greater capacity, woman the lesser, on purpose that she should give in to him: i.e. lest, with women being difficult about it, lust should compel men to look elsewhere and to go awhoring after another sex. She is called '*mulier*' from her femininity and not because of her weakness in having her chastity corrupted, for the language of Holy Writ is: 'And Eve was suddenly made out of the side of her man'. Not by contact with man is she called 'mulier'. The scriptures say: 'And he (God) formed her into a woman'.

Virgo the virgin is known as such because of her

greener age (*viridiori aetate*), just as the green twig is called '*virga*' and the heifer '*vitula*'. Others derive the word from her maidenhood, as in '*virago*', because she knows not womanly passion.

The Virago is named because she acts the man (*vir*), i.e. does the works of virility and is of male vigour, for the Ancients called strong women by that name. However, one cannot rightly call a virgin a virago, except when she does the office of the same. The woman who, like an Amazon, performs the masculine functions, is the one who is properly called a virago. As a matter of fact, what we now call a woman (*femina*) was anciently called '*vira*': just as we get '*serva*' from '*servus*' and '*famula*' from '*famulus*', so did they derive '*vira*' for '*vir*'. Some people think that the word virgin also comes from this.

Actually, '*femina*', a woman, comes from '*femur*' the upper part of the thigh, where the appearance of sex is different from man's. Others, by using a Greek derivation say that it is because of the fiery force with which a woman vehemently lusts, and that females are more longing than males, both in humans and in animals. Too much love was therefore thought to be effeminate among the ancients.

'Senior' means 'the maturer person among those present.' In the sixth book of *Ovid*, we find: 'And senior among the young . . .', while in *Terence* there is: 'By which ruling we are the more adolescent'. This latter implies, not that they were older than the young people who surrounded them, but younger than the old people who surrounded them, for here the comparative is a diminutive of the positive. So it is not enough just to say 'senior', in the sense that one uses the younger of two young people or the poorer of two poor people.[1]

Some people say that old men (*senes*) are so called from the lessening of their powers of perception (*sensus*), because they now begin to act silly, in a childish way. For the doctors state that people with colder blood are silly, while people with hot blood are sensible. And thus it is that aged men in whom things are now growing cold and little boys in whom they have not yet warmed up are the ones who are the least sagacious. That is why the states of infancy and senility are on good terms with one another. Old people are crazy from too much age, while the kids, through frolicsomeness and childishness, do not know what they are about.

'*Senex*' is the masculine and '*Anus*' is the feminine. You only use '*anus*' for a woman. She is called that from her many years (*a multis annis*), as in '*annosa*' (long-lived). For if the word were common to both genders, what would there be to prevent Terence from using '*senes*' for 'aged females'? Hence we also have the words '*vetula*' and '*vetusta*' for the old lady.

As 'senility' is derived from '*senex*' so is '*anilitas*' derived from '*anus*'. '*Canities*' (the hoary age) is derived from '*candor*' (pure whiteness) as if the 't' were a 'd'. Thus we get the quotation: 'Flowery youth and milk-white age (*canities*) are the main ones which we can call unblemished'.

Old Age brings with it many goods and ills. The

---

[1] i.e. 'more adolescent' may just as well mean younger as older. The question is, 'Senior to whom?' The good archbishop is already, in the seventh century, entangled with the theory of relativity. But, according to Cicero, a 'senior' was a man between forty-five and sixty.

At this point, the final leaf of our manuscript is missing. The text is supplied, with its illustration, from British Museum, Add. 11283.

advantages are that it liberates us from all-powerful urges, puts paid to the sensual pleasures, breaks the violences of lust, increases wisdom and gives maturer counsels. The bad things are that decline is very miserable with debility and hatefulness. Diseases and sad senectitude creep in, for there are two things with which the powers of the body are hemmed about, age and illness.

Death gets its name (*mors*) because it is bitter (*amara*), or else from Mars who is the maker of dead men, or else from '*morsu*', that bite of the first man, when, munching fruit from the forbidden tree, he merited death.

There are three kinds of death: premature, immature and natural. Premature is that of infants, immature that of young people, and the deserved or natural death is that of the old. Nobody knows from what part of speech the word '*mortuus*' is declined, for, as Caesar says, if it is the past participle of '*morior*' it ought to end up with one 'u', not with two of them. Because, if the letter 'u' is doubled, it is a noun, and not some difficult sort of participle. Whatever it is derived from, the idea which it expresses, to die, cannot conveniently be in an active mood, and as a noun it cannot be declined in speech.

Every dead man is said to be either a corpse or a cadaver. He is a corpse (*funus*) if he gets buried, and is called that from the '*funes*', the lighted twists of papyrus screwed up with wax which they used to carry before the bier. He is a cadaver if he lies unburied, for the word comes from falling down (*a cadendo*), because he cannot stand up any more. While the corpse is carried in the funeral procession, we call it the exequies (*exsequi*, to follow). We call cremated corpses 'the remains'. When put away or buried it is usual to call a corpse 'the body' (*corpus*), as in the quotation: '*Tum corpora luce carentum*'.

The Defunct is called so because he has finished the function of life. For we say that people have performed a ceremony (*functos officio*) when they have fulfilled the required rites. Hence we get the word '*functus*' for men and also '*defunctus*', because the fellow has been laid out dead, or put away from the rite of life, or else because he has done with the day (*die functus sit*).

'To entomb' means to hide away the corpses, for we call real burial 'inhumation': that is to say, it means putting them down in the MUD.[1]

[1] Our scribe, who has been taking St Isidore's philology at dictation speed for thirty pages, is so relieved to have done with him that he prints the last word in capital letters: *INICERE*.

There are F I R E - S T O N E S[2] in a certain oriental mountain, which are called in Greek T E R E B O L E M: they are male and female. When these are far apart from one another the fire in them does not catch light. But when by chance the female may have approached the male, at once the flame bursts out, so much so that everything around that mountain blazes.

[2] On a first inspection, it seems possible that the Firestones were lodestones and had something to do with magnetism. Early magnets were spherical. 'The first form of Magnet . . . is a large one in fashion of a round ball, boule or globe,

You, therefore, O Men of God, who wage this way of life of ours,[1] keep well away from women, lest, when you have got near to one another, the twin-born flame should break out in yourselves and burn up the good things which Christ has conferred upon you. For Satan hath his angels who are always in battle against the just, not only against holy men but also against chaste women.

In fine, Samson and Joseph were both tempted by the ladies, and the conqueror was conquered in his turn. Eve and Susannah were tempted, and both fell. Meet is the heart of man to be guarded and by all means to be admonished by the precepts of God. For the love of woman, by whom sin first arose, rages furiously in her disobedient children from Adam to the present day.

[1] i.e. the clergy.

---

and we do call it a *Terrella.*' M. RIDLEY, 1613. But the *Terrobuli* were in fact more than this: they were πυροβόλοι, Pyroboli, Pliny's Pyrites. Greene mentions them in 1589, 'a Pyrit stone, which handled softly is as colde as ice, but pressed betweene the fingers burneth as fire', and in 1590, 'like the pyrit stone, that is, fire without, frost within'. Phillips in 1706 defines, '*Pyritis,* a precious Stone, which burns the fingers if one holds it hard'. In 1796, Kirwan states that 'Pyrites is a name antiently given to any Metallic compound that gave fire with steel, exhaling at the same time, a Sulphurious or Arsenical smell'. *Early Man,* Dawkins (1880), has it that, 'fire was obtained in the Bronze Age by striking a flint flake against a piece of iron pyrites'. And the N.E.D. in 1909 informs us that the Firestones were: 'In modern use: Either of the two common sulphides of iron (FeS_2), pyrite and marcasite, also called distinctively *iron pyrites;* also, the double sulphide of copper and iron ($Cu_2S. Fe_2S_3$), chalco-pyrite or *copper pyrites'.*

NOTE. The illustration, which shows the scribe himself writing at his monastery desk with a pen-knife in his left hand, is taken from folio 63a of our manuscript: the section on Nature and Man which was summarized in a note.

Artistic conventions alter as the centuries pass, and so does the centre of interest. The 'anglo-saxon attitudes' mentioned by Lewis Carroll have become more and more attractive to the present limner, as he has traced the pictures one by one, from a photostatic copy of the original. The graceful formalism of the twelfth century was interested in things and in parts of the body which are no longer of prime importance to us. People were fascinated then by the pineapple knobs and by the cauliflower foliation of their verdure, by the stylized linenfold of their draperies, but above all by the bold, refined, tender and skeletal lines of chins, mouths, noses, hands, and of the feet, which are as sheer as wooden boot-trees. However unusual the other parts of their animals may be, the hocks, hoofs, paws, pads, claws and talons are always drawn with accuracy and love: while the fingers, heels, insteps, ankles and metatarsals of their humans have an air and a spring which is peculiar to no other style of beauty. 'Of these limbs,' says the Etymologist complacently, in his chapter on Man, 'the usefulness is great, and the look most becoming'.

APPENDIX

THE MANUSCRIPT

The manuscript which is here translated is a Latin prose Bestiary which was copied in the twelfth century. On f. 73a somebody has written in a sixteenth-century handwriting: 'Jacobus Thomas Herison Thys ys ye abbaye of Rev. . . .' There was an abbey at Revesby in Lincolnshire, so perhaps the manuscript was copied there. It is now preserved at the Cambridge University Library, where it is listed as II.4.26.

Its old number in the library lists is 278. How long it has been there the following inscription shows:

"*Ex dono integerrimi ornatissimique viri Osberti Fowler Collegii Regalis Registrarii 1655 Julii 16.*"

'The Registry of the College I take to have been an official, not necessarily a member of it; no Fowler occurs among the Scholars or Fellows entered in Harwood's *Alumni Etonenses* for the period, nor is an Osbert Fowler to be found in the Matriculations and Degree lists.' M. R. JAMES.[1]

---

[1] Mr John Saltmarsh, Fellow of King's College, informs the present translator that, although Osbert Fowler was never a member of the college, a member of the University, or an Etonian, and is not mentioned in Venn's *Alumni Cantabrigensis* or Sir Wasey Sterry's *Eton College Register:* 'The principal office which he held in this College was that of Bursars' Clerk. According to the *Year Lists of Members of the Foundation, etc., of King's College, Cambridge,* a manuscript in the College Muniment Room compiled from the College accounts and other sources in the early part of the present century by the late F. L. Clarke (who was himself then Bursars' Clerk), Osbert Fowler began to discharge this office in the second quarter of the year 1640–1 (i.e. between Christmas 1640 and Lady Day 1641), and ceased to discharge it in the fourth quarter (i.e. between Midsummer Day and Michaelmas) of 1658. F. L. Clarke has added a note that Fowler was buried on 9 July 1658. For this he does not add any authority;

The manuscript was edited for the Roxburghe Club by Dr James in 1928.

BESTIARIES

A Bestiary is a serious work of natural history, and is one of the bases upon which our own knowledge of biology is founded, however much we may have advanced since it was written.

There is no particular author of a bestiary. It is a compilation, a kind of naturalist's scrapbook, which has grown with the additions of several hands. Its sources go back to the most distant past, to the Fathers of the Church, to Rome, to Greece, to Egypt, to mythology, ultimately to oral tradition which must have been contemporary with the caves of Cromagnon. Its influence has extended throughout literature, and, as has been seen in the Notes, country people are still repeating some of its saws.

A full history of the subject would have to begin with oral tradition in various parts of the world, and to continue through Herodotus, Aristotle and Pliny, for many hundred years, before it reached the Physiologus which is the immediate ancestor of the work with which we are

---

but I suspect that he discovered it in the course of his researches on Cambridge parish registers.

It appears from the College Protocollum Books that Osbert Fowler did draw up the protocols of admissions of scholars and fellows, and he describes himself in this context as a Notary Public.

The office of Bursars' Clerk was not one which was normally held by a Fellow of the College. In the fifteenth century I believe the Bursars' Clerk was usually a full-time official of the College, but in later times he was frequently a lawyer of the town of Cambridge; and it seems to me quite likely that Osbert Fowler was a Cambridge lawyer.'

Dr Venn, the President of Queens' College, writes: 'I can find no Cambridge man with a surname anything like Herison (or its variants), whose Christian names were Jacobus Thomas. As a matter of fact, it was most unusual in the sixteenth century for anyone to have more than one Christian name.'

dealing. Some idea of this history can be gathered from the Family Tree which is printed on p. 233 and which the present translator has adapted from a very interesting diagram by Dr Ansell Robin. Unfortunately, Dr Robin's version does not mention the bestiaries as such.

The immediate ancestor of our manuscript is the Physiologus. His information may have come from any or all of the sources shown before him in the family tree, but the fact remains that an anonymous person who is nicknamed 'the Physiologus' appeared between the second and fifth centuries A.D., probably in Egypt, and wrote a book about beasts, possibly in Greek. The book was a success and was translated north and south into Syriac, Armenian and Ethiopian. The earliest Latin translation of him which we have is of the eighth century.

It has to be remembered that the circulation of ancient books was by manuscript. So popular was the work of Physiologus that, like a stone thrown into a pool, it proceeded to spread itself over the surface of the literate world in a series of concentric rings, as it was copied and translated from one language into another, century by century. 'Perhaps no book,' says E. P. Evans, 'except the Bible, has ever been so widely diffused among so many people and for so many centuries as the Physiologus. It has been translated into Latin, Ethiopic, Arabic, Armenian, Syriac, Anglo-Saxon, Icelandic, Spanish, Italian, Provençal, and all the principal dialects of the Germanic and Romanic languages.' The last hand-written manuscript known to the present translator, except his own, was copied in Iceland in 1724.[1]

Meanwhile, as the versions of the Greek Physiologus

[1] T. K. Abbott's *Catalogue of MSS in the Library of Trinity College, Dublin* (1900), p. 175, no. 1017.

THE FAMILY TREE

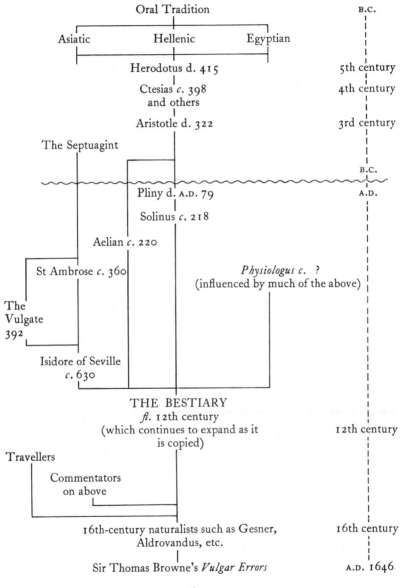

Oral Tradition

Asiatic   Hellenic   Egyptian

Herodotus d. 415

Ctesias *c.* 398
and others

Aristotle d. 322

The Septuagint

Pliny d. A.D. 79

Solinus *c.* 218

Aelian *c.* 220

St Ambrose *c.* 360

Physiologus c. ?
(influenced by much of the above)

The
Vulgate
392

Isidore of Seville
c. 630

THE BESTIARY
fl. 12th century
(which continues to expand as it
is copied)

Travellers

Commentators
on above

16th-century naturalists such as Gesner,
Aldrovandus, etc.

Sir Thomas Browne's *Vulgar Errors*

B.C.

5th century

4th century

3rd century

B.C.

A.D.

12th century

16th century

A.D. 1646

spread across the globe, other naturalists, some of whom may themselves have been influenced by him, were writing other natural histories.

There was no reason why a scribe, setting out to copy the original Greek but being aware of a later authority, should not expand his copy with interpolations from that authority. This in fact happened, and the Bestiary, as distinct from the Physiologus, began to grow like a living tree. There are forty-nine beasts in the Greek original: in the manuscript here translated there are between 110 and 150. The scribe himself says 144 in the sea.

It was in the twelfth century that the scrap-book as such reached its finest foliage in Latin prose, and that happened particularly in England. 'Indeed,' says Dr M. R. James, 'the Bestiary may be reckoned as one of the leading picture-books of the twelfth and thirteenth centuries in this country. It ranks in this respect with the Psalter and the Apocalypse. Leading, and influential: for researches such as those of Cahier and Martin in the last century and of Mr G. C. Druce in this, have shown how widely images and ideas taken from it have permeated medieval art.' Dr James examined thirty-four English copies. In this connection, it is perhaps a surprising fact that our own translation is the first full version to be published in English, although translations of much shorter works in Latin verse and Norman French have appeared. The version of Trevisa is not of the true bestiary. Those of Sylvester's *Du Bartas* and Topsell are very far from it.

Dr James, in editing this manuscript for the Roxburghe Club, took the trouble to trace every statement to its proximate source. Except for thirteen quite insignificant additions (from Rhabanus Maurus, the *Aviarum* of Hugo, the Pantheologus and a few untraceable) he found that the immediate ancestors of this version were (a) the Physiologus, (b) Solinus, (c) St Ambrose and (d) Isidore of Seville. All of them, of course, were liable to quote from the Septuagint, and from anybody who preceded them.

In short, if we are asked for 'the author' of the bestiary at its fullest, as here reproduced, we can only place a finger in the middle of the family tree on page 233, where the previous sources converge.

In adapting Dr Robin's Zoological Pedigree to the particular tradition of the bestiary itself, the present translator has omitted Theophrastus, Nicander, Oppian, Capella, Cassiodorus, Neckham, Vincent of Beauvais, English Bartholomew, Albertus Magnus, Marco Polo, Odoric, the supposed Mandeville, Belon and one or two general categories. These were associated with the remoter sources or with the subsequent influence, but the tree is complicated enough without them.

This brings us to the branches of the Bestiary in general, rather than to its roots.

Bartholomew Glanville (English Bartholomew) wrote his *De Proprietatibus Rerum* in the thirteenth century, as Neckham had written his *De Naturis Rerum* in the twelfth, and these books were extensions of the subject as we have seen it here.

Bartholomew was translated into English by Trevisa in 1397. A host of other writers had begun to appear, all of whom, with Bartholomew and Neckham, are included in our diagram under the comprehensive heading 'Commentators on the Above.'

In all probability, it would have been from people like Pliny and the commentators that Du Bartas (1578) and Topsell (1607), the translator of Gesner, derived some of their facts about animals, and from these latter that the poets like Spenser and Milton took theirs.

Meanwhile, the travellers and serious observers had begun to add their quota to the subject, people like Marco Polo and still more modern voyagers—there was even a Baron Munchausen of the subject, the pseudo-Mandeville, who resembled his predecessor Ctesias the Cnydian—until, with the sixteenth and seventeenth centuries, the voluminous sages like Gesner and Aldrovandus had vast stores of learning to collect. They were already beginning to have their doubts about the wilder statements.

In 1646, in England at any rate, which was the home of the bestiaries,[1] Sir Thomas Browne subjected what he called their 'tenents' to rational criticism in his *Pseudodoxia Epidemica*, and began to raise the subject of biology to a scientific level, for the first time since Aristotle.

This meant the end of the Physiologus as a serious authority, and memories of him declined as the factual approach of the eighteenth century gained in popularity. With the establishment of the Royal Society in 1662, direct observation and experiment had outmoded the old approach through the library shelves. Since the middle of the nineteenth century there has been a revival of interest, in an antiquarian sort of way, which has owed its impetus to the patient researches of people like Thomas Wright (1841), Cahier and Martin (1847–77), E. P. Evans (1897), G. C. Druce (1908–37), M. R. James (1928) and P. Ansell Robin (1932).

[1] The present translator has, for the sake of clarity, confined himself to the English side of the story. A fuller survey would deal particularly with Norman-French writers like Guillaume le Clerc, whom Mr Druce translated, with Jacob van Maerlant's *Der Naturem Bloeme* (1280) and with the *Bestiare d'amour* of Richard de Furnival.

The present translator has omitted much in this brief sketch of the manuscript's story. There is no mention of the Egyptian Horapollo, no conjecture about Tatian, and Ctesias the Cnydian exists as it were *in vacuo*. He hangs there, out on a limb, of the family tree. It is to be hoped that the explanation may have gained in simplicity what it has lost in erudition.

THE BACKGROUND

A medieval Bestiary, when one first comes across it in the twentieth century, is irresistibly reminiscent of Hilaire Belloc. But to approach it through the attitude of *A Bad Child's Book of Beasts* is to lose its fascination.

It can hardly be repeated too often that the bestiary is a serious scientific work: that even the great Dr James was perhaps a little mistaken when he referred, with a very faint touch of contempt, to its bread-and-butter-flies: that a Cameleopard, which does not appear in this manuscript, is a genuine animal, and by no means a bad attempt to describe an unseen creature which was as big as a camel while being spotted like a leopard, i.e. a giraffe: and that the real pleasure comes with identifying the existing creature, not with laughing at a supposedly imaginary one. Indeed, the more the reader is amused by the foolishness of Physiologus, the more he is liable to make a fool of himself. Who would have supposed that there really was a dragon with a head at both ends? Yet the incomparable Mr Druce easily ran it to earth in the official guide of the British Museum.

Our manuscript was carefully and beautifully written out, perhaps but not necessarily at the Abbey of Revesby in Lincolnshire, eight hundred years ago. Nobody at that abbey could possibly have seen an amphisbaena. On its way across Europe, over the roadless miles and through the slow centuries, it had passed through the hands of many scribes and limners who cannot have seen it either. What is surprising about the reptile is not that it should have appeared in a distorted way, but that it should have appeared at all. The reader who may smile at the Phoenix will probably get little pleasure compared with that other reader who can exclaim to himself: 'Why, it may have been the Benu, the sun-bird! They worshipped the sun at Heliopolis. Perhaps the priests wore purple robes. Perhaps it was the Purple Heron!'

Some slight idea of the conditions under which the manuscript was produced may be of assistance in visualizing its nature.

It was copied after the beginning of the twelfth century, for it contains the Ibex, which seems to have entered the mainstream of the bestiaries with MS. Stowe 1067, early in that century; but before the end of the century, for it does not contain the Barnacle Goose which came to the bestiaries from Giraldus Cambrensis after 1186. We might date it at the middle of the period.[1]

In 1150, King Stephen was supposed to be on the throne. It was little more than a man's lifetime since the

---

[1] A doubtful but closer guess about the actual date of this copy might run as follows: Revesby, if the manuscript was really written there, was a Cistercian foundation. The Cistercians, by the time that the influence of Stephen Harding had given place to that of St Bernard, had become an order whose face was consciously set against ornament. Their windows were of plain glass, their altars unpainted, their lovely architecture as austere as was their rule. The *Consuetudines* of 1134 proceeded to forbid illuminated initials in manuscripts. '*Litterae unius coloris fiant et non depictae*'. The actual pictures in a book such as ours could scarcely be left out, but it will be noticed that they cease to be coloured after the first four animals. It is within the bounds of possibility that this bestiary had been started before the *Consuetudines* reached Lincolnshire, and was completed there after.

Norman invaders had overturned the Saxon civilization of which Trevelyan has written: 'What a place it must have been, that virgin woodland wilderness of old England, ever encroached on by innumerable peasant clearings, but still harbouring God's plenty of all manner of beautiful birds and beasts, and still rioting in a vast wealth of trees and flowers . . . . In certain respects the conditions of pioneer life in the Shires of Saxon England and the Danelaw were not unlike those of North America and Australia in the Nineteenth Century—the lumberman with his axe, the log shanty in the clearing, the draught oxen, the horses to ride to the nearest farm five miles away across the wilderness, the weapon ever laid close to hand beside the axe and the plough, the rough word and ready blow, and the good comradeship of the frontiersman. . . . Every one of the sleepy, leisurely garden-like villages of rural England (today) was once a pioneer settlement, an outpost of man planted and battled for in the midst of nature's primaeval realm.' It was in such a backwood of the Wild West, with its sheriff's posse and its escaping slaves, the serfs, now rendered doubly a wilderness by the baronial wars of Stephen, that: 'By such men as these, in local possession of sovereign power, whole districts were depopulated. The Thames valley, the South-West and part of the Midlands suffered severely, but the worst scenes of all were enacted in the Fenland, where Geoffrey de Mandeville kept an army afoot on the plunder of the countryside. In the heart of this unhappy region, in the cloisters of Peterborough, an English monk sat tracing the last sad entries of the Anglo-Saxon Chronicle, first compiled under the patronage of the great King Alfred, now shrunk to be the annals of the neglected and oppressed. In it we hear the bitter cry of the English common folk against the foreign chivalry to whom the foreign kings had for a while abandoned them.

"They greatly oppressed the wretched people by making them work at these castles, and when the castles were finished they filled them with devils and evil men. They then took those whom they suspected to have any goods, by night and by day, seizing both men and women, and they put them in prison for their gold and silver, and tortured them with pains unspeakable, for never were any martyrs tormented as these were".'

The English monk of those tormented fenlands, who might just possibly have been acquainted with the scribes of our manuscript, for, though their abbeys were forty miles apart and belonged to different foundations, they might have shared a common interest in the Peterborough Psalter and Bestiary, which, like our own volume, was to be edited eight hundred years later by Dr James: that monk was sheltered by a Catholic and Apostolic Church which was at the time pre-eminently interested in learning and husbandry, as well as in morals. If there were a safe sanctuary to be found in the forest of England, over-run by outlaws and lawless barons, it was in the Abbey.

The Abbey of Revesby was a Cistercian foundation, between Tattershall and Spilsby. There, to that strict and reformed order at the outpost of European civilization, by lawless roads and tedious portages, a copy of the second family of bestiaries seems to have penetrated. Books were of great value in the twelfth century. They took so long to write, there were so few people who could write them, their durable materials were so costly, that, by 1331, Edward the Third was paying £66 13s 4d for a romance, at a time when ten oxen could be bought for £7 10s 0d. This would have been more lavishly illuminated than our own pages, however.

Since books could only be duplicated by hand, it was reasonable to duplicate as many as possible at the same time, by dictation. Several scribes seated at their desks round the Scriptorium could produce a limited edition as the text was read out to them. The present bestiary was probably dictated, for on folio 1a the words '*et simiis*' are written as '*eximiis*', which is a slip of the ear, not of the eye.

The effect of dictation was twofold. When a new arrangement of the manuscript penetrated to a district, it would set up a family similar to itself in structure, as it was loaned from abbey to abbey. Dr James has identified four families of English bestiaries, as if, in fact, four prototypes had circulated in the country. But, within the family itself, there were closer relationships. If two or more existing manuscripts are found to be almost identical, it is reasonable to suppose that they were simultaneously dictated in the same scriptorium. Our own copy has no blood brothers like this in existence, but the four bestiaries at Aberdeen (II.3.8), Bodley's Library (Ashmole 1511 and Douce 151), Caius College (372) and perhaps St John's College, Oxford (61), may have come from the same atelier. The bestiary seems to have been more popular in the north of England than in the south.

The scribe did not draw the pictures. These were left to the limner, who either filled them in afterwards or drew them before the writing was done. In our case, the scribes, for there were two of them and the handwriting

Rocodrillus a croceo colore dictus. gignit in nilo flumi
ne. animal quadrupes. intra 7 aq̄ ualens. longitudine
plerumq; uiginti cubitoz. dentiū 7 unguium inmanitate
armatus. Tantaq; cutis duricia. ut q̄muis fortiū ict̄ lapi
dum tergo repuciat non nocet. nocte inaquis. die inhu
mo q̄escit. Oua intra fouet. masculus 7 femina uices suant.
hunc pisces q̄dam serratam hn̄tes cristam. tenera uentr
um desecantes intimunt. Sol'autem p̄omnib; animali
b; supioza mouet. inferioza ū inmota tenet. Stercᵉ eī sit un
guentū. unde uetule 7 rugose meretrices facies suas pungunt.
fiuntq; pulchre donec sudor defluens lauet. Cuī figuram
portant hypocrite siue luxuriosi atq; auari. q̄q̄nuis uisco
supbie inflent̄ʰ. tabo luxurie maculent̄ʰ. auaricie morbo ob

changes, preceded the artist. Seated at their high desks like the professional craftsmen that they were; with quill pens and knives to trim them; with iron-gall inks, on skins which were difficult to prepare; with the strong downward strokes of their 'i's, which could reproduce '*munimini*' as 𝖨𝖨𝖨𝖴𝖴𝖴𝖬𝖨𝖨𝖨𝖨 , and their abbreviations by which ꝗ was '*igitur*' or ÷ was '*est*' or 𝖬𝖨𝖠 was anything from '*miseria*' to '*misericordia*'; with their attention concentrated upon the lector who dictated to them, or not concentrated, according to the mood of the moment; with no punctuation except to indicate the pauses of the dictation; with their words running over from one line to the next o r b e i n g s t r e t c h e d o u t like this to fill up a space ⁓⁓⁓⁓⁓⁓⁓⁓⁓⁓⁓ ; with their quotations from scripture which, if well known, were merely indicated by the initial letters of the words; immured in a not comfortable barracks, since the Cistercians were a self-denying order; surrounded by the dangers of a civil war and the difficulties of a frontier life; with their tongues between their teeth and their blunt, patient, holy fingers carefully forming the magic of letters: the producers of the scientific treatise which we have been reading presented us with the amphisbaena.

When we reflect how far it had come and through what perils, how lovingly it was treated and with what an innocent enthusiasm for learning, it seems impertinent in us to greet it with any other attitude than affection.

MORALIZATION

Symbolism is still one of the common interests of human life. Apart from half a hundred wild ducks in literature, like that of Ibsen, there are symbols at every street corner and in every newspaper that we pick up. The circle with the lettered bar across it symbolizes the Underground Railway, Mr Therm is the flame of the gas company, a dark figure in a cloak who holds a glass of red wine speaks all over England for Sandeman's port, as the sea-lion and the ostrich, without a word of explanation, speak for Guinness.

A true symbol is not only a badge: it is a brief sermon, a shorthand way of saying something. The circle of the Underground says, perhaps, 'I go round under London, like the Inner Circle'; while the ostrich, whose digestion is perfect—'Whose greedy stomack steely gads digests' says Sylvester—proclaims that 'Guinness is good for you.'

A symbol is a metaphor, a parable, a parallelism, a part of a pattern. The figure of Justice stands on the Law Courts with her sword and scales because, like these articles, justice is said to discriminate and to wield power. There is a pattern between scales and justice.

In the ages of faith, people believed that the Universe was governed by a controlling mind and was capable of a rational explanation. They believed that everything meant something. It was not only the ostrich of Messrs Guinness who stood at their elbow, waiting to give them a hint. Every possible article in the world, and its name also, concealed a hidden message for the eye of faith. It was hardly possible to play chess without reading a '*Jeu d'échecs moralisé*', in which the names of the various gambits would teach a man that 'he who gives not what he esteems, shall not take what he desires' or that 'he sees his play at hand who sees it at a distance'. He could not read a plain story in the *Gesta Romanorum* without finding its holy explanation at the end of it. Animals, like the didactic creatures of Aesop, conveyed him a parable. 'Ask the beast,' Job had said (XII, 7), 'and it will teach thee, and the birds of heaven and they will tell thee.' Even their names were meaningful—which is why we have had to put up with such a lot of the etymology of Isidore. Urica the canker burns (*urit*): but it also makes people urinate. Even words were hitched up and entangled with the universe.

The meaning of symbolism was so important to the medieval mind that St Augustine stated in so many words that it did not matter whether certain animals existed; what did matter was what they meant. '*Nos quidquid illud significat faciamus et quam sit verum non laboremus.*' Indeed, an apocryphal decree of Pope Gelasius I, supposed to have been issued in A.D. 496, placed a copy of Physiologus on the *Index Prohibitorum*, presumably because its 'moralizations', as they were called, were heretical.

Everything held together, was logically coherent. 'Why? Because' was the leit-motif of the ages of faith, which paradoxically made them able to say, '*Credo quia absurdum est.*' It was sufficient if there was a link in pattern. The Creation was a mathematical diagram drawn in parallel lines and, as we shall see in the next section, things did not only have a moral: they often had physical counterparts in other strata. There was a horse on the land and a sea-horse in the sea. For that matter, there was probably a Pegasus in heaven. There were physical comparisons as well as moral ones.

The reader who has come with us so far as this, will have ploughed through a good deal of moralization. If he has taken it only as admonition, he will have missed the point. It gave these people real pleasure to discover that Jesus Christ was an insignificant elephant, just as it gives pleasure to the theatre-goer of the twentieth century when he detects the parallel of Ibsen's wild duck.

There is one other point about the moralizations which has struck the present translator. He approached them, it has to be admitted, in a spirit of boredom, and for long considered the possibility of omitting them from the book. In later bestiaries, they often were omitted. But the actual charm of them, their holy simplicity, finally reached the heart. Quite apart from the intellectual interest of the symbol, in which a bird holds out its wings because Moses did so in the battle with the Amalekites, there is a gentleness of manner and a hopeful goodness which do touch the emotions. True, there is a good deal about Hell, but it strikes the pupil as being a little perfunctory. The reverend moralizer wags his finger at us about it, cautioning us not to gobble up other fishes for fear of being gobbled up ourselves, but he does not dwell upon it, does not relish it, does not describe its torments. He is no Dante, no sadist. He is a kind fellow. He is even kind to women. They brought about the fall of man, admittedly; they are bothersome creatures and need a good deal of lecturing; but . . . 'There is a catch in this for you too, my dear Man . . . Drive out the sulks when that solicitous wife does excite your affection. You are not her lord, but her husband, nor have you chosen a female slave, but a wife . . . Return sympathy for her misfortunes, kindness for her love . . . Thus you may be able to get her to accept you after all!'

Anybody who will read again the noble passage on the sea-urchin, the charming little sermons about that newly-wed, the Turtle-dove, and that poor but lovely mother the Nightingale, or the rather upsetting reflection on

Fishes (p. 208) about the Somebody Else who, like the frightful fiend in Coleridge, may close behind us tread: such a reader can hardly be sorry that the 'moralizations' were included.

The Bestiary is a compassionate book. It has its bugaboos, of course, but these are only there to thrill us. It loves dogs, which never was usual in the East from which it originated; it is polite to bees, and even praises them for being communists like the modern Scythians; it is tender to poor, blind Echinus; the horse moves it, as Sidney's heart was moved, 'more than with a trumpet'; above all, it has a reverence for the wonders of life, and praises the Creator of them: in whom, in those days, it was still possible absolutely to believe.

The Mantichora (Topsell's *Historie of Foure-Footed Beastes*, 1607)

THE MANTICORE AND THE MERMAID

The reader who has picked his way among so many fabulous creatures may be surprised, in looking back, to reflect that he has nowhere encountered a centaur or a mermaid. The manticore was nearly a centaur, but not one; and the syren, except for her picture, has lost her fishy tail. This is a measure of the essentially unfabulous nature of the bestiaries. Had our physiologist suspected that his manticore was a pagan myth, he would have suppressed it. For one thing, he was a christian.

But the Physiologus lived in the age of faith. He lacked, as we have seen, our modern means of communication and our apparatus of criticism. He was beset by a hundred traditions and fables which the March of Mind had not yet exploded. There was no *Encyclopaedia Britannica* for him, no *Oxford English Dictionary*. He was doing his best, and a wonderful best it was, when all things are considered, to write a serious text-book on biology.

So, when the critic of the twentieth century finds himself baffled by a satyr or a griffin, and unable to identify them for certain, it may be worth his while to consider the tangle of traditionary evidences among which the bestiarist was trying to discriminate.

In the first place, there were the usual rustic stories: the epidemic pseudodoxies with which anybody who has frequented the country inns of England will still be well acquainted. In public houses the English peasantry are at this moment assuring one another that owls cannot see in daylight, that hedgehogs collect fruit on their prickles, that mules never die (have you ever seen a dead mule?), that eels are bred from horse-hairs, that the moon without any combination of circumstances changes the weather and that adders swallow their young for protection. All this and much more must have beset the bestiarist. He had no reason to suppose that bears did not give birth to formless lumps. The hunters had told him that they did; and indeed, as we have seen in the notes, they seem to do so. He himself probably had no access to bears. Nature, moreover, really is a peculiar concern. What medieval dupe would believe the commonplaces of twentieth-century biology: that so many creatures really do give birth without fertilization (parthenogenesis) and that the life-cycle of the fluke in a sheep's liver depends upon a snail in a puddle? Where our own scientists can show that the amoeba is to all intents and purposes immortal, why should not the Phoenix have been so? Where we have scarcely touched the fringes of the deep seas and the creatures which may dwell therein, the sea serpent and the monster of Loch Ness, how can our ancestors be blamed for their Aspidodelone, in such undiscovered vastnesses? A little humility in this matter can hardly come amiss.

Human beings are liable to condescend to other animals, whose life is often better organized than their own, to foreigners who are known as Wops, Limeys and so forth, to savages, and to their own progenitors. We have invented the wireless telegraph, the motor car and the electric light, commodities unknown to previous centuries: and for that reason we assume that the twentieth century is the best of all, instead of being merely the most recent. An example of this attitude was provided by Jusserand, in his *English Wayfaring Life* (1889); although it is only fair to add that the author himself detected and amply apologized for the presumption. Dr John of Gaddesden (1280–1361) had claimed to have cured the son of King Edward II of smallpox by wrapping the patient in red cloth and by putting red hangings to the bed and to the curtains. The cure was held up by

Jusserand to the derision of his Victorian readers, until a Dr Niels Filsen of Copenhagen discovered in 1910 that red and infra-red light did have a beneficial effect upon the pustules of smallpox. 'One of the most depraved of all races,' wrote an excellent archaeologist in 1895, 'the now extinct Tasmanians, believed that stones, especially certain kinds of quartz crystals, could be used as mediums or means of communication at a distance!' W. G. WOOD-MARTIN. The exclamation mark of amusement was his own. Within a generation everybody was listening on their crystal sets, and one can only hope that the depraved Tasmanians did not become extinct through too much indulgence in this habit.

Perhaps it is always safer not to condescend. Civilization is a portrait which is being painted by the human race, and an artist is compelled to begin painting somewhere. Though he may rough in the general outline at the start, he must begin at some particular part of the canvas, whether it is at the hand or at the head, at the eye or at the nostril. The whole picture cannot be painted simultaneously. At the end of the Dark Ages it is true that there were no motor cars, but there was no Gothic architecture either. Perhaps it is a sobering thought that these people preferred to begin by inventing Westminster Abbey, leaving it to the leisure of our later times to perfect the bombs for it.

It used to be a common belief that everything on the earth had its counterpart in the sea. The horse and the sea-horse, the dog and the dog-fish, the snake and the eel, the spider and the spider-crab: these led the extremists to extend their classifications to the air, and even platonically to the metaphysical heaven itself, so that the Physiologus who could revisit our planet today would probably construct a parallelism between the ideal *Leviathan* in the Eternal Ocean, a barrage balloon, an elephant and a whale. What was more, if there were whales on sea and land, why should there not be men in both? Mermen? And if men, why not kinds of men? Why not bishops, for instance? In 1554, Rondeletius published the picture of a Bishop-fish (on page 252), deriving some of his information from Neckham in the twelfth century. The bishop-fish was accompanied by a monk-fish in his retinue and was presented in 1531 to the King of Poland, as we are informed by Gisbertus Germannus; but His Grace was not happy in Poland, and, after pleading for his liberty with the assembled clergy by means of signs, was reverently returned to his native element. Perhaps he was a walrus, for some bishops have looked like decayed walruses, but the matter is now beyond conjecture. The point was that, what with the belief in parallelism which had obscurely persisted since Plato, and the real oddity of animals like the manatee, there was, and is, nothing intrinsically impossible about the mermaid. There were mammals in the sea already, like the porpoise, so why not human ones? So far as that goes, Man, with his extension the machine, has in our own day in fact plunged beneath the waters. The sub-merman has become a submariner: he has become Spenser's waterman now,

> 'The griesly Wasserman, that makes his game
> The flying ships with swiftnesse to pursew.'

With ocean-going submarines, we may yet be confronted with a chaplain on board, and he will then be

The Makara (Indian reliefs, *c.* A.D. 200. From *Fabulous Beasts*, Peter Lum, Thames & Hudson, 1952). The Makara was almost any composite animal

Bishop-fish (Rondeletius, *De piscibus marinis*, 1554)

Babylonian water-god (after a relief from Khorsabad, 8th century B.C., from *Fabulous Beasts*, as are the next twelve illustrations)

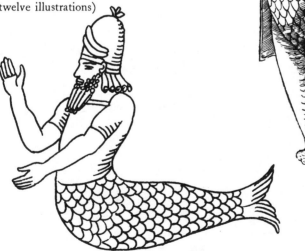

able to quote Sylvester's translation of *Du Bartas* (1578) with conviction:
> 'Seas have . . .
> Also Rams, Calfs, Horses, Hares and Hogs,
> Wolves, Lions, Urchins, Elephants, and Dogs,
> Yea, Men and Mayds: and (which I more admire)
> The Mytred Bishop, and the Cowled Fryer:
> Whereof, examples (but a few years since)
> Were shew'n the *Norway's*, and *Polonian* Prince.'

Man's Vampire Jet and his Walrus Amphibian have already joined the mammals of the air.

If there have been, are and always will be, more things in heaven and earth than were dreamed of in Horatio's philosophy, we must understand that one of the channels which led to the creation of animals like the Manticore was pure fact.

Apart from the rustic and the travellers' tales, there was a second tributary which went to swell the river of fable. This was the hearthside or mythological story, which is nowadays the hunting-ground of the anthropologist. When the dweller by the Nile saw the first Bedouin on horseback, or when Pizarro on his steed dawned dreadfully upon the Mexicans in the New World, the legend of the Centaur came into being. Of cavalry we still use the word 'horsemen': and what is a horse-man but a centaur? He has come to the bestiary by word of mouth,[1] through the fireside narratives of prehistoric bards. This interpretation is not incompatible with that of Mr Robert Graves (page 36), who claims that the origin is totemistic. It is reasonable to suppose that the tribe of the Horse Totem might well have become

[1] He appears in Bodleian 602, of late twelfth century. But see p. 86, his tears.

Egyptian Sphinx (Thebes, *c.* 1400 B.C.)

Persian Winged Bull (Susa, 5th century B.C.). Note that in silhouette the horns can become single

Assyrian Winged Bull (Khorsabad, 8th century B.C.)

a tribe of horsemen, on their way to becoming centaurs.

Another tributary was that of religion. The gods of primitive man, before he took to worshipping a Creator created in his own image, were generally animalistic. In Egypt Horus, Anubis, Sekmet, Thoth, Isis and Hathor; in India Hanuman and Ganesha; in Crete the Minotaur; in Greece Pan; in Christian Venice the winged lion of the Evangelist: all these out-moded gods and many others, which combined the attributes of men and beasts, were commemorated in sculpture or on papyrus. Their provenance having been forgotten or muddled by tradition, the bestiarist took them seriously. A winged bull of Assyria or a hieroglyph of a woman with a hawk's head, he assumed that these might have been real animals somewhere or other and tried to describe the Griffin or the Harpy.

Art itself has been a contributor to the confusion. The signs of the Zodiac, the sphinxes and murals of the Nile, the depicted Garudas and Tengus of the further east, perhaps the embroidered dragons of China, or the odd fact that in the science of heraldry it was possible to produce double-headed or double-natured monsters by the medieval practise of dimidiation: all these, with the prehistoric gods and myths and travellers' tales and rustic stories and the plain facts, are liable to crop up here and there in the biology of the twelfth century. It would be surprising if they did not. The impressive thing is that they appear so seldom. We have seen that ninety per cent of our animals were real ones. The charm about the remaining ten per cent, like the Leucrota and the Cockatrice, is that the interested reader remains free to construct his own theories.

There is one final tributary, and that an unexpected

Greek Sphinx (Metropolitan Museum of Art, 6th century B.C.)

Centaur (Etruscan gem, *c.* 450 B.C.)

Lion of St Mark
(Chartres Cathedral)

one: etymology. The scholars of what we are pleased to call the Dark Ages were intimately concerned with the problems of translation, transcription and interpretation. With the Bible itself hovering between Hebrew, Greek and Latin, the problems of language confronted them at every turn. It was hard enough to be faced with a horse-like animal which could move its horns at will, but when the Hebrew name for this creature had no Greek or Latin equivalent, the encyclopaedist was put to his wits. The reaction of the patristic writers, when puzzled by an animal, was to reach for the nearest copy of Pliny, not to examine the animal itself, and, if Pliny's two thousand sources failed them, they would seek for a linguistic relationship in the animal's name. In defining a Mermecoleon, the bestiarist and his commentator were unlikely to be able to study the habits of the Ant-lion. The nearest specimen might be five hundred miles away, and not by railroad, nor might they have any particular reason for supposing that

Ani and his wife, Tuta, standing on the roof of their tomb (Papyrus)

Benu (Papyrus)

Sekmet, Anubis, Horus, Thoth (Egyptian tomb-paintings)

the one was the other. In the haze of conflicting evidence which beset them, they would turn to the etymological approach and try to visualize the animal by fitting together the 'mer' of the mermaid and the 'leon' of the lion and the 'occeola' of the oyster and anything else which seemed appropriate to the philological fancy.

An ultimate muddle was the simple misprint. A Basilicock could always be helped on its way by writing an 'o' for an 's' in 'Basilisk'.

There used to be a nursery game called Russian Telegrams. The players sat in a line and whispered a message from ear to ear, from one end of the line to the other.

It was possible to begin with 'Nanny thinks this game is fun' and to end with 'Granny wants a currant bun'—or, indeed, if the line were a long one and the players more than usually average, to end with 'The Archbishop of Canterbury has ascended the Matterhorn with a mechanical grampus'. It is a form of message which is

Dragon (Chinese)

Garuda (Cambodian)

Ganesha (Indian)

still common in warfare, and in other forms of organized activity. When one reflects that the tenents of the bestiarists were not only communicated from man to man over a period of more than a thousand years, but also translated from language to language and scrambled with the traditions of hunters, travellers, mythologists, priests, artists and linguists, it is astonishing that the telegram should have altered so little: that the purely fabulous centaurs and mermaids should not have appeared among them, in our copy, as serious animals: and that the modern reader is yet in a position to construct some reasonable theory of his own, even about the identity of the Manticore and the Griffin.

THE ELIZABETHANS

It was in the Renaissance, and not in the Dark Ages, that the mind of man began seriously to sport with the fabulous. It was the Elizabethans, the Euphuists, the metaphorsicians, the poeticals, who elaborated the Gorgons, Harpies, Lamias, Tritons and Nereids. A visual comparison between the Doric simplicity of the Manticore (page 51) and Yale (page 55), as drawn by the bestiarist, and the Corinthian detail of their counterparts in Topsell (pages 247, 265) will show how the subject had proliferated by the time it reached the poets.

The later influence of the bestiaries, such as it was, is shown in the diagram on page 263, which may also serve to elucidate some of the references made in the notes.

Ariosto, publishing between 1516 and 1532, and Du Bartas, who published in 1578, were deeply influenced by the climate of Gesner. To Gesner, the Swiss naturalist who was beginning, however uncertainly, to collect

Ornithanthropus (Aldrovandus)

Whirlpoole or Physeter (Aldrovandus)

INFLUENCE IN LITERATURE

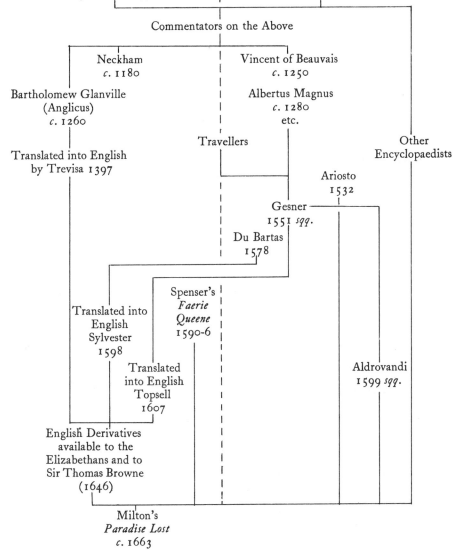

ENGLAND | THE CONTINENT

THE BESTIARY
(12th century)

PREVIOUS SOURCES

Commentators on the Above

Neckham
c. 1180

Vincent of Beauvais
c. 1250

Bartholomew Glanville
(Anglicus)
c. 1260

Albertus Magnus
c. 1280
etc.

Travellers

Other
Encyclopaedists

Translated into English
by Trevisa 1397

Ariosto
1532

Gesner
1551 *sqq.*

Du Bartas
1578

Translated into
English
Sylvester
1598

Spenser's
*Faerie
Queene*
1590-6

Translated
into English
Topsell
1607

Aldrovandi
1599 *sqq.*

English Derivatives
available to the
Elizabethans and to
Sir Thomas Browne
(1646)

Milton's
Paradise Lost
c. 1663

All these people could naturally have been influenced by any of the people who appear above them; and by many more who do not, such as Dante; Philemon Holland, for instance, had translated Pliny in 1601.

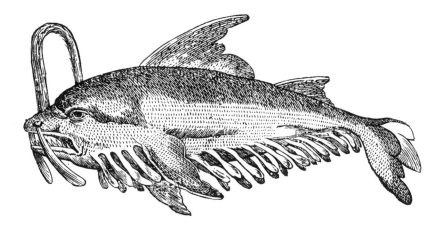

Scolopendra (Aldrovandus)

specimens at first hand as well as from the library shelves, our Physiologus was already *'author obscurus'*—an unimportant source. Among his contemporaries were Belon (1553) and Rondeletius (1554–5), authorities on fish, whose plates were widely reproduced and contributed to the poetry of the sea. It was through such authors as these and Du Bartas, rather than through the more direct English line of Trevisa, that the Elizabethans took their fabulous animals. Spenser was in this matter closer to the continent than to his native land; and Milton, when he listed his complicated monsters quoted on page 176, may possibly have been thinking of a similar list in Sylvester's translation of *Du Bartas*:

'O! wert thou pleas'd to form
Th' innammel'd *Scorpion*, and the *Viper*-worm,
Th' horned *Cerastes*, th'*Alexandrian Skink*,
Th'*Adder*, and *Drynas* (full of odious stink)
Th'*Eft*, *Snake*, and *Dipsas* (causing deadly Thirst):
Why hast thou arm'd them with a rage so curst?

Pardon, good God, pardon me; 'twas our pride,
Not Thou that troubled our first happy tide,
And, in the childehood of the World, did bring
Th'*Amphisbena*, her double banefull sting.'

OTHER BEASTS

A few animals have been mentioned here and there in
the notes, which do not figure in the text.

Spenser's 'Whirlpoole' was a whale: it whirled the
pool by spouting it. Sylvester calls it 'the Whirlpoole
Wale or huffing Physeter'. *Physeter*, its Greek name,
means 'blower'. It was not the maelstrom, though this
phenomenon had been known to Giraldus Cambrensis.

Scolopendras were centipedes or annelid worms, according to Aristotle. They were about two feet long.
Pliny, in his usual way, exaggerated them into the largest
marine animals, and made them swim with legs and

Gorgon or Catoblepas (Topsell, 1607)

265

bristles, like a trireme. The commentators of the sixteenth century divided them into two kinds: marine worms, which still exist as such, and the whale-sized monsters. Perhaps in this form their numerous legs may have been those of giant squids, or they may have been many sucker-fish attached to the belly of some large creature.

In the note on page 55, the Catoblepas was mentioned as a possible relative of the Yale. This animal was translated by Topsell into the Gorgon, and can be seen on

Sea-horse (Etruscan)

page 265. 'It is a beast all set over with scales like a Dragon, having no haire except on his head, great teeth like Swine, having wings to flie, and hands to handle, in stature betwixt a Bull and a Calfe.' Whatever the Yale and the Catoblepas may have been, the Gorgon of the sixteenth century has certainly become a composite creature. 'And thus much may serve for a discription of this beast, untill by gods providence, more can be knowne thereof.' TOPSELL.

The Sea-satyr must have been a species of merman or manatee. Anybody who has looked at a real sea-horse (Hippocampus) will acknowledge the possibility of parallels between land and sea.

Ziffius is xiphias, the swordfish.

Dr Ansell Robin says that Rosmarine is a walrus. The italicized parts of the following words all mean 'horse':

Sea-horse
(Hippocampus)

*Ros*marine, Wal*rus*. The N.E.D. thinks it is a *Hippo-*
potamus.

The Barnacle or Tree Goose deserves a paragraph of its
own. It was invented to account for the facts that (a)
some geese, being migratory, were not seen to breed in
the south and (b) shellfish like mussels do have the
general tulip shape and some of the coloration of wild

Barnacle Geese

geese with their wings folded. There is also an etymological muddle about wings, for translators had been
liable to render the two shells of an oyster as 'wings'.

'There are likewise here many birds called barnacles,'
wrote Giraldus concerning Ireland in 1187, 'which
nature produces in a wonderful manner, out of her
ordinary course. They resemble the marsh-geese, but are
smaller. Being at first gummy excrescences from pine-
beams floating on the waters, and then enclosed in shells
to secure their free growth, they hang by their beaks,

like seaweeds attached to timber. Being in process of
time well covered with feathers, they either fall into the
water or take their flight in the free air, their nourishment and growth being supplied, while they are bred in
this very unaccountable and curious manner, from the
juices of the wood in the sea-water. I have often seen
with my own eyes more than a thousand minute embryos
of birds of this species on the seashore, hanging from one
piece of timber, covered with shells, and already formed.
No eggs are laid by these birds after copulation, as is the
case with birds in general; the hen never sits on eggs in
order to hatch them; in no corner of the world are they
seen either to pair or build nests. Hence, in some parts of
Ireland, bishops and men of religion make no scruple of
eating these birds on fasting days, as not being flesh, because they are not born of flesh. But these men are
curiously drawn into error. For, if anyone had eaten
part of the thigh of our first parent, which was really
flesh, although not born of flesh, I should think him not
guiltless of having eaten flesh.'

Giraldus, like St Jerome, was fond of the theory that
the Irish were cannibals in any case.

THE TRANSLATION

The manuscript sometimes gives the impression of
having been written by a schoolboy who has suffered a
course of Bible reading. Most of the sentences are introduced by 'moreover', 'verily', 'therefore', 'thus' or 'and
so'. These repetitions have been cut out. There are
errors in spelling, or even mistakes in the general understanding of what the scribe is trying to report. Rather
than pester the reader with a series of notes on textual

criticism, for it is hoped that this is a book for the general public, as it can scarcely be one for the expert, the present translator has set these right without further ado. But he has not presumed to correct anything without investigation of the general sense in other bestiaries, in Aldrovandus, in the sources, or in the works of other students.

The following is a fair example of this kind of manipulation.

On the first page of our manuscript there appears the statement (about lions): '*Hujus genus tripharium dicitur*'. It is followed by a blank space, as if the scribe had paused to gaze upon his handiwork in some perplexity. '*Tripharius*' is not listed by Lewis and Short, while Baxter and Johnson give '*Triforium, trefoil*'. The tails of lions in the end papers, with which they rub out their tracks when pursued, are trefoliated. The idea that our sentence may mean something like 'the variety of this creature is said to be threefold' is weakened by the fact that the bestiarist immediately mentions only two varieties. The idea that it means 'the lion has three characteristics' is strengthened by the fact that Physiologus, in Greek, does later enumerate three. Yet, after some puzzling, and in the face of the subsequent statement that lions have five cubs, we have translated: 'The litters of these creatures come in threes.' The reason is that in other bestiaries also, not closely related to the present manuscript, and in ecclesiastical architecture all over Europe (see *Animal Symbolism*, E. P. Evans, pages 82–4), the litters are carefully represented as triple. This is evidently how the Middle Ages thought of them. *Triplasius* means threefold. This version has therefore been presented without explanation, for fear of frightening away the reader with a learned note, and that is the kind of thing which has happened more than once, after the same consideration, in the present translation.

It has to be admitted as an unfortunate fact, however, that the third version, which follows Physiologus, is probably the correct one. In a matter of little or no importance, the literal reading has been rejected for a second reason as well: it makes the general sense less scrappy.

A translator does have some right to give his original the benefit of a doubt.

Our book has tried to be an accurate version which will not be quite so halting as the dog Latin. It was a seventeenth-century student of the Bestiaries who said: 'As dutifull children let us cover the Nakednesse of our Fathers with the Cloke of a favourable Interpretation': and this is all that I have tried to do.

BIBLIOGRAPHY[1]

ADELINE, JULES: *Les Sculptures Grotesques et Symboliques (Rouen, et environs)*. Rouen, 1879.

AELIAN: see Fleming.

AHRENS, KARL: *Zur Geschichte des sogenannten Physiologus, Programm des Gymnasiums zu Ploen*, 1855, No. 251.

ALDROVANDI, ULYSSI: *Historia*, etc. Bologna, 1599–1642.

ALLATIUS, LEO: *S. Eustathii in hexahemeron commentarius*, ed. Leo Allatius. Lyons, 1629.

ALLEN, J. ROMILLY: *Christian Symbolism in Great Britain and Ireland before the Thirteenth Century*. London, 1887.

—— 'On the Norman Doorway at Alne in Yorkshire'. Article in *The Journal of the British Archaeological Association*, vol. xlii, pp. 143–58.

ANON: *Delectable Demaundes, and pleasaunt Questions . . . Newly translated out of the Frence into Englishe, this present yere of our Lorde God*. London, 1566.

ANON: *The Dialoges of Creatures Moralysed*. London, 150?.

ANON: *The Myrrour and dyscrypcyon of the Worlde*. London, 1527.

ANSELL ROBIN P.: *Animal Lore in English Literature*. John Murray, 1932.

ARISTOTLE: *History of Animals*, translated by Richard Cressell, Bohn Library. London, 1862.

AUBER, L'ABBE CHARLES AUGUSTE: *Histoire et Theorie du Symbolisme religieux avant et depuis le Christianisme*. 4 vols. Poitiers, 1872.

AUDSLEY, WM: *Manual of Christian Symbolism*. London, 1865.

BARTHOLOMEUS ANGLICUS (GLANVILLE): see Trevisa.

BERGER DE XIVREV: *Traditions Teratologiques*. Paris, 1836.

BRODERIP, W. J.: *Zoological Recreations*. London, 1847.

[1] Based on *Encyclopaedia Britannica*, M. R. James, P. Ansell Robin, E. P. Evans, Peter Lum, Daniel George and the translator.

BROWN, ROBERT, Jr.: *The Unicorn*. Longmans Green, 1881.
BROWNE, SIR THOMAS: *Pseudodoxia Epidemica*. London, 1646.
BOYLESVE, MARIN DE: *Les Animaux et leurs Applications Symboliques à l'Ordre Spirituel*. Paris, 1881.
BREYSIG, J. A.: *Wörterbuch der Bildersprache oder Angaben symbolischer und allegorischer Bilder*. Leipzig, 1830.
—— *Bulletin Monumental*. Vols. xi–xxix. Caen, 1846–54.
BYRNE, M. ST C.: *Elizabethan Zoo*. London, 1926.
CAHIER, CHARLES: *Mélanges d'Archeologie*. 4 vols. Paris, 1847–56.
—— *Nouveaux Mélanges d'Archeologie*. 4 vols. Paris, 1874–7.
—— *Monographie de la Cathedral de Bourges, ou Vitraux de Bourges*. Paris, 1841–4.
—— *Caracteristiques des Saints dans l'Art Populaire*. Paris, 1844.
CARLILL, JAMES: *Physiologus*. London, 1824.
CARUS, J. VICTOR: *Geschichte der Zoologie*. Vol. xii of *Geschichte der Wissenschaften*. Munich, 1872.
CHAMPFLEURY (pseudonym of JULES FLEURY): *Historie de la Caricature moderne*. Paris, 1865.
—— *Historie de la Caricature au Moyen Age at sous la Renaissance*. 2nd ed. Paris, 1875.
—— *Les Sculptures Grotesques et Symboliques*. Rouen, 1879.
—— *Histoire de la Caracature sous la Reforme et la Ligue*. Paris, 1880.
CLEMENT, FELIX: 'L'Ane au Moyen Age' (*Annales Archeologiques*, vols. xv, xvi).
COUCHOUD, PAUL-LOUIS: *Asiatic Mythology*. Harrap, 1932.
CROSNIER, L'ABBE: *Iconografie Chretienne*. Caen, 1848.
DAHLERUP, VERNER: *Bibliography of the Physiologus in Aarsboger for Nordisk Oldkyndighed og Historie udgiven af Det kongelige Nordiske Oldskrift-Selskab*. 1889.
—— *Denkwürdiger und Nützlicher Antiquarius des Neckar-Mayn-Lahn-und Moselstroms*. Frankfurt am Mayn, 1740.
DIDRON, A. N.: *Histoire de Dieu, Iconographie des Personnes Divines*, Paris, 1843.

Didron, A. N.: *Manuel d'Iconographie Chretienne*. Paris, 1845.
—— *Annales Archeologiques*. Paris, 1844–72.
Dietrichson, L.: *De Norske Stavkirker; Studier over deres system, oprindelse og historiske Udvikling*. Kristiania og Kjobenhavn, 1892.
Dietrichson, Dr. L. und Munthe, H.: *Die Holzbaukunst Norwegens in Vergangenheit und Gegenwart*. Berlin, 1893, pp. 25–7.
Douce, F.: *Dissertation on the Dance of Death*. London, 1833.
Douglas, Norman: *Birds and Beasts of the Greek Anthology*.
Druce, G. C.:

1. 'The Symbolism of the goat on the Norman font at Thames Ditton.' (Reprinted from *Surrey Archaeological Collections*, vol. xxi). London, printed by Roworth & Co., 1908.

2. 'The Sybill Arms at Little Mote, Eynsford.' (Reprinted from *Archaeologia Cantiana*.) London, Mitchell Hughes & Clarke, 1909.

3. 'The Amphisbaena and its connexions in ecclesiastical art and architecture.' (Reprinted from *The Archaeological Journal*, vol. lxvii, no. 268; 2nd Series, vol. xvii, no. 4, pp. 285–317.) Hunt, Barnard & Co., London, W., and Aylesbury, 1910.

4. 'The Symbolism of the crocodile in the Middle Ages.' (Reprinted from *The Archaeological Journal*, vol. lxvi, no. 264; 2nd Series, vol. xvi, no. 4, pp. 311–38.) Hunt, Barnard & Co., 1910.

5. 'Notes on the history of the heraldic jall or yale.' (Reprinted from *The Archaeological Journal*, vol. lxviii, no. 271; 2nd Series, vol. xviii, no. 3, pp. 175–99.) Hunt, Barnard & Co., 1911.

6. 'The Caladrius and its legend, sculptured upon the twelfth-century doorway of Alne Church, Yorkshire.' (Reprinted from *The Archaeological Journal*, vol. lxix, no. 276; 2nd Series, vol. xix, no. 4, pp. 381–416.) Hunt, Barnard & Co., 1913.

273

7. 'Some abnormal and composite human forms in English church architecture.' (Reprinted from *The Archaeological Journal*, vol. lxxii, no. 286; 2nd Series, vol. xxii, no. 2, pp. 135–86). London: Published at the office of the Royal Archaeological Institute, 1915.

8. 'The Legend of the Serra or Saw-fish.' (Extract from the *Proceedings of the Society of Antiquaries*, 1918, 2nd Series, vol. xxxi, pp. 20–35.) (No imprint given on cover.)

9. 'The Elephant in mediaeval legend and art.' (Reprinted from the *Archaeological Journal*, vol. lxxvi, nos. 301–4; 2nd Series, vol. xxvi, nos. 1–4, pp. 1–73, 1919.) London: Published at the office of the Institute, 1919.

10. 'The Mediaeval bestiaries, and their influence on ecclesiastical decorative art.' (Reprinted from the *Journal of the British Archaeological Association*, December, 1919.) British Archaeological Association.

11. 'The Mediaeval bestiaries and their influence . . . II.' (Reprinted from the *Journal of the British Archaeological Association*, December, 1920.) British Archaeological Association.

12. 'An account of the Μυρμηκολέων or Ant-lion.' (Reprinted from the *Antiquaries' Journal*, October, 1923 (vol. iii, no. 4). Society of Antiquaries.

13. 'The Sow and Pigs; a study in metaphor.' (Reprinted from *Archaeologia Cantiana*, vol. xlvi). Printed by Headley Bros., Ashford.

14. '*The Bestiary of Guillaume Le Clerc, originally written* 1210–11. Translated into English. Printed for private circulation by Headley Brothers, Invicta Press, Ashford, Kent. 1936.

15. 'The Lion and cubs in the Cloisters.' (*Canterbury Cathedral Chronicle*, April, 1936. No. 23.)

16. 'The Pelican in the Black Prince's Chantry.' (*Canterbury Cathedral Chronicle*, October, 1934. No. 19.)

17. 'Queen Camel Church bosses on the chancel roof.'

(Reprinted from the *Proceedings of the Somersetshire Archaeological and Natural History Society*, vol. lxxxiii (1937), pp. 89–106.)

18. 'The Stall carvings in the Church of St Mary of Charity, Faversham.' (Reprinted from *Archaeologia Cantiana*, vol. l, pp. 11–32.) Printed by Headley Bros., Ashford.[1]

Du Bartas, Guillaume de Saluste (1544–90) was translated by Joshua Sylvester as *Du Bartas His Divine Weekes and Workes*. London, 1592–1609.

Du Cange (Charles Dufresne): *Glossarium*. Festum, 1678.

Dumontier, G.: *Les Symboles, les Emblêmes et les Accessoires du Culte*. Paris, 1891.

Dursch, G. M.: *Der Symbolische Charakter der Christlichen Religion und Kunst*. Schaffhausen, 1860.

Du Tillot: *Memoires pour servir à la Fête des Fous*. 1741.

Ebers, Georg: *Sinnbildliches, Die Koptische Kunst, ein neues*

---

[1] It is a pity that the published papers of this bestiarist, which are definitive, have not been collected and edited in one volume. George Clarence Druce died on 11 May 1948, at the age of 88. He had been elected F.S.A. in 1912 and served on the Council in 1923. Born in Surrey, where he lived until 1923, when he retired from the managing directorship of a well-known firm of distillers, he settled at Cranbrook in Kent: was secretary of the Kent Archaeological Society from 1925 to 1935, and Vice-President. In 1947 he presented his unique collection of photographs and slides to the Courtauld Institute.

When he died in 1948, Druce made the following bequest to the Society of Antiquaries:

6 vols. photographs of misericords;
10 vols. containing notes, transcripts, cuttings and correspondence on Bestiaries;
1 vol. index of subjects to the above;
1 vol. index of places to the above;
4 albums of photographs of Bestiaries;
10 notebooks of reference to manuscripts containing Bestiaries;
1 large album of photographs of English medieval architecture and ornament, arranged in countries.

The present translator, who is resident in the Channel Islands, has unfortunately been prevented by that circumstance, and by the poverty of authors who are under the penal taxation of a philodemotic government, from moving his household to London in order to consult this important archive.

Gebiet der Altchristlichen Sculptur und ihre Symbole. With fourteen line illustrations. Leipzig, 1892.

EDWARDS, M. and SPENCE, L,: *Dictionary of Non-Classical Mythology. Dent,* 1912.

Encyclopaedia Britannica, 11th edition, article 'Physiologus'.

FIORILLO, J. D.: *Kleinere Schriften artistischen Inhalts.* 2 vols. Gottingen, 1803–6.

FLEMING, ABRAHAM: *A Registre of Hystories Out of Aelianus.* London, 1576.

FLORIO's *Montaigne.* London, 1603.

FRAZER, Sir JAMES: *Folk Lore in the Old Testament.* New York, Macmillan, 1923, and *The Golden Bough* (abridged), *ibid.* 1940.

GARRUCCI, RAFFAELE: *Storia della Arte Cristiana.* 4 vols. Prato, 1879.

GESNER, CONRAD: *Historia Animalium.* Zurich, 1551–87.

GOLDING, ARTHUR: *The excellent and pleasant works of Julius Solinus, Polyhistor...* Translated by Golding, London, 1587.

GOLDSMID, EDMUND: *Un-natural History.* Privately printed, Edinburgh, 1886.

GOULD, CHARLES: *Mythical Monsters.* Allen, 1886.

GOULD, RUPERT: *The Case for the Sea-Serpent.* Allen, 1930.

DU GUBERNATIS, ANGELO: *Zoological Mythology.* Trübenr, 1872.

GUERARD, F.: *Recherches sur la Fête des Fous.* Amiens, 1861.

GUERBER, H. A.: *Myths and Legends of the Middle Ages.* Harrap, 1909.

GUILLAUME, CLERC DE NORMANDIE: *Le Bestiaire Divin.* Best edition by Reinsch. Leipzig, 1890. *See* DRUCE.

HEIDER, GUSTAV: *Schöngraben uber Thiersymbolik und das Symbol des Löwen in der Christlichen Kunst.* Wien, 1849.

—— *Die Romanische Kirche zu Schongrabern in Nieder-Oesterreich. Ein Beitrag zur Christlichen Kunst-Archäologie.* Wien, 1855.

HOMMEL, Dr: *Aetheopic text of Physiologus.* Leipzig, 1877.

HUBAUX, JEAN, and LEROY, MAXINE: *Le Mythe du Phenix dans les Littératures Greque et Latine.* Paris, E. Droz, 1939.

HULME, F. E.: *Natural History, Lore and Legend.* Quarich, 1895.

JAMES, M. R.: *The Peterborough Psalter and Bestiary,* edited for the Roxburghe Club, and the present MS., C.U.L. 11.4.26, also for Roxburghe Club, 1928.

KNIGHT, GALLY: *Ueber die Entwickelung der Architectur vom x bis xiv, Jahrhundert unter den Normannen.* Leipzig, 1841.

KOLOFF, EDUARD: 'Die sagenhafte und symbolische Thiergeschichte des Mittelalters.' Raumer's *Hist. Taschenbuch,* pp. 179–269, 1867.

KRAUS, FRANZ XAVIER: *Kunst und Alterthum im Unter-Elsass.* Strasburg, 1876.

KREUSER, JOH.: *Der christliche Kirchenbau, seine Geschichte, Symbolik, Bildnerei nebst Andeutungen für Neubauten.* 2 vols. Bonn, 1851; revised edition, Regensburg, 1860.

KUGLER, FRANZ: *Kleine Schriften und Studien,* vol. i. Stuttgart, 1853.

LAND, J. P. N.: *Anecdota Syriaca.* Leiden, 1874.

LANGE, KONRAD: *Der Papstesel: Ein Beitrag zur Kultur-und Kunstgeschichte der Reformation.* Gottingen, 1891.

LANGLOIS, E. H.: *Les Stalles de la Cathedral de Rouen.* Rouen, 1838.

LAUCHERT, FRIEDRICH: *Geschichte des Physiologus.* Strasburg, 1889. (This exhaustive work contains a very full account of editions and translations.)

L'ESPRIT: *Histoire des chiffres et des 13 premiers nombres.* Paris, 1893.

LEY, WILLY: *The Lungfish, the Dodo and the Unicorn.* Viking, New York, 1949.

'LUM, PETER': *Fabulous Beasts.* Thames and Hudson, 1952.

LUTHER, MARTIN: *Abbildung des Bapstum.* Wittenberg, 1545.

—— und MELANCHTHON: *Deuttung der czwo grewlichen*

Figuren Baptesels czu Rom und Munchkalbs zu Freyberg ym Meysszen funden. Wittenberg, 1523.

LYCOSTHENES: *Prodigiorum ac Ostentorum Chronicon.* Basil, 1557. *Maxima Bibliotheca Veterum Patrum.* 27 vols. Leyden, 1677.

MAETZNER: *Altenglische Sprachproben*, Berlin, 1867.

MAI: *Classici auctores.* Rome, 1835.

MAPLET, JOHN: *A Greene Forest, or a Naturall History . . .* London, 1567.

MEISSNER: *Articles in* Herrig's *Archiv für das Studium der neueren Sprachen und Literatur* Vols. lvi–lviii.

MENZEL, WOLFGANG: *Christliche Symbolik.* 2 vols. Regensburg, 1854.

MERES, FRANCIS: *Palladis Tamia*, London, 1598.

MOBIUS, TH.: *Analecta norroena.* Copenhagen (?), 1877.

MULLER, SOPHUS: *Die Thierornamentik im Norden.* (From the Danish of J. Mestorf.) Hamburg, 1881.

MUNSTER, SEBASTIAN: *A Brief Collection.* London, 1574.

NAPIER, ARTHUR S.: *History of the Holy Rood-Tree, a Twelfth-Century Version of the Cross-Legend.* With notes by the editor, Professor Arthur S. Napier. London, 1894.

NEALE, J. M., and WEBB, BENJ.: *Du Symbolisme dans les Eglises du Moyen Age. Avec une Introduction, des Additions et des Notes par M. L'Abbé J. J. Bourasse.* Tours, 1847. (The second part (pp. 255–402) is an extended summary of William Durnad's Rationale Divinorum Officiorum, which was printed at Mayence in 1459.)

NORDSTERN (pseudonym of NOSTITZ und JANCKENDORF), GOTTL. ADOLF DERNST: *Sinnbilder der Christen.* Leipzig, 1818.

OUDEMANS, A. C.: *The Great Sea-Serpent.* Leyden, 1892.

OVID: *Metamorphoses.* Translated by Dryden, etc. London, 1807.

PAULUS, EDUARD: *Kunst- und Alterthums-Denkmale im Königreich Württemberg.* Stuttgart, 1889–93. Text, with numerous illustrations and large plates.

Peignot, E. G.: *Recherches sur les Danses des Morts et sur l'Origine des Cartes à jouer.* Paris, 1826.

Peters, E.: *Der griechische Physiologus und seine orientalischen Ubersetzungen.* Berlin, 1898.

Philippe de Thaun: 'Le Livre des Creatures.' Vide Wright's *Popular Treatises on Science during the Middle Ages,* pp. 74–131.

Physiologus: *See* Cahier and Martin, Carlill, Dahlerup, *Encyclopaedia Britannica,* Hommel, Land, Lauchert, Maetzner, Mai, Mobius, Peters, Strygowski, Tychsen, Volimöller, etc.

Pinder (Ulrich): *Der beschlossen gart des rosenkrantz Marie.* 2 vols. Nurnberg, 1505.
(According to the colophon this work was Gedrüch vn volendet zu Nürmberk durch doctor Vlrichen Pinter/am tag Dyonisiy/Nach Cristi vnsers lieben herren geburt M. funff hundert vnd funff jar.)

Piper, Ferdinand: *Mythologie und Symbolik der christlichen Kunst von den ältesten Zeiten bis in das 16. Jahrhundert.* 2 vols. Weimar, 1847–51.

Piton, Frederic: *La Cathedral de Strasbourg.* Strasbourg, 1861.

Pitra, J. B.: *Spicilegium Solesmense complectens Sanctorum Patrum scriptorumque Ecclesiasticorum anecdota hactenus opera selecta e graecis orientalibusque et latinis codicibus.* Tom. i–iv. Paris 1851–8.

—— Publications of Early English Text Society. Vols. xlvi–xlviii. London, 1865–6.

—— *Revue Archeologique.* Paris, 1844–92.

—— *Revue de l'Art Chretien.* Especially vols. vi–xx. Paris, 1845–77.

Pliny: translated by Holland. London, 1634.

Ponce de Leon: *S. Epiphanius ad physiologum.* Ed. Rome, 1587.

Rendell, A. W.: *see* Theobald.

Richter, Christian: *Uber die fabelhaften Thiere.* Gotha 1797.

Robinson, Phil: *The Poets' Birds.* London, 1883.

Ross, Alexander: *Arcana Microcosmi.* London, 1652.

Rudolphi, Friedrich: *Gotha Diplomatica oder Ausführliche Historische Beschreibung des Fürstenthums Sachsen-Gotha,* Vol. ii, p. 310. *Frankfurt am Main und Leipzig,* 1717.

Schadow, J. G.: *Wittenberg's Denkmäler der Bildnerei, Baukunst und Malerei, mit historischen und artistischen Erläuterungen.* Wittenberg, 1825.

Scheible, J.: *Das Kloster, weltlich und geistlich, meist aus den ältesten deutschen Volks-Wundercuriositäten und Komischen Literatur.* A curious compilation in 13 vols. Stuttgart, 1845–9. Vide especially vols. vii, ix and xii.

Schnaase, Karl: *Geschichte der bildenden Künste im Mittel-alter.* Especially vol. iv. Dusseldorf, 1843–64.

Sepet, Marius: *Le Drame Chrétien au Moyen Age.* Paris, 1878.

Shepard, Odell: *The Lore of the Unicorn.* Houghton Mifflin, 1930.

Smith, G. Elliot: *Elephants and Ethnologists.* Dutton, 1924.

Solinus: *see* Golding.

Strygowski: 'Bilderkreis d. griech.' *Physiologus, Byz.,* Archiv. II, 1899.

Swan, John: *Speculum Mundi.*

Sylvester, Joshua: *see* Du Bartas.

Theobald, Bishop: *his metrical Physiologus,* translated by A. W. Rendall, Bumpus, 1928.

Thompson, D'Arcy: *Greek Birds.*

Topsell, Edward: *The History of Four-footed Beasts.* E. Cotes, London, 1658. Abridged, *see* Byrne, M. St C.

Trever, C.: *The Dog Bird* (pamphlet). Leningrad, Hermitage Museum, 1938.

Trevisa: translation of Bartholomew (1397), subsequently appeared as Batman on Bartholomew, London, 1582.

Tychsen, O. G.: *Physiologus Syrus.* Rostock, 1795.

Viert, Peter: *The Schoole of Beastes.* Translated I. B., London, 1585.

Villette, Claude: *Raisons de l'Office.* Paris, 1601.

Vinycomb, John: *Fictitious and Symbolic Creatures in Art.* Chapman and Hall, 1906.

Viollet-le-duc: *Dictionnaire Raisonné de l'Architecture Francaise du 11ᵐᵉ au 16ᵐᵉ Siècle.* Paris, 1853.

de Visser, M. W.: 'The Tengu, Yokohama', *Transactions of the Asiatic Society of Japan.* Kelly and Walsh, 1908.

Volimöller, Carl: *Romanische Forschungen.* Erlangen, 1890. Bd. v., pp. 1–12, 13–36, 392–418.

1. *Zum Physiologus von Fried. Lauchert.* (An account of Cecco d'Ascoli's 'Acerba'.)

2. *Der äthiopische Physiologus von Fritz Hommel.* (A revised German translation.)

3. *Der waldensische Physiologus von Alfons Mayer.* (The first publication of the original text.)

(Vulpius, Aug.): *Curiositäten der physisch-literarisch-artistisch-historischen Vor- und Mitwelt zur angenehmen Unterhaltung für gebildete Leser.* 10 Bände. Weimar, 1811–23. Especially vol. vi, pp. 133–42.

Weerth, Ernst Aus'm: *Kunstdenkmäler des christlichen Mittelalters in den Rheinlanden.* 5 Bände Text und Tafeln. Leipzig, 1857–68.

Wessely, J. E.: *Die Gestalten des Todes und des Teufels in der darstellenden Kunst.* Leipzig, 1876.

Wright, Thomas: *Popular Treatises on Science during the Middle Ages.* London, 1841.

—— *History of Caricature and the Grotesque.* London, 1875.

—— and Halliwell: *Reliquae Antiquae.* London, 1841–3.

Zeddel, F. C.: *Beiträge zur biblischen Zoologie.* Quedlinburg, 1836. *Zeitschrift für deutsche Kulturgeschichte.* Vol. i, pp. 463–9; 708 *sq.*

Zockler, O.: *Geschichte der Beziehungen zwischen Theologie und Naturwissenschaft.* 2 vols. Gutersloh, 1887–9.

INDEX

Dekker, 121n
de la Pryme, Abraham, 113n
Delfines, 200
Delphi, 200n
Deluge, 31n
Devil, the, 8, 15, 21, 29, 34, 54, 59, 83, 135, 136, 161, 167, 188
Dictation, 241
Dipsas, 174, 181, 185n, 264
Dipsomania, 174n
Ditmars, R. L., 177n, 185n
Dittany, 37, 42n, 43n
Ditties, licentious, 134
Doctor, a learned, 46n
Dodo, 23n, 45n
Dog, 7, 22n, 31, 31n, 38n, 61 sqq., 217, 247
Dolphin, 200
Domestic Animals, 71 sqq.
Donkey, 82
Donne, John, 120n
Dorcas, 41
Doterell, a folyshe pek, 122n
Dove, 144 sqq., 159
Dove, Dr, 45n
Dragon, 14, 26, 159, 161, 165 sqq., 167n, 237, 259
Drinking horns, 78
Dromedary, 80
Druce, G. C., 55n, 115n, 177n, 199n, 202n, 234, 236, 237, 273, 275n
Drumbledary, 81n
Drunkards, sperm of, 190n
Dryden, 210n
Du Bartas, 20n, 24n, 111n, 117n, 128n, 140n, 167n, 172n, 179n, 199n, 207n, 234, 235, 244, 253, 261, 263, 264
Duck, 151, 243
Dugong, 201
Dunciad, 46n
Dyas, 61n

EAGLE, 105 sqq.
Eale, *see* Yale
Ebriety, 16n
Echeneis, 208
Echinus, 95, 212, 247
Echoic origin of names, 104, 104n
Edward II, King, 249
Edward III, King, 241
Eel, 170, 209, 248
Eel, electric, 210
Eggs, 49, 121, 152, 203, 205
Egredulae, 217
Egypt, 125n, 132, 255, 257, 258
Eland, 19n
Elephant, 10, 20n, 21, 24 sqq., 38n, 166, 167n
Elephant, insignificant, 26, 246
Elizabethans, 261
Elk, 19n, 26n, 53n
Emigramus, 193
Emilianus, 119
Emorris, 175, 185n
Encyclopaedia Britannica, 125n, 150n, 168n, 216n, 248
Enhydris, 169n, 179n
Epiphanius, 149n
Epopus, 131, 150
Equinox, 83n
Ercinee, 130
Erica, 19n
Ericius, 93
Eruca, 192, 194
Esau, 89
Escarius, 206, 208
Estridges, 121n
Ethiopia, 32, 35, 52, 55n, 61, 103, 167, 175n
Eton, 230n
Etymology, 37n, 52n, 169n, 217n, 226n, 245, 257
Eunuchs, 190n, 206. *See* Cut-offs and Castration

Euphrates, 18
Euphuists, 261
Evans, E. P., 8n, 15n, 26n, 71n, 93n,
    107n, 149n, 232, 236, 269, 271n
Ewes, Jacob's, 89

FABRICIUS, 19n
Falconers, 107n
Family Tree, 233. *See* also Influence,
    263
Family Tree, omission from, 235, 237
FeS$_2$, 227
Fellowes, Sir James, 67n
Fenix, *see* Phoenix
Fennel, 188
Ferret, 92n
Fig-tree, 159n, 218n
Fighter Pilots, 111n
Firestones, 226
Filson, Niels, 250
Fingers, 219n, 229n
Fish, 38n, 49n, 190n, 195 sqq.
Fish, anti-Jewish, 203n
Fish, flying, 199n
Fitchew, 92n
Flamingo, 125n, 133n
Fleas, 193
Flomus, *see* Mullein
Fowler, Osbert, 230, 230n
Fox, 7, 53, 94n
Fox, flying, 61n
Frog, 217
Fulica, 107, 122
Furnival, Richard de, 116n, 236n

GALANTHIS, 92n
Galatae, 85
Galen, 50n
Galli, 150
Gallus, 150
Ganesha, 255, 260
Ganges, 209

Garamantes, 62, 103, 103n
Garnett, David, 52n
Garuda, 22n, 255, 260
Gazelle, 41n
George V, King, 114n
George, Daniel, 113n, 271n
Gesner, 13n, 31n, 35n, 48n, 53n, 233,
    235, 236, 261, 263
Gesta Romanorum, 244
Gibbon, Edward, 70n
Giraldus Cambrensis, 197n, 238, 265,
    267
Gisbertus Germannus, 251
Gladius, 201
Glass, to glue, 153
Gnu, 55n
Goat, 35, 40, 42, 74, 172n
Goat, Holy, 41
Goat, blood of, 42, 190n
God, 213, 247
Goose, 152, 238, 267
Gold, medicinal, 151n
Golding, Arthur, 194
Goldsmith, 50n, 180n
Gorgon, 261, 265, 266
Gorreus, John, 177n
Goshawk, 121n
Graminia, 152
Graves, Robert, 36n, 253
Greece, 255
Griffin, 22, 48n, 52n, 190n, 255,
    261
Griffon Bruxellois and Vulture, 22n
Grus, 110
Guinness, 244
Guillaume le Clerc, 236n
Gulo, 31n

HAITI, 52n
Halcyon, 123
Halcyone, 124n
Hanuman, 255

287

288

295

White, Gilbert, 147n
Widowhood, 146
Wild West, 239
Williams, C. H., 25n
Willow, 218n
Wind, 137, 218n
Wine, 16n, 19
Wireless, 250
Wolf, 7, 56 sqq.
Wolf-hounds, 67
Women, 19, 89, 143, 146, 171 sqq., 219n, 222, 227, 246
Wood, Wild Men of, 36n
Wood-Martin, W. G., 250
Woodpecker, 115n, 138
Wordsworth, 145n
Worm, 10n, 191 sqq.

Wrasse, 208n
Wright, Thomas, 236
Wycliffe, 169n

XANAGARRA, 50n
Xiphias, 44n, 201, 266

YALE, 30n, 54, 77n, 261, 266
Ybis, see Ibis
Yena, 30 sqq., 48n
Yena Stone, 32
York, Duke of, 64n

ZABO, 32n
Ziffius, 44n, 201, 266
Zilio, 32n
Zodiac, 255

A CATALOG OF SELECTED
DOVER BOOKS
IN ALL FIELDS OF INTEREST

A CATALOG OF SELECTED DOVER
BOOKS IN ALL FIELDS OF INTEREST

CONCERNING THE SPIRITUAL IN ART, Wassily Kandinsky. Pioneering work by father of abstract art. Thoughts on color theory, nature of art. Analysis of earlier masters. 12 illustrations. 80pp. of text. 5⅜ × 8½.   23411-8 Pa. $3.95

ANIMALS: 1,419 Copyright-Free Illustrations of Mammals, Birds, Fish, Insects, etc., Jim Harter (ed.). Clear wood engravings present, in extremely lifelike poses, over 1,000 species of animals. One of the most extensive pictorial sourcebooks of its kind. Captions. Index. 284pp. 9 × 12.   23766-4 Pa. $10.95

CELTIC ART: The Methods of Construction, George Bain. Simple geometric techniques for making Celtic interlacements, spirals, Kells-type initials, animals, humans, etc. Over 500 illustrations. 160pp. 9 × 12. (USO)   22923-8 Pa. $8.95

AN ATLAS OF ANATOMY FOR ARTISTS, Fritz Schider. Most thorough reference work on art anatomy in the world. Hundreds of illustrations, including selections from works by Vesalius, Leonardo, Goya, Ingres, Michelangelo, others. 593 illustrations. 192pp. 7⅛ × 10¼.   20241-0 Pa. $8.95

CELTIC HAND STROKE-BY-STROKE (Irish Half-Uncial from "The Book of Kells"): An Arthur Baker Calligraphy Manual, Arthur Baker. Complete guide to creating each letter of the alphabet in distinctive Celtic manner. Covers hand position, strokes, pens, inks, paper, more. Illustrated. 48pp. 8¼ × 11.   24336-2 Pa. $3.95

EASY ORIGAMI, John Montroll. Charming collection of 32 projects (hat, cup, pelican, piano, swan, many more) specially designed for the novice origami hobbyist. Clearly illustrated easy-to-follow instructions insure that even beginning papercrafters will achieve successful results. 48pp. 8¼ × 11.   27298-2 Pa. $2.95

THE COMPLETE BOOK OF BIRDHOUSE CONSTRUCTION FOR WOODWORKERS, Scott D. Campbell. Detailed instructions, illustrations, tables. Also data on bird habitat and instinct patterns. Bibliography. 3 tables. 63 illustrations in 15 figures. 48pp. 5¼ × 8½.   24407-5 Pa. $1.95

BLOOMINGDALE'S ILLUSTRATED 1886 CATALOG: Fashions, Dry Goods and Housewares, Bloomingdale Brothers. Famed merchants' extremely rare catalog depicting about 1,700 products: clothing, housewares, firearms, dry goods, jewelry, more. Invaluable for dating, identifying vintage items. Also, copyright-free graphics for artists, designers. Co-published with Henry Ford Museum & Greenfield Village. 160pp. 8¼ × 11.   25780-0 Pa. $8.95

HISTORIC COSTUME IN PICTURES, Braun & Schneider. Over 1,450 costumed figures in clearly detailed engravings—from dawn of civilization to end of 19th century. Captions. Many folk costumes. 256pp. 8⅜ × 11¾.   23150-X Pa. $10.95

STICKLEY CRAFTSMAN FURNITURE CATALOGS, Gustav Stickley and L. & J. G. Stickley. Beautiful, functional furniture in two authentic catalogs from 1910. 594 illustrations, including 277 photos, show settles, rockers, armchairs, reclining chairs, bookcases, desks, tables. 183pp. 6½ × 9¼. 23838-5 Pa. $8.95

AMERICAN LOCOMOTIVES IN HISTORIC PHOTOGRAPHS: 1858 to 1949, Ron Ziel (ed.). A rare collection of 126 meticulously detailed official photographs, called "builder portraits," of American locomotives that majestically chronicle the rise of steam locomotive power in America. Introduction. Detailed captions. xi + 129pp. 9 × 12. 27393-8 Pa. $12.95

AMERICA'S LIGHTHOUSES: An Illustrated History, Francis Ross Holland, Jr. Delightfully written, profusely illustrated fact-filled survey of over 200 American lighthouses since 1716. History, anecdotes, technological advances, more. 240pp. 8 × 10¾. 25576-X Pa. $10.95

TOWARDS A NEW ARCHITECTURE, Le Corbusier. Pioneering manifesto by founder of "International School." Technical and aesthetic theories, views of industry, economics, relation of form to function, "mass-production split" and much more. Profusely illustrated. 320pp. 6⅛ × 9¼. (USO) 25023-7 Pa. $8.95

HOW THE OTHER HALF LIVES, Jacob Riis. Famous journalistic record, exposing poverty and degradation of New York slums around 1900, by major social reformer. 100 striking and influential photographs. 233pp. 10 × 7⅞. 22012-5 Pa $10.95

FRUIT KEY AND TWIG KEY TO TREES AND SHRUBS, William M. Harlow. One of the handiest and most widely used identification aids. Fruit key covers 120 deciduous and evergreen species; twig key 160 deciduous species. Easily used. Over 300 photographs. 126pp. 5⅜ × 8½. 20511-8 Pa. $2.95

COMMON BIRD SONGS, Dr. Donald J. Borror. Songs of 60 most common U.S. birds: robins, sparrows, cardinals, bluejays, finches, more—arranged in order of increasing complexity. Up to 9 variations of songs of each species. Cassette and manual 99911-4 $8.95

ORCHIDS AS HOUSE PLANTS, Rebecca Tyson Northen. Grow cattleyas and many other kinds of orchids—in a window, in a case, or under artificial light. 63 illustrations. 148pp. 5⅜ × 8½. 23261-1 Pa. $3.95

MONSTER MAZES, Dave Phillips. Masterful mazes at four levels of difficulty. Avoid deadly perils and evil creatures to find magical treasures. Solutions for all 32 exciting illustrated puzzles. 48pp. 8¼ × 11. 26005-4 Pa. $2.95

MOZART'S DON GIOVANNI (DOVER OPERA LIBRETTO SERIES), Wolfgang Amadeus Mozart. Introduced and translated by Ellen H. Bleiler. Standard Italian libretto, with complete English translation. Convenient and thoroughly portable—an ideal companion for reading along with a recording or the performance itself. Introduction. List of characters. Plot summary. 121pp. 5¼ × 8½. 24944-1 Pa. $2.95

TECHNICAL MANUAL AND DICTIONARY OF CLASSICAL BALLET, Gail Grant. Defines, explains, comments on steps, movements, poses and concepts. 15-page pictorial section. Basic book for student, viewer. 127pp. 5⅜ × 8½. 21843-0 Pa. $3.95

BRASS INSTRUMENTS: Their History and Development, Anthony Baines. Authoritative, updated survey of the evolution of trumpets, trombones, bugles, cornets, French horns, tubas and other brass wind instruments. Over 140 illustrations and 48 music examples. Corrected and updated by author. New preface. Bibliography. 320pp. $5\frac{3}{8} \times 8\frac{1}{2}$. 27574-4 Pa. $9.95

HOLLYWOOD GLAMOR PORTRAITS, John Kobal (ed.). 145 photos from 1926–49. Harlow, Gable, Bogart, Bacall; 94 stars in all. Full background on photographers, technical aspects. 160pp. $8\frac{3}{8} \times 11\frac{1}{4}$. 23352-9 Pa. $9.95

MAX AND MORITZ, Wilhelm Busch. Great humor classic in both German and English. Also 10 other works: "Cat and Mouse," "Plisch and Plumm," etc. 216pp. $5\frac{3}{8} \times 8\frac{1}{2}$. 20181-3 Pa. $5.95

THE RAVEN AND OTHER FAVORITE POEMS, Edgar Allan Poe. Over 40 of the author's most memorable poems: "The Bells," "Ulalume," "Israfel," "To Helen," "The Conqueror Worm," "Eldorado," "Annabel Lee," many more. Alphabetic lists of titles and first lines. 64pp. $5\frac{3}{16} \times 8\frac{1}{4}$. 26685-0 Pa. $1.00

SEVEN SCIENCE FICTION NOVELS, H. G. Wells. The standard collection of the great novels. Complete, unabridged. First Men in the Moon, Island of Dr. Moreau, War of the Worlds, Food of the Gods, Invisible Man, Time Machine, In the Days of the Comet. Total of 1,015pp. $5\frac{3}{8} \times 8\frac{1}{2}$. (USO) 20264-X Clothbd. $29.95

AMULETS AND SUPERSTITIONS, E. A. Wallis Budge. Comprehensive discourse on origin, powers of amulets in many ancient cultures: Arab, Persian, Babylonian, Assyrian, Egyptian, Gnostic, Hebrew, Phoenician, Syriac, etc. Covers cross, swastika, crucifix, seals, rings, stones, etc. 584pp. $5\frac{3}{8} \times 8\frac{1}{2}$. 23573-4 Pa. $10.95

RUSSIAN STORIES/PYCCKNE PACCKA3bl: A Dual-Language Book, edited by Gleb Struve. Twelve tales by such masters as Chekhov, Tolstoy, Dostoevsky, Pushkin, others. Excellent word-for-word English translations on facing pages, plus teaching and study aids, Russian/English vocabulary, biographical/critical introductions, more. 416pp. $5\frac{3}{8} \times 8\frac{1}{2}$. 26244-8 Pa. $7.95

PHILADELPHIA THEN AND NOW: 60 Sites Photographed in the Past and Present, Kenneth Finkel and Susan Oyama. Rare photographs of City Hall, Logan Square, Independence Hall, Betsy Ross House, other landmarks juxtaposed with contemporary views. Captures changing face of historic city. Introduction. Captions. 128pp. $8\frac{1}{4} \times 11$. 25790-8 Pa. $9.95

AIA ARCHITECTURAL GUIDE TO NASSAU AND SUFFOLK COUNTIES, LONG ISLAND, The American Institute of Architects, Long Island Chapter, and the Society for the Preservation of Long Island Antiquities. Comprehensive, well-researched and generously illustrated volume brings to life over three centuries of Long Island's great architectural heritage. More than 240 photographs with authoritative, extensively detailed captions. 176pp. $8\frac{1}{4} \times 11$. 26946-9 Pa. $14.95

NORTH AMERICAN INDIAN LIFE: Customs and Traditions of 23 Tribes, Elsie Clews Parsons (ed.). 27 fictionalized essays by noted anthropologists examine religion, customs, government, additional facets of life among the Winnebago, Crow, Zuni, Eskimo, other tribes. 480pp. $6\frac{1}{8} \times 9\frac{1}{4}$. 27377-6 Pa. $10.95

FRANK LLOYD WRIGHT'S HOLLYHOCK HOUSE, Donald Hoffmann. Lavishly illustrated, carefully documented study of one of Wright's most controversial residential designs. Over 120 photographs, floor plans, elevations, etc. Detailed perceptive text by noted Wright scholar. Index. 128pp. 9¼ × 10¾.
27133-1 Pa. $10.95

THE MALE AND FEMALE FIGURE IN MOTION: 60 Classic Photographic Sequences, Eadweard Muybridge. 60 true-action photographs of men and women walking, running, climbing, bending, turning, etc., reproduced from rare 19th-century masterpiece. vi + 121pp. 9 × 12. 24745-7 Pa. $10.95

1001 QUESTIONS ANSWERED ABOUT THE SEASHORE, N. J. Berrill and Jacquelyn Berrill. Queries answered about dolphins, sea snails, sponges, starfish, fishes, shore birds, many others. Covers appearance, breeding, growth, feeding, much more. 305pp. 5¼ × 8¼. 23366-9 Pa. $7.95

GUIDE TO OWL WATCHING IN NORTH AMERICA, Donald S. Heintzelman. Superb guide offers complete data and descriptions of 19 species: barn owl, screech owl, snowy owl, many more. Expert coverage of owl-watching equipment, conservation, migrations and invasions, etc. Guide to observing sites. 84 illustrations. xiii + 193pp. 5⅜ × 8½. 27344-X Pa. $7.95

MEDICINAL AND OTHER USES OF NORTH AMERICAN PLANTS: A Historical Survey with Special Reference to the Eastern Indian Tribes, Charlotte Erichsen-Brown. Chronological historical citations document 500 years of usage of plants, trees, shrubs native to eastern Canada, northeastern U.S. Also complete identifying information. 343 illustrations. 544pp. 6½ × 9¼. 25951-X Pa. $12.95

STORYBOOK MAZES, Dave Phillips. 23 stories and mazes on two-page spreads: Wizard of Oz, Treasure Island, Robin Hood, etc. Solutions. 64pp. 8¼ × 11.
23628-5 Pa. $2.95

NEGRO FOLK MUSIC, U.S.A., Harold Courlander. Noted folklorist's scholarly yet readable analysis of rich and varied musical tradition. Includes authentic versions of over 40 folk songs. Valuable bibliography and discography. xi + 324pp. 5⅜ × 8½. 27350-4 Pa. $7.95

MOVIE-STAR PORTRAITS OF THE FORTIES, John Kobal (ed.). 163 glamor, studio photos of 106 stars of the 1940s: Rita Hayworth, Ava Gardner, Marlon Brando, Clark Gable, many more. 176pp. 8⅜ × 11¼. 23546-7 Pa. $10.95

BENCHLEY LOST AND FOUND, Robert Benchley. Finest humor from early 30s, about pet peeves, child psychologists, post office and others. Mostly unavailable elsewhere. 73 illustrations by Peter Arno and others. 183pp. 5⅜ × 8½.
22410-4 Pa. $4.95

YEKL and THE IMPORTED BRIDEGROOM AND OTHER STORIES OF YIDDISH NEW YORK, Abraham Cahan. Film Hester Street based on Yekl (1896). Novel, other stories among first about Jewish immigrants on N.Y.'s East Side. 240pp. 5⅜ × 8½. 22427-9 Pa. $5.95

SELECTED POEMS, Walt Whitman. Generous sampling from *Leaves of Grass*. Twenty-four poems include "I Hear America Singing," "Song of the Open Road," "I Sing the Body Electric," "When Lilacs Last in the Dooryard Bloom'd," "O Captain! My Captain!"—all reprinted from an authoritative edition. Lists of titles and first lines. 128pp. 5³⁄₁₆ × 8¼. 26878-0 Pa. $1.00

THE BEST TALES OF HOFFMANN, E. T. A. Hoffmann. 10 of Hoffmann's most important stories: "Nutcracker and the King of Mice," "The Golden Flowerpot," etc. 458pp. 5⅜ × 8½. 21793-0 Pa. $8.95

FROM FETISH TO GOD IN ANCIENT EGYPT, E. A. Wallis Budge. Rich detailed survey of Egyptian conception of "God" and gods, magic, cult of animals, Osiris, more. Also, superb English translations of hymns and legends. 240 illustrations. 545pp. 5⅜ × 8½. 25803-3 Pa. $10.95

FRENCH STORIES/CONTES FRANÇAIS: A Dual-Language Book, Wallace Fowlie. Ten stories by French masters, Voltaire to Camus: "Micromegas" by Voltaire; "The Atheist's Mass" by Balzac; "Minuet" by de Maupassant; "The Guest" by Camus, six more. Excellent English translations on facing pages. Also French-English vocabulary list, exercises, more. 352pp. 5⅜ × 8½. 26443-2 Pa. $8.95

CHICAGO AT THE TURN OF THE CENTURY IN PHOTOGRAPHS: 122 Historic Views from the Collections of the Chicago Historical Society, Larry A. Viskochil. Rare large-format prints offer detailed views of City Hall, State Street, the Loop, Hull House, Union Station, many other landmarks, circa 1904–1913. Introduction. Captions. Maps. 144pp. 9⅜ × 12¼. 24656-6 Pa. $12.95

OLD BROOKLYN IN EARLY PHOTOGRAPHS, 1865–1929, William Lee Younger. Luna Park, Gravesend race track, construction of Grand Army Plaza, moving of Hotel Brighton, etc. 157 previously unpublished photographs. 165pp. 8⅞ × 11¾. 23587-4 Pa. $12.95

THE MYTHS OF THE NORTH AMERICAN INDIANS, Lewis Spence. Rich anthology of the myths and legends of the Algonquins, Iroquois, Pawnees and Sioux, prefaced by an extensive historical and ethnological commentary. 36 illustrations. 480pp. 5⅜ × 8½. 25967-6 Pa. $8.95

AN ENCYCLOPEDIA OF BATTLES: Accounts of Over 1,560 Battles from 1479 B.C. to the Present, David Eggenberger. Essential details of every major battle in recorded history from the first battle of Megiddo in 1479 B.C. to Grenada in 1984. List of Battle Maps. New Appendix covering the years 1967–1984. Index. 99 illustrations. 544pp. 6½ × 9¼. 24913-1 Pa. $14.95

SAILING ALONE AROUND THE WORLD, Captain Joshua Slocum. First man to sail around the world, alone, in small boat. One of great feats of seamanship told in delightful manner. 67 illustrations. 294pp. 5⅜ × 8½. 20326-3 Pa. $4.95

ANARCHISM AND OTHER ESSAYS, Emma Goldman. Powerful, penetrating, prophetic essays on direct action, role of minorities, prison reform, puritan hypocrisy, violence, etc. 271pp. 5⅜ × 8½. 22484-8 Pa. $5.95

MYTHS OF THE HINDUS AND BUDDHISTS, Ananda K. Coomaraswamy and Sister Nivedita. Great stories of the epics; deeds of Krishna, Shiva, taken from puranas, Vedas, folk tales; etc. 32 illustrations. 400pp. 5⅜ × 8½. 21759-0 Pa. $8.95

BEYOND PSYCHOLOGY, Otto Rank. Fear of death, desire of immortality, nature of sexuality, social organization, creativity, according to Rankian system. 291pp. 5⅜ × 8½. 20485-5 Pa. $7.95

A THEOLOGICO-POLITICAL TREATISE, Benedict Spinoza. Also contains unfinished Political Treatise. Great classic on religious liberty, theory of government on common consent. R. Elwes translation. Total of 421pp. 5⅜ × 8½. 20249-6 Pa. $7.95

CATALOG OF DOVER BOOKS

MY BONDAGE AND MY FREEDOM, Frederick Douglass. Born a slave, Douglass became outspoken force in antislavery movement. The best of Douglass' autobiographies. Graphic description of slave life. 464pp. 5⅜ × 8½. 22457-0 Pa. $7.95

FOLLOWING THE EQUATOR: A Journey Around the World, Mark Twain. Fascinating humorous account of 1897 voyage to Hawaii, Australia, India, New Zealand, etc. Ironic, bemused reports on peoples, customs, climate, flora and fauna, politics, much more. 197 illustrations. 720pp. 5⅜ × 8½. 26113-1 Pa. $15.95

THE PEOPLE CALLED SHAKERS, Edward D. Andrews. Definitive study of Shakers: origins, beliefs, practices, dances, social organization, furniture and crafts, etc. 33 illustrations. 351pp. 5⅜ × 8½. 21081-2 Pa. $7.95

THE MYTHS OF GREECE AND ROME, H. A. Guerber. A classic of mythology, generously illustrated, long prized for its simple, graphic, accurate retelling of the principal myths of Greece and Rome, and for its commentary on their origins and significance. With 64 illustrations by Michelangelo, Raphael, Titian, Rubens, Canova, Bernini and others. 480pp. 5⅜ × 8½. 27584-1 Pa. $9.95

PSYCHOLOGY OF MUSIC, Carl E. Seashore. Classic work discusses music as a medium from psychological viewpoint. Clear treatment of physical acoustics, auditory apparatus, sound perception, development of musical skills, nature of musical feeling, host of other topics. 88 figures. 408pp. 5⅜ × 8½. 21851-1 Pa. $8.95

THE PHILOSOPHY OF HISTORY, Georg W. Hegel. Great classic of Western thought develops concept that history is not chance but rational process, the evolution of freedom. 457pp. 5⅜ × 8½. 20112-0 Pa. $8.95

THE BOOK OF TEA, Kakuzo Okakura. Minor classic of the Orient: entertaining, charming explanation, interpretation of traditional Japanese culture in terms of tea ceremony. 94pp. 5⅜ × 8½. 20070-1 Pa. $2.95

LIFE IN ANCIENT EGYPT, Adolf Erman. Fullest, most thorough, detailed older account with much not in more recent books, domestic life, religion, magic, medicine, commerce, much more. Many illustrations reproduce tomb paintings, carvings, hieroglyphs, etc. 597pp. 5⅜ × 8½. 22632-8 Pa. $9.95

SUNDIALS, Their Theory and Construction, Albert Waugh. Far and away the best, most thorough coverage of ideas, mathematics concerned, types, construction, adjusting anywhere. Simple, nontechnical treatment allows even children to build several of these dials. Over 100 illustrations. 230pp. 5⅜ × 8½. 22947-5 Pa. $5.95

DYNAMICS OF FLUIDS IN POROUS MEDIA, Jacob Bear. For advanced students of ground water hydrology, soil mechanics and physics, drainage and irrigation engineering, and more. 335 illustrations. Exercises, with answers. 784pp. 6⅛ × 9¼. 65675-6 Pa. $19.95

SONGS OF EXPERIENCE: Facsimile Reproduction with 26 Plates in Full Color, William Blake. 26 full-color plates from a rare 1826 edition. Includes "The Tyger," "London," "Holy Thursday," and other poems. Printed text of poems. 48pp. 5¼ × 7. 24636-1 Pa. $3.95

OLD-TIME VIGNETTES IN FULL COLOR, Carol Belanger Grafton (ed.). Over 390 charming, often sentimental illustrations, selected from archives of Victorian graphics—pretty women posing, children playing, food, flowers, kittens and puppies, smiling cherubs, birds and butterflies, much more. All copyright-free. 48pp. 9¼ × 12¼. 27269-9 Pa. $5.95

PERSPECTIVE FOR ARTISTS, Rex Vicat Cole. Depth, perspective of sky and sea, shadows, much more, not usually covered. 391 diagrams, 81 reproductions of drawings and paintings. 279pp. 5⅜ × 8½. 22487-2 Pa. $6.95

DRAWING THE LIVING FIGURE, Joseph Sheppard. Innovative approach to artistic anatomy focuses on specifics of surface anatomy, rather than muscles and bones. Over 170 drawings of live models in front, back and side views, and in widely varying poses. Accompanying diagrams. 177 illustrations. Introduction. Index. 144pp. 8⅜ × 11¼. 26723-7 Pa. $7.95

GOTHIC AND OLD ENGLISH ALPHABETS: 100 Complete Fonts, Dan X. Solo. Add power, elegance to posters, signs, other graphics with 100 stunning copyright-free alphabets: Blackstone, Dolbey, Germania, 97 more—including many lower-case, numerals, punctuation marks. 104pp. 8⅛ × 11. 24695-7 Pa. $6.95

HOW TO DO BEADWORK, Mary White. Fundamental book on craft from simple projects to five-bead chains and woven works. 106 illustrations. 142pp. 5⅜ × 8. 20697-1 Pa. $4.95

THE BOOK OF WOOD CARVING, Charles Marshall Sayers. Finest book for beginners discusses fundamentals and offers 34 designs. "Absolutely first rate . . . well thought out and well executed."—E. J. Tangerman. 118pp. 7¾ × 10⅝. 23654-4 Pa. $5.95

ILLUSTRATED CATALOG OF CIVIL WAR MILITARY GOODS: Union Army Weapons, Insignia, Uniform Accessories, and Other Equipment, Schuyler, Hartley, and Graham. Rare, profusely illustrated 1846 catalog includes Union Army uniform and dress regulations, arms and ammunition, coats, insignia, flags, swords, rifles, etc. 226 illustrations. 160pp. 9 × 12. 24939-5 Pa. $10.95

WOMEN'S FASHIONS OF THE EARLY 1900s: An Unabridged Republication of "New York Fashions, 1909," National Cloak & Suit Co. Rare catalog of mail-order fashions documents women's and children's clothing styles shortly after the turn of the century. Captions offer full descriptions, prices. Invaluable resource for fashion, costume historians. Approximately 725 illustrations. 128pp. 8⅜ × 11¼. 27276-1 Pa. $10.95

THE 1912 AND 1915 GUSTAV STICKLEY FURNITURE CATALOGS, Gustav Stickley. With over 200 detailed illustrations and descriptions, these two catalogs are essential reading and reference materials and identification guides for Stickley furniture. Captions cite materials, dimensions and prices. 112pp. 6½ × 9¼. 26676-1 Pa. $9.95

EARLY AMERICAN LOCOMOTIVES, John H. White, Jr. Finest locomotive engravings from early 19th century: historical (1804–74), main-line (after 1870), special, foreign, etc. 147 plates. 142pp. 11⅜ × 8¼. 22772-3 Pa. $8.95

THE TALL SHIPS OF TODAY IN PHOTOGRAPHS, Frank O. Braynard. Lavishly illustrated tribute to nearly 100 majestic contemporary sailing vessels: Amerigo Vespucci, Clearwater, Constitution, Eagle, Mayflower, Sea Cloud, Victory, many more. Authoritative captions provide statistics, background on each ship. 190 black-and-white photographs and illustrations. Introduction. 128pp. 8⅞ × 11¾. 27163-3 Pa. $12.95

EARLY NINETEENTH-CENTURY CRAFTS AND TRADES, Peter Stockham (ed.). Extremely rare 1807 volume describes to youngsters the crafts and trades of the day: brickmaker, weaver, dressmaker, bookbinder, ropemaker, saddler, many more. Quaint prose, charming illustrations for each craft. 20 black-and-white line illustrations. 192pp. 4⅜ × 6. 27293-1 Pa. $4.95

VICTORIAN FASHIONS AND COSTUMES FROM HARPER'S BAZAR, 1867-1898, Stella Blum (ed.). Day costumes, evening wear, sports clothes, shoes, hats, other accessories in over 1,000 detailed engravings. 320pp. 9⅜ × 12¼. 22990-4 Pa. $12.95

GUSTAV STICKLEY, THE CRAFTSMAN, Mary Ann Smith. Superb study surveys broad scope of Stickley's achievement, especially in architecture. Design philosophy, rise and fall of the Craftsman empire, descriptions and floor plans for many Craftsman houses, more. 86 black-and-white halftones. 31 line illustrations. Introduction. 208pp. 6½ × 9¼. 27210-9 Pa. $9.95

THE LONG ISLAND RAIL ROAD IN EARLY PHOTOGRAPHS, Ron Ziel. Over 220 rare photos, informative text document origin (1844) and development of rail service on Long Island. Vintage views of early trains, locomotives, stations, passengers, crews, much more. Captions. 8⅞ × 11¾. 26301-0 Pa. $13.95

THE BOOK OF OLD SHIPS: From Egyptian Galleys to Clipper Ships, Henry B. Culver. Superb, authoritative history of sailing vessels, with 80 magnificent line illustrations. Galley, bark, caravel, longship, whaler, many more. Detailed, informative text on each vessel by noted naval historian. Introduction. 256pp. 5⅜ × 8½. 27332-6 Pa. $6.95

TEN BOOKS ON ARCHITECTURE, Vitruvius. The most important book ever written on architecture. Early Roman aesthetics, technology, classical orders, site selection, all other aspects. Morgan translation. 331pp. 5⅜ × 8½. 20645-9 Pa. $8.95

THE HUMAN FIGURE IN MOTION, Eadweard Muybridge. More than 4,500 stopped-action photos, in action series, showing undraped men, women, children jumping, lying down, throwing, sitting, wrestling, carrying, etc. 390pp. 7⅞ × 10⅝. 20204-6 Clothbd. $24.95

TREES OF THE EASTERN AND CENTRAL UNITED STATES AND CANADA, William M. Harlow. Best one-volume guide to 140 trees. Full descriptions, woodlore, range, etc. Over 600 illustrations. Handy size. 288pp. 4½ × 6⅜. 20395-6 Pa. $4.95

SONGS OF WESTERN BIRDS, Dr. Donald J. Borror. Complete song and call repertoire of 60 western species, including flycatchers, juncoes, cactus wrens, many more—includes fully illustrated booklet. Cassette and manual 99913-0 $8.95

GROWING AND USING HERBS AND SPICES, Milo Miloradovich. Versatile handbook provides all the information needed for cultivation and use of all the herbs and spices available in North America. 4 illustrations. Index. Glossary. 236pp. 5⅜ × 8½. 25058-X Pa. $5.95

BIG BOOK OF MAZES AND LABYRINTHS, Walter Shepherd. 50 mazes and labyrinths in all—classical, solid, ripple, and more—in one great volume. Perfect inexpensive puzzler for clever youngsters. Full solutions. 112pp. 8⅛ × 11. 22951-3 Pa. $3.95

PIANO TUNING, J. Cree Fischer. Clearest, best book for beginner, amateur. Simple repairs, raising dropped notes, tuning by easy method of flattened fifths. No previous skills needed. 4 illustrations. 201pp. 5⅜ × 8½. 23267-0 Pa. $4.95

A SOURCE BOOK IN THEATRICAL HISTORY, A. M. Nagler. Contemporary observers on acting, directing, make-up, costuming, stage props, machinery, scene design, from Ancient Greece to Chekhov. 611pp. 5⅜ × 8½. 20515-0 Pa. $10.95

THE COMPLETE NONSENSE OF EDWARD LEAR, Edward Lear. All nonsense limericks, zany alphabets, Owl and Pussycat, songs, nonsense botany, etc., illustrated by Lear. Total of 320pp. 5⅜ × 8½. (USO) 20167-8 Pa. $5.95

VICTORIAN PARLOUR POETRY: An Annotated Anthology, Michael R. Turner. 117 gems by Longfellow, Tennyson, Browning, many lesser-known poets. "The Village Blacksmith," "Curfew Must Not Ring Tonight," "Only a Baby Small," dozens more, often difficult to find elsewhere. Index of poets, titles, first lines. xxiii + 325pp. 5⅜ × 8¼. 27044-0 Pa. $7.95

DUBLINERS, James Joyce. Fifteen stories offer vivid, tightly focused observations of the lives of Dublin's poorer classes. At least one, "The Dead," is considered a masterpiece. Reprinted complete and unabridged from standard edition. 160pp. 5³⁄₁₆ × 8¼. 26870-5 Pa. $1.00

THE HAUNTED MONASTERY and THE CHINESE MAZE MURDERS, Robert van Gulik. Two full novels by van Gulik, set in 7th-century China, continue adventures of Judge Dee and his companions. An evil Taoist monastery, seemingly supernatural events; overgrown topiary maze hides strange crimes. 27 illustrations. 328pp. 5⅜ × 8½. 23502-5 Pa. $7.95

THE BOOK OF THE SACRED MAGIC OF ABRAMELIN THE MAGE, translated by S. MacGregor Mathers. Medieval manuscript of ceremonial magic. Basic document in Aleister Crowley, Golden Dawn groups. 268pp. 5⅜ × 8½. 23211-5 Pa. $7.95

NEW RUSSIAN-ENGLISH AND ENGLISH-RUSSIAN DICTIONARY, M. A. O'Brien. This is a remarkably handy Russian dictionary, containing a surprising amount of information, including over 70,000 entries. 366pp. 4½ × 6⅛. 20208-9 Pa. $8.95

HISTORIC HOMES OF THE AMERICAN PRESIDENTS, Second, Revised Edition, Irvin Haas. A traveler's guide to American Presidential homes, most open to the public, depicting and describing homes occupied by every American President from George Washington to George Bush. With visiting hours, admission charges, travel routes. 175 photographs. Index. 160pp. 8¼ × 11. 26751-2 Pa. $10.95

NEW YORK IN THE FORTIES, Andreas Feininger. 162 brilliant photographs by the well-known photographer, formerly with *Life* magazine. Commuters, shoppers, Times Square at night, much else from city at its peak. Captions by John von Hartz. 181pp. 9¼ × 10¾. 23585-8 Pa. $12.95

INDIAN SIGN LANGUAGE, William Tomkins. Over 525 signs developed by Sioux and other tribes. Written instructions and diagrams. Also 290 pictographs. 111pp. 6⅛ × 9¼. 22029-X Pa. $3.50

ANATOMY: A Complete Guide for Artists, Joseph Sheppard. A master of figure drawing shows artists how to render human anatomy convincingly. Over 460 illustrations. 224pp. 8⅜ × 11¼. 27279-6 Pa. $9.95

MEDIEVAL CALLIGRAPHY: Its History and Technique, Marc Drogin. Spirited history, comprehensive instruction manual covers 13 styles (ca. 4th century thru 15th). Excellent photographs; directions for duplicating medieval techniques with modern tools. 224pp. 8⅜ × 11¼. 26142-5 Pa. $11.95

DRIED FLOWERS: How to Prepare Them, Sarah Whitlock and Martha Rankin. Complete instructions on how to use silica gel, meal and borax, perlite aggregate, sand and borax, glycerine and water to create attractive permanent flower arrangements. 12 illustrations. 32pp. 5⅜ × 8½. 21802-3 Pa. $1.00

EASY-TO-MAKE BIRD FEEDERS FOR WOODWORKERS, Scott D. Campbell. Detailed, simple-to-use guide for designing, constructing, caring for and using feeders. Text, illustrations for 12 classic and contemporary designs. 96pp. 5⅜ × 8½. 25847-5 Pa. $2.95

OLD-TIME CRAFTS AND TRADES, Peter Stockham. An 1807 book created to teach children about crafts and trades open to them as future careers. It describes in detailed, nontechnical terms 24 different occupations, among them coachmaker, gardener, hairdresser, lacemaker, shoemaker, wheelwright, copper-plate printer, milliner, trunkmaker, merchant and brewer. Finely detailed engravings illustrate each occupation. 192pp. 4⅝ × 6. 27398-9 Pa. $4.95

THE HISTORY OF UNDERCLOTHES, C. Willett Cunnington and Phyllis Cunnington. Fascinating, well-documented survey covering six centuries of English undergarments, enhanced with over 100 illustrations: 12th-century laced-up bodice, footed long drawers (1795), 19th-century bustles, 19th-century corsets for men, Victorian "bust improvers," much more. 272pp. 5⅜ × 8¼. 27124-2 Pa. $9.95

ARTS AND CRAFTS FURNITURE: The Complete Brooks Catalog of 1912, Brooks Manufacturing Co. Photos and detailed descriptions of more than 150 now very collectible furniture designs from the Arts and Crafts movement depict davenports, settees, buffets, desks, tables, chairs, bedsteads, dressers and more, all built of solid, quarter-sawed oak. Invaluable for students and enthusiasts of antiques, Americana and the decorative arts. 80pp. 6½ × 9¼. 27471-3 Pa. $7.95

HOW WE INVENTED THE AIRPLANE: An Illustrated History, Orville Wright. Fascinating firsthand account covers early experiments, construction of planes and motors, first flights, much more. Introduction and commentary by Fred C. Kelly. 76 photographs. 96pp. 8¼ × 11. 25662-6 Pa. $7.95

THE ARTS OF THE SAILOR: Knotting, Splicing and Ropework, Hervey Garrett Smith. Indispensable shipboard reference covers tools, basic knots and useful hitches; handsewing and canvas work, more. Over 100 illustrations. Delightful reading for sea lovers. 256pp. 5⅜ × 8½. 26440-8 Pa. $6.95

FRANK LLOYD WRIGHT'S FALLINGWATER: The House and Its History, Second, Revised Edition, Donald Hoffmann. A total revision—both in text and illustrations—of the standard document on Fallingwater, the boldest, most personal architectural statement of Wright's mature years, updated with valuable new material from the recently opened Frank Lloyd Wright Archives. "Fascinating"—The New York Times. 116 illustrations. 128pp. 9¼ × 10¾. 27430-6 Pa. $10.95

PHOTOGRAPHIC SKETCHBOOK OF THE CIVIL WAR, Alexander Gardner. 100 photos taken on field during the Civil War. Famous shots of Manassas, Harper's Ferry, Lincoln, Richmond, slave pens, etc. 244pp. 10⅝ × 8¼.
22731-6 Pa. $9.95

FIVE ACRES AND INDEPENDENCE, Maurice G. Kains. Great back-to-the-land classic explains basics of self-sufficient farming. The one book to get. 95 illustrations. 397pp. 5⅜ × 8½.
20974-1 Pa. $6.95

SONGS OF EASTERN BIRDS, Dr. Donald J. Borror. Songs and calls of 60 species most common to eastern U.S.: warblers, woodpeckers, flycatchers, thrushes, larks, many more in high-quality recording.
Cassette and manual 99912-2 $8.95

A MODERN HERBAL, Margaret Grieve. Much the fullest, most exact, most useful compilation of herbal material. Gigantic alphabetical encyclopedia, from aconite to zedoary, gives botanical information, medical properties, folklore, economic uses, much else. Indispensable to serious reader. 161 illustrations. 888pp. 6½ × 9¼.
2-vol. set. (USO)
Vol. I: 22798-7 Pa. $9.95
Vol. II: 22799-5 Pa. $9.95

HIDDEN TREASURE MAZE BOOK, Dave Phillips. Solve 34 challenging mazes accompanied by heroic tales of adventure. Evil dragons, people-eating plants, bloodthirsty giants, many more dangerous adversaries lurk at every twist and turn. 34 mazes, stories, solutions. 48pp. 8¼ × 11.
24566-7 Pa. $2.95

LETTERS OF W. A. MOZART, Wolfgang A. Mozart. Remarkable letters show bawdy wit, humor, imagination, musical insights, contemporary musical world; includes some letters from Leopold Mozart. 276pp. 5⅜ × 8½.
22859-2 Pa. $6.95

BASIC PRINCIPLES OF CLASSICAL BALLET, Agrippina Vaganova. Great Russian theoretician, teacher explains methods for teaching classical ballet. 118 illustrations. 175pp. 5⅜ × 8½.
22036-2 Pa. $3.95

THE JUMPING FROG, Mark Twain. Revenge edition. The original story of The Celebrated Jumping Frog of Calaveras County, a hapless French translation, and Twain's hilarious "retranslation" from the French. 12 illustrations. 66pp. 5⅜ × 8½.
22686-7 Pa. $3.50

BEST REMEMBERED POEMS, Martin Gardner (ed.). The 126 poems in this superb collection of 19th- and 20th-century British and American verse range from Shelley's "To a Skylark" to the impassioned "Renascence" of Edna St. Vincent Millay and to Edward Lear's whimsical "The Owl and the Pussycat." 224pp. 5⅜ × 8½.
27165-X Pa. $3.95

COMPLETE SONNETS, William Shakespeare. Over 150 exquisite poems deal with love, friendship, the tyranny of time, beauty's evanescence, death and other themes in language of remarkable power, precision and beauty. Glossary of archaic terms. 80pp. 5³⁄₁₆ × 8¼.
26686-9 Pa. $1.00

BODIES IN A BOOKSHOP, R. T. Campbell. Challenging mystery of blackmail and murder with ingenious plot and superbly drawn characters. In the best tradition of British suspense fiction. 192pp. 5⅜ × 8½.
24720-1 Pa. $5.95

THE WIT AND HUMOR OF OSCAR WILDE, Alvin Redman (ed.). More than 1,000 ripostes, paradoxes, wisecracks: Work is the curse of the drinking classes; I can resist everything except temptation; etc. 258pp. 5⅜ × 8½. 20602-5 Pa. $4.95

SHAKESPEARE LEXICON AND QUOTATION DICTIONARY, Alexander Schmidt. Full definitions, locations, shades of meaning in every word in plays and poems. More than 50,000 exact quotations. 1,485pp. 6½ × 9¼. 2-vol. set.
Vol. 1: 22726-X Pa. $15.95
Vol. 2: 22727-8 Pa. $15.95

SELECTED POEMS, Emily Dickinson. Over 100 best-known, best-loved poems by one of America's foremost poets, reprinted from authoritative early editions. No comparable edition at this price. Index of first lines. 64pp. 5³/₁₆ × 8¼.
26466-1 Pa. $1.00

CELEBRATED CASES OF JUDGE DEE (DEE GOONG AN), translated by Robert van Gulik. Authentic 18th-century Chinese detective novel; Dee and associates solve three interlocked cases. Led to van Gulik's own stories with same characters. Extensive introduction. 9 illustrations. 237pp. 5⅜ × 8½.
23337-5 Pa. $5.95

THE MALLEUS MALEFICARUM OF KRAMER AND SPRENGER, translated by Montague Summers. Full text of most important witchhunter's "bible," used by both Catholics and Protestants. 278pp. 6⅝ × 10. 22802-9 Pa. $10.95

SPANISH STORIES/CUENTOS ESPAÑOLES: A Dual-Language Book, Angel Flores (ed.). Unique format offers 13 great stories in Spanish by Cervantes, Borges, others. Faithful English translations on facing pages. 352pp. 5⅜ × 8½.
25399-6 Pa. $7.95

THE CHICAGO WORLD'S FAIR OF 1893: A Photographic Record, Stanley Appelbaum (ed.). 128 rare photos show 200 buildings, Beaux-Arts architecture, Midway, original Ferris Wheel, Edison's kinetoscope, more. Architectural emphasis; full text. 116pp. 8¼ × 11. 23990-X Pa. $9.95

OLD QUEENS, N.Y., IN EARLY PHOTOGRAPHS, Vincent F. Seyfried and William Asadorian. Over 160 rare photographs of Maspeth, Jamaica, Jackson Heights, and other areas. Vintage views of DeWitt Clinton mansion, 1939 World's Fair and more. Captions. 192pp. 8⅞ × 11. 26358-4 Pa. $12.95

CAPTURED BY THE INDIANS: 15 Firsthand Accounts, 1750–1870, Frederick Drimmer. Astounding true historical accounts of grisly torture, bloody conflicts, relentless pursuits, miraculous escapes and more, by people who lived to tell the tale. 384pp. 5⅜ × 8½. 24901-8 Pa. $7.95

THE WORLD'S GREAT SPEECHES, Lewis Copeland and Lawrence W. Lamm (eds.). Vast collection of 278 speeches of Greeks to 1970. Powerful and effective models; unique look at history. 842pp. 5⅜ × 8½. 20468-5 Pa. $12.95

THE BOOK OF THE SWORD, Sir Richard F. Burton. Great Victorian scholar/adventurer's eloquent, erudite history of the "queen of weapons"—from prehistory to early Roman Empire. Evolution and development of early swords, variations (sabre, broadsword, cutlass, scimitar, etc.), much more. 336pp. 6⅛ × 9¼. 25434-8 Pa. $8.95

AUTOBIOGRAPHY: The Story of My Experiments with Truth, Mohandas K. Gandhi. Boyhood, legal studies, purification, the growth of the Satyagraha (nonviolent protest) movement. Critical, inspiring work of the man responsible for the freedom of India. 480pp. 5⅜ × 8½. (USO) 24593-4 Pa. $6.95

CELTIC MYTHS AND LEGENDS, T. W. Rolleston. Masterful retelling of Irish and Welsh stories and tales. Cuchulain, King Arthur, Deirdre, the Grail, many more. First paperback edition. 58 full-page illustrations. 512pp. 5⅜ × 8½. 26507-2 Pa. $9.95

THE PRINCIPLES OF PSYCHOLOGY, William James. Famous long course complete, unabridged. Stream of thought, time perception, memory, experimental methods; great work decades ahead of its time. 94 figures. 1,391pp. 5⅜×8½. 2-vol. set.
Vol. I: 20381-6 Pa. $12.95
Vol. II: 20382-4 Pa. $12.95

THE WORLD AS WILL AND REPRESENTATION, Arthur Schopenhauer. Definitive English translation of Schopenhauer's life work, correcting more than 1,000 errors, omissions in earlier translations. Translated by E. F. J. Payne. Total of 1,269pp. 5⅜ × 8½. 2-vol. set.
Vol. 1: 21761-2 Pa. $10.95
Vol. 2: 21762-0 Pa. $11.95

MAGIC AND MYSTERY IN TIBET, Madame Alexandra David-Neel. Experiences among lamas, magicians, sages, sorcerers, Bonpa wizards. A true psychic discovery. 32 illustrations. 321pp. 5⅜ × 8½. (USO) 22682-4 Pa. $7.95

THE EGYPTIAN BOOK OF THE DEAD, E. A. Wallis Budge. Complete reproduction of Ani's papyrus, finest ever found. Full hieroglyphic text, interlinear transliteration, word-for-word translation, smooth translation. 533pp. 6½ × 9¼. 21866-X Pa. $9.95

MATHEMATICS FOR THE NONMATHEMATICIAN, Morris Kline. Detailed, college-level treatment of mathematics in cultural and historical context, with numerous exercises. Recommended Reading Lists. Tables. Numerous figures. 641pp. 5⅜ × 8½. 24823-2 Pa. $11.95

THEORY OF WING SECTIONS: Including a Summary of Airfoil Data, Ira H. Abbott and A. E. von Doenhoff. Concise compilation of subsonic aerodynamic characteristics of NACA wing sections, plus description of theory. 350pp. of tables. 693pp. 5⅜ × 8½. 60586-8 Pa. $13.95

THE RIME OF THE ANCIENT MARINER, Gustave Doré, S. T. Coleridge. Doré's finest work; 34 plates capture moods, subtleties of poem. Flawless full-size reproductions printed on facing pages with authoritative text of poem. "Beautiful. Simply beautiful."—Publisher's Weekly. 77pp. 9¼ × 12. 22305-1 Pa. $5.95

NORTH AMERICAN INDIAN DESIGNS FOR ARTISTS AND CRAFTS-PEOPLE, Eva Wilson. Over 360 authentic copyright-free designs adapted from Navajo blankets, Hopi pottery, Sioux buffalo hides, more. Geometrics, symbolic figures, plant and animal motifs, etc. 128pp. 8⅜ × 11. (EUK) 25341-4 Pa. $6.95

SCULPTURE: Principles and Practice, Louis Slobodkin. Step-by-step approach to clay, plaster, metals, stone; classical and modern. 253 drawings, photos. 255pp. 8⅛ × 11. 22960-2 Pa. $9.95

THE INFLUENCE OF SEA POWER UPON HISTORY, 1660–1783, A. T. Mahan. Influential classic of naval history and tactics still used as text in war colleges. First paperback edition. 4 maps. 24 battle plans. 640pp. 5⅜ × 8½.
25509-3 Pa. $12.95

THE STORY OF THE TITANIC AS TOLD BY ITS SURVIVORS, Jack Winocour (ed.). What it was really like. Panic, despair, shocking inefficiency, and a little heroism. More thrilling than any fictional account. 26 illustrations. 320pp. 5⅜ × 8½. 20610-6 Pa. $7.95

FAIRY AND FOLK TALES OF THE IRISH PEASANTRY, William Butler Yeats (ed.). Treasury of 64 tales from the twilight world of Celtic myth and legend: "The Soul Cages," "The Kildare Pooka," "King O'Toole and his Goose," many more. Introduction and Notes by W. B. Yeats. 352pp. 5⅜ × 8½. 26941-8 Pa. $7.95

BUDDHIST MAHAYANA TEXTS, E. B. Cowell and Others (eds.). Superb, accurate translations of basic documents in Mahayana Buddhism, highly important in history of religions. The Buddha-karita of Asvaghosha, Larger Sukhavativyuha, more. 448pp. 5⅜ × 8½. , 25552-2 Pa. $9.95

ONE TWO THREE . . . INFINITY: Facts and Speculations of Science, George Gamow. Great physicist's fascinating, readable overview of contemporary science: number theory, relativity, fourth dimension, entropy, genes, atomic structure, much more. 128 illustrations. Index. 352pp. 5⅜ × 8½. 25664-2 Pa. $7.95

ENGINEERING IN HISTORY, Richard Shelton Kirby, et al. Broad, nontechnical survey of history's major technological advances: birth of Greek science, industrial revolution, electricity and applied science, 20th-century automation, much more. 181 illustrations. ". . . excellent . . ."—Isis. Bibliography. vii + 530pp. 5⅜ × 8¼.
26412-2 Pa. $13.95

Prices subject to change without notice.
Available at your book dealer or write for free catalog to Dept. GI, Dover Publications, Inc., 31 East 2nd St., Mineola, N.Y. 11501. Dover publishes more than 500 books each year on science, elementary and advanced mathematics, biology, music, art, literary history, social sciences and other areas.